THE
HANDLER

THE
HANDLER

M. P. Woodward

BERKLEY
New York

BERKLEY
An imprint of Penguin Random House LLC
penguinrandomhouse.com

Copyright © 2022 by Michael Woodward
Penguin Random House supports copyright. Copyright fuels creativity, encourages
diverse voices, promotes free speech, and creates a vibrant culture. Thank you for buying
an authorized edition of this book and for complying with copyright laws by not
reproducing, scanning, or distributing any part of it in any form without permission.
You are supporting writers and allowing Penguin Random House to continue to publish
books for every reader.

BERKLEY and the BERKLEY & B colophon are registered trademarks of Penguin
Random House LLC.

Library of Congress Cataloging-in-Publication Data

Names: Woodward, M. P., author.
Title: The handler / M.P. Woodward.
Description: New York: Berkley, [2022]
Identifiers: LCCN 2021061887 (print) | LCCN 2021061888 (ebook) |
ISBN 9780593441633 (hardcover) | ISBN 9780593441640 (ebook)
Subjects: LCGFT: Spy fiction. | Thrillers (Fiction) | Novels.
Classification: LCC PS3623.O6857 H36 2022 (print) | LCC PS3623.O6857
(ebook) | DDC 813/.6—dc23/eng/20211223
LC record available at https://lccn.loc.gov/2021061887
LC ebook record available at https://lccn.loc.gov/2021061888

Printed in the United States of America
1st Printing

Book design by Ashley Tucker

For John and Evelyn

CAST OF CHARACTERS

THE AMERICANS

Meredith Morris-Dale—Senior operations officer in CIA's Counterproliferation (CPT) Division; ex-wife of John Dale.

Grace Morris-Dale —Daughter of John and Meredith; midshipman at the US Naval Academy.

John Dale—Indefinitely suspended CIA case officer living in rural Washington State.

Ed Rance—Department head of CIA's CPT Division based in Langley, Virginia.

Jeff Dorsey—Director of CIA's National Clandestine Service.

Rick Desmond—Junior CIA analyst in the CPT Division; Meredith's deputy.

Steve Chadwick—CIA Istanbul chief of station; Meredith's occasional boyfriend.

THE RUSSIANS

Yuri Kuznetsov—Russian SVR (Foreign Intelligence Service) (Directorate PR) officer based in Damascus.

Maria Borbova—Russian SVR (Directorate S) officer based in London; internally in SVR, her code name is Zoloto.

Genevieve Lund—Maria Borbova's alias when working undercover.

Colonel Vladimir Niskorov—Russian SVR (Directorate PR) commander at SVR HQ Yasenevo.

Vasily—Russian Spetsnaz operative in SVR's Aslan (Alpha) elite foreign operations team.

Leo—Russian Spetsnaz operative in SVR's Aslan (Alpha) elite foreign operations team.

Oleg—Russian Spetsnaz operative in SVR's Aslan (Alpha) elite foreign operations team.

Putov—Yuri Kuznetsov's number two SVR officer in Damascus.

Nikita—Russian scientist shadowing Zana Rahimi at the Tabriz enrichment facility.

THE IRANIANS

Zana Rahimi (*Cerberus*)—Nuclear physicist working in the Iranian centrifuge arrays; Cerberus is his CIA code name.

Nadia Rahimi—Wife of Zana Rahimi living in Tehran.

Sahar Rahimi—Daughter of Zana and Nadia; student at McGill University in Montreal.

Kasem Kahlidi—Quds lieutenant colonel based in Lebanon; a former adjutant to the late General Soleimani, former head of Quds Force.

Naser Maloof—Iranian Ministry of Intelligence and Security (MOIS) colonel based in Tehran; in charge of Iranian counterintelligence.

Javad Mirzadeh—Zana's supervisor at the Tabriz enrichment facility; an active-duty Iranian Revolutionary Guard Corps (IRGC) major.

Kasra—Girlfriend of Kasem Kahlidi, living in Tehran.

Major General Qasem Soleimani—Commanding general of the Quds Force killed by an American drone strike in Iraq in January 2020.

Brigadier General Hossein Salami—Commanding general of the IRGC.

THE
HANDLER

PROLOGUE

SAHAR RAHIMI ARRIVED AT THE AIRPORT EARLY ONLY BECAUSE HER
mother had insisted on it. The smart, lithe, yoga-loving nineteen-year-
old had pushed back on the early hour, trying to tell her mother that
she worried too much. But her mother, Nadia, had lived in Tehran for
all of her fifty-one years. Somewhere in that instinctual space between
maternal wisdom and middle-aged pessimism, the older woman had
just known she'd be right.

"They'll find a way to hold things up," she'd kept saying during the
pack up. "An unscheduled search, a long interview, a fivefold check of
your visa, a dispute over the weight of your luggage—doesn't matter.
There will be something. It's *Tehran*. Trust me."

A premed student near the top of her class, the nineteen-year-old
had responded with a subtle eye roll and a stream of text messages to her
boyfriend, Esfan. The one-month trip home from university had been
insufferable. Thank God, it was all nearly over.

With a long, labored breath, Sahar had gone on to explain to her
mother that the world was no longer quite so jammed up as it once had
been, even in Iran. The magic of technology had smoothed things out.
Today's Tehran was *not* her mother's Tehran. It was, the daughter had
advised, perhaps time for a more optimistic outlook.

Waving all of that away, Nadia had replied with a mantra of near
religious clarity, "You don't know these people the way I do. There will
be something," she'd said again.

Recalling their conversation now, Sahar stifled a yawn and looked blearily at the queue in front of her. She checked her phone again. Still no reply from Esfan. The last she'd seen him was at a shuttle stop as she was leaving Montreal's McGill University for the airport weeks ago, a scene she'd replayed in her mind at least a hundred times since. Because they'd both pledged to keep their relationship a secret from their meddling parents, texting had been the only way to stay in touch.

But to her liking, he'd been a little too quiet. Of late, his sometimes hours-long silences would cause her to create wild, spine-tingling fantasies of a forthcoming breakup. Even now she was imagining he'd found some new way to avoid her at the airport, wobbling her faith in the one immovable thing she'd been counting on: their shared flight back to Canada. This morning's flight.

At a little after four thirty in the morning, trapped in an overengineered glass tunnel somewhere between security and immigration, she stood among a crowd of fellow travelers with nervous faces, none of them Esfan's. Adding to her anxiety, in the close confines of the tunnel, the line had ballooned and lost its shape. There was some kind of delay up ahead. Grudgingly, she'd begun to think her mother might have had a point.

Someone behind her accidentally kicked her heel. Her elbow touched the man next to her. She balled her fists in frustration and shifted the strap of her shoulder bag away from someone else. This was not coming off at all the way she'd hoped.

Compounding it, her despair rang with a certain sense of inevitability, a pang of foreboding. She'd intuited it as soon as she'd stepped out of bed a few hours earlier. She told herself that her mother's dour outlook, coupled with the disquiet of her relationship, had morphed into this stubborn sense of dread and that it would all go away soon enough. But it hadn't. If anything, it had gotten worse.

In the car on the way in, the reporter on the all-news station had been going on about the Iranian missile attack on the American base in Iraq, payback for the US bombing of a top Revolutionary Guards general named Soleimani. Forty dead American soldiers, invaders, the newsreader had kept saying, repeating the number as though it were a football score.

Hearing this, her mother had stabbed the steering wheel with an index finger. "That's it," she'd said. "The fools."

Now, ignoring the jabs of the crowd, Sahar could picture her mother sitting in the parking lot out there somewhere, waiting in their snow-mottled sedan, obsessing on the news. Nadia had lived through the Iran–Iraq War, so anything of a military nature always made the woman jumpy. As though in concert with Sahar's own dark presentiment, Nadia had vowed to stay at the airport until Sahar's plane had safely taken wing.

Her spirits at a low ebb, Sahar supposed that whatever was happening up there might cause her to miss her flight. With a shaking thumb, cramped against fellow travelers, she began to compose a signal to her mother to wait for her, just in case.

But her typing was interrupted with an incoming message. It was Esfan finally. She savored the few words glowing in front of her, the weight of her fears suddenly lifted. She canceled the message to her mother and opened a dialog with him instead.

He was also in the throng, somewhere back behind her, around the corner where she couldn't see him. Predictably, he complained about being too early. No doubt, she replied, adding that he was lucky his mother wasn't as much of a psycho as hers. She restrained from further comment, attempting to play it cool, giving him a taste of his own taciturnity.

The line narrowed and re-formed. Travelers were moving forward. Things were happening. She felt a rising sense of confidence. While Esfan remained out of sight some hundred yards behind her, his presence had made all the difference.

Over the next quarter hour, she passed through the gauntlet with a smile, eventually selecting a red vinyl chair in the waiting lounge where she could block the seat next to her with her bag. Aiming for a look of metropolitan sophistication, she adjusted the pink hijab across her throat and crossed her legs, checking her lipstick in a glass railing. Comprehending nothing at all, she flipped through a censored—but mostly intact—*Vogue* magazine, preparing for Esfan's arrival.

It wasn't that hard to tune out a ceiling-mounted TV that went on and on about the missile attack. Now and then she glanced up at the reporter, but tried not to. Nearly departed from this besieged country, she was determined *not* to be her mother.

Yet ten minutes on, there was still no sign of Esfan. The gate agent ran through the boarding procedures over a squawking PA. The foreboding reemerged. The connection time in Kiev was painfully brief. If he missed this flight, then she wouldn't see him for another day, perhaps even three, given the sparse schedules out of Tehran.

A tortured breakup fantasy bubbled up from the depths. Who was she to think she could hold on to him during this long time apart? She stewed on her shortcomings for another few minutes before her substantial reasoning powers finally won out. Even if he was going to dump her, she reminded herself, he still had to come. He had school starting in a few days and responsibilities of his own. It made no sense that he would turn around now.

Then where was he?

She leaned forward and looked up the concourse in a fruitless search. It made no sense. She lost control of her fingers, texting him three times in forty-five seconds with essentially the same message: *WTF?* But no response came. She soon regretted sending them and melted under a hot wave of self-incrimination. Exasperated with her overactive imagination, she stuffed the magazine into her bag and stared at the carpet, her phone on her lap, just in case it should come back to life.

But it didn't. When her row was eventually called, she proceeded glumly through the door, down two flights of stairs, and out onto the tarmac. It was still dark, only five thirty in the morning. A cold breeze ruffled her headscarf.

Sahar gaped at the big blue airplane before her, which hissed from its ground turbines and gleamed under the floodlights of the terminal building. She climbed the boarding stairs and squeezed into the cabin, where she was greeted by an enviously pretty Ukrainian flight attendant. Sahar thought that a flight attendant with those looks would have no problems with men.

She settled into her seat and waited; in order to distract herself, she watched the other passengers stow their bags. She watched the luggage streaming into the belly of the plane. It was going to be another gloomy day, but there was a small gleam of pink as dawn crested an eastern ridge.

Pulling out her phone, she snapped a picture of it. She coached herself to stop caring about Esfan. If he wasn't coming, then so be it.

She thought about posting the photo to Instagram with a few words about a new day, a new year, a new semester, faintly hoping he'd see that she'd turned the page. But nothing clever came. *Better to leave it alone than say something stupid,* she thought. Besides, her father had told her to avoid Instagram while home in Iran. She was suddenly glad of the excuse. Reminded of her parents, she texted her mother, letting her know she was safely on the plane.

The incoming text found Nadia a half mile away through a cordon of security fences. On seeing it, she closed her eyes and thanked her god. Despite all her misgivings, Sahar was safely on the plane.

Nadia was sitting in her car with the engine running, her chai thermos empty and cold. She'd been firing the engine in three- to four-minute intervals, just long enough to ward off the chill while still conserving gas, which had been rationed for the last eight months. She stared out at the orange line cresting the ridge and ran her hand through her hair, tension draining from her fingertips as she massaged her scalp.

Her phone rang. It was her husband, Zana. Though he'd also planned on staying to see Nadia off, he'd been recalled three days early to his work site, a few hours off to the northwest, over toward the Caspian.

Nadia had been angry with him for that, which had led to a nasty spat. But in her suddenly expansive mood, she'd let it all go, appreciative that he'd thought to call. While she didn't like his job, she admitted that he was well looked after by the government. They had a pleasant home up in the foothills and a daughter in her second year of premed at a Canadian university. On balance, she thought now, it seemed one of life's more equitable trade-offs.

"Everything going okay?" he asked through the phone tentatively, the fight over his early exit still fresh in mind.

"Yes, it's fine now," she replied. "But you know your daughter. She's obsessed with that Taghavi boy. And believe it or not, she still thinks we don't know."

"Hmph," he said with a chuckle. "She thinks we're idiots."

Nadia smiled. She glanced in the mirror on the back side of the visor. There were some wrinkles on the forehead, some skin gathered below the chin. But her hair was still thick and black. "I was once that way about you, eh? Sneaking around behind our parents' backs."

"A long time ago. Not so sure about now."

"Hmph," she said, imitating him. She tucked some hair behind an ear and closed the mirror.

Seeing Sahar step out onto the airport curb in the dark a few hours prior had made Nadia wistful. The old argument with her husband was gone now, displaced by the sentimentality of parenthood.

"Am I so terribly old?" she asked her husband.

"Whatever you are, you're younger than me."

She'd hoped he might say a little more, but let it go. *Trade-offs.* Through the phone she heard the sound of papers rustling, the creak of a chair.

"So," he said, anxious to get to more practical matters, "she's on the plane? On her way to Canada?"

"Yes, she's on. Ukraine first, remember? It connects in Kiev." In the spare gray light, Nadia could see that they'd removed the boarding stairs. A squat yellow tractor was pushing the jet back toward a taxiway. "Late but leaving now."

"That's a relief," he said. "You know Tehran."

Sahar gasped aloud when she saw Esfan walking down the plane's aisle. Flustered, she tidied the empty middle seat to make room. She smoothed her scarf and pulled out a thick lock of hair across her shoulder. Esfan dropped into the seat, grabbed her hand, and brushed his lips across her cheek.

"My bag was too big," he said, grinning. "Apparently the plane is overweight. I had to make arrangements to get it back to my mother."

Abandoning another particularly cruel breakup fantasy, Sahar sucked in a shaking breath and held it for a moment. The very smell of him gave her vertigo. To steady herself, she squeezed his hand.

"They'll ship it" was all she managed to say.

"Yes," he answered. "And . . . in all the confusion, they missed this." He pulled a small bottle of Listerine from his carry-on and took a sip. "Canadian Club," he added, smiling widely. "Minty fresh."

She leaned in conspiratorially to catch a whiff of the whiskey. "Oh, do I ever need that."

"What was the big rush to get back to work?" Nadia asked, grateful to see Sahar's plane rolling toward the end of the runway.

"I assume you've been listening to the news," Zana answered tersely.

The Americans, she thought. He had a rule against talking politics over the phone and dropped into this monotone whenever she ran afoul of it. "Never mind," she said. "I understand."

He changed the subject. "How is the new medicine doing? Been long enough to tell?"

Nadia, who'd developed multiple sclerosis in her early forties, looked unconsciously at her hand. No shaking. The headaches had dissipated as well. Come to think of it, the new medicine had been a blessing during Sahar's long visit home.

"You know," she replied, "I think it's very good. You can get me more?"

"Good," he said. "Yes, I can get more."

In a wide dirt clearing three miles away, a twenty-five-year-old third lieutenant in the Iranian Air Defense Force had just assumed the watch.

It was now after six and the January sky was brightening, but the young officer had no sense of that. There were no windows in the corrugated metal box where he worked, which was roughly the size and shape of a shipping container. Inside he had only the gray-green pall of optical TV and radar screens with which to render the world.

His eyes were pink and narrowed, his uniform rumpled. He'd been up until two at an after-hours party at a friend's house a few miles away. Though Iran was a dry country, the after-hours-cocktail circuit was something of an open secret among Tehran's Snapchat set.

The interior of his trailer was a steady sixty degrees in order to keep the electronics happy. The unending whir of computer fans made him sleepy, while the disapproving glances of the three sergeants in front of the radar scopes made him jumpy. More than anything, he wished he could simply crawl back in bed and sleep off the thumping in his head.

He thought about grabbing one of the Toyota four-by-fours to drive around the Tor missile batteries a few hundred yards away just to get away. The fresh air would be a tonic, he told himself, just the thing he needed. Moreover, driving around the missile site would buoy his mood. He liked mixing it up with the crews, inspecting the tank-tracked vehicles, glimpsing the spotless white missiles.

But as the platoon commander, his job was in here, the trailer, the nerve center. Especially since his commanders had called in the alert. There'd been some kind of attack on the Americans. All crews had been recalled. They were at the highest state of alert.

He and the sergeants wore their working green fatigues and heavy winter coats, shivering against the chill. A diesel generator chugged outside, keeping the systems running. Raising his voice over the hum of machines, one of the men said something about a status report. The young officer rubbed his face, put his communications headphones over his black beret, and shifted in his chair. He read aloud from a checklist into his microphone, just as he'd done a thousand times before.

8

He'd been coming to this particular tac trailer on the outskirts of Tehran for going on two years now. It was his first assignment as an officer of the ADF and he had decidedly mixed feelings about it. On the one hand it wasn't a particularly prestigious billet, manning a button to launch surface-to-air missiles against an air raid that would probably never come. But on the other, it allowed him to live in the city and go to after-hours parties.

"Say status," he said to the lead radar operator, continuing the exercise.

"Clear sweep sectors one, two, three, and four" came the rote response.

They could all do this in their sleep. The lieutenant's mind drifted back to the party.

"*Contact!*" the sergeant suddenly shouted. "Designate unknown target Alpha One."

Jarred by the sharp tone, the young lieutenant stiffened. He rose and approached the sergeant from behind, the cord from his headphones stretching back to his console. The operator repeated the information, the words tumbling out in haste.

The lieutenant looked dubiously at the scope. But there it was, a blip moving at about two hundred knots, circling in toward them. Headed toward his sector, it had already been designated a target by HQ. A suspected American Tomahawk cruise missile, according to the scope's marker.

"Range nine kilometers, speed two-five-zero knots, altitude one thousand feet and holding. Bearing two-eight-five. Heading three-zero-zero. Turning south now."

The officer studied the glowing red dot, his mind running through calculations. The profile didn't seem quite right to him, too slow for a Tomahawk. He noted the bearing.

"That's near the airport," he said to the sergeant at the scope. "How do we know that's not just civilian traffic? Check the squawk."

The sergeant rattled off some instructions into his microphone and punched a few buttons. "IFF showing a negative response, sir. No plane would be out there without a squawk." The experienced operator angled toward him. "Sir," he said, "they've marked it hostile—it's right over the city."

His mind still reeling with calculations, the lieutenant turned away and gave a grudging nod. It didn't add up. But he had no time to override procedure. It was all happening too fast.

"Fire-control radars ready," he said automatically. "Batteries one through four. Standing by."

The sergeant barked out the changes in altitude, bearing, speed, and heading of target Alpha One. The radar operators reported a solid track, a good targeting solution. The missiles were armed and ready.

No, the lieutenant thought. It didn't add up. The contact was too slow. Its altitude was rising rather than falling. The profile was just plain wrong. The young officer tugged at his shirt collar, bit his lip. To the man at the scope he said, "This has to be a drill." But the older sergeant dismissed him with a crisp shake of the head.

The target was now in sector four, the one he commanded. Through his own headset, the lieutenant heard the order from the ground-control-intercept operator in the hardened underground bunker some six miles south.

"Sector four: *fire, fire, fire!* Target Alpha One. *Fire!*"

Though trained to accept them, in all his time at this site, he'd never heard those exact words. This was no drill.

The young officer hesitated. He couldn't believe his own ears. The sergeant at the scope glanced at him. The lieutenant started to say something, then thought better of it and cleared his throat. He wet his lips.

"Lieutenant!" the sergeant yelled. "Did you hear?"

The young officer put a hand over his microphone. "No. I mean, yes, I heard. But it doesn't look right. . . ."

All three of the sergeants were looking at him now.

"It's an *order*," the lead one said, eyes wild and searching.

The lieutenant turned around, facing his own desk. He put a hand to his forehead and pressed his eyes shut. One of the sergeants said something else, something about duty. The lieutenant pinched his temples sharply, ignoring him, thinking. His head pounded. He was the final safety check, the arbiter as to whether the missiles raced off the rails or not. It was his call. If he was right and they were wrong, he would be a hero. If the other way round, he'd catch the blame, regardless of the orders coming up from the bunker.

Two seconds later, he pressed the button to key his microphone, still not quite sure what he'd say. When he eventually spoke, the voice seemed distant, like it belonged to another.

"Battery two: fire on target Alpha One," he said.

Nadia Rahimi was still on the phone with her husband discussing Sahar's next visit home in May. Watching the big blue Boeing gain altitude in the silvery overcast, she was already growing sad at the thought of driving back to an empty house. With a husband working remotely in another part of the country and a daughter off in Canada, she struggled to think how she would occupy herself for the rest of the winter.

Her husband was going on about a certain project associated with his work, using the casually vague terms that had come to define his professional life. Watching the plane, she tuned him out until he said they might grant him another leave soon. That got her attention.

Listening, her eyes still fixed on the aircraft, she noticed a bright white light move across her windshield. Initially, she thought it was the reflection of a headlight somewhere behind her. Then she thought it was another plane. But it moved so quickly and burned so brightly, like nothing she'd ever seen before. There was a smoke trail behind it, curling gracefully up from the ground.

"I think Friday the thirty-first will work," he was saying. "I could probably get the cargo flight on Thursday and make it a long weekend. That would be—"

"Zana, wait," she interrupted. "I'm seeing something here. It's fast, a white light. Like a ball. It's . . ." Nadia watched as the object streaked in a long J pattern up toward the blue Ukrainian 737. The curl of smoke grew longer and longer. She watched the bright object merge into the plane. A heartbeat later there was a yellow flash, reflected like lightning against the surrounding clouds.

"*Zana!! Zana!!*" she screamed.

She watched as the airliner caught fire. A wing dipped. Black chunks came loose and fell like dead birds. Two seconds later she heard a thunderous crack in the air, one loud bang.

"What is it? What? *What?*" her husband yelled in alarm.

She struggled to speak. How to describe the impossible? "The plane . . . Something came from the ground. It was . . . a missile. It struck the plane. A missile. Sahar's plane . . . it . . ." Her hands were trembling.

"How . . . ?"

"There was an explosion. The plane's on fire. It's turning, dipping. No. No. *No!*" she wailed piercingly into the phone.

"Maybe an engine blew? They have two. It probably looks worse than it is. Surely it will land. It can't be far from the field."

She took a ragged breath. She was hoarse now, her voice low, a sound her husband had never really heard before. "No. No, no, *noooooo*. There's another one. A long streak of smoke coming from the ground. It's coming apart. It's . . ."

The phone fell to the floor as she screamed at the windshield, driving the heels of her shaking hands into her eyes.

PART ONE

READY

CHAPTER 1

MEREDITH MORRIS-DALE WINCED AT THE NYLON WEBBING GOUGING her thighs as the hulking Air Force C-17 banked over the field. The flight from Doha to Norfolk had been tortuous, droning on for some twenty-odd hours at the monster's lumbering pace. She glimpsed the rising brown landscape through a narrow porthole, shifted her weight, and cursed the sadistic straps that passed for seats.

But it wasn't just the seats that had her wincing. She'd been writhing, pacing, or straining all the way across the Atlantic, often the only passenger awake. She'd stalked the cargo bay as the others, military men for the most part, slept in heaps of camouflage scattered across the vast metal deck. They'd collapsed into Ambien-induced comas immediately after takeoff from Qatar.

Not Meredith. She'd channeled her overtaxed central nervous system into a twisted decathlon of self-loathing. Somewhere over Cyprus, she'd cranked out fifty push-ups. Over the Azores, she'd found a cross-strut where she devised a pull-up challenge. By Bermuda, she'd cleared a space for wall-sits that made her thighs burn.

She'd blown the op. God, had she ever blown it.

Sagebrush. Mother-effing Sagebrush. That was the name of the asset she'd lost in an effort to expose a bioweapons network with designs on Syria. Lost him—probably for good.

Of course for good, she corrected herself as the C-17's flaps came down with a clunk.

Sagebrush had been snatched right under their noses in a teeming

Dubai market district. Pained by the recollection, she twisted her legs. It had to have been SVR, she thought, Moscow's latest incarnation of the KGB. The tradecraft was just too good for it to be anything but. They'd not only absconded with Sagebrush, her asset, but also her money for the buy, a cool two million bucks.

But a goddamned bargain, she'd argued seemingly ages ago, back in the conference room of the Agency comptroller. Remembering it now, she shuddered and slammed a bootheel against the cargo deck.

A lot of money, sure, but not the kind of dough that could lead to Congressional hearings, she'd said with worldly bravado back then. For a measly two million, CIA would stop the sale of a weaponized virus with an R-naught communicability score of six capable of decimating a rebel-held city in a week. By comparison, the novel coronavirus had been a tepid three.

She'd argued that it would have been irresponsible *not* to fund the buy. *A goddamned bargain,* she'd said two or three more times, damn near pounding the table. In the end, she'd gotten them all to agree. Budgets were arranged, funds wired. As one of the few women field leaders trying to crack into the upper ranks, she'd been proud of her own forcefulness.

They'd all remember that now, that meeting where she'd been so forceful.

The plane descended into more turbulence, jostling her. The handful of other passengers were zipping up their mil-spec gear, yawning, shaking off the seven thousand miles.

Meredith closed her eyes, listening to the straining jets, reliving the disaster, cringing to the point of facial cramps. Her team had developed an enviously detailed countersurveillance plan, posting watchers on every corner, setting up a real-time Echelon link with NSA to monitor local calls. They'd done all the difficult due diligence that was supposed to happen.

And yet Sagebrush had been pulled right off his bright green Ninja and tossed into the back of a Mercedes in traffic, right under their noses.

She glanced up at some rough-looking Special Forces types tightening up their equipment cases. *Wish I had their job,* she thought, admiring the cruel simplicity of combat. *See a bad guy in the scope, take his head off.*

The fantasy ended. She had *this* job, a department head in CIA's Counterproliferation Division—at least for another couple of hours.

God, had she ever blown it.

At last, the brakes shook and squealed on the taxiway. Frigid air streamed over the ramp, reminding her she was home to another gray Virginia winter. She grunted into her green field jacket, muscled a khaki rucksack over her shoulders, and trudged through the freezing rain. A dark Suburban with blacked-out windows was idling just on the other side of the chain-link fence, its wipers batting away sleet. Lights were flashed; a door opened. The fact that her boss, Rance, had sent an escort team made her want to stow away on the plane's return flight to CENT-COM. But they'd seen her now. There'd be no going back.

Minutes later, she was hurtling up I-64 in the backseat toward McLean. She'd had a brief exchange with the two beefy security men up front, but that was it. CIA drivers were used to tight-lipped passengers. That suited Meredith. She was in no mood.

Staring at the blur of barren trees, thinking of what awaited, she wondered if there could be silver linings. She could be a present mother for her nineteen-year-old daughter for once. Maybe she'd pull a Beltway rebound as a consultant with one of those overstuffed defense contractors, make a pile of cash. Life would go on, sort of. Just not the life that . . .

Knock it off, she commanded herself, straightening on the bench seat. They'd just passed Fredericksburg, according to a sign that whizzed by. Not much time before Langley.

"Would you gentlemen please avert your eyes?" she asked. "I need to change."

They stuttered an awkward assent and Meredith went about transforming herself from GI Jane to corporate exec, girding for an ambush of a different sort. She pulled a skirt, heels, and a clean blouse out of her bag. A fit brunette with thick dark eyebrows, now forty-three, she could still turn a male head when it counted. If the two drivers stole a glance or two in the rearview while she was in her bra, Meredith didn't much care. She reached for her makeup kit.

An hour later, the Suburban was waved through a security gate off Virginia Route 123 and flew down a couple of driveways, coming to a stop in an underground parking garage. Once on foot, she encountered more gates, more guards, and eventually an elevator that took her to the seventh floor, home of CIA senior management. There she found more security, including a TSA-style millimeter-wave-detection machine.

As though she were about to board a flight to Cleveland, Meredith threw her bags on a conveyor belt. She pulled a Glock 17 out of her backpack, ejected the ten-round magazine, pulled the slide to open the breach, and handed it to the guard. *So long, old friend,* she thought, watching the guards tag and stow it. She'd oiled and babied that thing for years, to the point that it felt like an extension of her hand. She supposed she would never see it again.

Rance's administrative assistant was pacing on the other side. "He's waiting," the plump woman said unhelpfully.

Meredith logged a small triumph when she caught Rance's hungry eye. He was just on the older side of good-looking, fiftyish. His once reddish-blond hair was thinning, a second chin just beginning to form. About five years earlier, he'd made a boozy pass at her. Two years after that, he'd made a sober one, which had been far worse.

Meredith smelled his cologne from five feet away. He was standing in his doorway, showily checking his expensive watch, turned out, as usual, in a suit he shouldn't have been able to afford.

"About time," he started with a quick halfhearted handshake.

She wasn't about to give him the satisfaction. She smiled breezily, muttered a greeting.

He stood there looking at her for a moment, barring the way into his office, a little too close. "No point in sitting down," he said. "We're off to see Dorsey."

A gut punch. Dorsey was the big boss. It was even worse than she'd feared.

"That's great," she replied through her smiling teeth. "Lead the way."

Walking through a maze of cubicles, he leaned in to ask her what the hell had happened to Sagebrush. She responded that if she hadn't had to interrupt her work to answer his summons, she'd have been working on the answer to that question right now. As the words came out, she was thinking that after she'd been fired, it would all be his problem. At least there was that.

He nodded without comment. There were people around them now.

Midway to Dorsey's office, Rance indicated a restroom and stopped. He said, "You might want to step in here and freshen up. You look tired."

Asshole.

Balding and wiry with ropy veins spidering toward his hands, Jeff Dorsey was the head of National Clandestine Services, two rungs below the director of CIA. When it came to spies undercover in the field, Dorsey ran the show. After ascending to his post a few years back, he'd swapped the bad habit of smoking for the nervous tic of chewing on cheap plastic pens. One dangled from his whiskered lip when the door opened before he snatched it away and stood. Tie askew, sleeves rolled, leaning on knuckles, he let his eyes linger on Meredith one second longer than they should have.

Two for two, she thought. Not bad for a backseat dressing room.

He motioned Meredith and Rance to a conference table, and called for coffee before asking for an update on things. The question was open-ended. She spoke broadly for twenty seconds, avoiding Sagebrush. Dorsey listened, saying nothing. Before long, she was running out of topics, wondering what to do, gesturing with her hands a little too much.

She was saved by an opening door.

Sheffield, the general counsel assigned to Counterproliferation, entered with a red-striped manila folder stamped with exotic classification markings. Dorsey held up a palm, cutting her off. The moment had apparently arrived.

Fine, she thought. *Let's get it over with.*

The boss placed an open metal box on the table. "Phones and watches in the casket, everyone. We need to have this next conversation in the SCIF."

SCIF, pronounced *skiff,* stood for Sensitive Compartmented Information Facility. It was a hardened room, a vault impervious to radio waves. No watches or phones allowed, not even secure ones. Meredith couldn't understand why her firing would be of such a sensitive nature, but supposed it didn't much matter.

Once installed around another table in the claustrophobic SCIF, Dorsey looked at the lawyer Sheffield. "All right, Dave, let's have her review and sign."

Head in guillotine, blade rising. She smiled woodenly.

Sheffield passed her a three-page document. It was a nondisclosure agreement, but one with the promise of prison if she were ever to acknowledge the existence of a code-word program called Active Archer. Bewildered, Meredith signed her name and dated the document. Sheffield applied a stamp and countersigned. He said his goodbyes and left.

"Glad that's out of the way," Rance said, pushing some of his thin hair over his forehead. "Now we can finally tell you why you're here."

She nodded, speechless, saliva returning to her tongue.

Dorsey chewed furiously on the end of a Bic, watching her. "I'm going to ask Ed to do the honors," the spy chief said, eyes narrowed in appraisal. "He'll read you in."

Rance nodded, tapped the document, and cleared his throat with theatrical purpose. "Meredith, you've been on the bioweaps end of the doomsday spectrum for a while, so let me start by refreshing your memory on uranium enrichment."

"You don't have to, Ed. I know how—"

"It starts with dirt pulled out of a mine, usually somewhere in Africa," he continued, oblivious. "After sifting, the raw ore is ground down to a uniform particle size and chemically leached, isolating the natural U238 in a powdery residue called yellowcake, due to its light color."

He cleared his throat again and waved off another protest from Meredith. "Now, U238 is fissionable, splittable, usable as fuel for power plants. But if a neutron can be separated from it, turning it into U235, it becomes *fissile*, comparatively easy to bombard with force, setting off the atomic chain reaction that results in a mushroom cloud."

Meredith plastered a neutral look on her face. Rance was a world-class mansplainer. *But why is he telling me this?*

Her boss went on. "To separate that neutron, you ionize the U238 into gas form and apply massive centripetal force through a centrifuge. Since you need about a hundred pounds of it for the critical mass to make a bomb, you need a lot of centrifuges. Thousands of them spinning at the speed of sound, night and day, perhaps for years."

Dorsey removed the Bic from his mouth and levered it back and forth between his fingers, watching her reaction. "Meredith, Iran has had tens of thousands of centrifuges spinning secretly for years. You ever wonder why they haven't achieved breakout?"

"Breakout" was intel slang for nuclear-weapons-capability enriched U235.

"I'm guessing it's this, Active Archer?" She tapped the papers she'd just signed.

"You bet your ass." The pen returned to Dorsey's mouth, angled up by a modest paternal grin. "Welcome aboard."

She nodded, relieved—but confused. "Right . . . so how does the op work?" she asked, stalling, thinking this must be some sort of demotion.

The pen returned to Dorsey's fingers. His voice fell by five decibels. "We have an asset in their enrichment program. A senior scientist code-named Cerberus. Simply put, if it weren't for him, all of these escalations going on right now—our hit against Soleimani, their retaliatory strike against us in Iraq—all of it would be under the threat of an Iranian nuclear response."

"A relief, of course," she said. "I'm just a little confused about my role in it. . . . Why the sudden flight back from Doha when . . ." She let the sentence drift, avoiding self-incrimination, Sagebrush.

Dorsey looked away suddenly, tossing the crumpled pen in a bin. Rance recrossed his legs, turning away from her, fiddling with his tie.

What's this?

"Well," Rance said from his peculiar angle, "here's the thing. We need you to bring your husband back."

"*What?*" she blurted. It came out an octave higher than she'd have liked.

The two men suddenly looked very worried. Eye contact was lost.

She pressed on. "First of all, he's my *ex*-husband. Second of all, you have way more control over him than I do. You're the ones that PNG'd him off to the wilderness two years ago, stripping him of his pension. You know he's flat broke now? And what the hell does John have to do with all this anyway?"

Still no eye contact. The pressure release of offense felt too good to stop now. She glared at Rance, speaking to the end of her breath. "You actually want me to run an op where the first task is to recruit my own ex-husband. *That's* why I just crossed the Atlantic in the middle of an op? Of all the *bullshit*. What the *fuck*, Ed?"

Dorsey fumbled with a fresh box of pens. Rance told her to calm down.

"*Stop*, both of you," she said. "You have to tell me how John is even remotely involved in this. *Now.*"

"Meredith," Rance replied, running a hand over his scalp, "remember the circumstances under which you met John? Back in Montreal?"

"What of it? He was a junior case officer. I ran him. And I had the

22

bad judgment to fall in love with him. Nothing ever came of the op it-self."

"Actually, that's where you're wrong," Rance said.

"John never told me anything about it."

Dorsey leaned in. Eye contact returned. "He couldn't, Meredith. See, in 2005, while he was posing as a student at McGill, he somehow came in contact with an Iranian national studying, we think, quantum physics. At the time, it didn't seem to mean much to John . . . or to you for that matter. There were no contact reports, nothing mentioning him that we could find."

"Okay." Her mind was racing, groping.

Her job back then was to supervise greenhorn CIA case officers who were trying to build up a network of contacts through various means. One of the officers in her employ was John Dale, ex–military intelligence with a Persian background, fresh off the Farm on his first under-cover assignment. Since Dale spoke a little French and Farsi, the Agency had shipped him up to Canada to recruit students because the Iranians sent all their promising academics to school there.

She and John Dale had fallen for each other and married soon after, too young. An accidental baby followed, too young. But that was an-other story.

"We logged *dozens* of contact bumps over the two years I was run-ning John. But you're saying one of them actually came through? What's his name? Maybe I'll remember him."

"We don't know, Meredith," said Dorsey. A fresh pen had made its way to his mouth. "We got a ping to the LinkedIn page of John's alias back in 2012, which we kept alive through another intermediary. Long story short, the query referenced John's time at McGill. After bona fi-des, we assessed it as coming from a scientist in Iranian weapons re-search. The real deal. But still, after all these years, Cerberus has managed to keep himself a mystery to us."

Rance nodded, picking up where Dorsey left off. "John recruited him based on the ping in 2012, well after your time in Montreal. Who-ever Cerberus is, he, *uh*, likes John. They seem to have developed some sort of trust with each other. After John moved on from the Agency, we just kept running the scientist. It wasn't that hard because Cerberus simply kept software doors open for us, doors that we used for operations to throw off their centrifuges. That changed a week ago. Cerberus is demanding to work with John now. Only John."

"Well . . . John can be very likable," Meredith said. Her ex had never spilled any of this. Of course, that was something of an occupational hazard, a fault line in their marriage. "So what's John supposed to do anyway? What does this guy want?"

Rance smoothed the fabric over his crossed knee. "We think Cerberus wants John to bring him out. We'd prefer he keep doing what he's doing, of course. If we lose him, we lose Active Archer."

"I don't see why you need John for *that*," Meredith said, desperate to leave her train wreck of a personal life out of this. "Why don't we do what we always do to defecting assets? Blackmail him, lie to him. Let him know that if he leaves, he's a dead man because we'll out him as a spy. You guys know how this goes."

"We do," said Rance. "But this is different. Cerberus is telling us that if he doesn't get to John, he'll expose the whole operation through some kind of code embedded in the Iranian system long after he's gone. We'll lose everything."

"He's *reverse*-blackmailing the CIA? That takes balls. Why not take him out? We're good at that sort of thing."

"Yeah," said Dorsey, chewing. "He seems to have thought of that already."

"Oh?" She raised a thick eyebrow.

Dorsey pushed his drooping sleeves up past his elbows. "We don't know who he is or where he is. And as of last week, he's cut off our access to their program. We're blind now. That's why we need you . . . why we need your husband."

"*Ex,*" Meredith said. She leaned back in her chair, pushed out a short sigh.

A long moment passed. She felt the need to fill the void. "So, in summary, my mission is to talk John into rejoining the Agency that called him a traitor so he can go bring out an asset that he may have recruited almost ten years ago. Or maybe kill him. All of this from the woman that asked him for a divorce eighteen months ago. That about it?"

Dorsey grimaced. "More or less." He tossed his second crimped Bic in a bin. "Look, Meredith, Cerberus is our best asset in this little quasi-war with Iran. He'll only talk to John. John's not going to listen to Ed—or me for that matter—after what happened. Without John, without Cerberus, we're looking at the very real possibility of a nuclear strike against us one of these days. You've simply got to make this happen. *I* need you."

She didn't have a good response to that. She nodded quietly, lowered her eyes to the table.

Dorsey's assistant arrived then, holding the door open so he could shuffle off to his next urgent catastrophe.

On his way out, the spy chief pushed up his drooping sleeves again and glanced back at Meredith. "Sheffield will fix everything legally for John to come back." He nodded once at her, then turned to Rance. "All yours, Ed."

With Dorsey gone, Rance looked at her sideways, one brow lowered. "We still haven't talked Sagebrush."

She felt her stomach tighten. "No," she said.

He nodded curtly. "We know John's living somewhere out near Seattle. I'm authorizing a plane for you. Leaves Andrews in the morning."

She stared at the table.

"Look," Rance said, softening. "I'm sure you can handle John, bring him back. You're good at that sort of thing. And we can talk Sagebrush later—this is frankly more important. Get home and rest up a bit. You *really do* look tired."

Asshole.

CHAPTER 2

FIVE HOURS LATER, ED RANCE GLANCED AT THE SPOT ON HIS WRIST where his Panerai would have normally sat. But his watch and phone were still in the leaden box outside the SCIF.

Sheffield, the gray-haired general counsel, caught him doing it. "In a hurry, Ed?"

The CIA division chief had been busy performing calculations of driving times between Langley, the city, and his home in Silver Spring. *Yes,* he thought. *I am in a goddamned hurry.* By his math, in order to slip into bed next to his wife at a reasonable hour, say ten thirty, he'd need to be on the road by six.

But outwardly, he'd been aiming for stolidity. "Of course not," he said, dropping his wrist below the table. "We have to do this right."

Sheffield nodded briefly before canting over a document with striped classification markings, initialing various lines. "This is a highly unusual situation," the lawyer added. He spun the document toward Rance and looked up. "How's it look to you?"

Rance barely read it as his eyes went the length of the three pages. "Yup, all good."

"Okay. Then here, take this." Sheffield handed him a lapel microphone. There was a video camera at the end of the table. "Technically we should probably get the signature of a Congressional oversight staffer for a reinstatement like this, just to cover ourselves. But that'll take too long. We'll have to settle for the director." Sheffield grinned. Lawyer humor.

"Right," said Rance, absently drumming his fingers on the table.

They were in Sheffield's conference room, a SCIF reserved for the attorney's personal use. Even by CIA standards, the lawyers had more secrets than anyone else.

Rance wanted to check his phone to see if maybe Genevieve had called, but the damn thing was forty feet away. Feigning a stretch so he could catch a fleeting glimpse of the clock over the door, he thought her plane should have landed by now.

"Okay, let's get started."

Sheffield flipped a switch. A red light blinked and then remained steady. The unblinking lens above it watched ominously, a HAL 9000 redux.

The lawyer recited a formal introduction of their names, the time, the date, the subject of the interview. He gave several classification warnings, noting that they would be discussing SCI code-word-access programs called Broadsword and Active Archer.

Formalities done, he looked directly at Rance, his eyes as expressionless as the camera behind him. "For the record, Mr. Rance, please give me the history of your interactions with former CIA Special Activities operative John Dale, suspended case officer nine-eight-one-one-two."

Now that the tape was rolling, Rance's mind kicked into gear. "Sure," he started slowly, running the angles. "John Dale was assigned to me as an operational clandestine case officer in February 2012, when I was deputy chief of station, Baghdad. He was detailed to me from Ground Branch on an ad hoc basis for an active operation."

"Right. What operation was that?"

"It was called Broadsword."

Sheffield said into the microphone, "For the record, Operation Broadsword is no longer an ongoing concern. It remains classified SCI code-word access, refer to case number one-five-seven-one." He nodded back to Rance. "Mr. Rance, please state the nature of Broadsword and Dale's role in it."

"Sure. The objective of Broadsword was to infiltrate ISIS cells in eastern Syria and Iraqi Kurdistan. We were to establish contact with Syrians that we could turn as assets and gather intelligence on ISIS."

"Why was John Dale assigned to it? How was he qualified? What was his role?"

Rance cleared his throat elaborately to buy some time. He started to say something, checked himself, and then started over. "John Dale worked with CIA Special Activities Ground Branch to lead renditions of suspected ISIS members. Because the Jihadists were usually far from the front lines in Syria, Dale and his Special Activities team were embedded with friendly Syrian Kurds so that any attempted attacks on suspected terrorists could not be traced back to the US military, which we believed would force them to change tactics."

"Right. And what was the success rate of John Dale's team as part of Broadsword?"

"Mixed. His team eliminated five suspected cell members over the course of about six months, but we never took down a primary cell. On his last mission in August of 2012, Dale was captured by ISIS forces in an operation near Mosul. Five days after his capture, he escaped and we recovered him."

Sheffield nodded. He knew the story. Everyone above a certain pay grade knew the story. But he needed it for the tape. He glanced at a paper clipped to a manila file, then turned back to Rance.

"Mr. Rance, John Dale's record shows that he was recruited into the Agency in 2004, direct from the Navy, where he served as an intelligence officer. As his former managing case officer, can you describe his qualifications and training while at CIA?"

Rance nodded. On safer ground now, he spoke quickly. "Dale's early work was as a recruiter for Iranian agents at a Canadian university. His mother was an Iranian refugee if I recall. After Canada he applied for additional Ground Branch operations training. I think he spent about five years on and off in the Middle East with the counterterrorism division before being transferred to me as part of Broadsword."

"Why did you select him for Broadsword?"

"Because he was at least conversationally proficient in Farsi. Iranian intelligence was active in the region, so we thought Farsi would be useful. I, along with others, including Deputy Director Dorsey, believed

John's tactical and language skills would be valuable contributions to the effort."

"So you thought he was *uniquely* qualified? Particularly well suited for the role?"

"Yes. Well, myself *and* Deputy Director Dorsey thought so."

"Did you have any hesitation before assigning him to Broadsword?"

"Yes."

Sheffield looked at him, surprised. He arched his eyebrows as if to say, *Well?*

Rance continued. "My hesitation was that he had a reputation for being hard to control. He was also married to another case officer, Meredith Morris-Dale, who was stationed here at Langley. They had a young daughter. Given the dangerous and occasionally autonomous nature of John's assignment, I didn't want a case officer that could become emotionally unstable."

"I see. And did you voice these concerns to Deputy Director Dorsey?"

Rance hesitated. *Careful.* "I . . . may have. It's been several years. Knowing what I know now, I regret not having done so more forcefully at the time."

"Right. But in the end, you accepted Dale into your operation."

"Along with the concurrence of others, yes. As I said earlier, he had a unique background for what we needed. I'd also add that the operation had been cleared by National Command Authority with some urgency." Rance wasn't about to let the bastards who might come after him one day for Broadsword pretend it had all been *his* idea alone.

"How did John Dale's career with the Agency end?"

"Dale was captured by an ISIS unit operating near Mosul. After analyzing his escape and debriefing him, we couldn't rule out the possibility he'd been turned, and initiated a preliminary inquiry report."

"Turned by ISIS? Is Mr. Dale a Muslim?"

"Not that I know of. But I can't rule it out."

"Why did you think he had been turned after only five days?"

"He'd been independent and invisible to us for more than eight months, living among Kurds, targeting Syrian or Iraqi contacts for solicitations of agency. In so doing, we believed he may have developed . . . sympathies . . . a distaste for his mission. We assessed that this confusion of loyalty may have had something to do with his escape."

"What evidence did you have to support the initiation of an inquiry?"

"After his capture, we obtained drone footage of his quote-unquote escape. In the drone video, he's seen conversing with a hostile. They wave to each other before John walks off to be picked up by friendly forces."

Sheffield looked at a legal pad, made a note. He said into the camera, "Reference case file nine-five-six-five-zero dated August tenth, 2012, preliminary inquiry submission six-seven-two-one." He turned back to Rance. "Did the inquiry expose the identity of this hostile that he waved to?"

"No. Mr. Dale wouldn't reveal anything about him. He only acknowledged that he was a fellow captive and that they had worked together on an escape plan. But the suspected hostile wore clothing more typically identified with ISIS members. He was also clearly of ethnic Middle Eastern origin."

"What happened then?"

Rance sighed, thinking of the time. He could have strangled Sheffield for his thoroughness. "Under questioning, we felt that Dale had, in fact, become emotionally unstable, just as I had thought. His wife, a fellow officer with unique insights into his state of mind, concurred. Dale leveled some accusations against the Agency—unsettling accusations, baseless. But unable to support these, he walked out, resigned, refused to cooperate. With the inquiry still pending, we tagged him as a possible compromise. We suspended his career with conditions, which remain in effect. But we took no . . . punitive action, given his service."

"What are the conditions of Mr. Dale's suspension?"

"We've taken his passport. He has to report in from time to time on his whereabouts. Otherwise he is free to live his life as he chooses. And, of course, live up to his confidentiality obligations."

"Since you are the division chief for Counterproliferation, Mr. Dale's suspension continues based on your recommendation. For the record, Mr. Rance, why do you recommend reactivating him for assignment to Active Archer, which is, after all, a Counterproliferation operation?"

"For the record, General Counsel Sheffield, I am acting on the orders of Deputy Director Dorsey. Director Dorsey has asked that we reactivate John Dale because he has been requested by a specific asset with whom he appears to have a unique relationship. The deputy director sees the reactivation of Dale as unfortunate but necessary."

"Understood. And so your next action is to reinstate him on your authority?"

"No. Case Officer Meredith Morris-Dale is to evaluate his fitness for duty and, if suitable, recruit him back with limited duty for Active Archer—on Director Dorsey's authority." Rance crossed his legs, quietly congratulating himself on the nuance.

After rattling off the reference numbers for Active Archer, Sheffield punched a button and stopped the recording. "Good. That should do it. I'll have this officially transcribed so you can countersign it. If you see anything you don't like, you can rewatch the tape for accuracy. But let me be clear. Until the director endorses with his signature, you can't take any action toward Dale."

Rance turned to glance at the clock again. "Is it okay with you if all of that goes down tomorrow? Nothing is going to happen before then. I really do need to run. You know, the wife . . ."

"Sure," said Sheffield, grinning.

Rance unclipped the microphone from his lapel and pushed through the SCIF exit like a man released from jail. He retrieved his watch and phone from Sheffield's secretary and hustled down the elevator to his office. Barely breaking stride, he let his secretary know he was leaving and would be incommunicado at the gym for the next couple of hours. He hurried to his BMW in the parking garage.

By six thirty he was speeding out the HQS exit gate toward I-66 through Arlington, on his way to DC. He received a text and, risking collision, glanced down to read it. Genevieve had already checked in. Room 505. God, even the number sounded sexy.

As he was entering the freeway ramp, he inwardly rejoiced at the sparse traffic. He headed to the left lane and sped to seventy-five, one eye monitoring the rearview for cops. But just as he slipped into a reverie of the evening ahead, he had an abruptly uncomfortable thought. He'd forgotten to set up Meredith's travel so that she could get out to see John Dale and sign him on to Archer. He'd promised an Agency jet out of Andrews to make it happen quick. That had been Dorsey's idea.

But now, he realized with growing alarm, it would be too late, since it required multiple signatures. Rance didn't have the clout to scramble an Agency Gulfstream on his own authority; he sure as hell wasn't going to bother his superior with this kind of minor detail after hours. Thinking it over, he decided to do what most bosses do: make it a subordinate's problem.

Meredith could figure out a commercial flight on her own. Not much of a security risk anyway. Wouldn't it make sense that a co-parent would make the occasional trip out West to see the father? Not a stretch at all. *Problem solved,* he thought.

He needed to call Meredith to get her moving, but didn't have the inclination to open the encryption app required for a secure call. That would require him to enter a lengthy complicated code and his fingerprint for two-factor authentication. He wasn't about to slow down, not even a little bit. Instead he dialed her in the clear, listening to her phone ringing through the Bluetooth. Voice mail. *Good enough.*

"Hi, Meredith, it's Ed. About that flight out to see your husband. I wasn't able to line up a company plane after all, so probably best if you just fly commercial to Seattle. Sorry for the change of plans. Time is of the essence. Also . . . no phones, obviously. Need you to speak to him in person only about . . . that thing. I trust your judgment. Please report back in after you've made contact. Oh—and why don't you say hello to John for me?"

He smiled at that last bit, knowing that John Dale was most definitely not an Ed Rance fan.

There, he thought. He sped up to eighty.

Less than an hour later, he was hammering on the door of room 505 of the Hay-Adams Hotel. Genevieve Lund opened the door with a drink in her hand. She wore a short dress that sent his heart rate to three digits.

Handing over a cut-crystal glass, she ushered him in, explaining that she had a meeting with the Office of Maritime Security tomorrow to defend the legality of a Panamanian flagged ship owned by a certain client that had never once been to Panama, not even the canal. After the morning meeting she was to whisk right back to London. Could he believe it?

He couldn't, but at the same time, he didn't care. They'd met in London six weeks earlier when Rance had been on a tour through the Agency's European field ops. She was an executive with a shipping insurance company called Stoke Park, tasked with external government relationships. As a safety precaution, Rance had run a quiet background check on her. But given his intentions, he'd done it back channel with an underling as a discreet favor, without the full force of Agency investigators. She'd been born in Finland, emigrated young to England, had an economics degree from Newcastle. He'd had another case officer make a few quiet inquiries in the UK. She'd come up clean. *Good enough.*

Now, as she stood before him, the only thing his addled mind processed was that he had only a couple of hours to play with between work and home. Why on earth was she using some of that up by making him endure a drink? Were they really going to sit and talk about their respective workdays like some old married couple in Baltimore?

"Come on," she said, pressing the glass into his hand. "A splash of bourbon will do us both some good."

The Finnish-English accent was a nuclear turn-on. Particularly that tendency to drag out certain words. His face was hot.

Fine. He would have the drink. One.

He sat back in the plush club chair and crossed his legs, his foot bobbing.

She noticed it. "You seem anxious, darling. Rough day? I'm the one who's just crossed the Atlantic and is still living on Greenwich Mean Time. I'm near *stupefied*. Is everything okay on your end?"

He'd made Genevieve believe he was a long-suffering civil servant in some boring branch of the State Department. "Yes," he said, "everything's fine. It's just been an unusually hectic day, what with your hard Brexit and all." He smiled winsomely.

She returned it. "Oh, do tell me your opinion on our *hard* Brexit. Old Bo-Jo does have *balls,* doesn't he?"

He spoke through his grinning teeth. "Must we?"

"Finish your drink," she said, laughing, toying with him. "You're staring at me like you're going to eat me *whole.*"

"The thought had crossed my mind," he returned. *Fuck it.* He tossed off the bourbon in one gulp and stood, loosening his tie. He couldn't take it anymore.

Later, his naked body lay sideways across the tousled sheets. He was snoring.

Genevieve Lund skillfully slid out from under him. The athletic thirty-four-year-old blonde found Rance's suit jacket lying across the suite's white velvet sofa. She slid her hand through the silken lining, past the Zegna label, and located the phone in the breast pocket. Naked from head to toe, she slipped around the corner into the bathroom, out of sight, but with the door still open, cupping the phone in her hands.

CHAPTER 3

SHE'D MIXED A SPECIAL BOURBON-TRANQUILIZER CONCOCTION FOR Rance that should keep him out solid for another two hours. She listened to him breathe heavily for a moment before picking up her small clutch purse, already positioned by the sink. With one eye on Rance's bare white ass, his freckled back rising and falling on the bed, she retrieved a small device disguised as lipstick.

She extended a thin cord from its cylindrical bottom and plugged it into the phone's power port, which lit up. After about ten seconds, she checked the screen, which was dark, indicating that it had done its work. She retracted the cord into the lipstick container, wiped the phone free of fingerprints, and reinserted it into his pocket. She carefully replaced the coat and slipped back into bed next to him.

God, she thought, listening to him snore, staring at a finely plastered ceiling medallion. *Why do we always have to do this in my hotel room?* If it had been his room, she could have just gotten up and left. The disciplined Russian SVR Directorate S officer lay like a marble statue until a quarter to nine, then shook Rance hard and reminded him he needed to get home. Best not to jeopardize this collection op by tipping off the wife.

Around ten, after Rance had finally left, complaining of a pounding headache, she took a hot shower to scrub herself clean. That unpleasant task over, she donned a tight black running outfit and tucked her hair in a watch cap. To disguise her face and shield herself from the cold, she wore a balaclava over her mouth and neck. She strapped on a small Camelback backpack with a water bladder, as well as a cargo pocket filled with her tools of the trade. She made her way to the lobby, past the night bellman, and out the front door.

A blast of cold mist greeted her on H Street. She picked up the pace, hoping to warm up, while turning variously to random streets, some lit, others dark. Every now and then she stopped to watch for movement through the reflection of shopwindows, disguising it by retying her Nikes.

Her target, Rance, was a sloppy senior case officer. One of these days the intelligence he provided would be traced back to him and the FBI would start tailing him and all of his private contacts. But she saw no sign of that comeuppance this evening. Just a city asleep on a typical Thursday night.

After a jog down Independence and out three-quarters of a mile toward Union Station, she sprinted across Constitution, past the Capitol rotunda, and onto the Mall. Somewhere in the middle, near an enormous oak, she stopped.

She pulled down her balaclava and noted the thick cloud of steam coming from her lungs. On this freezing night she saw no one, save for a sleeping derelict on a park bench well over a hundred yards away. She removed her backpack and sat under the tree, her back against the trunk, stretching her hamstrings, crunching against the frozen grass.

Genevieve, whose actual name was Maria Borbova, plugged the fake lipstick device into a port on her Android tablet. She donned a set of earbuds and went through a preprogrammed series of gestures, apps, and codes to turn the generic tablet into an SVR field computer. After all of this digital voodoo, she uploaded the filched audio file from Rance's phone.

The spyware program was only moderately effective. Through trial and error, SVR had learned that in order to avoid detection by CIA forensics, the file had to be very, very small. It also couldn't upload its payload over a wireless connection. Anything that violated these two parameters would tip off info-tech specialists, who were constantly on the lookout for it. Rather, the embedded Android APK recorded conversations only when the phone was on, tapping into the passive microphone.

So far, regrettably, the snoop had been moderately effective at best. Since case officers went into secure rooms for conversations without their phones, most of what she heard was inconsequential bureaucratese. That was the trouble with this kind of op. It was all so damned random. If it were up to her, she would scuttle this surveillance tool. But it wasn't up to her. Far from it.

Rance's job, though officially the head of the Counterproliferation Division, was mostly one of administration. Still, SVR had assigned her to him because, when it came to peddling weapons to embargoed countries around the world, many of the foreign agents they faced reported up through his case officers. The thinking was that they could piece together enough fragments of information to be able to assemble a credible hierarchy of the spy network. That was the way Yasenevo saw it anyway.

Regardless of the reasoning, Maria had had to sleep with the man four times over the last three months and had little to show for it, other than a degraded sense of self. Her professional training allowed her to endure it all without too much psychological harm; but she was only human. If the take remained slight, she hoped fervently that SVR would move her onto something else—*someone* else anyway.

Listening now to Rance's one-sided conversations, she took notes on her tablet to an encrypted app. The tiny size limit of the captured audio file allowed only about twenty-four hours of recording, which were encoded at an ultraefficient bit rate. The sound quality was terrible.

Just like her previous two hauls, this one started with Rance leaving home, saying a few words to the wife. Just like the last two, he started his day by complaining to her about the lethargy of their fifteen-year-old son. Rance's kid seemed to have a marijuana problem. Maria sighed. She'd slept with him for *this*?

But then, as Rance got to the office, the recording changed. He was busily barking to his secretary about the arrival of someone. He wanted his schedule cleared to be able to meet with this arrival and also, significantly, the deputy director of Clandestine Services, Jeff Dorsey. Maria paused the recording and jotted several notes. *Finally,* she thought. Something worth reporting.

The meeting was with a person named Meredith Morris-Dale. She was to come in and see Rance as soon as she landed. He wanted the secretary to send drivers to pick her up. She was landing at Langley Air Force Base about two hours away, down near Norfolk.

After that, there was more bureaucratic grumbling, on and on about budgets, head count, real estate. By now the sweat in Maria's clothes was freezing her. She needed to move this along. She fast-forwarded through snippets of Rance's day that were uninteresting.

Finally, she landed on the conversation with Meredith Morris-Dale. She knew it because Rance used her name liberally. Maria was able only to catch fragments of Morris-Dale's voice through the passive mic, but his was loud and clear.

There was a brief reference to SVR. This caught Maria's attention. She heard enough of Meredith's voice to catch "Dubai." An operation called Sagebrush. Maria transcribed furiously, her fingers flying over the small keyboard.

There followed references to the Dorsey meeting. After that a lot of chitchat with Dorsey himself. Morris-Dale doing most of the talking, but inaudibly. Then nothing until the end of the day. Maria stopped typing and went back over certain sections of the recording to make sure she had it right.

The last voice conversation, before Rance arrived at the Hay-Adams to see her, was him leaving a voice mail. From the background noise she could tell he'd been driving. Meredith Morris-Dale was to get out to Seattle to see her husband. The fact that Rance ordered her to do so with haste and instructed her not to just call him seemed significant. He ended it with "Oh—and why don't you say hello to John for me?" Knowing Rance as she did, she thought he was being sarcastic. Strange.

She typed a note to herself:

John and Meredith Morris-Dale: married officers (?) central to
some kind of follow-up from a suspected SVR rendition of asset
Sagebrush, Dubai (?). Operational security advised; no phone
conversations allowed. Directed personally (?) by Dorsey.

She reread her own note. Maybe worth something. Maybe not.
She'd let Yasenevo figure it out.

She blew warm air through her cupped hands and thought of another angle. A Google dive of Meredith's name on the tablet's browser
revealed nothing. The absence of any search result was in itself interesting, she thought. She knew the Agency had strict rules about online
presence. However, those rules didn't apply to family; or if they did, the
Agency seemed to have a hard time enforcing them. She did a search on
just the name Morris-Dale, Washington, DC.

Bingo: a girl named Grace Morris-Dale had been a student at
Georgetown Prep, a soccer player in her senior year.

Daughter? Sister? Cousin? She opened Facebook. Grace Morris-
Dale had a public profile. There was a graduation picture from somewhere. The girl looked to be about seventeen in the picture. She was
standing between her parents, wearing her mortarboard. "With Meredith and John," read the caption.

Maria zoomed in on the image of the parents. Good-looking family.
She'd come to think of Americans as congenitally fat and lazy. But these
three were fit and healthy, standing on an outdoor stage somewhere.
Meredith's face was behind sunglasses, a lean face, pretty in a severe way.
The father had brown hair bronzed by the sun, brown eyes, olive skin,
and a beard with gray streaks. He looked like he could have been Middle
Eastern himself, or Greek or Italian. Hard to say. Though he wasn't
obscured by sunglasses, he seemed to be shrinking before the camera,
eyes down, chin sideways, only a faint closemouthed grin.

Maria snapped a screenshot and saved the image to her tablet. She
then Googled the name John Morris-Dale, Seattle. Nothing. Figuring
he might go by just John Dale, she tried that. A number of people came

up; none of them seemed to be the man in the picture. But it was a poor image of him to begin with. She was shivering.

She opened a second encrypted app. It took her five more minutes to file the contact report to her superiors at SVR HQ in Yasenevo. She described Meredith Morris-Dale as a possible lead case officer in an undetermined operation in the Middle East, likely Dubai, resulting in a CIA-suspected SVR rendition. She added a sentence about a meet with her husband, John, also a possible case officer but undetermined. She annotated the report with the photo from Grace's Facebook.

By the time she was done typing on the glowing glass screen, her hands were shaking with cold, her teeth chattering. She encrypted the file and hit the send button, launching it off to an SVR server, somewhere out there in the ether.

Sitting there in the dark before a now-empty screen, she thought about the report she'd just sent. It seemed obvious to her that this was important. If it was obvious to her, then it would be obvious to her superiors. She knew what they would ask her to do.

She reopened her browser and Googled flights to Seattle. It took five more minutes to buy a first-class ticket on a six o'clock out of Reagan National, using the Genevieve Lund alias.

There wasn't even a need to enter a passport. All of this while standing here in the middle of the National Mall in the middle of the night.

You have to love America, she thought.

CHAPTER 4

A FEW HOURS LATER AND HALF A WORLD AWAY, YURI KUZNETSOV SAT drinking tea in the little café on Al Khateeb Lane, just across the grassy park from the Russian embassy in Damascus.

As the SVR's number one man in the greater Middle Eastern theater, he had a car, a driver, and a murky agenda. But of all the things he might do, he liked lunching at this little café best. He lingered here often, sometimes for hours.

A mustachioed waiter appeared at his elbow, poured Darjeeling from a samovar, and placed sliced meats on the table with colonial formality.

It was early afternoon and the sun warmed his face through a large street-facing window. Though well into winter, it was a pleasant, cloudless sixty-five-degree day. After dozens of winters in Russia, the balding forty-nine-year-old reminded himself of his good fortune in being assigned here. Not Paris by any stretch, but it would do. An old friend of his in the twilight of his career had been just been assigned to Chechnya. Thinking of that old friend now, chewing his sliced chicken, Yuri shuddered. *Chechnya.*

He folded his day-old printout of the *Moscow Times* and bit into a pita, positioning the newspaper to his right, settling in for a long read, another of his secret indulgences. He always printed the online edition and took it with him to this café. He wasn't able to enjoy the *Times*, an opposition paper, in the embassy, where someone could look over his shoulder. The uptight pricks over there only permitted *Pravda*, party-line pablum.

Today, the *Times* headline that caught his eye was about an oil deal between Gazprom, the state-owned Russian energy company, and the Iranian government. In exchange for drilling access to the Iranian oil fields just to the east of Iraq, the Russians would complete the construction of a half-finished nuclear reactor at Bushehr, an Iranian port city on the Persian Gulf.

Yuri had heard rumors about such a deal, but only just. Though he was the senior-ranking SVR spy in the Middle East, this was clearly one of those lucrative ruble-driven ventures that rolled down from the top. The kleptocrats that ran his country would have said it was none of his business—which only made sense in Russia. Nevertheless, he liked what he read, which was rare enough.

For once it wasn't all about money.

Well, he corrected himself, *of course it was about money.*

But at least there was a strategic predicate. Russia had long coveted access to these fields. The pipeline would let them ferry oil directly to Russian tankers in the Caspian Sea, where Gazprom already had substantial refining operations. It was a bonanza for the company, sure, but it was also a bonanza for the *Rodina* herself, whether the greedy bastards had meant for it to be or not.

The Molotov cocktail throwers at the *Times* disagreed, of course. Given that the vice-chairman of Gazprom was a former puppet-president of Russia, Putin's number two, the opinion writers used two columns to criticize the enormous payoff sure to head the way of Gazprom execs and, by extension, Russian government officials.

After finishing the editorial, Yuri looked up from the paper and removed his reading glasses, enjoying the sun on his face. He squinted against the street, framed by white government buildings of the austere, postmodern Islamist style. There weren't many cars on the road—or pedestrians for that matter.

Damascus felt oddly at peace, despite the civil war raging away in the north, up past Homs. Yuri much preferred it down here in the quiet south, just over the hill from Lebanon and the balmy Mediterranean. A perfect climate.

Chechnya . . . He smiled and stirred three sugar cubes into his tea.

By the time he returned to the embassy, he had digested the rest of the *Times* along with a plate of cheese. He'd been putting on weight here. His pants were sticking to his thighs, hard to ignore in the rising afternoon heat. He knew he needed a new, fuller-cut suit. There was a tailor in Beirut, highly recommended by the Foreign Ministry pretty boys. In the meantime, he forced himself to take the three flights of stairs up to his office at the embassy. He arrived at his door puffing.

Breathing hard, the SVR Directorate PR major sank into his chair and looked over the report of one of his field teams. Though it was in the secure in-box on his computer, his secretary had printed it and laid it on his desk, per his standing instructions. He donned his reading glasses and soon forgot about his labored breath, his mouth falling open as he read.

A report on the Macedonian arms dealer he'd nabbed in Dubai.

Under Yuri's orders, his team had executed the snatch because the dealer had been advertising a sensitive strain of the tularemia virus that could be weaponized. Assad's army chief was interested since it would allow him to clear out the rebel population in Aleppo without blowing up more infrastructure. Because he was the head of the region's SVR counterintelligence bureau, Yuri's counterparts in Syria's Military Intelligence Directorate had asked him to vet the deal first, see if it was legit.

Complying, Yuri's operatives set up a first-rate surveillance package only to discover that the Macedonian seller had been in contact with suspected CIA officers right smack in the middle of Dubai. Without telling the Syrians, Yuri had ordered his men to scoop the Macedonian for questioning. He'd taken direct action because he thought he might expose a CIA operation against Syria, something he could use, a feather in his cap career-wise.

Reading the report now, he realized the take was even better than he'd hoped. Under "enhanced interrogation" at the SVR safe house in Al Aweer, the Macedonian had told of a two-million-dollar payoff to come from the Americans. He'd given the names of accounts and contacts. The SVR team asked him to confirm the identity of the CIA operatives they'd surveilled. On and on.

Amazingly, the dealer hadn't even had access to the virus strain. He was going to use the money from the CIA to try to go buy it himself from another set of criminals. In effect, he had bluffed the CIA.

Ballsy, thought Yuri, leaning back in his chair, its springs clicking under the strain. He couldn't believe what people would do for a couple million bucks. The report went on with some pictures of the suspected CIA officers. One of them was a woman, good-looking, late thirties maybe, intense face, thick eyebrows, dark hair dangling beneath a hijab.

The Macedonian thought she might have been the leader, according to the lead interrogator. She'd been to a meet once, the asset said, but she'd worn a blond wig then. He said she'd ordered the other guys around like they worked for her, but she was never identified. He didn't have a name for her, of course. But in one of the photos, there was a reasonably clear view of her face.

Yuri went to the digital dossier on his aging desktop PC. He clipped the most prominent photo of each of the CIA operatives, but especially the woman. He attached it to a general cable for SVR headquarters, along with a request for information. If he could figure out who she was, he could set up more surveillance and beat the CIA at whatever game they were playing.

Not a bad day. Not bad at all.

Around sunset, there was a knock at his office door. It was Putov, Yuri's weasely faced deputy. Putov looked at Yuri and tapped his watch. They were on their way to a meet at a brothel where they intended to lure a Syrian official for blackmail. The idea was to get him to rat out rebel sympathizers. It was work.

Still. Work at a brothel.

But the next morning, Yuri awoke in a funk. Things at the whorehouse hadn't gone as planned. He'd found himself too preoccupied with the implications of uncovering the CIA team operating in his midst to get in the mood.

In the main drinking parlor, he'd ignored his girl, who, he'd sensed, had been making ill-considered references of him to the others. Coming to this drunken realization, he'd lost his temper and backhanded her like an annoyed bear coming out of hibernation. A ruckus with security, hushed words in the corridors, Putov spiriting him out into a waiting car.

In the end he'd come home to his apartment alone, where he'd sat up until three, smoking and drinking vodka. Now, this morning, he poured himself strong coffee and shouldered into his too-tight suit jacket, his head splitting.

Back at the office he logged on to his secure messages and found that the SVR Operations Center in Yasenevo had replied to his request for information. Their reply made Yuri sit up straight. The head splitting abated.

They knew the CIA woman.

While their reporting was light on sources and methods, Yuri figured they must have done an AI facial recognition search and returned with a hit. She was reportedly a high-level CIA operative who had exited the UAE under a different alias and disguised with an auburn wig. There was a picture of the passport. Yuri knew SVR had a line into the passport agencies of a number of countries; evidently, the UAE was one of them.

The completeness of the SVR information was breathtaking. Her real name was Meredith Morris-Dale and she worked, they believed, for Edward Rance, the head of CIA's Counterproliferation Division. She and Rance had met with Jeff Dorsey, CIA's head of National Clandestine Service, only twenty-four hours earlier.

Incredible information, thought Yuri, rubbing his temples. A big fish. She'd been in Dubai for the Syria bioweapons operation only forty-eight hours ago and was sitting down with CIA's top spy in Langley immediately afterward. This meant that she was likely the mastermind behind CIA operations in his neck of the woods.

It also meant that if the CIA went snooping around the new Russia–Iran deal, she would probably play a leading role.

The information referenced reports from an SVR undercover officer code-named Zoloto, Russian for "gold." Given the detail of the reporting, Yuri assumed Zoloto to be an illegal SVR operative who worked in the US under nonofficial cover—the shadowy world of Directorate S. Gold indeed.

His head was beginning to clear. He made a request to his superiors to initiate a full-surveillance operation on Meredith Morris-Dale in the hopes of intercepting whatever her next operation was. He marked it priority one, mission critical, a *Krasniy Odin*. For extra insurance, he noted that it was critical to the success of the Russo–Iranian nukes for oil deal.

That would get the fat cats' attention.

CHAPTER 5

MEREDITH WAS ALL SET TO FLY TO SEATTLE THAT FRIDAY MORNING TO chase down her ex in Washington State, per Dorsey's orders. Since returning from Dubai, she'd had just enough time to swap suitcases, bathe, and grab a few fitful hours of sleep before this sudden trip to the West Coast. Now she stood shivering on the stoop of her Dupont Circle brownstone at seven o'clock, her black TUMI roller bag at her side, an Uber four minutes out.

But remembering something Rance had said, she abruptly stepped back inside, initiated the encryption app on her smartphone, and made a secure call to Sheffield, the CIA general counsel assigned to Counterproliferation. After authenticating, she asked the attorney whether the director had signed the authorization papers.

Nope, the big man hadn't gotten to it yet. Sheffield followed with a lawyerly harangue about how Meredith shouldn't initiate contact until authorized, the perils of illicit disclosure, the danger of crossing lines, given John's special status, and two other things she ignored.

Very well, she thought, hanging up. *Screw Rance and his hurry-up offense.* She'd just been ordered to enjoy a weekend at home by none other than Agency legal. She nixed the Uber and sent a text to her daughter.

Forty-eight hours and several soaking baths later, she sat across from her nineteen-year-old daughter, eating brunch. Grace was a midshipman third class at the US Naval Academy, the imposing white walls of which stood only fifty yards away, abutting a canal that led to the Severn

River. It was a dark, icy day and the few boats moored to the seawall creaked against frozen ropes.

The daughter looked pale and serious in her service dress blue uniform, brown hair at the collar, eyebrows knotted at an angle. As usual, she could spare only a few hours for the visit. January was a notoriously strenuous time at the USNA—all inspections, exams, and frozen marching.

After a plate of eggs and a catch-up on gossip, the conversation lulled with the waiter's arrival. When alone again, Grace said, "So, Mom, what's going on with you? I'm worried."

Meredith cocked her head without expression.

Grace carried on. "I mean, you look good, as usual. A little thin maybe. You've got a nice suntan but I won't bother asking you where it's from. But still . . . you seem even more preoccupied than usual." She placed her hand across Meredith's.

Meredith smiled and patted her daughter's knuckles before stowing her own hand beneath the table. "I'm fine," she said. "Things have just been a little hectic."

"How so?"

Meredith smiled silently, a practiced family signal.

"You must be able to tell me *something*."

The CIA officer looked off toward the frozen docks, thinking about what to say. She wondered at the extent to which she would ever be able to share her whole self with her daughter. *Probably someday,* she concluded.

But not today.

She began, "I can tell you that I'm still on the counterproliferation detail. I can tell you that I find the work rewarding and important. It's fast-paced . . . it's my life, and—you're right—it takes a lot out of me. But hey, look at this tan." The smile weakened as she rolled up her sleeve.

Grace nodded, coolly mature. As Grace sat there in her regimented wool coat, sipping coffee, Meredith could picture her daughter in command of some large naval enterprise someday, a future filled with gold braid.

In that respect, she supposed, the Academy seemed to be doing its job, equipping Grace for life. But while it should have been enough to make a mother proud, she'd been nursing a nagging concern that Grace might still be too young for it all. Meredith didn't want Grace to repeat her own mistake of rushing into adulthood too early. That made her think of John, the mistake's manifestation. Then she pushed it all aside.

Don't get sappy.

After brunch they walked around campus, looking up at the leafless trees, the leaden sky, the imposing granite buildings. Grace escorted her mother to Bancroft Hall, the thirty-three acre, five-story barracks of the brigade of midshipman. She introduced her mother to a handful of other uniformed "mids," mostly girls sharing Grace's serious, confident outlook.

Later, as they sat at a just off-campus Starbucks about to say their goodbyes, Meredith had the depressing thought that maybe Grace had chosen the Academy to provide the structure she'd been missing at home. Here they were, supposed to be catching up, but with very little to say to each other.

About to get up and leave, Meredith blurted, "I almost forgot. I'm on my way out to see your father."

Since the trip was for CIA business, she hadn't been planning on sharing that; but she felt the need to say something that would break through—anything, really.

Grace blinked rapidly. "Really? Out in Washington State? Why?"

"I need him to sign some papers. It's nothing, really, just some legal paperwork the Agency asked me to take care of."

"Can't that sort of thing be DocuSigned? Why go in person?"

"You know how the Agency can be."

Grace touched Meredith's hand on the table. "Mom. Is he . . . okay?"

Meredith was never quite sure what Grace knew about John's situation. Like any child of divorce, she was guarded in her discussions with her parents.

"I'm sure he's quite fine out there, doing his thing," Meredith replied, withdrawing her hand again.

"Yeah, that's Dad. . . ." Grace sipped her coffee, then abruptly put it down. "Wait! I have something for him. I was going to mail it—if he were a normal human, it would be e-mail, but you know how he is." Grace fished through her Academy-issued backpack to find the letter. "Anyway, Mom, would you deliver it for me?"

Like some form of diplomatic correspondence, the letter was sealed in a five-by-seven manila envelope with Grace's signature across the flap. It lay in the seat next to Meredith in her handbag on the flight to Seattle later that afternoon. It was folded in treble, buried in one of the covert document slots sewn into the handbag's lining.

Built by Agency specialists, the slot required a special combination of pulls, prods, and slides to open. The envelope next to Grace's letter contained an encrypted USB drive with information she was to give to John.

Staring out at the faded Midwestern landscape sliding beneath her window, her mind should have been on the contents of the USB drive.

But it was on Grace's letter.

CHAPTER 6

JOHN DALE SAT ON THE DECK OF HIS MOUNTAINSIDE HOME, ADMIRING his work. It was almost four thirty on Sunday afternoon and the sun was already low. Here on the eastern side of the Cascade Range, which roughly divided Washington State into wet and dry halves, the temperature was in the forties and the sky a crystalline blue. In the unfiltered sun it was almost warm.

He was leaning back in his Adirondack, enjoying a beer as he looked at his art, the product of the last several hours' effort. The IPA, the chair, and the late-afternoon vista constituted something of a ritual whenever he finished a painting.

Some people even said he was pretty good. There were five of his paintings on display at the touristy watering hole over in Roslyn, a few miles up the road. A few more at the steak place in town. Three others had already sold for about five hundred bucks apiece at a little gallery in Ellensburg. One lady had asked him to sign an exhibit program when he visited. That was cool.

Dale had spent the cold, clear day near the top of the mountain ridge on which he lived. In the early-morning dark, he'd loaded up his portable easel, a small canvas, and his converted fishing tackle box full of oils into the cargo hatch of his snowmobile. He'd headed uphill on a well-groomed track in the dark, using his aging government-issue night-vision goggles to find the way around the mountain switchbacks.

Since the gray wolf population had been growing in this part of the Cascades, he'd also slung over his back his hunting rifle with its high-end thermal scope, another remnant of his former life. Having seen all manner of wolves, bears, and cougars in these mountains, he never set off into the backcountry unarmed. Especially in the dark.

His idea had been to try to get up early enough to capture the morning view of a big granite mountain across the valley called Peoh Point. In this stretch of clear winter weather, Peoh was majestic, revealing deep shadows and subtle snows that would glow pink in the morning light. Every morning the river valley at the monolith's feet sent wisps of fog upward, where they evaporated to clear air as they reached the peak. By ten, the glowing veil would be gone.

But it had been crazy cold for plein air brushwork—colder than he'd ever attempted before. To fight against the freezing temperatures, he'd prepped his snowy painting site the day before with the fixings for a campfire and a portable heater powered by a propane tank big enough for a barbecue.

He finished his beer and set it down on the cedar planks of the deck, further admiring his work, thinking about what he had to do in his studio to finish it up. His outdoor speakers were playing an old country-western ballad full of slide guitar. With the sun sparking on the snowmelt, he considered this to be one hell of a fine moment. He wanted it to last.

And then his phone chirped, ensuring it wouldn't.

Another text from Meredith, his ex. She'd announced on Friday that she needed to see him about something in person, and she wasn't the type to be denied.

He hadn't responded at first. She'd upped the ante by saying it was about their daughter. But Dale figured that was a ruse. He and Grace traded letters now and then. His daughter seemed fine, probably more stable than her parents.

Playing along, he'd asked Meredith to just call him so they could discuss it on the phone. Nope. Meredith had insisted it had to be in person. She was on her way out to Seattle one way or the other. She was like that.

Whatever this was all really about, Dale had been guessing that it wasn't going to be good. Meredith, the trained covert-asset handler, liked to take on conflicts in person. Her superpower was reading people—more like seeing through bullshit with X-ray vision. She'd been Dale's boss, his wife, the mother of his child, and now his ex. He'd been on the other side of that penetrating glare more than once.

He tipped a fresh bottle to his mouth, wishing her away.

Not much point to that. Seeing her one-way messages come steadily pulsing in as the sun went down was like receiving intelligence reports of an invading force. She'd left Dulles. She'd landed at SeaTac. She'd made it to the freeway. Soon she'd be getting close to the pass that held back the Pacific storms.

But it wouldn't hold her back. He glanced at his chunky diver's watch. About an hour out now. *Shit.*

Her arrival was extra vexing since it had forced Dale to break a date with a wealthy, just-divorced Seattle housewife who'd gotten the family's fancy mountain vacation house as part of the settlement. She'd bought one of his paintings out of the touristy bar two weeks ago, and they'd been on a texting relationship ever since.

She'd hung the painting and invited Dale over to see it, along with other sundry hints. The hints had been escalating to the point that Dale was now pretty sure that tonight was going to be the night. But now he'd done a last-minute putoff until next weekend. The divorcée had sounded pissed. Really pissed.

There goes another one, he thought, rising from the Adirondack.

With a sigh, he dropped the dead soldiers into a trash can and decided he'd better tidy the place up.

His two-bedroom house stood at the northern, uphill end of a sloping forty-acre plot. It was of a stacked-log-cabin style, its four big gables framed by large Doug firs felled right there on the property by the builder. In addition to the house, there were a barn and a couple of other outbuilding sheds, mostly for his hunting or painting gear.

The rocky, tree-studded property was only three miles up the hill from the little town of Cle Elum, Washington, which billed itself as "the Heart of the Cascades." *Cle Elum* was a Yakima Indian phrase that meant "swift waters," in reference to the river that bisected the valley.

Dale had owned the place for two years now. He liked it for the solitude, the painting, the hunting, and the high-altitude trail runs through the mountains to stay in shape. It was also only a few hours' drive over the mountains to Puget Sound, where he moored a small sailboat. He liked to spend at least half the summer sailing the San Juan Islands, fishing for salmon and closing down the occasional marina bar.

When he'd left the Agency under duress and lost half his assets in the divorce, he'd been pretty well broke. Figuring he couldn't sink much further, he'd pooled his remaining assets to buy this fixer-upper, then spent a year doing the handiwork himself. He was still pretty well broke, but at least he had a house he liked.

And it turned out he didn't need nearly as much money as he'd always thought. He spent most of the year painting landscapes, hunting big game when in season, and sailing in the summers. The paintings were an all-cash business and kept him in groceries. He didn't have a family to support anymore. As far as he was concerned, he was doing fine.

Meredith texted again. She was in Easton, forty minutes out. Looking around at his leathery living room with the massive stone hearth he'd built himself, Dale decided he didn't much like the idea of her showing up here at his house. Like the former spook he was, he much preferred meeting his contact at a neutral location, incognito.

He texted her back that he would meet her for dinner in town at Owen's, the local steak place. He could use a steak. He'd make her buy.

Meredith brought her rented Explorer to a halt in the parking lot of Owen's well after the shy winter sun had sunk behind the mountains. She wore jeans, a black wool shawl, and knee-high boots. She walked briskly across the parking lot with her ever-present bag over her shoulder, zigzagging to avoid the puddles of snowmelt. Every other vehicle seemed to be a jacked-up pickup with fat tires. She was definitely outside the Beltway now.

As she made it around the building to the Old West Main Street sidewalk, she and John locked eyes through the front window. He was in a back booth with a clear view of the door. He nodded toward her with a mildly amused look that she knew well.

Meredith entered and breezed purposefully past the hostess. It was a slow Sunday evening and the place was half full at best.

Dale stood when she approached. They traded an awkward hug.

She smiled as she slid into the booth across from him. "You look good, John," she said. "Fit. Almost like you're still operational."

She meant it. As an ex-wife, she'd been secretly hoping to see more gray in his hair, maybe a bit of a beer gut. As his soon-to-be managing case officer, she was delighted to see he was in shape.

Dale nodded and returned the smile. "I try." He leaned back and took her in. "You look tired, Meth."

Meredith smiled through her irritation. First of all, other than John, she hadn't been called Meth by anyone since her training days at the Farm. Second of all, why the fuck were people always telling her she looked tired?

She looked around at the small-town restaurant: red booths, hundred-year-old oak floors, brick walls, a few elk heads on the wall, the smell of roasted meat. "Little early for dinner, isn't it?"

Before he could answer, the bell at the door rang. It opened with a cold blast of air and an elderly couple. The hostess helped them to a booth.

"Nah," John said. "I'm starving. Besides, you look like you've been hanging out with the vegan set on the seventh floor. You can get a steak the size of a hubcap here. Oh, and also, I humbly wanted to impress you with this."

He pointed at a three-by-five painting over his head. It was of a distant valley view with farms, a river, and a sweeping mountain range in the distance captured in a dusty golden sunset. In the corner there was a small red signature: *Dale*.

Her eyes widened. "One of yours? *Wow.* It's good, John!"

"It's okay."

"Okay enough for you to want six hundred bucks for it. Hell, I think you could get a couple grand. Life must be getting pretty good out here at those rates."

Dale nodded. "Keeps me from panhandling. Barely."

"How many have you sold so far?"

"I don't know. Like five. Maybe it will plug the hole of that pension your bosses decided to deny me." He smiled to show he didn't blame her for his situation with CIA.

"Yeah," she said awkwardly. "Would be nice to straighten that out one of these days, wouldn't it?"

The waitress came. Dale ordered a beer, Meredith a Diet Coke.

They said nothing to each other for a while. But then, in spite of everything, they couldn't help but fall into the pattern of any one of their former relationships: officer-handler, husband-wife, mother-father.

Meredith could read enough of John to see that he was somewhat happy, somewhat healed. He'd endured so much. It made her hate herself for having to pull him back in.

"Well," she said after a while, her voice softening, "I know I forced you into this meeting. Thanks for doing it."

"You'd have found me one way or the other," he said. "You have the resources for it." He stopped smiling and looked earnest. "But honestly, Meth, it's been too long. Just one look at you and I'm already jealous."

"*Jealous?* Of who? Of what?"

"Of what's-his-name, whoever he is." He took her hands in his, stretching over the table. He caressed the top of her knuckles, pinched her fingers. "You're still smoking hot, Meth. Sexier than the day we met. Please don't tell me you're getting married. I'm begging you." His face molded into that faintly amused look again.

Meredith pulled her hands back with a jerk. She'd almost fallen for it. *Idiot.* "Married to the work, John. You know how it is. You can be jealous of Charlie-India-Alpha."

"Yeah, right," he replied, leaning back. "Seriously, Meth, if you've come to break my heart, do it quickly. Have mercy."

"Does this act work on the local talent?" she asked, regaining her footing. "Where was all that charm a few years ago when I really needed it?"

"Right here, baby." He tapped a fist over his heart, looking wounded. "You were just working too hard to see it."

"*I* was?"

"Yes."

"You mean, when I was stuck at that crappy condo in Arlington and you kept re-upping for paramilitary ops in Iraq?"

"What can I say? You're good at kissing the brass's ass and I like to kick in doors. Maybe you should've joined me over there."

"Couldn't. Remember? Had a daughter to raise."

He paused. Something in his eyes changed. The spell was broken, the nerve struck. "Yeah. So did I."

"You know what I mean. We had our respective duties."

"Yeah." He lifted his hands, cracked two knuckles. "But my duty kind of fucked me over in the end, didn't it, Meth?"

"Didn't have to. You're the one who left the Company. It was your call, holing up out here like Ted Kaczynski. We still have a daughter who needs raising, if you want to come down from your mighty mountaintop."

Dale maneuvered one leg out of the booth, about to stand and leave. "I don't need this shit," he said with a grunt.

But just as he was about to get up, the wide matronly waitress arrived, blocking him. At the same time, Meredith put her hand on his, holding it in place on the red-checked tablecloth, shooting him an apologetic look.

The motherly old server, witness to at least a thousand of such confrontations in this small town, lightened the mood by talking about the approaching snowfall, about how rough the roads had been up on old Route 97 two nights back. The old gal knew what she was doing. She wasn't about to let this handsome young couple go at each other like that. And besides, she didn't want to lose their tip. Things were slow this time of year.

Boxed in by all this feminine guile, Dale shifted his leg back under the table. Neither of them said anything for a while.

Meredith made the first move. She touched Dale's calf with the toe of her boot beneath the table. "I really shouldn't have said any of that. I'm sorry."

"Bygones, Meth," Dale replied after a few seconds, warming again, the amused look coming back to life. "Enough venom. Let's chase it with something useful." He looked at her Diet Coke. "It may not look like it, but they make a hell of a Manhattan here."

She looked up at the elk heads on the wall. "We're a long way from Manhattan. But fuck it. I could use one."

Maria Borbova slowed the Audi to a stop on the far side of the parking lot from Meredith's rental Explorer. Over her earpiece, she told Leo and Vasily, the two Spetsnaz Alphas in the black SUV somewhere behind her, to keep moving until she developed a plan. They'd hastily changed into clothes appropriate for tourists in the mountains, with new Gore-Tex coats, jeans, Sorels, and hats, gratis from the clever SVR planners at the Seattle consulate.

Maria stood in the gravel parking lot at the back of the building, listening, watching. She held her phone in front of her to act like she was thumb-typing, but she was really making sure she was alone. After a few moments, she walked to Meredith's Explorer and attached a magnetic GPS tracker, about the size of a deck of cards, to the underside of the SUV.

She then studied the back of the old building. It was a cold, clear night and the stars fired away in the mountain setting. Beyond the town, there were only a few scattered lights on the surrounding ridges. Vehicle traffic was intermittent.

She noticed what appeared to be a kitchen door that led to a dumpster. She also noticed that the second floor of the old Main Street brick building had drawn blinds over dark windows. Whatever was up there was either vacant or closed. This gave her an idea. But first she had to see what her surveillance target was doing.

She ratcheted her knit cap over her blond hair and yanked her zipper all the way up to hide her mouth. She went to the front of the building and walked past the window to see what was happening. This put her on the prominent sidewalk of the town's main drag.

In about ten rows of booths, she saw a handful of diners. The Morris-Dale woman was in the last booth, facing away from the front door, not far from the restrooms. To case it further, Maria kept moving, looking down at her phone as she walked. Using the phone's glass screen like a mirror, she was able to keep her head down as she passed right in front of the restaurant. She saw Morris-Dale and her husband turn their heads to look at her as she passed. Not a problem, but interesting to note their level of awareness.

She took a right at the next street to circle the building, ending up back in the rear parking lot. Now having a better understanding of what she was up against, she studied the second floor. There was a rusty metal staircase on the side of the building that rambled like a fire escape up to the second floor.

After pausing to ensure she was still alone, she jogged up the stairs to find a heavy fire door, locked. Maria fumbled through her jacket pockets to retrieve her wallet-sized pick kit. The lock was ancient, maybe from the forties. She had the second-floor door open about three minutes later.

Once inside, she saw a few desks, laptops, filing cabinets, and posters on the windows. It appeared to be a small independent real estate office. The floor was bare wood planks, very old, probably original. It smelled musty.

She spoke softly into the encrypted UHF radio, connected to her ear with a voice-activated microphone via Bluetooth. "Alpha One, this is Bravo. Park at the street around the corner and meet me on the second floor of the building. Targets near the window on the street, eastern side of building. Bring the equipment up to me."

CHAPTER 7

OUT OF HABIT, MEREDITH AND DALE BOTH NOTICED THE YOUNG WOMAN bundled up in a down Patagonia jacket hustling up the street. Neither of them thought much about her, though it was a little odd for someone to be walking in this small town on such a cold night.

Meredith was a third of the way through her T-bone and ready to raise the white flag. She hadn't eaten this much in a long time, but she stuffed it down to equalize the bourbon. Though it was still early, she had a red-eye back to Dulles leaving around midnight. She needed to get sharp.

"So, Meth," Dale said, "you still haven't told me what was so important."

Her eyes darted to the corners. A napkin went over her mouth. "Yeah. Look, I need to. I do. But I don't think I can get into detail here."

Dale held his fork and steak knife stock-still. "What do you mean? Why not?" He studied Meredith's face. It suddenly dawned on him: this was about work. "Wait. Really? What could anyone with your company want from me these days that we couldn't discuss here?"

"It's about something you used to do. Something that's popped up again. It's important enough that I've been ordered here to discuss it with you. Let's just put it at that." She turned toward the waitress and signaled for the check.

Dale studied her. He pushed his plate away and sank into the red vinyl of the booth, shaking his head. "Negative," he said.

"John, it's important."

"Doesn't matter."

"It does. But we can't talk about it in public."

"You act like we're in Vienna or Prague and the bad guys are around the corner. It's Cle Elum, Meth. People around here get suspicious of anyone without a don't-tread-on-me bumper sticker. You can give me something. Right here. Otherwise, fuck off."

Ten feet above them, Maria and Leo crouched on their knees with headphones on, listening. Leo had drilled a tiny hole all the way through the floor, just to the left of a light fixture on the ceiling of the restaurant below. The upturned glass cup of the fixture had caught the small amount of ceiling dust.

Through this tiny hole, he'd inserted a glassy wire with a directional mic on its end the size of a matchstick. They had had to fiddle with the amplifier in order to squelch out electrical interference and adjust the fade to overcome ambient noise, but they were now able to listen to the conversation, if faintly.

Meredith wiped her hands on her napkin and dropped it on the plate. "All right. I'll see if I can come up with a public version. What's your favorite news channel?"

"Don't have one," said Dale. "I find my mind stays clearer if I avoid the news."

"Of course you do. Must be freeing to have such an empty mind." He frowned at her. "Well, I was reading an article in the *New York Times* on the flight over. It made me think about Grace."

"Uh-huh. What about her?"

"When she gets commissioned, she may find herself in the Gulf. Maybe as a pilot, maybe as a ship driver," Meredith said.

Dale nodded slowly. He knew what she was doing, so he just listened.

"As a mother, I'm worried. I need your help. I need to get your perspective on it," she said. "You were Navy over there once. You know what it's like. We are all very, very worried. It's just been terrible."

His eyes narrowed. "Terrible how?"

"Oh, you know. Same thing that's been happening for years. The *Times* laid it out pretty convincingly. Goes all the way back to the eighties, when the *Vincennes* shot down the Airbus. Then all of the IRGC-sponsored terror ops with Hezbollah in Lebanon, Syria . . . all of that. Now the nuclear deal has fallen apart and we've taken out that Quds general, Soleimani. The *Times* was talking about how the mullahs are getting desperate, barely holding on to power. That's why I'm so worried about Grace. I was hoping you could calm me down."

Dale slumped, listening. Meredith went on. "I mean, at this point it keeps escalating. They've seized a British oil tanker in the Straits of Hormuz. They lobbed some missiles into our base in Iraq. Expecting more, their air defenses are so keyed up that they shot down a Ukrainian airliner by mistake." She tilted her head forward. "It's just a lot of bad shit, John. Wondered if you'd heard and thought you might be able to help."

"Too bad I'm no longer involved," Dale said. "And no, I'm not worried about it. These things have a way of working out. Neither side wants a war. I certainly don't."

"Yeah. But I wonder if one can be avoided. The *Times* thinks it can be done only if we take some actions to *de*-escalate things, rather than what's been happening. Maybe behind the scenes. You know?"

Dale slowly shook his head. "Like I said, I don't think about things that don't affect me anymore."

The check came. Meredith pulled her credit card out of her bag. "I got it," she said. "Business." She signed and pocketed her copy of the receipt. She stood by the table, looking down on him, absently tapping her foot. "We need to talk more about it somewhere privately. How about your place? I don't have much time before I have to get back for my red-eye. I'd really feel better about it."

On the floor above, Maria looked at Leo. She spoke through her Blue-tooth to Vasily, who was still in the Yukon outside, watching for threats. "We need to find his house. They're taking the conversation there. It's the only place we'll get anything valuable."

Vasily answered over the radio. "The database isn't returning an ad-dress for Morris-Dale or just plain Dale. He must go by something else. It's coming up empty."

"*Govno*," Maria cursed. "We need to tail. If they take his car, you need to follow. Leo and I will take down the rig and be behind you. Try John with both an H and without. Hurry it up."

She listened to Meredith on the ground floor below, thanking the waitress on her way out. Whatever was driving this, it was about Iran. Since Rance ran the Counterproliferation Division of CIA and Mere-dith reported to him, it made sense that she would be focused there. But what did it have to do with this scruffy mountain man she used to be married to?

Vasily answered. "Think I've got something . . . on the open web. There's an artist, a painter, named John Dale. He displayed his work in Ellensburg, about twenty miles from here. Not much more about him. We could submit an RFI to Yasenevo to get his address. They could pull up something through Motor Vehicles."

"No time," said Maria. "Whatever it is they're going to talk about is going down right now."

Out on the street, Dale slid behind the wheel of his 2014 Ford F-150 Crew Cab and fired the truck up. Meredith had forgotten how to get to his house, so he told her to follow behind in her rented Explorer. Wire-less coverage and Google Maps were both dodgy out on the mountain roads where Dale lived.

Meredith was uncomfortable following directly. In a fake embrace outside his truck, she whispered to him that she would perform an

SDR, a surveillance-detection route, in the town first, then approach at the corner of the road that led to his property. The corner with the old antiques store. Dale nodded reluctantly.

As he warmed up his truck and Meredith drove off, he shook his head, sobering up. Seeing her, listening to her talk about tradecraft, the need to do an SDR . . . it left him numb. The mild two-beer buzz he'd been enjoying when dining with Meredith was gone now, replaced by a cold, empty feeling in his gut.

He'd left this life behind. Patiently, deliberately, and finally. He wanted nothing to do with it. But here was Meth, referencing Grace as a kind of code word to pull him back in. She wouldn't do that if she wasn't deadly serious about needing his help. He'd told her to fuck off, appropriately in his estimation; but he also knew he'd have to hear her out.

He made it to the corner and waited in the dark with his parking lights on, as they'd agreed. A few minutes later, he saw her headlights blink and knew they were in the clear. He turned onto the slushy road and started making his way up the mountain, skidding here and there, her headlights a few hundred yards behind him.

It was a slow climb of about two miles of switchbacks before they came to his property. Snow was beginning to fall. A few flurries at first, but picking up with big fat flakes. It was often that way here in the mountains. A perfectly sunny day could end with a blizzard. You never knew.

"Headed up a gravel road now," said Vasily into the encrypted UHF. "Hard to follow on the GPS. Roads aren't marked. But I can see their tracks in the snow."

Maria and Leo acknowledged with two transmitter clicks. Vasily gave them further directions on where to go.

A few minutes later, he said, "They've entered a private property. There's a gate. I can see what looks like a cabin behind some trees with lights on. They must be in there. I'm going to double back. Tracks would be too obvious. We'll want to find another way up."

Two clicks came as a response. Vasily moved the switch on the dash to the Four High drive position and spun around. The snow had accumulated about an inch so far, but it fell on top of many older snows that had melted and refrozen in the sunny weather. He heard one of his wheels spin. He pulled over and studied a trail map. He saw another way. They'd have to hike for a quarter mile through some cover, but there was at least a parallel road.

Leo and Maria found it hard going. Eventually they got to the point Vasily had signaled, pulled over, and killed the Audi's engine right behind him. They'd already rigged their cars so that the interior lights would stay off with the doors open. Vasily was gathering their gear under the light of a red-lensed flashlight.

He emerged with two sets of night-vision devices. They strapped them over their ski hats like miners' lights.

Maria switched hers on and flipped the two optical tubes down over her eyes, waiting for them to warm up. With the half-moon lighting the clouds, she was able to see the wintry landscape in shades of green, punctuated by the black dots of snowflakes falling in front of her like static.

"Let's go," she said to the two Spetsnaz men.

Meredith had been to Dale's home once before. But it had been summer then, right around the time the divorce had finally settled. She and Grace had taken a vacation out here, on which they hiked and camped at a nearby glacier lake. John had stayed with them for one of those nights and the three of them had slept here at his home, almost like the family they'd once been. But that was over a year ago. Meredith hadn't been back since.

Dale let her in and turned on some lights. There was a large stone hearth with a woodstove. Dale went about splitting kindling and tearing newspaper. Within a few minutes, he had a fire going.

Now that she was fully operational, Meredith wandered around the house, looking for vulnerabilities. She didn't want to freak him out, but she needed to have this conversation in a professional manner, which meant tradecraft. She turned on the kitchen tap, letting the water run.

"Really?" he said, looking over his shoulder from the fireplace.

"Yes." She looked out at the driveway. No headlights. "What kind of security do you have here?" She started pulling down window shades up front.

"Because my paintings are so valuable?"

"No, asshole." She crossed to the back windows and started lowering blinds. "Because I need to make sure this is a secure conversation."

"This is about as safe a safe house as you're going to find. I may not look it, but I'm still armed and dangerous."

"Okay, okay," she said, stopping in front of a window that still had the shades up. "I'll leave this one alone so we can at least watch the snow." She collapsed into a leather chair, sighing, rubbing her forehead. "This job made me paranoid a long time ago." She sighed again. "In my defense, it's sort of a prereq."

He nodded, watching her. She was tense. Whatever was on her mind, it was bad. "You have to tell me what's going on, Meth. For real."

Meredith riffled through her handbag. She pulled out her secure covcom—agency shorthand for covert-communications device. To anyone else it looked like a normal Microsoft Surface tablet with a flexible keyboard. She performed a number of sequences with codes and gestures before it brought up a separate home screen of secure Agency apps.

Accessing his Wi-Fi over a VPN, she pulled up a LinkedIn page with John's picture on it. He looked darker in the picture. The name on the profile was Reza Shariati. She tilted the tablet for him to see. "Remember this guy?"

Dale leaned over and examined his own photo. It was a younger version of him. His hair was shorter and his eyes were darker because they'd deliberately changed his skin tone with makeup. "Yeah. Good to see old Reza's doing so well."

The legend of John's former alias had progressed. According to his

LinkedIn profile, he'd gone on to a number of professional jobs with little-known consultancies that were all Agency front companies.

"Well, a certain asset just reached out to you, Reza, right here. Through this profile." She tapped the Surface's screen.

"Who? What asset?"

"Cerberus."

Dale closed his eyes and shook his head. He couldn't believe he was having this conversation. He said, "I guess you've been read in, then. You know the op or am I about to get water-boarded?"

"I know it. Dorsey himself. Active Archer."

"Right."

"Well, the guys that took over running Cerberus for you have a problem. He's gone off-grid."

Dale stood up, opened the door to the woodstove, and poked at the fire. A gust of heat warmed the room. Turning back to her, he said, "I would agree that that's a loss. He was good. Probably my best work at the Company. But how is this my problem?"

"Because he says he will talk only to you. He trusts only you."

Dale laughed in spite of himself. "Yeah, that's probably hard for you guys to believe."

"It's not. You were always a better case officer than you ever acknowledged. A great handler."

"Uh-huh. Keep working me, Meth. I like it. Handle me."

"I'm serious. Look, he's gone away at the point where we need him. We don't know where or why."

Dale nodded, remembering his correspondence with the man. It had always been on Cerberus's terms. "Is his wife still alive?"

"Yes. As I dug into the file, I learned we've been feeding her MS meds. I assume that started with you."

"Right. That was a big part of it for Cerberus. Do we know where he's working now? He was on the research side when I had him. We communicated through the company I was supposedly working for—Baramar, based in Dubai . . . machine-parts distributor. One of those parts happens to be Swiss-made centrifuges for medical research. With a little work, they're sanctions-proof."

"Who is he?"

"I never knew. Somebody that remembered me from my rabble-rousing at McGill. But I never knew who he really was."

"How did you establish his bona fides?"

"The Agency did. He claimed he could manage the code of their centrifuges. We didn't know if it was true or not, but we didn't see the harm in passing him some tainted code of our own. If it was a trap, what were they going to do? The only damage would have been to my cover. We all thought it was worth the risk since I didn't have any other real business going in Iran. None of us did."

"So what happened?"

"We sent him some code and he installed it. Their Swiss-made centrifuges have been a tiny bit off ever since. It must be driving them nuts."

"That's what Dorsey and Rance said. According to them, Cerberus is the only firewall we have that's keeping them from going nuke."

"Rance . . . ," Dale said, shaking his head. "He's in this?"

"He's running Counterproliferation. My boss."

"Fuck, Meth. You need to get away from that guy. He's dirty."

"I'd love to. But you know him. He keeps climbing. Look, I wouldn't be here if this were just Rance. Dorsey's on it. So's the director."

"I need a drink," said Dale.

He went around the corner to his kitchen. He offered something to Meredith but she declined. He threw in some ice and poured himself two fingers of Maker's Mark. He sat by the fire, sinking into a worn leather club chair, taking a sip, looking through the one unblocked window at the falling snow.

"You shouldn't," said Meredith. "This is serious."

"I should. Because it's serious."

"Fine, have it your way."

Dale took another sip. "So what am I supposed to do? Be his pen pal? Become old Reza again?"

Meredith nodded. "For starters, yes. We need you to come in. We need you to communicate with him closely . . . and we need to be ready for anything he does. How is your Farsi these days?"

"How do you think? It's rusty as hell. But that doesn't matter."

"Why doesn't it matter?"

"I told you. I'm not participating in any of this. I'm out."

Meredith leaned forward. A vein sprouted where her neck met her collarbone. "*What?* John, are you fucking *kidding me*? We're just about at war with the Iranians. The only thing keeping them from enriching enough uranium to build their own nukes is one guy. That one guy will only talk to *you*. And you won't do it? What the fuck?"

Dale took a slug of bourbon this time, a real mouthful. How many times had he endured arguments with this woman?

"Listen," he said, pausing, letting her profanity echo off the stone floor. The booze burned his throat. "It may be that cut-and-dried to you, Meth. But let me remind you of something."

He held his right hand before her, stretching out his fingers. The pinkie had been severed at the middle knuckle, healed over now as a stump. He wiggled it.

"The last time I worked for you fuckers, I lost this little guy, thanks to some Stone Age cave dwellers. They did that to show me what my beheading would be like. It was supposed to be the opening act."

His hand started to shake. He brought it down to his side and clenched the fabric of his jeans to stop it.

He leaned forward. "Then when I fight my way out of that hellhole, the very people that sent me into it call me a traitor. *Me*, Meth! *Me!*"

His whole arm was shaking now. He kicked a stray log into the woodstove with a loud metal clang before tossing the rest of the bourbon over his teeth.

CHAPTER 8

LEO LAY IN A PRONE POSITION IN THE TREES. SNOW FILTERED TO THE ground around him. He was aiming a three-foot directional mic shaped like a giant shuttlecock at the house.

"Anything?" he whispered to Maria. She lay next to him, tuning the amp.

"No," she said. "Garbled voices. Hissing. I think some water's on."

They'd climbed down from a parking spot up the hill, having snaked up a narrow logging road. They had a downhill view on the side of the house, about fifty yards from the deck, in the dark of the tree line.

"That means tradecraft. Must be important. I'm going to try video."

There was one window where they hadn't drawn the blinds. Now and then Maria could see them pacing.

Speechreading had been part of her training as an SVR spy. If she could capture the exchange on high-res video, she thought she might be able to read their lips. Worst case, she could make a tape for expert analysis later. She pulled a long-lensed electronic device similar to a spotting scope from her bag and set it up on a tripod. She powered it up and ensured it was recording.

"Alpha Two, security check," she said into her mic, turning the knobs to bring the cabin windows into focus.

"All clear," Vasily answered.

He was stationed up at the vehicles to make sure a lookie-loo neighbor didn't chance upon them. Since their position on this desolate mountain road would be hard to explain, Vasily had taken a nine-millimeter

HK machine pistol from his bag, hiding it below a coat on the seat next to him. It was unlikely anything like that would be necessary, but this was a K1, a *Krasniy Odin*. Anything was authorized.

Meredith let John's storm pass. There wasn't much else she could do. His anger was certainly justified—and familiar. The same old rage that had split them up. Still, she had to get him back off the ledge. She had no choice.

He was standing now, his hands trembling. He stood before the window that looked out on Peoh, invisible now in the dark. He stared out into the falling snow, his elbows quivering. He shoved his hands into his pockets.

Meredith approached from behind and touched his shoulders gently. She turned him toward her and embraced him, burying her face into his flannel shirt, pulling him in tight. He smelled smoky, bourbon on his breath.

She held him there for a long time, silently, no other sound in the cabin beyond the crackling fire. His body shook softly against her. Eventually it slowed and stopped. She felt his arms encircle her back and squeeze. She thought she felt his shoulders rise and fall in a long breath, maybe even a muffled sob. None of this was right. None of it.

She pulled back and caught his eye. "Hey, John, it's okay. It's me. I agree with everything you've said. You know that."

He breathed deeply again and let go. His eyes shone. She was glad now that he'd taken that drink. He seemed to gather himself and sat in a leather chair, near the fire. Meredith took the matching chair across from him. He nodded and stared into his glass, the booze gone, some ice remaining. He cleared his throat. Started to say something, then stopped.

"John," she said. She spoke softly, quietly. "You're the best man I know. Best man I've ever known. What they did to you was bullshit. You'll get no argument from me."

A nod.

"You deserve peace. You do. I'm going to ensure you have it. I can do that. That's why I'm here personally."

Another nod. He stared at the melting ice in his glass.

"But you have to understand, we're at the end of our rope. All of us. You're all we've got."

"No, Meth. No." His voice was ragged, hoarse. He kept staring into the glass. He cleared his throat again. "You can't lay that kind of trip on me, man. Not after everything they did to me."

She nodded and sat silently for a time. The fire hissed. The wind rattled. Snowflakes pelted the windows. She said, "Now that you know what we're up against, what if we were to use it to get some justice for you?"

He shook his head. "Justice? Who are you kidding?"

"Hear me out. What if we—I mean, you—dictate terms back to the Agency?"

"Terms like what?"

"Like you're fully reinstated with all honors. The inquiry would just go away."

"I don't need that," he said. "I left *because* of my honor. Fuck them."

"You do have your honor. You have more honor than anyone I know of. And it's why you're going to do this. We both know it."

"Nope. I'm not. The Agency ruined that man. You know that too."

"Bullshit. That man is indestructible."

Maria had a good view of them now; Dale seemed to be looking out the window, almost right at her. "Got 'em," she said into the mic. "I have a visual. Recording."

Somewhere up the hill Vasily answered with two clicks. Leo said, "Still no audio here."

"I've got eyes," Maria said. "Keep trying."

She watched the couple in the window, picking up a few words by lip-reading when she could. They embraced, and Maria thought she was going to witness a love scene. But then they came back apart and sat across from each other. She now had a perfect view of Dale's face. He looked distraught, irrepressibly sad.

"Can you at least tell me why Cerberus trusts you? Any hints?" asked Meredith.

"No, not really."

Meredith looked at him sympathetically. "I know you hate talking about this. I do. But you can at least give me context."

He nodded. "Yeah, okay." He seemed to pull himself together. He crossed his legs, set the glass on an end table. "I never met him. He was a good asset and we had him right where we needed him."

"In research?"

"Yes, but he would never tell us where that really was. He was very, very careful."

"What motivated him?"

"He never said. But it wasn't money or religion. I also don't think he had any particular affinity for America."

"Then why spy for us?"

Dale stood up and returned to the fire, poking at it. He put a heavier log on. Sparks flew out and he tamped them dead with his boot.

"Few of the Iranians I met in Canada liked the US, even the ones who hate the mullahs. They blame CIA specifically for Ajax, the overthrow of Mossadeq. They blame us for keeping the shah on the throne while he crushed all opposition. They blame us for giving the shah exile when he was finally tossed out." He returned to his seat. "But they also think that what they got after the shah was worse. I heard that a lot up there in Montreal."

"Right," she said. "Frying pan to fire."

He nodded. "Before '79, Iran was a country tilting toward modern Western values. The mullahs were the outliers, lowbrow hicks from Qom. A lot of the students I knew thought of themselves as true Persians, with a proud liberal tradition that wanted to save their country from the mullahs. I always figured Cerberus for one of these."

"But to risk your life for it?" Meredith asked. "Has to be more than that."

Dale sighed. "I suppose he saw himself as a bulwark against a mad country, a mad world. He didn't share much, but that was my take-away." He looked up at her. "That's what I got, Meth. That's it. Sorry."

"If you had to guess, why do you think he would stop?"

"I don't know. Maybe he's finally had it with the US. Maybe he's worried about his security. Maybe he's finally become one of them. You know as well as I do that the good assets are in it for ideology . . . or even better, their version of morality. Sometimes it shifts."

"Sometimes it does."

"Could be his family," Dale said. "You know about the sick wife. There was a daughter too. I used to use that. She'd be about the same age as Grace now."

They talked for another few minutes. Meredith kept her distance, quietly gleaning as much as she could. She looked at her watch. She had a red-eye in four hours. Dorsey wanted a briefing the next morning.

"I have to leave," she announced.

Dale nodded, said nothing, stared at the fire.

Meredith realized he was hurt. "John, I'd consider staying. I didn't mean to crush you with all of this. It's just that I have to brief Dorsey personally tomorrow."

"It's okay. I remember how it is. Will you see Rance at your briefing?"

"Yup."

"Tell Dorsey I might consider doing this if Rance is off the op. And make sure to say it when the dick is in the room."

"I'm not going to tell him that."

"Well, you know my answer, then."

"Remember what I said about this being an opportunity for justice, John."

"In that case, why don't you go back and see what they're willing to do? If this is the only thing keeping the Iranians from building the bomb, I'm thinking the offer is going to be pretty sweet. I could use my back pay and pension reinstated. Tell them to double up both."

Meredith stood and gathered her things in her bag and glanced out the window. "All right, I will. Snow's picking up. I need to get down that hill and back over the pass now or I'm never going to make my flight."

Dale nodded. "Go, Meth, go. Do what you have to do."

"I'm supposed to leave this with you." She dropped a USB stick on his coffee table. "It's encrypted. For OPSEC reasons, since you haven't yet agreed, I'm going to wait to send you the password until I get back. The file is good for only another day or two. Then it deletes itself on access." Meredith put an Android phone on the table. "I'm leaving this too. It's secure. Please keep it on you so we can communicate about this. Okay? If nothing works out, we'll send someone back for this stuff."

"Yeah, I know the drill," John said. "Save yourself the trouble and drop that shit in the fire."

She went on, unruffled. "There's also this." She dug through her bag and produced Grace's letter. "She wanted me to give it to you . . . to save time on the mail." She laid it on the table. "Before you throw that USB in the fire, you should really think about Grace. Think about what the future means for her."

Dale snorted. He picked up Grace's letter and held it to the light, studying it. "Did you read this, Meth, or more likely have some Agency clowns write it?"

She ignored him. "John, I know this has been a lot. Please, for me, sleep on it . . . the whole thing. You probably have a couple of days to decide. Keep at least enough of an open mind that I can get back to you after my meeting with Dorsey. And keep that phone on you. I mean it."

He nodded and stood. She hugged him for a long time. "I know you're going to do the right thing," she said at last, meeting his eye. "You're the best man I know."

She kissed his cheek, then made her way to the door and out to her car.

"She's moving," Maria said, watching through the high-res. "I'm going to come back up to follow in the Audi."

Reading his lips, she'd seen Dale mention Rance. She also now knew it was an operation that involved an asset in Iran, which seemed to dominate their conversation. But she didn't know why it pivoted around Dale.

Based on the records they'd hacked, she knew Meredith was flying back on a Delta red-eye out of SeaTac. Now she knew it was for a meeting with Dorsey and Rance. If she could get Rance back into bed the next night, she might be able to get something out of his phone. This was certainly hot enough to try.

"We know she's going back to the airport," Leo said next to her. "What's it matter?"

"Don't worry about that," Maria barked. "You two need to stay here. She gave him something—looked like a USB and a document. We need both. Search the house for them. Bug it while you're in there." She repeated these instructions into the microphone.

Vasily replied over the radio, "How far are we authorized to take this? Can we eliminate him if necessary? I have the Chukavin." The Chukavin was special forces' newest sniper rifle, accurate for over a thousand yards.

Maria wasn't sure what to answer, so she dodged the question. Her job was to collect intelligence. Probably best to keep the two Spetsnaz men focused on that.

"We need him to let his guard down. I need those documents and to know what he's doing. That's your mission. Clear?"

Two clicks came in reply.

About ninety minutes later, Maria pulled over in the cell phone waiting lot at the Seattle airport, some sixty miles away. Having watched Meredith return her rental car, she felt sure the CIA woman was well on her way to her scheduled flight.

In the dark confines of the Audi interior, she recovered her tablet, signed in, and uploaded the report on the activities of Meredith Morris-Dale and the knowledge of the suspected mole in Iran to Yasenevo. She included still photos, captured from the video, of John Dale's face.

Then, switching gears, she retrieved her burner phone. Getting back into the mindset of Genevieve Lund, she sent a racy text message to Rance.

CHAPTER 9

YURI KUZNETSOV OPENED THE SLIDING-GLASS DOORS AND INHALED
deeply. Beyond the hotel's wide white beach lay the glittering green
Mediterranean, the late-afternoon sun bouncing off blue. Salt air blew
in through the open door, ruffling the drapes of the fourth-floor room.
He exhaled happily and looked at his phone. No messages. The meet
must still be on.

He'd always had a thing for Beirut. Where Damascus had shit hotels
and bland food, Beirut had it all. This, the five-star Riviera, had long
been his favorite. It sat on Général de Gaulle Avenue with an Olympic-
sized pool and a midcentury modern vibe that echoed the KGB Cold
War glory. Some of the old-timers could tell some pretty good stories
about this place.

Having survived multiple Lebanese civil wars, Beirut was somewhat
at peace again—superficially anyway. Gone were the days of rockets
and rubble. The fighting now was below the radar, among Mossad,
Hezbollah, and Quds killers.

Still, Europeans with fat wallets and long memories were loath to
consider it the jewel it had been. That was A-OK with Yuri. Since business was slow, it meant he could stay here in this oceanfront suite for
under three hundred, just within SVR per diem. A shame he couldn't
stay longer.

The two-bedroom suite's phone rang. He picked it up.

"Room service," said a male voice in French.

Yuri's cover when he traveled to Beirut was as a Russian immigrant turned Parisian. *"Très bien. J'ai hâte de la soupe."* His French had a Slavic accent but worked.

"Oui. La soupe est très bonne aujourd'hui."

With that predetermined authentication out of the way, he hung up and waited. He stood by the window, looking at the Med, smoothing his suit jacket. It was new. He'd found the tailor that the diplomats favored.

A minute later, there was a knock at his door.

A dark, clean-shaven man in his mid-forties walked into the suite's marble foyer. He wore a well-tailored gray Armani, a white shirt, a navy tie. There were strands of gray near his temples. He had a newspaper conspicuously folded under his arm: a pink broadsheet, the *Financial Times*, international edition. Hard to miss.

They greeted each another in French, but didn't shake hands. Neither man smiled.

"Nice view," the newcomer said, looking out to sea, advancing toward the living room.

"Oui. A pity to have to work today, isn't it?" Yuri answered in French.

The man dropped the *Times* on the table. They sat on opposing beige sofas, perpendicular to the view, the paper between them. "What's it been . . . five years?"

"At least," replied the Russian. "Nice to be meeting under more charming circumstances." He swept his arm.

The man, whom Yuri knew only as Kasem, nodded, but didn't bother to look around. They'd met in the smoking ruins of the Syrian–Kurdish city of Al Hasakah in '15. Kasem had been running kill squads against Kurdish rebels. Educated in the UK, he'd been one of the few Quds men who seemed capable of negotiating with foreigners. SVR had him marked as an up-and-comer. A crucial contact within the opaque Iranian hierarchy.

At best the relationship had been a marriage of convenience. Both were in the Syrian fight to prop up Assad, but for different strategic reasons. Iran wanted to build an arc of Shia dominance across the region; Russia wanted access to hydrocarbons.

"Anything good in the news?" Yuri asked, acknowledging the paper. It was a conspicuous prop, so why not?

Kasem unfolded the thin pink pages, spreading them on the glass coffee table. The sea air lifted a corner. "You've seen this?"

Yuri didn't bother to look. He gave a dismissive shrug.

Kasem said, "I don't usually like the business papers, but the headline caught my eye, so I picked it up in the lobby. I forget, Yuri—do you read English?"

Now Yuri looked. His English was poor, but good enough to make out most of a news story. There was a subhead about a pipeline deal between Iran and China, part of China's Belt and Road Initiative.

Belt and Road, aka the New Silk Road, was a growing source of inflammation for the Kremlin. If successful, it would create a worldwide artery for oil and trading flows that were controlled by Chinese security and infrastructure, free from Western—and Russian—interference. A substantial portion of the overland route cut straight across Northern Iran, pointedly bypassing Russia.

Abutting the article was a large photo of Iran's prime minister in Beijing, shaking hands with Chinese president Xi.

"I saw it," Yuri said. *Très intelligent.*

The Iranian closed the paper. He stared at Yuri, a dark Persian gaze.

Yuri let the Iranian have his moment. He said, "A good thing you brought this up. It's somewhat related to what I wanted to see you about: the other pipeline deal you have. The one between our two countries." He waggled his index finger back and forth. "Bushehr."

"Amazing how all these things seem to come together at once," said Kasem with a supercilious smile.

Yuri understood the Quds man's gloat. Iran had a long history of playing world powers off one another. It went all the way back to their manipulation of the Brits by flirting with the Soviets toward the end of the big war.

"I'd hoped to speak with you about it," Yuri said. "An off-the-record chat . . . less conspicuous than a presidential delegation for the consumption of the papers."

"Right," said Kasem, sitting back, crossing his legs. "Like the old days. What is it about *our* deal that has your attention? A great thing to bring efficient nuclear power to the far reaches of the Islamic Republic."

"Yes, and a wonderful thing for Russia to refine and make use of Iranian oil." Yuri grinned. He grabbed a bottle of water off an end table. "If you weren't a man of faith, I'd suggest a *real* drink to celebrate."

Kasem remained still. A seagull screeched just off the balcony. He said, "You didn't come to Beirut and ask me here to celebrate, Yuri, now, did you? You that lonely these days?"

"No. But here we are. Two old friends. Colleagues. Just talking."

The seagull chirped again, the sound wheeling away as the bird lost altitude. Yuri continued smiling, until gulping down a third of the water bottle.

"Well, old friend," the Iranian said, leaning forward, "my position here in Beirut remains busy. Especially now. You must have a point in here somewhere? Perhaps I could help you find it?"

The Russian had decided to pull this string, the only one he had, after reading the latest update from Yasenevo on the American operation the night before. Something was up, something big. The intel seemed to indicate the Americans had a mole in the Iranian nuke program. If Yuri could get to it first, he'd be able to round up the entire operation, gain Russian leverage over Iran, and emerge as a superstar within the SVR ranks. Given the enormously profitable nature of the Iran–Russia deal, he would be a real hero.

But he hardly knew anything, really. Thus, the meeting. If he could spin up Iranian counterintelligence as a bird dog, he thought he might be the one to find the mole by following CIA's reaction. He'd be able to do so through that wonderful new SVR Directorate S source, the illegal called Zoloto.

He said, "Let me put it this way, Kasem. Since we've worked together before, I thought I might do you the favor of a certain line of thinking from our side, one that you might not have anticipated."

Kasem stared hard at him, eyebrows pressed.

Yuri went on. "You see, old friend, there are those on our side who might think about reconsidering our deal if we thought there were unnecessary risks."

"Are there?" said the Quds man, eyes unblinking. "And what risks might there be?"

"One hears things."

"What things?"

Subtle, Yuri thought. "Do you know much about nuclear reactors, Kasem—like the one in Bushehr?"

The Iranian said nothing.

"Maybe you don't," Yuri continued. "Let me tell you about them. You see, reactors are dangerous. They leak. If mismanaged, they can leak many things, toxic things, unpredictably volatile things. We would know. We learned a lot from Chernobyl."

The Iranian hadn't moved.

Yuri paused, downing the rest of the water. "And the funny thing about radiation . . . when it leaks, it can be detected all over the world. Everywhere. What a mess. Because of our own experience, we'd all be a little more comfortable if we knew Iranian reactors weren't at risk of such exposure. Leaks, I mean. Leaking is very bad."

He tossed the empty plastic bottle toward a trash can. It missed, bounced, and rolled on the carpet.

The Iranian watched him carefully. He finally shifted in his seat, his dark eyes steady. "Leaks, you say. And you think Iranian reactors are prone to them? Even ones built by Russians?"

Yuri shrugged. "This is what I'm hearing. Built by Russians, managed by Iranians. Leaky management."

"Yuri. Enough. Just tell me what exactly you're hearing."

"Kasem, old friend. You know I would if I could. But we have to protect our sources in this business. You of all people would understand that."

The Quds man shifted farther sideways.

Yuri could see that he was freeing his arm for a clear reach at the pistol under his jacket, just in case he wanted the Russian to be *much* more specific.

"Oh, I shouldn't have been so rude," the SVR man said abruptly, angling his arm toward one of the doors over his shoulder. "This is Putov."

Putov, Yuri's vulpine-faced deputy, stepped from the bedroom. His suit jacket was open, revealing the ballistic nylon strap of a shoulder holster. The SVR deputy hitched his belt to show that his hands were free. He cracked his knuckles to show they were restless.

Kasem looked at Putov and back to Yuri, who sat there grinning. The Iranian leaned back against the quilted white upholstery, saying, "I forgot, Yuri. Like most Russians, you're not comfortable traveling without friends."

The Iranian kept his hand poised on his lap. It would have been a fast maneuver to withdraw his pistol, one that he'd probably practiced a thousand times. But it would still have been two against one. He added, "Perhaps I have friends in the hotel as well."

"Oh, good," said Yuri. "Because I definitely do. They're downstairs now. You must have passed them in the lobby. Maybe we could rent the penthouse and have a party, no? The view up there is even better than this. . . . Celebrate our deal."

Kasem had had enough. He stood up, smoothed his trousers. "I wouldn't see the point of that. As you said, as a man of faith, I rarely celebrate the same way you do."

"A pity," said Yuri, also standing. "But like I said, you should maybe check on some of those leaks. That reactor of yours is pretty old. Even though it's of good, solid Russian construction."

Kasem nodded. "You may keep the newspaper." He began walking to the door. "You may recall that the original Silk Road went straight through Tehran," he said. "Founded during the Persian Achaemenid Empire, if memory serves. Cyrus the Great, king of kings."

Yuri nodded. "So enlightening chatting with an Oxford man. You always learn so much."

"Oh, but I don't bother to try to read the Queen's English anymore.

Don't think that language matters around here as much as it used to. Perhaps Mandarin?" He smiled and turned his back on Yuri, walking through the door with a wave.

"*Au revoir,* Kasem," Yuri called after him.

"What the fuck do you mean, he said no?" Jeff Dorsey asked.

Meredith, Sheffield, and Rance had been waiting for the director of the National Clandestine Service in the SCIF. It was three hours after sunset.

Meredith had waited all day, having returned on the red-eye the night before. She was more than ready to get out of here and slide into a hot bath. The meeting had been postponed three times, as Dorsey had apparently run from one crisis to the next.

The deputy director stood over the table, leaning on his fists, knuckles white.

"It's not a definite no," offered Meredith. "He may come around yet. I'm just giving you his first reaction."

"I knew we shouldn't've bothered," said Rance. "Dale's a risk one way or the other. I, for one, still question his loyalty."

She bit her tongue, fighting the urge to say something stupid. Having seen her ex twenty-four sleep-deprived hours ago, she felt dangerously combative.

"I don't know," said Dorsey. He began to pace. "Dale was a hell of a handler. One of our best field operators too. Remember Basra? Skills like that rarely come in one package."

"But then, there was Mosul," Sheffield reminded everyone.

"Yeah, yeah," Dorsey muttered. *"Mosul . . ."* He waved dismissively. "Still . . . I'd really hoped this would come together. It'd solve a lot of problems for us. Whether John's up to it or not—he's got the chops."

"Had," said Rance.

Dorsey's eyes lowered like a pair of howitzer barrels. "Ed. *We* didn't pick Dale for this op. Cerberus did."

Rance looked at the table.

Sheffield, the gray-haired attorney, asked, "Meredith, did John give any hints as to why the asset trusts only him? Or anything on why he's gone dark? He must have some insights."

"John said he thinks Cerberus isn't a particular fan of the US, but rather someone that's just against the mullahs running the country. He always figured Cerberus wanted to keep them from getting the bomb and that's why he was spying for us. John also said there's a daughter, if that matters; otherwise he's in the dark."

"You believe him?" asked Rance.

She felt her pulse surge. "What the hell kind of question is that?"

"Come on, Meredith," Rance said, inspecting his cuticles. "John has an ax to grind—we all know it. Don't you think he might be holding back? He's probably enjoying this."

"Holding back for what?" she replied. "Spite? *Really?* Frankly, I thought John's life looked pretty damned good out there. I don't think he wants to come back in because he's basically happy. Recovered. Maybe we should all take a lesson."

Her words hung in the SCIF's cloistered atmosphere.

Dorsey paced. After a few steps, he said, "Well, we are where we are." A quick sigh. "What do we do about it?"

"Give me a little time," Meredith said. "Let me work him. Just a few days."

"That's not something I have right now. The director's asking for insights into this Iran–China deal, the whole Belt-Road nightmare. He wants an analysis in tomorrow's PDB," he said, referring to the President's Daily Brief.

Meredith nodded. Rance seemed content to stare at his fingernails.

The deputy director quit pacing and stared up at the ceiling. "Fuck," he said to no one in particular. "Suddenly the Iranians have a bakery full of yellowcake, right when we've pasted Soleimani to the asphalt. Be great if we could provide some reassurance that we aren't going to wake up to a mushroom cloud over Manhattan next week."

"Yes, sir," answered Meredith.

"And of course," he continued, "the carefully cultivated asset we have that could do just that will talk *only* to an officer that we cashiered five years ago and probably justifiably hates our guts. The director is going to love this shit."

Rance looked at the floor, crossed his legs, played with a loafer tassel.

Meredith ventured, "I'm asking for only a day, maybe two. John's an honorable man, a patriot. My money's on him coming around."

Dorsey's assistant knocked. He held up a halting hand, freezing her at the cracked door. She turned and left, shutting the door behind her. He put a pen in his mouth, chewed, removed it. A flinty eye settled on Meredith.

"I need it to work," he said.

Rance sniffed.

"You have another idea, Ed?" Dorsey turned toward him, pointing with the Bic. "'Cause I'd sure love to hear it."

"I do, sir. I think we just tell Cerberus that John *isn't* an option. We tell him he's dead, out of the service, completely insane. Whatever. He obviously doesn't know how to find John himself. We'll just get someone else to handle him."

Dorsey shook his head. "We don't know what Cerberus knows. We'd risk him quitting on us altogether and never reaching back out."

"That's putting a lot of trust in Dale, sir."

"No," Meredith said, "it's putting a lot of trust in me. Obviously, I know John. He's going to come around on this."

Neither man answered. She felt her pique rising.

"Maybe we *lean* on John," said Rance, looking up at his boss. "Give him a little push."

"Meaning what?" asked Dorsey.

"Meaning, why don't we tell him that if he doesn't do it, he'll be violating an oath, breaking the law, something along those lines? This would be a lot better than prison. Surely we have some leverage."

"What are we going to do?" asked Meredith, her voice rising. "Suspend him all over again? Take away his passport and pension? Check and check. You try to throw him in prison, Ed, and you will be reading all about it on the front page of the *Washington Post*. I'll make sure of that."

Rance crossed his arms. He looked at Sheffield, who shrugged, adding, "I don't see what else can be done, Ed. Legally speaking."

"Right," Dorsey said. "No one is suggesting anything that's not legal or improper or overly harsh. Let me be clear about that."

Another sigh. The Bic went into a waste bin. "This is no longer a debate. I need him back on board. Meredith, you figure it the fuck out. Ed, David, make sure we're clearing a refresher course for John at the Farm in case things get kinetic. If we have to do something about Cerberus in-country, John needs to be ready. Was he fit, Meredith? You think he'd be capable of operating like he used to?"

"He's still got Farsi, sir, a little rusty maybe. I'd suggest having him go through a weapons refresher and an update on comms tech. But yes, he looked very fit, said he'd been running mountain trails or something."

Dorsey stood silently, his hands in his pockets. He looked at the carpet and then back toward the rest of them. "All right. Two days," he said, pointing at her.

Nods all around.

A few minutes later, Meredith walked a half step behind Rance over the long expanse of the seventh floor to the cluster of the Counterproliferation cubicles. She'd fully expected to be led into his office for a smackdown. She kept herself in a state of coiled tension, waiting for the first punch.

But her boss was distracted, busily carrying on some kind of texting session as they walked. His face was flushed. Something from the wife, she supposed. Rance's wife had a reputation as the controlling type— probably why Rance had hit on Meredith all those times. She secretly hoped now that his personal life was a living hell.

When they finally reached Rance's threshold, he announced to his secretary that he'd be leaving, heading to the gym, not to be disturbed for the rest of the evening. Hustling to the elevator, he said something to Meredith over his shoulder about making sure to get Dale on their side, as though it had been his idea all along.

But he'd said it almost as an afterthought, his thumbs working feverishly over his phone. The usual condescension was muted.

Odd, Meredith thought, watching the elevator doors close in front of him.

CHAPTER 10

ZANA RAHIMI, THE MAN THE CIA KNEW AS CERBERUS, LIVED ON THE north end of Tehran in the rising foothills of the Zagros Mountains, near Golabdarre Park. Just up the hill lay the headwaters of the Golab Darreh river, which began as a mountain spring but swelled to feed the smoggy sprawl of eight million in the valley below. One of the first homes it passed was his home—a single-story colonnaded house of white masonry.

Along the cobbled street that led to the Rahimis' was a wide gutter, built in the nineteenth century to irrigate the valley. Here the Golab Darreh gurgled, sluicing over tiered drops of dimpled stone as it made its way downhill to the city. Its stature decreased as it descended, changing from a source of drinking water, to bathing pool, to laundry tub, and eventually, some five miles downstream, to latrine.

All of the guests of the memorial remarked on the beauty of the canal. It reflected in the cold winter sunset, a glowing ribbon of orange wending its way through the terraces as far as the eye could see.

Several had commented that the glowing thread was a sign from God that Sahar had been accepted into heaven. The visiting imam reinforced this with a quote from the Prophet, saying, "When the *ruh* is taken out, the eyesight follows."

The normal procedure would have been to bury her immediately after death. It was believed that the *ruh*, the soul, would be reunited with the body in the afterworld, come judgment day. To mar the sacred body in any other sort of undertaking ritual would be to make it impure in heaven.

But the Rahimis were never afforded that type of funeral, as Sahar's body had never been recovered. There'd been gloomy memorials of a sort, but they'd been rushed, confusing affairs without proper ceremony. The government had been careful not to dwell on the tragedy and had sent out men to ensure there was nothing too public.

Now that some time had passed, this ceremony was different, marking Sahar's twentieth birthday. It had been Nadia's idea, a small act of defiance against the government and a deliberate attempt to keep Sahar's memory alive. Zana had gone along with it on the condition that the local imams be left out of it, for they were never to be trusted. But once they'd heard of it, there was no keeping them away.

Now, looking at the glowing canal, the imam added that Sahar Rahimi's *ruh*, freed from her nineteen-year-old body so many months prior, remained pure. He went on to say that it would certainly be reunited with her intact body, come judgment day. Until then the *ruh* would be in heaven, freed of its earthly burdens.

Zana Rahimi had listened to all of it dolefully, privately thinking it all nonsense. This ceremony was for closure, because Nadia wanted it. He'd hosted his friends from the neighborhood, his wife's distant relatives, the clergy, and a few former colleagues from his days at the University of Science and Technology. He'd made the correct motions of public grief. But as far as religion went, he'd only seen it ruin his country.

Nadia had arisen at six that morning to begin the food preparations. She'd made several stews—an eggplant, a mushroom, and a mutton with walnuts. She'd produced a large batch of adas palow, a rice dish with raisins, lentils, and dates.

The cooking had at least given her a distraction. It might even have provided a bit of light in the darkness that enveloped them.

The guests were finally saying their goodbyes. They were hugging the Rahimis, kissing them on each cheek in the Iranian tradition, going on and on about Sahar's assured ascension. They made their way in a long chain of half hugs and handclasps across the stone tiles of the courtyard and toward the parked cars.

When the last of them had finally gone, Zana strolled about his courtyard in the front of the house, alone, listening to the stream. To block the rising waters of the thaw, there was a built-up section of the bank like a long stone bench. As he stood there taking in the fading sunset, he could see the two Guardsmen sitting there on this bench, watching, the water at their backs.

They were dressed in the olive-green uniform of the IRGC. Per their tradition, they wore thick dark beards and long-billed ball caps.

As the name implied, the Guards had been established shortly after the revolution by Ayatollah Khomeini himself to ensure the regular secular armed services of the shah's regime remained in check. They'd even fought off a regular military coup in the early days of the revolutionary government.

With the Imam Khomeini's trust, they'd since evolved to operate all the elite branches of the military and intelligence arms. It was the Guards who manned the barracks at Tabriz. It was the Guards who had launched missiles at the American base in Iraq. It was the Guards who had murdered Sahar.

These two had been polite enough. It wasn't their fault they had to escort him everywhere he went during his funeral leave. It wasn't their fault they had to drive him to Tehran and set up a watch station outside his front door.

But it was the fault of their organization that Sahar was dead at all. The cancerous fanaticism that had ruined Zana's once proud country had grown to take his father, his brother, and now his daughter.

Taking one last look at the river darkening with the dusk, Zana Rahimi turned back toward the front door, ignoring the Guardsmen.

CHAPTER 11

DALE BLEW OFF MEREDITH'S REPEATED TEXTS, SETTING HIS PHONE ON Do Not Disturb. As far as he was concerned, he'd given his answer. Hurricane Meredith had blown through and done its worst. He was looking to repair and rebuild. He had no interest in that USB she'd left behind.

He tried as best he could to forget about her visit. She'd go away and the CIA would figure something out eventually, as they always did. It wasn't his battle to fight anymore, not his world.

Grace's letter had been interesting. With uncanny intuition, Dale's daughter had written a few paragraphs about how much she admired her father's honor. She said they'd been taking a military ethics course at the Academy and it had gotten her to thinking about her dad. She wrote that while she knew that she'd never really know what had happened to her father during his service, her bedrock belief was that he was the most honorable man she'd ever known.

Just like Meredith had said. Uncanny. Had he gotten that letter a week ago, he would have reveled in it. But having been delivered by Meredith along with that USB, it wasn't sitting quite right.

He went back to thinking about how to finish the Peoh painting, hoping to observe some live details of its northern face to add to the work. But the weather had turned sour and the mountain kept disappearing behind fog. *Of all days,* he thought dispiritedly, *this would have been a good one to paint.*

With that option closed, he went to the little gym carved out of a corner of his barn and pumped iron for an hour, trying to kill the remainder of the morning. He followed the weights with a run on the frozen road, up to the peak and back. After, he showered and settled into his worn leather club chair with a book.

Meredith's USB drive sat on his coffee table. He glanced at it intermittently, interrupting the flow of his eyes over the page. To head off the distraction, he blocked it with a magazine. But then he just kept glancing at the magazine cover.

Annoyed, he finally took the USB to the small digital gun safe in his bedroom closet, where he kept a Glock and three magazines. He punched in the code and tossed it in. *Out of sight, out of mind,* he told himself, resuming the book.

He read the same page three times and put the book down. He stared out the window at the white sky, waggling his foot. He fixed a sandwich but was only able to eat half of it. He sighed. It was no use.

Cerberus. Yeah, of course he remembered Cerberus. Goddamned Meredith had flipped over the rock and now the memories flew like bats from a cave, rattling around his head.

It'd all started back in the early 2010s. By then Dale was off his recruitment mission in Canada and had transitioned over to CIA's Special Activities Division, Ground Branch, as a paramilitary operator. He'd been up in the border area between Iraq and Syria, a lead sniper hunting for ISIS scumbags, when the ping had come in.

Broadsword. That was the name of the counter-ISIS op. Rance had been the senior officer in charge of Broadsword back then, based at Forward Operating Base Sykes, near Tal Afar, Iraq. Dale had been Rance's muscle out in Indian Country, leading a team of five other Ground Branch operatives, a kill squad. His mission had been to grant the fanatics their most fervent wishes of martyrdom with both alacrity and generosity, courtesy of Uncle Sam.

He'd just been hitting his stride in the wilds, living with the Kurds, having picked up a bit of the dialect. He'd also gotten a line on some Iranian Quds spies inserting themselves with the Syrians, and he had been following them too. Then, out of nowhere, the radio call came summoning him back to CIA regional HQ in Bahrain.

It'd pissed Rance off that he was going to be losing his best field weapon, the one making him look good back at HQS. Or maybe not look good. At that point things were just beginning to get out of hand with Broadsword. Bodies were piling up and Rance had begun taking more liberties with targeting assignments, some of them questionable.

For the Agency to reach out and tap Dale to come in to work on another op must have rattled Rance, made him wonder if the inspector general was finally going to start checking up. No wonder he'd been so pissed. But it wasn't up to Rance. Before Dale knew it, a Blackhawk popped over a hill and scooped him up. He was off to Bahrain, like it or not. Orders were orders.

It wasn't until he was at the safe house in Bahrain that he realized that Rance had nothing to worry about. He'd been tapped for another reason, something from his past—back when he'd first worked for Meredith, back in Montreal.

Out of the clear blue sky, an Iranian had reached out to John's old alias, Reza Shariati. The CIA had given him the code name Cerberus.

Cerberus said he remembered Reza from his days at McGill University in Montreal, where he'd been a member of the Muslim Student Association. He said he remembered John's casual ramblings off hours about supporting the opposition, the MEK, the People's Mujahideen, which maintained that Khomeini's rise had been a coup against their man, Banisadr. He said he remembered that John, aka Reza, had seemed approachable, anxious to discuss such things, a kindred spirit.

The whole thing had struck Dale as eerie. Somehow Cerberus seemed to know that Reza was an alias, a front for CIA. Though John had successfully recruited a few assets to go on to do some low-level reporting in Tehran, none of them were this man. None of them had had the background.

That probably meant one of his other assets had talked, giving Cerberus the lead. That kind of thing didn't happen without someone ending up in Evin Prison, the sprawling den of evil where IRGC tortured suspects into "confessions." If John's alias was blown, there was a chance he'd end up there himself one fine day.

But then, there were a lot of things about Cerberus that were hard to figure.

Whoever he was, he was altogether different. Dale guessed he was older, more mature, wiser to the ways of the world. Once secure communications had been established, the would-be spy said he had important info on his government's plans for nukes. He wanted someone, presumably the US, to stop them.

Normal procedure should have been to establish a face-to-face. Plenty of walk-ins approach with offers to spy, but most are nutjobs, low level, or opposition doubles. After the face-to-face, the next step should have been to hook him up to a lie detector to ensure bona fides. Provided he passed, they'd push him through a training program at a neutral location, probably London. They'd teach him how to avoid detection, establish a communications procedure. They'd work out logistical things like payment.

Cerberus wouldn't have any of it. He was the one who came up with the protocol and schedule. He wouldn't take money or submit to a face-to-face. It was unorthodox to say the least. Eerie.

As a final validation step, they tried an experiment. The potential double Cerberus claimed to be working on uranium enrichment, in charge of the lab. CIA created a virus to install on the Iranian SCADA network. SCADA—Supervisory Control and Data Acquisition—is the software that runs machine labs, where scientists make small tweaks to the equipment, learning through rapid automated experimentation. Through John, the CIA sent him the code to install on the SCADA network, a nasty little virus called Stuxnet.

Within a few weeks, there was a massive explosion at the Tehran complex where Iran ran its centrifuges. It actually tipped the Richter scale.

A few days after that, Cerberus was back, reporting for duty, asking for more.

And with that, he was in. Not only was he in, he was pure fucking gold. Operation Active Archer was born. Working on Cerberus's unusually one-sided terms would be just fine with CIA.

Those terms were actually pretty simple. Cerberus would provide information on the SCADA system, including back doors that CIA could use to hack directly. CIA would work out subtle ways to infiltrate the software and develop malware to ensure enrichment remained unsuccessful. Through one of the suppliers that was selling equipment to an Iranian front company, the Agency would communicate with Cerberus via encrypted documents uploaded to the supplier's technical support site.

Langley could hardly believe its luck.

There was one area where John had gained some insight. Per his request, CIA provided Cerberus with drugs for multiple sclerosis. This was how John learned about the wife. Over time, Cerberus trusted John enough to also tell him about the daughter; but even that had been cryptic. He'd learned of her only because Cerberus had asked John to develop an escape plan for the whole family in case the Iranians ever closed in on him. He was even fussy about the design of the plan.

Once Cerberus was up and running, communication became infrequent, almost nonexistent. But Cerberus held up his end of the bargain anyway. John passed him off to another handler and went back to hunting ISIS zealots.

As far as he knew, Cerberus barely ever checked in again, but dutifully installed CIA software updates whenever asked. Dale hadn't really thought much about him again—until Meredith dropped that USB on his coffee table.

His mind found its way back to the present. He stared down at the stub of his pinkie, thinking about how it had all ended.

He looked up through the window at the solid white sky, then at the barometer on his mantel. Both pressure and visibility were dropping. He couldn't see much beyond the trees now. If there was a sun up there somewhere, it was in deep hiding; there'd be no painting today. How he wished that weren't the case.

He drummed his fingers on his thighs. Too quiet in this house. The solitude, normally calming, was choking. Classic cabin fever. He put on a Johnny Cash record and returned to his chair with a glass of water. To get his mind off his past, he picked up the letter from Grace and tried to reread it. He put it down halfway through.

"Music," whispered Leo, lying prone in the snow some fifty yards to the west of John's house. "The Monk has finally made a sound."

Vasily lay next to him, nodding.

They'd taken to calling Dale "the Monk." Other than for exercise, he hadn't left his property since the CIA woman had departed two nights before. Nor had he made a single sound, other than moving about his kitchen making coffee. He'd sat up reading in his bedroom much of the night. He went to his gym. He read in his chair. It was perhaps the most boring surveillance op the two of them had ever been on.

Vasily and Leo had improved their hide in the tree line. They were still operating the directional microphone and the long-range video recorder. They hadn't heard from the uptight SVR targeting officer called Zoloto since she'd left them there on that freezing mountain. Settling in for the long haul, they'd draped themselves in camouflage netting and down sleeping bags. To keep warm, they were lying on chemical heat packs the size of throw pillows. Twice, Leo had snuck off to town to resupply.

Every now and then, one of them would have to climb up the hill to take a piss or grab food out of the SUV. Things were not so bad as far as tactical surveillance ops went. Just boring as hell.

"Oh, hang on," Vasily said, looking through the video scope. "I think he's on the move. He just put on a coat."

"I hear car keys," confirmed Leo.

He pulled off his headphones and rose to his knees. Their agreement was that if the target left the home, Leo would follow him while Vasily stayed behind to improve their surveillance capability. Zoloto had said not to let Dale out of sight.

"Finally," said Vasily. "When he goes, I'll search the house for the USB and the documents. I can also get a real microphone in there."

Dale couldn't take it anymore. He had to get out of the house—even Johnny Cash wasn't helping. He kept wondering about Cerberus, why he'd be reaching out, why now.

Maybe the jig was finally up. Maybe the wife was sicker and he had to get the hell out of the country, triggering the egress plan. Probably so. Dale felt bad about that. He felt bad about a lot of things. He thought about Grace's letter.

Time to get out of here.

He slipped into his blanket-lined Carhartt, pulled on his Blundstones, and locked up. He debated whether to take the secure burner that Meredith had left and decided at the last second to pocket it. Coverage was better down in town, and if she had something really important to say, he figured he'd better actually listen.

Anyway, there was something he'd been planning to do this week and he needed to go to town. What a blessing to have something to do.

Back in October he'd applied for a permit to hunt bighorns on the Cleman preserve over near Ellensburg. The state had said that due to the lack of natural predators, the bighorn population had become unsustainable and a few animals could be hunted out, an extremely rare occurrence.

Dale had been pretty pumped about it. Bighorns required long-distance shooting. Since he was a trained sniper, it was right in his wheelhouse.

He started up the F-150 and scraped the falling snow off the window, thinking about the ammo supplies he'd need. He used an M91 rifle for this type of hunting, which he'd picked up on the black market after leaving the CIA. Bullets for that thing weren't exactly off-the-shelf.

It was the same model he'd been trained on and used in Iraq. He'd outfitted it with a thermal scope for hunting at night, just like in Iraq. He had to get powder, shot, and brass jackets down at the gun shop in town to make his own cartridges. He'd build them up in the little shed on his property, where he kept his snowmobile and gun vault. He already had about twenty rounds done, probably enough, but he needed this excuse to go to town, so what the hell?

Once the truck's heat got going, he climbed in, slipped into four-wheel drive, and made his way out across the driveway. A few inches had fallen and he felt the wheels spin once before they bit.

A half mile above Dale, Leo rode the brakes of the black Yukon XL down the hill, thinking that this was the worst possible kind of surveillance. A single black vehicle against an all-white background with no concealment. But the logging road they'd taken to get up there would have been impassable and he'd lose sight of Dale.

Farther down the hill on the occasional switchback, he could see Dale's truck. The trick would be to remain far enough back that Dale didn't notice him, but at the same time not to move so slowly that he would lose him in town.

At least the town was small, Leo reassured himself. The way Dale had left so quickly, Leo wouldn't expect this to be a complicated trip. He was confident he'd be able to find the truck. But still, better to keep Dale in sight.

Vasily updated him on the encrypted UHF. Leo heard his voice crackle in his Bluetooth.

"I'm in the house," Vasily said. "Looking for the documents."

Leo answered with two clicks.

After Dale hit the gun shop, he decided to drive the twenty miles over to Ellensburg to go to the big outfitter he favored. He stocked up on propane bottles, freeze-dried food, some artificial game scent to help disguise his human smell, and some new Gore-Tex snowmobile gloves.

After a few hours in the city, he angled the F-150 back to I-90 and headed home toward Cle Elum. Whatever weak sun that had been hiding up there had finally given up. The sky to the west was gunmetal gray. Dale turned on his headlights.

Rolling down the highway, his eyes swept over the rearview. *There,* he thought. There was that black Yukon XL again.

He'd spotted it back in Cle Elum, parked down the street from the gun shop. There were plenty of wealthy SUV owners from Seattle who drove nice trucks around those parts. But it'd been parked in front of a Laundromat. Rich people driving Yukon XLs didn't use Laundromats.

Out of habit, Dale had filed this tidbit away. He'd gone on to hit the NAPA near the tracks and bought some two-cycle oil for the snowmobile. But then, exiting on the far side of town, he'd noticed the Yukon parked near the equipment-rental place.

Plenty of wealthy SUV owners rented equipment for yard work, log splitting, and other types of maintenance on their vacation homes. But the place closed up between Thanksgiving and Memorial Day. Something was up.

Now, rolling down I-90 in the gathering dark, he saw the suspect vehicle six or seven cars back. That was the last straw. He was pissed.

He called Meredith on the phone she'd left with him. It went to voice mail but he was too mad to hang up.

"Meth, it's me. Not cool that you left a couple of your people to watch me. I'd appreciate if we could just keep this between us. Call off your goddamned dogs." He hung up and punched the gas, fuming.

Leo called Vasily on the satphone since they were out of the range for UHF. "I think I'm blown," he said.

"What?" replied his partner. "Why do you say that?"

"He's starting to drive like a madman."

"Where's he going?"

"He was over at this town called Ellensburg. We're about fifteen miles away, headed back to Cle Elum. I think he's probably heading home. Are you back in the hide?"

"No, I'm still in the house. Couldn't find the USB. The letter was nothing related to the mission. Just something from a kid, a daughter. Now I'm wiring up some passive audio."

"Well, the Monk is on his way home."

Dale had the F-150 up to ninety, moving fast down the right lane. He'd heard on the radio that the snow was falling up at Snoqualmie Pass some thirty miles ahead and there was a big tractor trailer on its side. If that was the case, he was pretty sure the highway patrol would be occupied with it for this stretch of road. He accelerated through ninety-five, weaving to avoid traffic, looking at the rearview. He lost sight of the Yukon.

That ought to teach those fuckers, he thought. He came up with some ideas about how he'd screw them up when he finally got home.

The satphone by Leo's seat rang. "I'm out of the house," said Vasily. "I got two transmitters installed. Would have been better to get three or four. Where's the Monk now?"

"He's somewhere ahead of me. He jumped up to a hundred miles an hour trying to lose me. There's no sense in my attracting that kind of attention, so I fell back. Where are you now?"

"I'm back in the trees, freezing my ass off."

"Good. There shouldn't be anything to worry about. Even though I'm burned, he'd have no reason to suspect anything off at the house. Let's see what he does."

"Okay. But get back here, just in case I need a ride."

"On my way."

Dale chose an exit three miles before Cle Elum to use the back way into town. He skidded through the backstreets, anxious to keep the tail from catching up. When he finally got to the gravel road that led up to his house, he noticed a second set of tire tracks. Fresh truck tracks overlaid on his own. He swore under his breath. Meredith's CIA surveillance team had set up to watch him at his house, he thought. Now he was really pissed.

He flew up the snowy mountain road in the half dark, gunning the engine out of anger, his tail skidding around corners. Once up to his gate, he hopped out, drove through, and closed it behind him. He drove straight down to the shed, where he kept his snowmobile and his hunting gear. He slammed the truck door.

He went into the shed and opened up his large gun safe with a few spins of the dial. He pulled out his sniper rifle, leaving it unloaded. He put away the new gear and returned to the rifle, setting it on a workbench. Though it would mean he'd have to resight it, he detached his expensive thermal scope from the weapon. If Meredith's surveillance team was out there in the snow, seeing them on IR was the way to find them.

But the last thing he wanted to do was wave his rifle around, looking for them through the scope. That'd be a good way to get himself killed. Controlling his temper, he detached the scope and turned it on, giving it a quick inspection.

He walked up to the cabin, unlocked the side door, and entered with the lights off. Kicking snow off his boots, he went upstairs in the dark to the deck, the place with the best view of the surrounding woods. He put the thermal to his eye and swept the tree line. The secure phone in his pocket buzzed.

With the scope still to his eyes, Dale put the phone to his ear with his free hand.

"It's Meredith."

"Hold on," he said.

He saw something in the trees. A heat signature of a man. The man was lying on his stomach, a classic prone surveillance position.

Gotcha, dickhead.

"Yeah, Meth," Dale said, angry. "You get my message?"

"Of course. But I don't know what you're talking about."

"I'm talking about your goon squad. I've got eyes on a surveillant in my tree line right now. You need to call him off. Tell him to get the hell off my property. Go ahead and make the call. I'll stay on the line and watch him as he leaves or I'll call the fucking cops. Deal?"

The timbre of her voice surprised him. "John, *listen* to me. We don't have anyone watching you."

"Yeah, right," he said, waving away the doubt. "If you don't, then Rance probably does. We both know how that asshole works."

He focused his eyes in on the man in the tree line, a hot white blob against the blackness of the snow. As he spoke, the gray-white man shifted, then raised himself to a crouch. In silhouette, John could see what looked to be a snubbed-off rifle with a long mag. It looked like an HK machine pistol.

Her voice now had that professionally firm quality he knew so well. It chilled him. "*Listen* to me, John. Just listen. It's not us. Whoever it is, I don't know—but get the fuck out of there. You hear me? Call me back from a secure spot and we'll figure this out. Get out now and evade. You hear me? *Go!*"

Dale hung up and slipped the scope back into his jacket pocket. He turned and ran to the rail of his deck and vaulted over the side, landing five feet below in the snow. He slid a little farther down the hill on his side, keeping his profile low, then jumped to his feet and sprinted full speed for his shed.

CHAPTER 12

VASILY WHISPERED INTO THE SMALL SATPHONE MIC DANGLING BY HIS ear. "I think he's onto me."

He squinted through the low-light video lens. He could see the Monk had some sort of scope to his face, sweeping the tree line. He also seemed to be on the phone. Vasily could hear the Monk speaking but he was too far away for Vasily to make sense of it. Feeling exposed, he rose to a crouch and shuffled sideways behind a bush.

"How far out are you?"

"Bottom of the hill," answered Leo. "Just hitting the gravel. Five minutes."

"If we're blown, what do we do?"

It was a good question. As the more senior of the two operators, Leo thought about how to answer as he skidded up the switchbacks.

Zoloto had said that the most important thing was to retrieve the USB and any other documents in the house. She'd also directed them to keep the surveillance target in sight. But what if the Monk bolted or, worse, came after them? Their first order of business was to avoid detection. Second was to gain intel. Leo thought of a way to do both.

"Snatch," he replied.

While extreme, this was a *Krasniy Odin*, the highest-priority op, and he was definitely in extremis. They couldn't afford to lose the Monk, whoever he was, and they couldn't kill him—could they?

If they took him alive, they'd at least have options. Leo ran down the logic. "If you think we're blown, he's going to call the police. That can't happen. And we need him—alive. Take him and let's get out of here."

"Okay," said Vasily. "He's running. Recovering target. Out."

Dale sprinted at full speed back to the snowmobile shed. He pulled the bare bulb's chain as he entered, killing the lights. He felt his way to his workbench and found the old NVGs. He put them over his head while fumbling through his still-open gun safe.

Whoever the armed man in the trees was, he wasn't going to be open to reasoning. Dale knew he had to arm up fast. He wanted his Glock for mobility, but it was up in the small digital safe in his bedroom. He had the sniper rifle, unloaded, which wouldn't be too helpful since he'd taken off the scope. He also had a twelve gauge he used for hunting geese. He knew it was loaded with five shells. He took it.

He figured the NVGs, now warmed up and functioning, would be his advantage. If the man out there was coming for him, he'd be entering the house first. But Dale knew his way around his own home, which would be another edge. Shotgun in hand, he ran from the shed to the basement below his two-bedroom cabin.

Once inside the cellar, he found his fuse box and killed the master power. The lights had been off anyway, but now his pursuer wouldn't be able to turn them on. He pressed his back against the stony foundation walls and slowed his own breathing, feeling the cool of the concrete through his jacket. He listened to the creak of the stringers a few feet over his head.

He heard footsteps on the deck and the sliding grind of his back door opening. The footfalls advanced into the living room. They were slow, deliberate, gentle, hard to discern against the subfloor, but enough that Dale could follow. Because the pursuer was moving so easily in the dark house, Dale guessed he might have night vision too.

With a tactical eye, he surveyed the contents of his basement in the spooky green light of night vision. There was a washer and dryer. A basket of dirty clothes. A water heater. A sink and a counter with a pair of scissors on it.

He slithered along the wall toward the washer and fished a cotton sweat sock out of a basket. He pocketed the scissors from the counter. He continued on until he was within arm's reach of the water heater. He quietly unscrewed the long metal magazine of the shotgun and carefully withdrew two shells.

Listening to the footfalls above, Dale could hear the man going from room to room. In less than a minute, the assaulter would find the obscure basement door next to the kitchen pantry.

He used scissors to cut off the sealed plastic cap of the shotgun shell and dumped the exposed metal pellets into the empty sock. He removed the plastic wadding and poured the exposed black gunpowder into the sock, over the top of the pellets. After repeating this process with the second shell, he twisted the end of the sock, knotting the powder and shot in a tight, massed-up ball. He set the loose, twisted end of the sock on fire with the pilot light at the bottom of the water heater.

As the long end of the sock began to burn, acting as a fuse, he crept outside and made his way quietly up the side of the house on his way to the deck. He silently slipped onto the wooden planks and crept forward through the open back door.

His pursuer was facing the front of the house now, scanning the small foyer and dining room. Dale could see from the other man's profile that he also had night-vision goggles over his forehead. The assaulter kept his back to the wall, sweeping the rooms of Dale's cabin with the HK machine pistol. He looked like a pro.

The assaulter found the basement door and carefully opened it.

Bang!

The blast rang out, plinking the water heater with shot. The tank began to hiss and gurgle. Dale saw the man fall back into the kitchen and assume a crouch toward the open door, ready to return fire, assuming he was under attack from below. But showing good fire discipline, the assaulter held off and shunted sideways to the threshold, waiting.

Dale couldn't get a reliable shot with the twelve gauge since the man was partially blocked by the kitchen island. The shotgun was notoriously slow to reload and a half hit against a man with a machine pistol would be certain death. It was now or never. Dale set the shotgun down on the deck.

As the man stayed focused on the basement stairs, Dale launched himself, springing forward past the island, blindsiding the assaulter violently on the stone floor. Smashed together, the two men slid into the gas range, where Dale smacked his own head.

Dale ignored the jolt to his skull. He quickly reached for the HK with a twisting motion, trying to wrench it free. He thought he felt it move in his direction. But he realized it was slung around the man's back. It wasn't going to work.

While the tackled man concentrated on retaining his weapon, Dale thrust the heel of his right hand into the man's face with wicked force, crunching the assaulter's nose. He ripped off the man's NVGs and jabbed him in the middle of his face with a closed fist, working on the already smashed nose. He hit him with a third jab to the eyes, which turned the bridge of his nose to pulp. The man let out a guttural scream, as much in anger as pain.

The younger, stronger assaulter thrashed furiously, raising the weapon. Dale wouldn't be able to hold it down with one hand. With the assistance of his shoulder sling, it was just a matter of time before the assaulter regained control of the HK.

Seeing the inevitable, Dale released his grip. In one smooth motion, he jerked himself free of the struggle and flung his own back flat on the floor. He raised his right leg and kicked the man with the heel of his boot, slamming it upward into his chin. As the assaulter took the blow and raised his weapon, Dale rolled to his side and twisted. He got a leg jab into the man's knee, feeling it buckle. As the man reacted, Dale scrambled up and behind him. He kicked the knee again from the other direction, knocking him off-balance. Dale ended up behind him, gaining a choke hold. They were leaning back against the kitchen counter, both struggling for advantage. Dale pulled his own wrist to tighten the vise around the man's neck.

The assaulter pulled the trigger of the automatic HK, attempting to raise the gun over his shoulder to hit Dale. But the burst was wild and erratic, splintering the kitchen cabinets, echoing loudly off the stone floor, hot brass shells skittering.

Dale pulled the man backward toward his kitchen sink. He risked a free hand to fumble for the knife block that he knew was on the counter, next to the sink. He found it and knocked it over, spilling a few blades. Cutting his hand in the process, he managed to get a steak knife by the blunt end.

The man fired another burst. Dale felt something graze his shoulder. Another inch to the left and it would have hit him in the head.

His shoulder burned now. He couldn't know how bad it was, which also meant he couldn't know how much time he would have to continue to act with strength. He ignored it. He squeezed the man's neck harder in the vise between his left elbow and forearm, slightly angling his victim's chin. With as much strength as he could muster in the awkward position, Dale inserted the steak knife just below the man's jawline, near the rear of his head. He savagely buried the serrated blade up to its handle and twisted, screaming in fury as he did so. It had been a long time.

The assaulter got off one more burst of machine pistol fire before jerking his legs in a death rattle, then going abruptly limp.

His arm covered in the blood, Dale slid to the ground with the man in his arms, slapping away the business end of the red-hot HK barrel.

His breathing was out of control as adrenaline surged. His kitchen smelled of cordite and the metallic tang of blood. Chunks of broken wood were splayed across the floor. He pulled the gun from the dead man, raising the sling over the inert, slumping head.

Shaking, Dale stood, the smoking machine pistol in his hands. He could see from the mag's orange dot that the HK had burned through its thirty-eight nine-millimeter rounds. He laid the body on the floor and looked it over in the bilious, otherworldly light. He forced himself to take several deep breaths.

The dead man wore an expensive ski jacket with a tactical H-harness, Gore-Tex snow pants over jeans, and Sorel snow boots. He was clean-shaven with a short but not-too-short civilian haircut. He looked like any other jackass coming off the slopes around here. He was a fit, otherwise average-looking white guy with blond hair, maybe thirty years old.

His hands quaking, Dale patted down the pockets of the nylon H-harness. He found a spare magazine for the HK. He ejected the used mag and inserted this one, cocking the slide.

He slung the HK over his neck and backed his way to his deck, sweeping the house for additional threats. He noticed his shoulder was wet and realized it was his own blood dripping down his forearm.

That was when he heard the truck coming up his driveway.

Its lights were off but a floodlight with a motion sensor on Dale's barn lit it up. Dale carefully backed himself all the way to his deck, his eyes continuing to focus forward into the house. The deck was on the opposite side of the driveway. He wasn't sure what was going on with the vehicle, but he recognized the black Yukon XL.

On the deck now, Dale saw his shotgun where he'd left it. With the dead man's loaded HK in hand, he wouldn't need the shotgun. But he'd been trained as an operator to create options whenever possible.

He stood on the arm of an Adirondack and put the shotgun in the roof gutter. He lodged his healthy left elbow into the gutter and swung his right leg like a pendulum, gaining momentum. After a few swings he had enough centrifugal force to rotate his body sideways onto the roof. He lay there, gasping for a moment, marshaling his strength.

Dale's house had four roof gables pointed in each direction, like an X. Except over the back deck, which had a flat extension, the metal roofs were steep in order to let the snow slide clear. In order to ascend to the top, Dale had to wedge his body between the angled gables with his shoulders against one end, his feet on the other. Using his body as leverage, he inched to the peak, where the four gables came together. From this high perch, he looked down at the Yukon in the driveway.

It sat there idling, lights off. He couldn't see the driver behind the blacked-out windows. The engine stopped and a door opened. A man crept out, moving slowly in a tactical crouch. He had a longer weapon than the dead man in the kitchen. Dale recognized the shape instantly—its banana-shape clip gave it away as an AK-12, the modern Russian assault rifle, the descendant of the famed AK-47. This assaulter also wore a set of NVGs over his eyes. He had a pistol strapped to his thigh. Other than the pistol, he was outfitted exactly like the man now lying dead on Dale's kitchen floor.

Dale's shoulder stung and burned. He could feel the moisture of his own blood running cold down his arm. With that kind of loss, he knew he wouldn't have much time to eliminate this new threat.

But he also knew the threat wouldn't just go away. It was pretty clear that Yukon man was going to enter the house just like his partner had, but with a more accurate rifle. He was going to find his dead buddy and then start hunting for Dale directly. Who knew what other weapons he had stashed in that SUV?

Even if Dale opened up a gunfight from this position on the roof, tactically a superior position, he estimated he'd lose. Yukon man had a far-more-accurate weapon and loads of concealment to work with. Dale studied the SUV. He was now willing to bet that the man was alone. Tactics would dictate that a second assaulter should have crept out and swept toward the house in the other direction.

Dale's borrowed HK was a PDW—a personal-defense weapon—designed to spew lead at a target only a few feet away. It was horribly inaccurate outside of close range. The only way to kill Yukon man would be to draw him in and shock him.

Dale watched the other man advance carefully in a practiced crouch, making no noise whatsoever in the snow, sweeping for targets. Dale heard wind in the trees. He might be able to get a shot off here, he thought. But then he guessed he would make too much noise squaring up on the metal roof before the man ran under the eaves for cover. He held off, waiting for an option with a higher PK, probability of kill.

Dale watched to see whether the assaulter would head straight into the house via the front door or move down the sides. If it were Dale, he would have moved down the sides and inspected the quiet, dark interior before entering.

Sure enough, that was what the man did. He turned left, moving toward Dale's right, his weapon before him, ready to fire.

There was accumulated snow in the angled corner between the gables on this side of the roof. The old snow was as hard as ice, having thawed and refrozen several times in the recent stretch of sunny weather. Some of it was even blue, a tiny glacier. On the ground below lay the snowbank where the snow would eventually fall.

But on this cold night, the roof snow was frozen in place, not about to move anywhere. Dale climbed on top of it, slinging the HK to his back. He lay on his stomach, his face toward the ground, watching the man. He could barely get a view of the man's head, moving slowly along the house. There was a large window just below the gable here. Dale guessed the man would pause to watch through the window with his night-vision goggles.

He guessed right.

As the man paused, watching and listening at the window, Dale pushed himself into position on the sheet of icy snow, aiming himself. The whisper of night wind in the trees was just enough to conceal the sound of his maneuvering. He pushed forward with his hands. Within seconds he was sliding quickly, silently, gaining speed, flying off the roof in a suicidal luge.

He shot off the gable with his arms extended, flying downward toward the top of the man's head. He managed to hook the assaulter's neck in his elbow as he flew forward, toppling him into the snowbank, where they both landed.

Stunned by the hit and the plunge into the frozen snow, the man took a moment to get his bearings. He rolled onto his back and raised the AK toward Dale, who lay right next to him. But the longer barrel of the Kalashnikov was a hindrance in the short space between them. Dale blocked it with his leg, swung the HK out from behind his back, and cooked off a burst of three machine pistol rounds that obliterated the top half of the other man's head, shattering the large picture window behind him, spraying blood over the snowbank.

Dale lay back in the snow, panting. He looked up at the bright stars in the clear sky above, listening to the wind and his own breathing. He dropped the weapon by his side. He wanted to just lie there, getting his breath, trying to make sense of it.

But he knew there was no time for that. He had to get the hell out of here.

CHAPTER 13

THE SILVER MERCEDES S550 GLIDED SOUTH, DOWN THE RIGHT LANE OF Tehran's Jenah Expressway. It entered the turning circle surrounding the ivory Azadi Tower, then went east onto a frontage road. Here it slowed and exited, turning onto a driveway that ended at a gate. An arched sign over the gate announced it as the main entrance to the Iranian Meteorological Center. To either side, opaque razor-topped fences surrounded five acres of nondescript buildings, communications antennae, and a heliport.

The Mercedes driver, clad in the dark green working uniform of the IRGC, pressed a laminated card against the window. Two uniformed Guardsmen emerged with MP-5s hanging from their shoulders. One spoke to the driver. The other moved to the far side and leaned through a rear window to inspect the passenger.

Inside, relaxing with crossed legs, Kasem Kahlidi bowed his head in greeting. Dressed in a striped Savile Row, the clean-shaven Quds man looked like a banker. That didn't keep the IRGC sergeant from saluting him.

After digging through the trunk and surveying the under chassis with a mirror, the Guardsmen backed away, motioning the long sedan through. One of them waved to the driver as it passed.

The Mercedes proceeded to a reserved spot in front of a white building framed by old, thickly painted artillery guns that had last seen service by the Russians in World War Two. The sign above the front door announced the building as the Center's administrative office.

Once inside, Kasem passed through two sets of heavy double doors, where his ID was checked again. Then another Guard stepped forward to wand him with a metal detector. A third looked through his attaché case and confiscated his phone.

The well-dressed intelligence officer finally made it to a reception desk manned by another bearded Guardsman proffering a logbook emblazoned with the green all-seeing-eye logo of the Iranian Ministry of Intelligence, MOIS. Kasem signed his name on the indicated line, annotating it with his official Quds service number.

Now almost forty years old, MOIS could trace its roots back to prerevolutionary days. It had morphed from the despised SAVAK intelligence wing of the shah era.

With the shah's ouster, Khomeini's Guards had taken control and promptly cleansed SAVAK with the torture and execution of thousands of its men. It was rechristened as SAVAMA, then VEVAK, then VAJA. Though the acronyms evolved, its mission did not.

"*Salaam, baradar* Kasem," said a potbellied older man emerging from an office in the uniform of the Guards. His beard had gone gray and his face was marred with pits. He leaned forward and kissed Kasem on each cheek, hugging him. "It has been too long," he said. He leaned back, smiling, his hands still on Kasem's shoulders. "Look at you. Every inch the successful businessman."

"*Salaam, baradar* Naser," Kasem replied, returning the smile, displaying even white teeth. "Yes, business has been good."

Kasem posed as president of an import-export company with suppliers in Switzerland, France, and Germany—a front for weapons smuggling into various Quds hotspots around the world. Only the best got that job. Both of them knew it.

The older man relaxed his hold on Kasem's shoulders and shifted his grip to a handshake. Noticing the scar that crept up from the younger man's collar, he nodded toward it. "I suppose there's a story behind that, old friend," he said with a wink.

Kasem withdrew his hand, suppressing the urge to touch the scar on his neck. "I'd be surprised if you didn't already know it." He winked back.

Naser Maloof nodded and laughed. Indeed, he did know it. The old colonel had a dossier on just about every Quds operative, since he led the MOIS Internal Security Department, charged with rooting out spies. And Naser Maloof wasn't just *any* special Quds officer. He'd been the adjutant to the late, great General Soleimani himself, a highflier.

Colonel Naser Maloof, now well into his sixties, had worked his way up from his early days as a lowly lieutenant in the Guards, distinguishing himself in the Iran–Iraq War ages ago. Much later, during interdiction operations against the Americans' invasion of Iraq, he'd been young Kasem's battalion commander. They'd rarely seen each other since, though Maloof kept tabs on the brilliant young officer's rise.

Once the two men were installed in Maloof's spacious office, an orderly delivered tea. The two former colleagues spoke of old times for a while. The older man asked after Kasem's trip, his flight from Beirut, his plans in Tehran. All the while he was anxious to maneuver the conversation toward the purpose of Kasem's mysterious mission here; but he didn't want to show it.

When the small talk had run its course, Maloof lit a cigarette and creaked back in his chair, stroking his gray beard. "I'm glad you called me," the MOIS colonel said. "I've often felt that MOIS and Quds could work together more often. Perhaps you and I, brothers of the *pasdaran*, could take that first step."

"I completely agree," said Kasem, his face pleasantly neutral. "I believe the Americans' killing of General Soleimani should be a wake-up call for all of us. We shouldn't be slaves to politics."

"Ah," replied the colonel, frowning. "You are so right. Praise be to the martyr. We will have our revenge on *Amrika, inshallah*. I only hope that you are here to give me some information I can use to pay them back in kind, the motherless dogs."

In the wake of Soleimani's death, the various branches of IRGC were tripping over themselves to be the first to come up with a retaliatory plan that would meet with the defense minister's approval. The colonel wondered whether Kasem might be there to pump him for information in order to get the jump on a retaliatory strike.

Kasem nodded and sipped his tea, letting the silence stretch. "May I?" The Quds man reached forward and pulled a cigarette from the pack on the colonel's desk. He sat back and lit it, crossing his legs.

"Colonel," he began, inhaling, the tip of the cigarette glowing. He shook the match flame out. "A man in your position knows a lot. But a man like me assumes nothing." A jet of blue smoke curled over his head.

"You have a gift for mystery, Kasem *jon*. Do I need to outright ask you why you're here?"

"I will spare you the trouble, sir, I promise, I promise," Kasem said, chuckling. He cycled through another lungful of smoke before turning serious. "I'm sure you know I spend most of my time these days in counterintelligence, like you." He gestured toward the colonel with his cigarette. "But unlike you, my efforts are tilted toward rooting out Mossad snakes intent on disrupting our work with the Hezbollah. Homegrown traitors are not quite my specialty, as they are yours."

"You are too modest, Kasem *jon*. I have read many times of your exploits. You are a true *pasdar*. Nothing makes me prouder than when I hear of your heroics."

The Quds man angled his head in deference. When upright again, he said, "I understand the Russians are sending a delegation to the reactor in Bushehr as part of the new deal."

"Yes," said the colonel warily. Finally, the Quds man was getting to it. But almost everyone knew about the Russians coming to Bushehr. "They're coming a few weeks from now. We've been readying work on the plant for months with our technicians and a dozen or so Chinese contractors."

Kasem looked on in his impassive way, sipping his tea, smoking.

The colonel felt the need to fill the void. "I should also say that we've been beefing up air defenses," the older man added. "The last thing we want is to expose ourselves to an Osirak-style strike. We have a half dozen new SAM sites going in—even the S-400."

The Quds operative raised an eyebrow. "I didn't realize we'd taken delivery of the S-400. That's very good news. Very wise."

"Yes, Kasem *jon*. It was all part of the larger deal. The Russians give us their best SAMs and the plant. We give them oil at the Caspian. American sanctions can't stop it."

Flattering the colonel, Kasem asked after a few more details, offering his approval of the secret program's layered aspects. He flattered him with comments about the equally impressive bargain with the Chinese.

After burning through two-thirds of a cigarette, he got to the real point. "Colonel, this is all incredible news for our republic. But let me ask you something of a more . . . delicate nature . . . as it pertains to this. I believe the Russians are providing us other things as well. Yellowcake perhaps and some expertise on refining it." He sipped some tea and stubbed out the smoke.

The colonel grew pale and squinted.

"It's all right," said the Quds man. "I'm read in on *Zaqqum*."

The colonel's cigarette angled down as his face fell. *Zaqqum*, the tree that grew in the depths of hell, fruited with the heads of demons, as noted in the Quran.

It was the code name for the overall program to obtain sustainable nuclear weapons capability. It was the Iranian government's version of the Manhattan Project, with a government resource allocation of a proportionally similar scale. Only a handful of people even knew the code name. How the hell had Kasem gotten close to it without the head of MOIS Internal Security even realizing it?

"We should not speak of *Zaqqum*, Kasem *jon*. I do not know how to—"

"Let me reassure you, *baradar*. General Soleimani himself read me into the operation. He had me performing counterintelligence missions against the Americans and Israelis to keep it secure. The CIA and Mossad are everywhere with respect to this. We can't be too careful."

The colonel blinked. Soleimani had been the most influential man in the intelligence service. If the general had brought his best man into the program, then so be it. But he'd need to add this revelation to Kasem's dossier.

"I see," the colonel said. "So why bring it up with me?"

Privately, he now feared the Quds man was looking for leverage from the colonel's security lapse. Perhaps this was some sort of play to take Soleimani's position as head of Quds?

"As part of my counterintelligence operations to protect our work on *Zaqqum*, I had an interesting meeting a few days ago. In Beirut."

"With . . . ?"

"The Russians. The head of SVR for the Middle East. He works out of Damascus. We monitor his movements closely. He came to Beirut specifically to see me."

The colonel looked worried. He snubbed his cigarette in an ashtray. "And?"

"And he too is preparing for the Russian visit to Bushehr. Only, interestingly, he seemed to imply that he has an intelligence source within our nuclear program, within *Zaqqum*."

"No," said the colonel flatly, shaking his head. "Not possible. Every man in *Zaqqum* has been heavily vetted. There can be no such mole. What did he say?"

"He wasn't specific. Pointedly so."

"You see?"

"Colonel, with respect. I believe him. He is a fat little Russian. Corrupt as a two-bit whore. But he is smart . . . and he was unusually smug in his inferences, even for him. I've worked with him in our Syrian campaigns, killing Kurds, trading intelligence. His information has always been good. And I don't think he's capable of bluffing. Why would he?"

"*Ach,*" grunted the colonel with a wave. The smoke dissipated. "How can you know with Russians? The most duplicitous people. I far prefer the Chinese."

Kasem smiled. "The Russians are too coarse to manipulate anyone well. The Asians are much better liars. I find it interesting that you prefer the better liars."

"Come, come. Russians produce the world's best chess players," parried the colonel.

"True." Kasem smiled. "But I believe this Russian. I think he is both serious and credible. He may be playing chess . . . and admittedly I don't know why. But that doesn't mean he's wrong."

The colonel sighed, shaking his head.

Kasem knew what the older man was thinking. If there was indeed a mole in *Zaqqum*, the costliest development project ever undertaken by the theocratic government, then it would be the colonel's head. Even to suggest an investigation into a mole would be catastrophic to his career. Possibly his life. Kasem was sure the poor old man was now in a full-on panic.

"What do you suggest?" asked the colonel weakly.

"Simple," said Kasem. "I can come back to Iran for a while. I can work undercover here just as well as I can work undercover overseas." He ran a hand under his smooth chin. "Though of course I'll have to grow my beard back." He smiled charmingly.

The colonel was too worried now to return it. "And what would you do?"

"What I do best. I'd poke around, leverage my foreign sources, and sniff out this mole. But I'd work only for you. If I find him, I root out the entire spy network . . . on behalf of MOIS. A joint MOIS–Quds operation."

"And you would report only to me?"

"Only to you."

"Who else would know about this?"

"No one."

The colonel ran several possible scenarios through his mind. Though he could never fully trust Kasem, he couldn't come up with any better outcome.

"When can you start?"

CHAPTER 14

DALE SPENT ABOUT FIVE SECONDS STARING UP AT THE STARS, LISTEN-
ing to the breeze in the trees, just breathing. All was quiet on the property. No one else had emerged from the Yukon. There were no additional
engine noises chugging up the hill. He didn't hear the crunch of an assassin's boots coming up through the snow from the tree line. Other
than the two dead assaulters, his property was as still and peaceful as the
surrounding mountain forest.

He probed the wound to his shoulder with his fingers. Intact but
moist, throbbing and stinging. He scooped some snow and jammed it
under his shirt, pressing it into the pain. The numbing cold was an instant relief.

He haltingly rose to his knees and then feet, stumbling once. He
looked down at the dead man in the snow next to him. Half his head
was missing. As he unshackled the man's AK-12 from his harness, he
kept his eyes averted from the mess that had been his face.

Dale pulled the assaulter's shattered NVGs up from where they lay
beside him. He wiped away some blood and tissue to examine them.
They were military issue, a five-tube sensor model not available on the
open market. He patted down the rest of the dead man's H-harness and
found an additional mag for the AK, which he wrestled free.

With the rifle in his hands and his own NVGs flipped back down
over his eyes, Dale went into his house. In the dark of his kitchen, he
dragged the first dead operator through the foyer and out the front door

into the night air, leaving a smear of blood on the stone floor. He laid both dead men on the snowbank, side by side like two fish in a market.

He went back inside and scrounged through a closet to find a flashlight. With this, he rummaged through a bathroom to find his trauma kit. He removed the NVGs and chanced a look at his shoulder in the bright white of the beam. After stripping off his shirt, he washed himself clean of the attackers' blood and took a close look in the mirror.

A bullet had nicked the top of his deltoid but hadn't actually penetrated. It was a deep groove of flesh that wouldn't be closing on its own anytime soon. Dale poured some peroxide on it and dabbed at it with gauze. He affixed a bandage that he wrapped around his arm, making it tight. The wound would need stitches, but his makeshift bandage would have to do for now.

It hurt like hell. There was a vial of morphine in the trauma kit, but he tried not to think about it. He didn't want to cloud his reasoning or reflexes.

In his bedroom closet, he dug out his largest waterproof backpack and began stuffing it with clothes. He opened his small digital gun safe and removed the Glock, shoving it into his waistband. He saw the USB Meredith had left behind right where he'd laid it earlier. He zipped it into the trauma kit and stashed it in the bag. He stuffed his laptop in an outer pocket. Finally, he changed his clothes, tossing his bloody ones in a trash can. He circled through his great room to pick up Grace's letter, stuffing it in a breast pocket.

On his way back outside, he carefully shouldered himself into his heaviest down parka. He slung the backpack over his good arm and the sling of the AK over his wounded shoulder. He trotted through the snow, past the two dead men, down to the snowmobile shed. In the dark confines of the shed, he placed the AK on a workbench. Using his flashlight, he riffled through the big gun vault that he'd opened only twenty minutes before, looking for a hidden seam at its rear. He explored the walls of the vault with his fingers and eventually found the edge of a twelve-by-twelve panel.

He froze when he heard something, ready to spin around and take up the AK. It was an owl hooting in the woods. He went back to work.

Behind the panel he recovered a small nylon bag. He zippered it open, conducting a quick check of the contents with a sweep of the flashlight. There were three passports—UK, US, Canada—three grand in twenty-dollar bills, and four loaded magazines for the Glock. He zipped the go bag closed and stuffed it into the larger backpack.

Dale poured some gas into his snowmobile and cranked it up. He rode it up the small trail to his driveway. He dismounted in front of his house and angled its headlight onto the two dead bodies. He shut the machine down and walked over to them.

One by one, he dragged the dead men to the rear of the Yukon, leaving a red streak of blood on the snow. He opened the driver's door and scanned the interior. The backseat was folded forward, maximizing the truck's cargo area. He saw the satphone on the center console and three military-style duffels behind the front seats. The keys were still in the ignition.

He pocketed the phone and went about inspecting the duffels. He found only clothes, regular American labels. Oddly, there was a mish-mash of outfits including dress and casual wear, even extra shoes. He noted that one of the bags was filled with women's clothing. He left the bags where they were.

The snow was picking up. Dale looked back at the bloodstains. Already they were fading under the big flakes.

He opened the truck's lift gate and tried to pull one of the dead men into the cargo area. But the effort was too much and the weight too awkward. His shoulder was killing him. He had another idea.

He jogged to his barn and found a length of rope among his rock-climbing gear. He wrapped it around the ankles of the two dead men and then dropped to his back, sliding under the truck to tie it to the rear axle.

With the two bodies dragging five feet behind, Dale drove the truck off his driveway and into the far trees, snapping branches of bushes and saplings on the way. At this side of the house, his property fell away into a shallow ravine with a small seasonal creek. As the truck rolled slowly toward it, idling in four-wheel drive, Dale opened the door and hopped out into the ankle-high snow. He watched the SUV plow over more scrub until it found its way to the edge. Finally, it tipped forward and disappeared over the bank with a crash, whipping the two corpses along behind it.

He went back to his snowmobile and took a last look around his property through his NVGs, shaking his head. All he'd wanted to do that day was finish that painting of Peoh.

Meredith's secure cell phone rang at seven a.m. eastern standard time, just as the Virginia sunrise was beginning to brighten the otherwise drab walls of her Langley office. She was on her fourth coffee. She leapt at the phone, almost knocking her cup over.

"Meth, it's me," said Dale.

"John, where the fuck have you *been*? What happened? Why didn't you answer my calls? I've been up all night. I've spun up a team that will be out there in your area about now. I've . . ." She realized she was ranting. "*Shit, John!* Just tell me."

"Yeah, I got a little busy."

"Tell me. *Now.*"

"How secure is this line?"

"I can see you're on the phone I gave you. We're good."

"You're alone?"

"Yes, I'm alone. I'm at HQS. If this isn't secure, then nothing is. What *happened*?"

She heard him take a breath. "You're burned, Meth. No doubt about it. They followed you to my place."

She hunched over her desk as though she'd just been gut-punched. She buried her face in one hand while she held her phone with the other. "Shit. I'm sorry."

"You should be."

"Just give me the details. We'll figure it out."

He paused. She could almost hear him thinking through the way to handle this conversation.

"There were two of them. One of them was following me in an SUV. I spotted the tail—that's when I called you. As it turns out, the other was back at the house watching me from the tree line. I picked him up on IR when we were on the phone. He had a machine pistol. He meant business. I ended up taking him down in the house."

"*Christ*, John. I'm so sorry."

"Yeah."

"What about the other guy?"

"The second one came hauling down my driveway in an SUV. That was the guy that was following me on the highway. He had an AK. I got him before he made it in the house."

Still cradling her head, Meredith tightly closed her eyes. The morning light, the coffee next to her, the conversation with her ex-husband about killing people, the fact that she'd been stupid enough to be followed . . . it was all too surreal. She started to feel nauseous. She swallowed hard and opened her eyes, pulling herself back into the job.

"Okay," she said. She picked up a pen and paper. "You know I'm going to need a lot more information. But give me the current tactical picture."

"Yeah, yeah. Okay. But let me just say, Meth, I don't fully trust your organization. Don't expect me to come in to some briefing center. You guys created this mess, not me."

There was rightfully a quavering edge to his voice. But Meredith knew how to deal with adrenaline-soaked operatives. "I understand. Just tell me the current tactical picture. We'll figure out how to deal with it. You're not alone in this."

He was quiet for a moment. "All right. But only you. Okay?"

"Yes."

He made her promise it. She did. He went on.

"I wasn't sure what else was coming up the hill. I also wasn't sure of the nature of the threat, so I wanted to conceal the scene as best as I could before I got out. I sank the SUV and the two dead guys in a creek bed on the side of the house. Then I did an exfil up over the hill to avoid any new threats coming up from town. That's about it."

"What kind of exfil? How? You took your car up over the mountain?"

"No, I figured my car is off-limits. If you're burned, then I am too. Let's just say I'm off-grid."

She wasn't going to press him. Not yet. "I'm sure you did an SSE of their vehicle and equipment. Who were they? Iranian?"

"Negative. Russian."

"Russians?" Meredith almost choked as she said it. She stood and paced. "How do you know?"

"Their night-vision gear had Cyrillic engraving. High-end military issue. Also one of them had an AK-12 with Russian ammo. It looked military issue, not the shit rednecks build themselves. They looked Russian too, ethnically speaking. Military-age males and all that."

Meredith paced in a tight oval in front of her desk, the phone squashed to her ear. *Russians?* "All right. You're probably right. I'm just having a hard time grokking this whole thing."

"Are you guys going to clean it up?"

She thought that over. She'd need to get clearance from Rance, maybe even Dorsey. Legally, the CIA wasn't supposed to go around killing foreign adversaries in the USA, plastering over the mess. Counterespionage was the FBI's turf. But FBI was law enforcement—cops. FBI would mean stringing up yellow crime scene tape and explaining a whole bunch of things that she wouldn't have the time or inclination to do.

Since it was her ex-husband's house high on a mountaintop and only two foreign operatives, she thought she could get away with keeping it in the CIA family. At least that was how she'd pitch it to Dorsey; he'd hate the whole thing and probably make her sign a bunch of nondisclosure forms. But he'd play along.

"Yes," she said, sighing. "I'm going to ask Ground Branch to secure the site. We'll want to get a look at these guys, their equipment. It'll be low profile, I promise."

"Not HRT?" HRT stood for "hostage rescue team," FBI special operators who would descend into a hostile environment.

"No, not yet. But let me worry about that."

"Good. I don't want my name in the papers. Look, I'm going to drop. I'll check in with you later."

"Wait," she said, stalling.

She stopped pacing. She could see Rance through the vertical window next to her office door. She'd been calling him all night, trying to bring him up to speed, but he hadn't bothered to answer. She saw him now, leaning against a cubicle in his gray suit, talking to his executive admin. He looked pale. *Wait till he gets a load of this,* she thought. *That will be world-class pale.*

"John," she said. "We still have to talk about Cerberus. I still need that. Did you look at the file I left you? I texted you the password. It's good for another day."

"Not now, Meth. This is way too fucked up."

"You realize this thing is with the director at this point? It's going to go before the National Security Council."

"I don't care."

"Listen to me. I can't make sense of what happened to you. But the Cerberus thing hasn't gone away. If anything, if the Russians really are involved, then it just underscores how serious this is. Have you seen the news? The Russians are heavily involved in the Iranian nuke program via that reactor in Bushehr. That means yellowcake going in right past our sanctions. You're still the only way we're going to keep this thing . . ."

Meredith suddenly realized she was talking to dead air. He'd hung up.

Rance scheduled the meeting with Dorsey for two that afternoon. By then, Meredith had done what she could. At least Dorsey had given her the authorization to take care of it. A Ground Branch paramilitary team that had been training in the mountains of Idaho was flown in to the tiny Cle Elum Airport, where they were met by a hastily dispatched case officer who worked on recruiting Chinese immigrants in nearby Vancouver, Canada.

Posing as county inspectors, the team drove up to John's property in a white SUV with government plates. They found the vehicle, the site of the gunfight, and the two dead operatives. They didn't have the equipment to haul the SUV out. Instead, after searching it for intel, they cut down a beefy lodgepole pine to bury the vehicle under a mountain of branches.

Rance was furious about the whole thing. He was pissed at her for being burned, pissed at John for disappearing, pissed at himself for having to explain all of this to higher-ups.

Aside from his general surliness, Meredith thought he looked terrible, like he'd been awake all night. His skin was gray. He kept belching into a closed fist as though he were on the verge of throwing up. When she asked him if he was all right, he just got more pissed. She assumed it was a hangover. But a pretty thick one for a garden-variety Wednesday.

Dorsey leaned on the conference table in the SCIF, steadying himself with two fists, a pen in his mouth, his standard crisis-management pose. After hearing a recounting of the saga, he said, "All of this and we're still no closer to getting someone to talk to Cerberus." He lowered his head, frustrated, chewing furiously. "What intel did we get from the bodies?"

"Everything seems to indicate they're Russian," said Rance. "The clothing labels were American, but we found Russian equipment. The Yukon was rented at the Seattle Airport. We traced the bill back to an SVR front company. We're running a picture of the one guy's face through our recognition database."

"Why not both of them?" asked Sheffield.

"Because the other guy's was shot off," said Rance.

"My guess is they're Spetsnaz Alphas," said Meredith. "That was John's assessment too."

"Operating in the US?" Dorsey shot. "What the fuck? Why go after Dale?"

Meredith started to say something but Rance cut her off. "I think you remember the WMD buy Meredith was coordinating in Dubai, sir, the bioweapons-Syria thing. Our asset there, the seller, got snatched. We think it was SVR. I'd say this confirms it."

"I remember it. You're saying Meredith got burned on that op? Led them straight to Dale?"

It galled her that they spoke about her like she wasn't in the room. "Yes," she said, inserting herself. She had to reluctantly admit to herself that Rance might be right. "That appears to be the case."

"But why would they be following you so closely back in the US? Even if you were burned back in theater, why would they be following you back here? The beauty of your cover was that you are an actual wife visiting an actual husband."

"Ex-wife, sir," she corrected.

"I don't know," said Rance. "It could be something fishy about Dale too."

"*What?*" Meredith blurted. "How the hell could it be John's fault?"

"I mean, we just don't know what he's been up to."

"Oh, come *on*," she said. "It's not that. John's not been in any of this stuff. He's retired . . . by us, I might add. No. This is an Occam's razor thing. You guys are right that my cover was blown in Dubai. I picked up an SVR tail and it stayed active when I got back for whatever reason. That's all." She looked toward Dorsey for support.

"A tail that went all the way from here to Seattle, to the mountains. Two Spetz Alphas in the woods," Dorsey replied, looking back at her. "Smells bad. But I doubt it's a Dale problem. I'm with you, Meredith. You're blown and they followed you. Somehow they got a bead on Dale as being important, which he unfortunately is." He sighed, shaking his head. "Has Cerberus surfaced at all?"

"No," said Rance. "He left pretty explicit instructions that we're not to come back to him without Dale. He's still dark."

"And Dale? Where's he now? We need to bring him in, obviously."

Rance looked at Meredith. "You want to tell him? Or should I do it?"

She took a deep breath. "John's spooked, sir. As you might imagine, he's taking extreme measures to protect himself. That means, unfortunately, that he's not answering his phone right now."

"Of course not," said Dorsey. He crossed his arms and raised one hand to his brow, smothering his eyes, chewing on the pen. "Jesus, it's almost like we're *trying* to fuck this up."

CHAPTER 15

AFTER ABANDONING HIS PROPERTY, DALE HAD RIDDEN THE SNOWMO-
bile over the mountain trails in the dark, arriving in the neighboring
town of Roslyn around nine p.m. He pulled up to a low-rent used-car
dealer on the edge of town. There were a dozen cars for sale sitting out
in a gravel lot with a single-wide trailer as a sales office.

He'd long ago noted that there was no security fence on this lot and
only one sputtering overhead light. Somewhere in the recesses of his
mind, the meager little business had lodged itself as a stepping-stone in
a potential egress plan, should the need ever arise. The need had arisen.

On the back edge of the lot, he found the type of vehicle he was
looking for: a beat-up mid-seventies Chevy pickup sporting three different colors, one of which was plain Bondo Gray. He retrieved a
bundled-up tool kit from a cargo recess under the snowmobile's seat
and spread it out.

He used a slim jim from the tool kit to access the truck and a screwdriver to pry the steering column loose. He closed the circuit of the
truck's ignition system by touching two stripped wires together. The old
beast roared to life with the squeal of a slipping fan belt.

After throwing his backpack in the cab, he returned to his snowmobile and scraped away the registration decals. He purposely left the keys
for the machine in the ignition. Though he was stealing the truck, his
conscience was clear. The expensive two-year-old snowmobile was more
than a fair trade for the beat-up Chevy. By the time the car dealer put it
all together, he'd accept the trade.

Knowing he had limited time before the truck was reported stolen, he headed north to the touristy town of Leavenworth on Highway 97. There were dozens of motels in Leavenworth and he drove around their parking lots, looking for a target. After casing three, he found an early-eighties Chevy pickup with a camper top sandwiched into a dark spot. Close enough.

Using pliers and a screwdriver, he swapped out the license plates between the two trucks. He figured he now had even more time before the cops would look twice at his ride.

Around eleven, he headed west through the mountains and eventually north on I-5, stopping only for gas, food, and coffee, paying cash the whole way. By one a.m., he'd made it to Bellingham, just below the Canadian border. Here he found a small mom-and-pop motel with a red neon vacancy sign. He parked the truck around back, paid the manager in cash, and trudged up the outdoor stairs to his room, dead-dog tired. The freeway roared by just outside the metal door.

It was from this bed that he called Meredith at four the next morning, having bagged a few hours of sleep. After hanging up on her, he went into the bathroom, showered, and removed his shoulder bandage. It was soaked with blood.

Dale knew what he had to do, but the thought made him cringe. Facing the inevitable, he dug through his pack and found the trauma kit.

He cleaned the wound while perched on the bathroom's Formica counter, his eyes close to the mirror. With the substantial blood loss, he knew that if he gave himself any morphine, his blood pressure would drop. He'd have to tough this one out. He bit down on the end of a towel, ready to scream.

Pinching the skin closed over the wound, he used a medical stapler to insert ten sutures, trying hard not to pass out from the extraordinary pain. He finally got it done, though it felt like his arm had been torn out of its socket. He dabbed the sealed wound with gauze, coated it with Neosporin, rebandaged himself.

He caught sight of his face in the mirror. The skin was ashen. Sweat beaded on his forehead. The coppery brown hair was ragged and stringy, hanging down to his three-day beard. Not pretty but appropriate for the look he wanted to cross the border, since it was closer to the picture on his passport.

Hours later, he was rolling north on I-5, a plastic bag of ice on his shoulder and an IV in his wrist. The IV tube was hooked to a plasma bag hanging from the empty gun rack in the truck's rear window. When he'd taken in half the bag, he pulled over and stowed it in the trauma kit, hoping like hell he'd never have to use it again.

Starving, he found a nearby greasy spoon where he threw down a plate of eggs and forced himself to take in a quart of water. On his way out the door, he liberated from a hook by the men's room a filthy mechanic's jacket that smelled of old engine fluids. At his next stop for gas, he bought a ball cap with a Budweiser logo. He checked the truck's oil and smeared some engine grease on the hat, giving it a black patina.

The sun broke free of the Cascades, affording a brilliant view of Mount Baker. The dashes in the highway whizzed by. It was just a matter of time now.

The tires hummed along with his thoughts. He'd grown up not too far from here, fifty miles south in the little port town of Anacortes. His dad had been a Navy man, an A-6 bomber pilot based at Naval Air Station Whidbey Island. In the twilight of his flying days, the old man had retired and taken a job with a defense contractor on base, which had allowed Dale to grow up without moving the way other military brats usually did.

He passed by a taco stand at exit 126. He and the old man used to stop there on road trips. Things had been great back then for a while. But then Paul Dale died suddenly of a heart attack at the age of forty-six, the summer between Dale's junior and senior years of high school. That was a raw deal if ever there was one.

He saw a road sign: CANADIAN BORDER, PEACE ARCH, THIRTY MORE MILES. Dale's mom was Canadian, a Quebecer.

Her parents had emigrated from Iran in the mid-seventies in the grim lead-up to the revolution. When John was a kid, his mother had spoken to him in both French and Farsi. She was a strong woman, but the death of her husband at such a young age had turned her life upside down. Weekend social drinking became daily. She was dead now, so it didn't matter anymore.

The border was only fifteen miles now, the cars beginning to bunch up.

His life had been conventional till then, a paint-by-numbers kind of kid. He'd done well, gotten into Notre Dame, won a Navy ROTC scholarship. He was going places. He was going to do it for his dad. He thought about Grace. The letter in his pocket.

Five miles. He pulled over, rummaged around the seat, and found his passport. The truck's temperature was rising. Not good. He'd have to find another ride on the other side. He took a pull of water. He didn't feel great.

After commissioning, Dale had taken all the requisite tests for the Navy to determine the direction of an officer's career. He figured he'd be off to Pensacola and flight school, just like his dad had done back in the seventies. But much to his disappointment, the Navy billeted him as an intelligence officer, with orders to report to some command in a Virginia town he'd never heard of. He protested, but the needs of the Navy always came first. They liked to say stuff like that.

He took down some water and looked at his phone, looking over Google Maps for a less traveled crossing. If someone had a clue, they'd get the ping on his phone and know he'd gone out through Canada. But he'd be long gone. Didn't matter.

He hadn't loved that intel job out in Bahrain, boring as hell. He applied regularly to become a SEAL, a pilot, a sub driver . . . anything else. But the Navy didn't oblige—its needs were still coming first. He'd started thinking about what he'd do as a civilian when his tour of duty was up.

Thumbing through the digital map, he found a small two-lane that went east. Surely that crossing would be sparser. He exited I-5 and doubled back south, looking for the exit. The truck rattled along.

It had gotten better over time, he had to admit, back there in Bahrain. In his second year, he was assigned to monitor the movements of the IRGC Navy and prepare briefings for the commanding admiral. In one of them, he translated some raw Farsi between Iranian patrol boat crews in the Shatt al Arab. Stunned by this surprising knowledge of native tongues, the admiral made him his main man. That was when shit really changed.

He was headed due east now, squinting into the sun as it rose higher over the brilliant white mountains.

The admiral had known John wanted to be an operator. He must have said something to somebody. John was invited to an interview with a Navy captain from JSOC, the Joint Special Operations Command, which oversaw all American Special Forces, including the SEALs. Dale couldn't have been more excited at the time—he was going to get a real shot at his dream.

He'd been directed to a nondescript building in the middle of Manama, the capital of Bahrain. But when he entered the office there in his snowy dress whites, he found that the people waiting for him weren't JSOC. One of the interviewers was a gorgeous young brunette named Meredith Morris. She had a proposition for him.

The small border checkpoint was just ahead. There was a line of three cars before him. He put the truck in park and killed the engine, waiting. The weak winter sun warmed his shoulder. The Canadian passport was on his lap. There was a black-and-white Holstein cow lowing in a field on the Canadian side of the border. More of them were lazily walking toward it, joining in, mooing from a distance.

He absently tapped the passport with the gold seal of the Canadian government. The photo page had his picture from six or seven years ago: Reza Shariati, resident of Montreal, graduate of McGill University.

He wasn't worried about getting flagged at the border. The CIA had a division that did nothing but apply for real documents from passport agencies, DMV offices, and other state-run bureaucracies all around the world. In effect, it manufactured law-abiding citizens out of thin air. These invented people, "legends," were carefully tracked and cultivated over time.

When the Agency had placed him on inactive suspension, they'd confiscated his CIA ID, his handgun, and his real US passport. He'd been told to surrender all other related agency equipment and materials by a certain date. But he never had. If they wanted the shit so damn bad, let them come and get it.

They'd never followed up. He knew why. The Agency needed to keep legends alive so as not to have to explain to any real government entity why the person they'd manufactured had ceased to exist. Since he was on inactive suspension, they weren't inclined to kill off his personas, which continued to maintain contacts with real assets in the intelligence world, like Cerberus.

He'd always believed his past would catch up to him somehow. It was why he kept the passports of these legends and a wad of cash close by. It was why he had every intention of getting through to the Vancouver airport and flying to the Caymans, where he had a few more thousand dollars stashed. From there, he intended to switch to another legend on a UK passport and get to France, where he'd once paid cash for a little shack in Bordeaux a long time ago. There was a moldy old cellar at that house, where Dale had locked away a cache of supplies, including weapons. The CIA never knew about it. He never even told Meth.

So there he sat in line, fingering the Canadian passport of a person manufactured by the CIA, the agency that had legally barred him from leaving the country. The agency that was now apparently begging him to come back to run a mission. Not only was he breaking their suspension deal with them; he was turning his back on them. He supposed that technically it meant he was about to become a fugitive from the United States government wanted by the CIA.

The car ahead of him moved forward. Dale cranked the truck and followed, then shut it down, listening to the cows mooing away just past the fence. Canadian cows.

Fugitive. The word rattled around in the engine of his brain like a loose part. He recalled the still-open inquiry, the nature of the punitive suspension that had kicked in when he resigned. The Agency had told him it would be illegal to leave the US without their permission. He'd signed a bunch of papers.

Up till now he hadn't really cared. He had his home in Cle Elum and his growing renown as a local artist. But he could do that anywhere. Hell, weren't all the great impressionist painters from France?

The Cle Elum home was in Grace's name, held in trust; Dale was a tenant who paid rent into the trust. Meth would figure a way to clear his name.

It wasn't like he was a real criminal.

But now that he was actually fleeing the country—with stolen credentials—he wondered about that. He was breaking multiple laws, felonies. That would make him ipso facto a felon, a fugitive, even if he had a very good excuse.

He started the truck, slipped it into gear, and moved forward another vehicle length before shutting it down again.

He suddenly recalled a story from his middle school years. A young pilot in his father's squadron had so indebted himself to a shady loan shark outfit that the officer had just up and fled to Canada one day. In doing so, the young lieutenant had become a deserter from the US military, breaking the oath of his commission. The scared kid had probably even used this very border crossing. Once over that line, he'd become a fugitive, never able to return to the US. Dale remembered his dad telling him how he'd had to brief the FBI on the deserter. A youthful indiscretion leading to a lifelong mistake, his dad had said.

Dale shook his head, listening to the cows. *That's not me,* he thought, removing his hat, running his hand through his hair. The two scenarios were nothing alike.

He'd served his country admirably, *unquestioningly* for most of his life. He'd risked his life for it, killed for it. He had more stories of valor than anyone he'd ever even met. He'd always met the tenets of his oath to his country. Always. He was a man of honor who had done his duty. *Deserter?*

A cow looked at him dumbly, unblinking, then went back to chewing the ground. *Deserter.* It was even worse than technically being a fugitive, if not a real criminal. He looked at the vehicle behind him. A VW van with Canadian plates. He accidentally caught his own eye in the rearview mirror.

He thought of Cerberus. The Agency would figure something else out. They'd been more than ready to send him packing just a few years ago. How could he possibly be the only tool they had to deal with this nuclear problem? And how dare they show up on his doorstep and drop the whole mess in his lap, nearly getting him killed by a pack of *fucking Spetsnaz!*

Irritated, he rotated his arm, testing the wound on his shoulder. It burned.

More of the cows seemed to be looking at him now. They'd all gone silent for the moment. Driving forward another thirty yards to the barbed wire where the animals stood would mean becoming a deserter, the object of stories that others would tell one day. *That* would be his legacy. Would his own daughter be telling that story to his grandkid one day? What about his wife? *Ex-wife,* he reminded himself.

Meth had damn well better understand his extenuating circumstances, he thought. Of course she would. John wasn't going for good—he was just getting out while things were hot. A team of operatives had tried to kill him for Christ's sake. He'd be back soon enough when it was safe. She'd understand.

But would Grace? He tapped his shirt pocket, heard her letter wrinkling beneath. *Whatever happened, Dad, you're the most honorable man I've ever known. I couldn't be prouder of you.* Would his daughter understand that the Agency had treated him like a traitor when he wasn't? Would she understand that he'd had to leave because their reckless mismanagement had put him in danger? Would she understand why he hadn't wanted to work for them again, even when asked? That he'd had no choice? It was a lot to ask of a kid.

He pictured Grace in the same khakis he'd worn years ago, manning the bridge of a ship in the Persian Gulf, doing her part to keep the world safe from the mad mullahs. Would she understand that her father had also served there to keep the world safe? That he'd gone above and beyond?

Had he?

The car ahead of him moved on into Canada, past the cows. Dale sat frozen, unable to turn the ignition to start the truck up again. The VW van guy honked. Dale waited three more seconds, staring at the dingy old speedometer in front of him. He looked at his own eye in the rearview and then at the van behind him. It honked a second time. VW man had his hands raised, palms up, the universal WTF gesture of drivers everywhere.

Dale reluctantly started the pickup and inched it forward. After ten seconds he found himself looking into the mildly pleasant face of a Canada Border Services officer.

He thumbed the passport on his lap, flicking the pages. He kept it below the window, out of sight.

"Good morning, sir. Canadian or American?" the officer asked, the sun behind him blotting his face, the cows beyond mooing loudly again. "Sorry about the cows," the border officer said, glancing away. "The dairy farmer over there comes out to feed them about this time every morning." He smiled. "Just like my dogs. Passport?"

Dale stared back at the immigration officer, saying nothing. It was now or never. The cows were going nuts.

"Sir?"

"Shit," Dale said out loud, staring straight ahead. "Shit, shit, *shit*!" He slapped his hand on the top of the steering wheel, rattling it.

"Sir, excuse me?" The officer's voice took on that law enforcement edge. His hands were now on his hips, his hat tilted toward Dale.

Dale let his passport fall to the floor of the truck by angling his knee. He covered it with his boot and slid it under the bench seat. He made a show of patting down the pockets of the greasy jacket.

He removed the Budweiser hat and wiped his sweating forehead. "I just realized I forgot my passport," he said. "I'm an American. I'll need to turn around."

Ten minutes later, two miles south of the border, he pulled over next to a dewy alfalfa field thawing in the sun. He found the secure phone Meredith had left with him in an outer pocket of his backpack. He'd taken the battery out so they couldn't track him. But it didn't matter anymore. He put the battery back in, powered the phone up, waited for the signal.

He stared at it for ten more seconds, thumb over the first digit. Then he dialed. He called his ex-wife. His handler.

PART TWO

SET

CHAPTER 16

ZANA LEANED AGAINST THE THICK WINDOWS THAT OVERLOOKED THE lab, watching the busy floor. His face was reflected in the dark sheen of the lead-infused coating. Staring past it, he observed teams of techs working below as he sipped black coffee from a foam cup.

They wore either blue or yellow surgical-style suits, puffed up with radiation-resistant materials. The bulky, brightly colored unisex outfits gave them a benign, cartoonish quality. They trundled awkwardly through the bulging rows of equipment in their heavy uniforms, occasionally disappearing into one of the protected warrens to either side of the raised white floor, like so many Smurfs at work.

Standing there at ten in the morning, drinking his coffee, the former quantum physics professor was counting the heads of the blue smocks, the Iranians. For every ten of the blues, he noted, there was at least one yellow, a Russian. One of those yellows, he thought, was going to be a problem.

From this angle, Zana couldn't quite tell which of the yellows on the floor might be the Russian disguised in protective gear who troubled him. But he knew the man was down there somewhere asking questions. He had that old Soviet way about him: brusquely impersonal until loaded up with vodka after hours, oafish but perceptive, smarter than he looked. Zana had never liked Russians much.

He crumpled the cup and dropped it in a trash bin, then settled at his desk. He fired up his e-mail, scrolling immediately to the message that had been on his mind all morning. It was simple, only one line, but he'd reread it over and over.

Not much to go on, really. The commander of the facility wanted to see him in his office tomorrow morning at 0700. The message from the commander's adjutant said to leave a deputy in charge of the lab, as the meeting might go long. Full stop.

Zana had parsed each of the fifteen words that formed the e-mail at least a dozen times.

He was 80 percent sure it would be about the exit travel stamp for himself and Nadia. It had been two weeks since his request, and thus far, he'd heard nothing. His immediate superior, Javad, a thirty-five-year-old nuclear scientist with a streak of Islamic fervor, had told him that due to the extraordinary circumstances of the Russian visits, he wouldn't be able to grant the stamps.

Though Zana was still in the traditional forty-day mourning period, Javad had said to put the exit travel stamp out of his mind, get back to work, take advantage of the Russian expertise.

That was Javad in a nutshell—a zealot, a revolutionary, a *pasdar*. People like him were why Zana had been sabotaging the entire operation. Javad believed they were on a mission from God. He believed a nuclear weapon would bring about the Mahdi, the messiah, the Twelfth Imam hiding in the Occultation since the year 872. He'd launch it the day he could.

Outsiders, Westerners, wouldn't take these purported beliefs seriously. But the reality was, Javad and the other Twelvers who ran the IRGC really did believe they were akin to apostles, specially appointed ambassadors, the only ones in the current world who could cleanse it and return the world to God's embrace. With the mysterious powers of the universe emanating now from their labs, why wouldn't they? A former president, Ahmadinejad, had spent half a billion dollars building a palace for the Twelfth Imam's return, to be installed after the first mushroom cloud. They weren't kidding.

As apostles, they wanted to destroy the roots of decadence and resistance—America, Europe, Israel—in order to restore the divine world order. In their twisted logic, the fastest, most efficient way to do that was a nuke. And right now they were desperate for it. All these tensions with America . . . they saw it as the end of days.

But only the insiders, like Zana, knew just how serious they were. He thought it all nuts, an organized, terrified madness, a group suicide cult. He kept thinking he would wake up one day to find that they weren't on a race toward the end of the world, with himself as the enabler in chief.

Iran deserved better. Iran, Persia, the empire that had first established international commerce and postal communications under Cyrus the Great. That was the real Iran. And it was under siege by all these Javads. They should have been driving toward modernity, not going the other direction. Instead, they would become death, destroyer of worlds, to borrow Oppenheimer's famous line, lifted from the *Bhagavad Gita*.

Maybe there was still some sanity somewhere, Zana thought, leaning back, chilled. Not all were pure Twelvers like Javad. Some were more moderate, more pragmatic. They still believed in the vision of the clerics, but saw the path as more evolutionary, less doomsday. They saw Iran to be an ascendant world power, rebuilding the world in God's vision without immediately destroying it to bring that vision about.

Thinking of that e-mail again, he'd always considered the commander to be of that stripe: committed to the IRGC, committed to nuclear weapons development for Iran, but not quite prepared to immolate millions. The commander at least had a speck of humanity buried in his DNA. It hadn't yet been hijacked by the fervent, overwrought interpretations of ancient texts—had it?

And so it was to the commander Zana had appealed for the travel stamps, going right over Javad's head. That was two weeks ago. Since then, nothing. Now the commander wanted to see him in person.

He moved the cursor up and down the message, thinking about it. Yes, that must be it—the exit visa. Why else?

The commander was a busy man, constantly working with dignitaries, plainclothes MOIS intelligence men, clerics, Russians, Chinese. In fact, he'd just been in Tehran for the last few days and was supposed to return tonight. It was strange that his first order of business would be an early-morning meeting with Zana. Troubling.

There was a distant noise in the lab beneath his feet. Zana could hear hatches closing, the warning bells of the equipment, a few shouts among techs over the rising hum of machines. He could feel a faint vibration through his rubber-soled shoes. Another test was starting up, the fourth that morning.

He checked more e-mails. Several from Javad asking him to prepare reports for the Russians. He reread the one from Nikita, his new Russian "helper" down there on the floor right now, running around in his yellow suit, probably the one demanding this fourth test.

In his gruff style, the Russian had said he wanted to spend a few hours with Zana that afternoon to learn about the SCADA design. Nikita said he considered himself an expert in Zippe centrifuges, but acknowledged that he was less familiar with this particular one, built by a French–German consortium but of the classic Swiss type.

Yes, Zana thought, thinking about that request. The array was nothing if not unique. It had been built in another research facility in Arak, three hundred miles away, at a civilian research site. It was then disassembled and transported secretly here to Tabriz to be rebuilt deep belowground in this hardened bunker in order to create highly enriched uranium (HEU) with at least a 90 percent concentration of U235—weapons grade.

But the unique enrichment environment had never made it to weapons grade. The purity had never made it above 50 percent and, even then, not in sufficient quantities for the critical mass of a weapon. And now the commander wanted to see him. *It could go long. . . . Leave the deputy in charge.* Not good.

Zana lit a cigarette and slouched in his chair, thinking about how he would approach the discussion with the Russian. He inhaled smoke and kept it in his lungs, staring but not seeing, his eyes drifting toward the window on the far side of the office. He blew the smoke out, feeling the nicotine. Should he take the Russian's word at face value? Was it true he didn't know much about the Franco–German array? Or was he trying to draw Zana out? Why the insistence on meeting today? Why the day before the appointment with his commander?

He thought of Nadia at home in Tehran, more than three hundred miles to the southeast, waiting to hear from him. He hadn't been in touch with her for a week. The last time they'd spoken of his plans, in the bathroom next to running water, he'd directed her to be ready to leave on a moment's notice. Perhaps, he thought, he should give her a call now to check in, to make sure she'd followed through, communicating it in their own special code. Perhaps, he thought darkly, it would be the last time he'd ever be able to speak with her. He blew a jet of smoke through his nose, stubbed out the cigarette.

He stood, stretched, walked to his door. He looked down the hall and saw the normal pair of Guardsmen standing there, leaning against a wall, talking to each other. One of them noticed him and waved. The scientist waved back and headed to the men's room down the hall, empty. His entire team was down on the floor with the Russians. He was alone. Good.

He hurriedly washed and dried his hands and returned to his office, waving again at the Guardsmen. He shut the office door behind him and carefully, quietly, pressed the button on the knob. The locking click seemed too loud and he waited a moment before backing away.

Sitting down at his computer, he accessed the web, moving the mouse quickly. It was actually a "walled garden" of the real Internet, hemmed in by the Guards' firewall to limit access. But that wasn't a problem for Zana, not today. He navigated to the site of the lab's equipment supplier, a company called Baramar, Dubai-based.

Baramar did business with the Iranians through another ex-im company, an IRGC front. But Baramar itself was a legit systems integrator and reseller of industrial equipment, including the Franco–German array that was humming away now just twenty yards below Zana's office.

He logged in to the site and landed on a technical support page. Since he knew his web traffic would be tracked, he went to an archival page that maintained technical manuals for the lab equipment. He began downloading one, thinking he'd use it to keep Nikita busy by giving it to him as a preread before their discussion. He'd bury the fat Slav with data.

As the file was downloading, Zana opened another tab and accessed another Baramar site. He went through a series of URLs in a complicated sequence. He eventually found his way to an obscure page dense with nonsensical terms and conditions for the warranty of an industrial cooling fan. He scrolled down the page to find a particular sentence and a particular eight-point-font word: "indemnification."

This word was a regular HTML link, though one would never know it, since it looked just like the rest of the text. He clicked on it. Another window opened up with another log-in screen. He authenticated again, this time with different credentials known only to him.

Once on this page, he looked at a simple plaintext message board, not unlike the ones from the early days of the Internet. There were about fifteen messages stacked up, all of them from the Americans. They went back about six weeks, to when he'd stopped communicating with them, telling them that he would only work with his original handler from now on—or else.

The nature of each message was a query, each building in urgency as he read down the stack. They were asking him why he hadn't checked in as scheduled. They were asking him where he was. They were asking him if he was safe. Their intensity grew until they were virtually pleading with him.

But on the final, fifteenth line of the in-box there was an altogether different message from only a day ago. The subject line simply read, *Hi—This Is Reza*. There were no other words in the body of the message itself, only an attached file, encrypted.

Zana's hands recoiled, then hovered over the keyboard. He felt his pulse in his ears. *Reza. Finally.*

The centrifuge test was in full swing now: the red lights strobing, the bells ringing, the Smurfs hiding. Zana ignored the noise. He went back to the office door and pressed his cheek against the cold metal, listening for footsteps that might be headed his way. The Guards' boots tended to make an audible click on the hall's polished linoleum. If anyone was coming, he'd be able to hear it.

Besides, he wasn't too worried about the Guards. When the bells were ringing, the Guards tended to stand back, as though an extra twenty feet of air would protect them from a radioactive disaster. He was more concerned about Nikita.

He was worried the Russian might have decided to come up and monitor the test here in the office. It would take him about five minutes to free himself from his yellow protective suit and make his way upstairs. Zana guessed that more than five minutes had elapsed since the test had begun. But with his ear pressed to the door, he heard nothing unusual.

He turned around, pressed his back hard against the door, pushing against it. While braced, he hurriedly tugged the lining of the right front pocket of his twill trousers, letting it flop on his thigh. He fingered the inseam of the exposed white cotton and found a small flap secured by Velcro. He opened the cavity and retrieved a tiny black MMC memory card, the approximate size of a postage stamp.

He approached his PC and, with the delicate card between finger and thumb, loaded it into the appropriate slot. He kept one eye on the door as he navigated to the message from Reza and right-clicked it. He started to download the small encrypted file onto the MMC card.

Though small, the download was queued up because the PC was still digesting the technical manual. He was faced with the ubiquitous Windows hourglass. *Come on,* he thought, cursing the slow network. The test in the lab was over. The red light had stopped. Zana tapped his foot and leaned over the keyboard, willing it to hurry the hell up.

The tech manual was done downloading. The PC had just started on the encrypted file now. In the absence of the lab test below, his office fell quiet. Then he heard a pounding noise.

Someone was knocking on his door with an open palm. *Javad.*

The encrypted file finished downloading. Zana removed the card and shoved it in his pocket, hurrying to the door.

"Come on," Javad said, bursting into the room, looking around, nostrils flaring. He'd been running. "Hurry. The commander wants to see us now. He got back from Tehran early."

CHAPTER 17

MEREDITH MORRIS-DALE SAT AT A SMALL TABLE IN A DIMLY LIT
French restaurant in the tony Barracks Row neighborhood of central
DC. Though she wore a strapless black dress and the new black satin
Manolo Blahnik shoes that she'd picked up for half price on her last trip
to Dubai, she wasn't in much of a date mood. Perhaps the wine would
help.

She'd forgotten about this interlude, a setup from one of her George-
town college friends. Seeing it on her calendar today, she'd figured she
would break it. But now that she was a known surveillance target, the
"CI" counterintelligence specialists at the Agency had instructed her to
keep as many appointments as possible, including this one. There was
nothing more convincing, the CIs had said, than going out and visibly
relaxing.

Meredith's instinct had been the opposite. She wanted to slip into a
different alias, don a different disguise, get back in the field quickly.
She'd always been more comfortable operating overseas, stalking prey
from the tall grass.

But the brass at HQS would have none of that. Word in Clandestine Services was out that she'd been burned on the Sagebrush op in
Dubai and, worse, surveilled on a domestic contact bump in Washington State that had left two dead Spetz Alphas in its wake. She was officially radioactive, in the fitting jargon of the Counterproliferation
Division.

Dorsey had ordered her to sit through a bunch of mandatory brief-ings with the CI specialists and stand down on covert activity until she had a clean bill of health. She was to keep a sharp eye out and keep her service weapon on her at all times. She hadn't been able to do much more than nod. She was busted.

The CI spooks had said she should assume she was an active target and do anything she could think of to bore the hell out of her watchers. The more mundane, the better. The idea was to try to show that there was utterly nothing unusual going on. She was to keep her life boring, pretend like she was clueless about the mess that had gone down out West. *Mission accomplished,* she thought now, sipping the wine. This guy was above and beyond when it came to boring.

She'd met him here, arriving in an Uber. She was pleased to see that she could still turn a few heads when she shined herself up. She re-moved the wrap from her bare shoulders and handed it to a coat-check guy. With her freshly styled hair, the thousand-dollar Manolos on her feet, the tautness of her exposed back, and the loaded Glock in her clutch, Meredith strolled through the pretentious, overpriced restau-rant with all the confidence of a lioness. Every straight man over the age of thirty snuck a glance as she breezed past the hostess.

Her date, David, was standing at the table. Not bad-looking, a tad soft, a little narrow shouldered. Thinning blond hair and a well-cut suit. A legislative aide for a Democratic senator, a Harvard man, of course. She knew it because he wore the ring. She felt it through his soft hand-shake.

Right after the initial hellos, a sommelier showed up with a bulky book. She reached for it but David got there first. Before she knew it, amid some kind of exposition on minerality, David had picked the wine, a Sancerre, without even asking. *Strike one.*

When the sommelier came back for the pour, David made a show of the sip. After some swirls around his mouth, he announced to Mere-dith that he was sending it back. Too tart. *Strike two.*

To shift the focus from the wine drama, she ordered cassoulet, figuring it as the comfort food of France. David ordered escargots. Meredith almost laughed out loud when he did it in perfect French. *Escargots? Strike three!*

She carefully checked the Apple Watch strapped to her wrist, ready to punch out on old David. But she hesitated. Maybe they'd just gotten off to a poor start. She took her finger off the watch face. She'd give him one more chance.

He started talking about the job. He was particularly proud of his senator's work in curbing defense appropriations. To hear him tell it, he was the real senator; the famous, fatuous one he actually worked for was more of a figurehead. He gave example after example of his cunning.

As she listened to this, her mind wandered. Her free hand crept closer to the watch on her wrist beneath the table. The CI guys should give her a medal for enduring this, she thought. At least there was that.

"So what do you do at State?" he finally got around to asking her after chewing his way through a buttery snail. The first substantive question he'd asked in a half hour.

"I lead the trade mission for East Africa under the deputy undersecretary for East African Affairs," she began. "We're developing partnership programs among American corporations and Kenyans that . . ."

She went on for another thirty seconds. It was all a lie, a well-rehearsed DC cover. This bozo would never rate knowing anything about her real job.

"That's fascinating," he said, trying to make his eyes sparkle in the candle flame.

He raised a glass in toast to her career. She responded in kind, flashing her widest, fakest smile.

He added, "I was in Kenya last year on a delegation. Perhaps our paths crossed?"

They played the who-do-you-know? Washington-insider game and Meredith started to get uncomfortable. If this guy really had spent any time in East Africa, then her cover was going to grow thin fast. Even a professional liar like her had limits.

Worse, men who were top lieutenants for senators might be dull, but they were definitely not dumb. Time for plan B. She dropped her wrist below the table and firmly pressed her finger to her watch, activating the phone in her clutch via Bluetooth. A preprogrammed message went out. She put her hands back on the table, waiting. Ten seconds later the watch lit up and buzzed.

"I'm sorry," Meredith said, looking at it conspicuously. "My daughter." She pulled her phone free from the clutch, careful to keep the Glock concealed. "Give me a minute." She removed an earring and placed the phone to her head while she shimmied between chairs, away from the table, the purse in her other hand.

"Mom—really? It's like seven thirty," said Grace.

Meredith stood in the hallway that led to the ladies' room. She ducked inside and took a quick scan beneath the stalls. Empty. "Yeah, it's that bad. Worse, I'm going to make my goodbyes and get out of here."

"Mom, you have to finish a date one of these days. At least dinner."

"Said the girl who has never had a relationship longer than two weeks."

"Whatever. Bye."

The senator's aide stood when Meredith made it back to the table.

"I'm sorry," she said.

He awkwardly made his way around her and pushed the chair in behind her as she sat. She felt his hand linger near her bare shoulder blade as she got settled. It was cold and soft.

"How old is your daughter?" he asked.

"Nineteen. A third-class midshipman at the Naval Academy."

"*Uch,*" he said, grimacing. "That's a rough place for a girl."

Strikes four through ten. I'm out, she thought.

"Is everything okay at home?" he asked.

Meredith suddenly realized she hadn't come up with a good cover story as to why she had to leave. She was about to make something up. Anything. Mercifully her watch buzzed again. She pulled out her phone and looked at it. It was ringing through the secure app used by the Agency. Now she didn't even have to lie.

"I'm so sorry, David—I really do have to take this. Be right back."

She answered, hurrying back to the ladies' room. "Morris-Dale."

"We're on," said a rushed voice on the other side of the call. It was Todd Olsen, one of the technical operations specialists on her team.

"What do you mean? Say more."

"Your man Cerberus is back up. It took him a couple days, but he's finally responded to your husband."

Meredith smiled for real this time. She gave herself a small fist pump in the bathroom mirror. "*Ex*-husband," she said. "I'm on my way in."

Ed Rance was walking across the lobby of the Four Seasons in George-town, his eyes darting. It was the first time Genevieve had texted him in more than two weeks. She'd been off at some conference for international shipping insurance in Amsterdam, she'd said . . . or something like that. He hadn't bothered to keep all the details lined up, except one.

The detail he cared about was that she'd said to meet him here at the Seasons. She also said she'd text him the room number. It was *on*.

But she hadn't yet.

He found himself with nowhere to go, standing there like some Nebraska shit heel at a convention. To avoid looking stupid, standing here at eleven on a Friday night by himself, he sauntered up to the lobby bar and ordered an old-fashioned. He installed himself in a velvety chair with a reasonable view of the lobby, watching for her.

Her call had surprised him. She'd never reached out on a Friday before. He'd been so desperate to see her that he'd told his wife he'd have to stay at a safe house down in midstate Virginia tonight.

Being able to lie liberally was *one* advantage of life in the CIA, he'd thought many times before. Why not a Friday? For once he'd have plenty of time to really enjoy himself, not watching the clock like some sort of stud on loan to another farm.

He didn't know what it was about Genevieve. Something in their liaisons took everything out of him physically. Every time they'd completed the sacred act, he'd fall asleep, blissfully, dreamlessly. He'd have the deepest hour of unconsciousness, not a care in the world.

He took a sip of the sweet bourbon, relaxing for the first time in several days, his mind wandering lazily. It had been a hell of a week. The Russians and the Chinese were in cahoots with the Iranians, building a new nuclear reactor down at Bushehr on the Gulf. That meant importing uranium from the Kazakhstan mines and cooking it down into yellowcake, which could then easily be turned into nukes.

Even the *New York Times* was writing about it. It was all over the news. Every journalist from here to Tibet seemed to be writing about it.

Of course, the one organization in the world that should have been able to verify the information was the CIA. Specifically, the Counterproliferation Division, which Rance ran. And yet he couldn't verify it. It had been the worst professional week of his life.

He wasn't smiling now. He sipped the drink. The sips got larger.

Yellowcake. He shuddered at the merry little word. He was so sick and tired of trying to keep track of every ounce of uranium ore in the world. With all the heat from the Russians, he'd been pressured into coming up with something . . . anything . . . to figure out what the fuck was happening. Even better, to actually *do* something about it. Iranian yellowcake had been in the headline in every PDB for the last two weeks. But CIA had zilch, zero, nada. The president was furious.

Not that Rance cared too much about the politics, but the administration was losing its collective mind. SecState was galled that the Russians were breaking all of the tenets of the NPT, the Nuclear Non-Proliferation Treaty, monitored by IAEA. Without any proof, the secretary couldn't do diddly-squat by way of real diplomacy.

The Russians were playing it like a Stradivarius at the UN, talking about all the benefits of the new Bushehr reactor. Why should the West have a monopoly on clean power?

That left it to CIA. The administration wanted some kind of covert action to ensure the Iranians weren't spinning their way to U235. And that meant Active Archer and Cerberus and—Rance paused to take a lusty gulp—John *fucking* Dale.

Just running that name through his mind made Rance take another quick swallow, jangling the ice with his tongue, finishing the drink off.

He raised the glass over his head, rattling it, getting the bartender's attention. Time for another. He checked his phone. Still no texted room number from Genevieve.

The thing about Dale, he thought, sucking a cube, was his utter unpredictability. Rance had seen it close up back in Mosul. To have this loose cannon banging around now on the ship of state made no sense to Rance at all. Who knew what damage Dale would do? Who knew what he'd do to screw over Rance personally?

It hadn't always been this way. Rance could remember some heroics back in Basra, when Dale was younger, less complicated, less *moralistic*. A tough, talented operator back then. Still, he'd always been a handful, hard to control . . . and in unpredictable ways.

Rance could see the bartender mixing. *Faster,* he thought, checking his phone again, stanching a rising irritation with Genevieve for making him wait.

When Rance had wanted to take operations to the next level back in Iraqi Kurdistan, he'd made the mistake of trusting Dale. Dale had gone soft on him. Then he'd gotten himself captured and then—though Rance could never really prove it—Dale had gone *really* soft. Classic Stockholm syndrome. He'd let one of the terrorists walk. They had the whole thing on tape!

The second drink came. Rance stirred it. He felt the warm, easy flow of booze in his bloodstream. It was like medicine. *Dale.* He simply couldn't believe that the only guy who could help him with his current predicament, this gap in intelligence for the Iranian enrichment program, ended up being John *fucking* Dale. And now here he was, pulled off of suspension, working on an op that would probably determine the balance of Rance's Agency career. *What the fuck?* he thought bitterly. *Why does this shit happen to me? Some kind of weird karma, that.*

And where the hell is Genevieve?

He needed to stop thinking about Dale. It was taking him out of the mood. If there was one thing he wanted to avoid, it was *that*. He had enough performance pressure at work. He didn't also need it in a five-star DC hotel room with a beautiful young woman in his arms.

He leaned back into the velvet chair at his small table, crossing his legs, looking around the rest of the bar. It was the standard DC crowd. A bunch of lawyered-up suits, some not-too-bad women in their forties, and a piano player. His phone chirped. There she was. *Thank God.*

He looked down at the phone and frowned. Not Genevieve. It was ringing through the secure communications app. Work. Probably an issue with the goddamned PDB again. Those poor bastards never slept. Rance reluctantly answered.

"Rance."

"Ed, it's Meredith."

Fucking great, he thought. If there was anyone who could spoil a mood more than John Dale, it was his wife, Meredith.

"Yeah," he said.

"You at home?"

Here we go. "Uh . . . no, actually. I'm having a drink with a buddy from State. Former Agency guy. You ever know Phil Haskins?"

There was a pause before Meredith answered. "No, but that's fine," she said. "Are you in a place where you can talk?"

Rance looked around. The nearest occupied table was about fifteen feet away. "I can talk," he said. "But maybe not too much."

"Okay. Listen, I just—"

"Meredith, sorry. Hold on. Phil just got here. Let me shoo him away. He'll understand."

Genevieve was approaching his table in a short dress tight enough to affect her circulation, he thought, delighted. He stood up, smiled, and politely motioned her away, pointing at his phone, his hand cupped over it. She kissed his cheek anyway.

"Sorry," he whispered, squeezing the phone hard. "It's work. Can you give me one second?"

She nodded, jutted her lower jaw in a pout, and placed her finger over her pursed lips in a my-lips-are-sealed gesture. She walked toward the bar, swaying her hips. Utterly transfixed, Rance could see the line of her skimpy underwear as she departed.

"Hey, you there still?" Meredith.

"Yeah," he said. "Sorry. I'm here."

"Okay, listen. I have good news. We've got a message from Cerberus. He and John are in contact."

"Great!" said Rance, genuinely relieved, raising a hand to his forehead. "What's the story?" He had to force himself to lower his voice.

"He and John are trading messages."

"Yeah, you said that. But what's the story? What's the situation?"

"I don't know yet."

Rance turned away from the bar toward a window. He leaned forward, his hand cupping his mouth. "What the *fuck*, Meredith? Why not? What did the message say?"

"It's with John."

"Meaning Dale won't tell you?"

Meredith paused before answering. "It's early. Let's let it percolate a little bit."

"Ah, hell, Meredith. You're playing me. Your husband won't tell us, will he? I told you we couldn't trust him."

"*Ex*-husband, Ed. For fuck's sake, settle down. John is his handler. Don't we need to trust him to do his job?"

Rance sighed. "Sure. Why are you calling me, then?"

"I thought you'd want to know. It's good news."

"Right."

"Also . . ."

"What?"

"There's an extract plan. John said Cerberus may be punching out."

"Bullshit," said Rance. "If that's his message, you tell John to turn him around. We need that bastard right where he is right now."

"It's not up to John."

"It's up to the handler to convince the asset to stay in place, isn't it?"

"Yeah. I'm just saying, John may not be able to do that."

"Well, you're John's handler, per our little agreement with Dorsey. You need to convince him, Meredith. You need to do *your* job."

"You know what, Ed? I'm sorry I called. Let's discuss this tomorrow. Okay?"

"Fine," Rance said, hanging up. He missed the old flip-phone days when you could really hang up with force. With his current phone, the only thing he could do to express his frustration was stab the red button. Not even a button, just a dot on a screen. He jammed it anyway and thrust the glass thing into the breast pocket of his suit jacket.

"My, *my*," said Genevieve, approaching his table from the bar. "Someone's having a rough day. You're as red and prickly as a lobster, darling."

"You don't know the half of it," said Rance. He stood up. He'd had enough. He offered her his elbow. "Shall we?"

"You okay with going to the room *together*, dear? I thought we had rules for this sort of thing."

"Right," Rance said, tossing off the rest of his drink as he stood by the table. "Fuck the rules. Let's go."

CHAPTER 18

THE FOLLOWING WEDNESDAY, MEREDITH ROSE EARLY ENOUGH TO GET in a run. She exited her flat, the first floor of a Dupont Circle brownstone, and hit the pavement on a shining wet Massachusetts Ave. Picking up speed, she took a right and veered toward Embassy Row.

The rain that had been falling all night wasn't about to let up. She was decked out in her black Gore-Tex windbreaker, bounding over puddles, her hair tied behind her head. She ran with a fanny pack weighted down by her Glock. She had yet to pick up any of the surveillance that was supposedly on her, but if they were Russians, they were going to be very, very good. She couldn't be too careful. Every hundred yards or so she took an abrupt turn and stopped, monitoring her would-be watchers through window reflections.

But she saw no one. Relieved, she went on with her workout, thinking of the day to come. A half mile on, she passed the high white spire of the Islamic Center of Washington. The sun was just coming up beneath the overcast, coating the minaret in an orange aurora. She stopped, allowing herself to catch her breath and stretch her hamstrings. The faint chant of the *azan* was barely audible, drifting over the parked cars. She thought of Cerberus. She thought of John. She hadn't heard from him in almost two weeks.

Her hair was still wet ninety minutes later as she drove along the Potomac via Route 123 on her way in to HQS in her Volvo SUV. There was no point in doing an SDR on her way into the office. If anyone out there was watching, they sure as hell knew where she worked. Besides, they'd be fools to expose themselves anywhere near the hidden banks of cameras that studded the approach to Langley.

Her guard at its ebb, she thought about the meeting she was about to attend. Dorsey wanted answers. He wanted to know what was going on with Active Archer and Cerberus. He'd put himself way out on a limb by going to the director, stumping for John's return from suspension. Now he expected a payoff, results, answers as to what was going on with the Iranian nuke program. Rance was even worse, reminding Dorsey at every turn that they never should've trusted John. She wished to her bones that she could show them up.

But she hadn't heard from John either. She was beginning to have her doubts.

Her phone rang through the secure app. She answered it via Bluetooth. "Morris-Dale."

"Hey, Meth."

"*John.* Where the hell are you?"

"Good to talk to you too."

She groaned. "Not today. I need a real status report. You've got to do a better job of staying in touch. I'm on my way in to see Dorsey this morning—driving there right now. You do realize he's going to take my head off. If this is going to work and I'm to be your handler, then you've got to check in more. It is a *major* problem. Do you hear me? Do you *understand* that, John?"

There was a long pause on the other end of the line. Eventually he said, "Never mind. I'll call you later."

She sighed. "Sorry, sorry. I didn't mean to rip into you like that."

"Yeah, you did."

"No, I didn't. But you can see the predicament I'm in. I'm a little freaked out."

"Yeah, that's pretty obvious. But that's also why I'm out here trying to take care of that little problem we have."

There was a sudden break in the clouds. The rising sun beamed through the windshield, gleaming silver off the river. Meredith dropped the visor to ease the glare and slowed the pace of her wipers. "Oh, yeah? And where is *out here*? Where exactly are you?"

"Not far. Take a look in your rearview."

She did. A dark gray Dodge Challenger swerved into the lane behind her and flashed its high beams. John was behind the wheel, grinning like a high school kid, his face bright in the sunlight.

"What the *fuck* are you doing, John?" she said a little louder than she probably should have.

"I think you would flunk the SDR course, Meth. No wonder you got burned."

"Fuck off."

He chuckled into the phone. His car dropped back, lining up to exit to the right. He said, "Meth, take the exit at Highway One Twenty. There's a place just off the road called the Madison Community Center. Park there and go in. You can walk all the way through to a kitchen and out the back. They run some kind of art class for seniors this time of day. Nobody will even notice."

"*Really*, John?"

"Yes, really. Once you get out the back door, shoot across the street into Glebe Road Park. We can talk there. Later." He hung up. His car was gone.

Twenty minutes later, Meredith walked along a jogging trail lined with cedar bark in Glebe Road Park. A big black cloud had blown in and the rain had picked up, but she at least had an umbrella with her now. Her dark pants suit was otherwise not well equipped for a walk in the woods. Her low heels were unsteady in the soft bark.

Just as she crested a low hill, John stepped out of the trees. He was wearing Levi's, his Blundstone boots, a green Helly Hansen raincoat, and a lopsided grin.

"Okay," Meredith said as he approached. "Is this how it's going to be?"

His hair and beard were longer than when she'd last seen him a few weeks ago. He looked darker, like he'd been in the sun for weeks.

"It's almost like you're not happy to see me," he said, smiling.

She thought his teeth looked extra white against his dark beard. They briefly hugged.

"Glad to see you're getting into character."

"Yeah," he said, stroking his beard, "I bought the double-XL package at the tanning place. Been practicing my Farsi too. Thought you'd be proud."

"I am . . . sort of." She pulled back from him. "But seriously, John. You get it, right? You've set this whole deal up with the Agency where I'm the only one you'll talk to."

"Right."

"So that means you actually need to *talk* to me. They're busting my proverbial balls over your silence. They think I'm a gullible idiot for trusting you. They feel like gullible idiots for trusting *me*."

He nodded. "Yeah, I know." He smiled again. "But here I am. What more could you ask for?"

"You could've just called like I asked you to. Now I'm going to miss the meeting with Dorsey."

Dale nodded, the grin fading. He looked out toward the rest of the park, into the rainy, woodsy reserve. On this nondescript Wednesday morning, the place was deserted.

He said, "I'm not trusting phones. You're burned, remember?"

"That doesn't mean the Agency phones aren't secure."

"Maybe we should check that with the two dead Spetz you guys pulled out of my front yard." The rain picked up. He leaned into her. "Hey, pull that umbrella over my way a little, will ya?"

She angled the umbrella toward him. They were standing in tandem, their shoulders touching, both looking out across the greenbelt toward the community center.

"So here we are," she said. "I'm waiting to hear your report."

He leaned closer to her ear, brushing her hair back a little. "Okay, Meth, here's the deal. Cerberus wants out. He wants to activate his egress plan. He wants to leave soon. He said he'd let me know when exactly."

"It's definite?"

"Yeah."

"Why?"

"He said the Russians are all over him. They've brought them in to fix the problems they've been having with the centrifuges." He paused to let that sink in. "He says it's just a matter of time before they figure out what's going on. With a little more work, they're going to pin it on him. So Cerb thinks anyway."

"Shit."

"Yeah, shit."

"How close are they to weapons grade?"

"According to Cerb, we should start getting ready to welcome the Twelfth Imam back into the regular world," Dale said.

She blew out a long sigh. "Not funny."

"No. They're getting a ready supply of yellowcake from the Russians, spinning it up night and day."

"Why are the Russians so hell-bent on arming up the Iranians?" she asked.

"Cerb has no insight on that, but you can read about the politics in the open. My guess is the Russians think a nuclear Iran will keep us out of the Gulf for good. Once we're out, the Saudis and the rest of the A-rabs will stop playing nice with us."

"So what?"

"So I bet the Russkies figure it nets out as a win for them, because they can open up trading routes free from sanctions and there won't be jack shit we can do about it. They also want to curry favor with Iran before the Chinese beat 'em to it."

"Quite a gamble, giving a bunch of madmen nukes," she said.

"Yeah, I doubt the Kremlin's too concerned about a lasting legacy of peace. They're in it for the dough. And to screw us."

"This is depressing," she said. They briefly looked at each other and then turned away. She said, "So, not to overstate it, but the infrastructure your man Cerberus set up may very well be our last defense—and it's crumbling."

Dale shrugged. "You know our defenses better than me."

"I think he's it," she said. "It's why Dorsey's been coming unglued." She shook the umbrella to divert some water. "We need to talk Cerberus into staying. He can change the way we sabotage it. Different software, harder to find."

"Not an option."

"Why?"

"'Cause he may have already taken off. If not, he's dark, about to leave."

"*What?* To where?"

Dale put his hand behind her back and leaned in close. "Look, Meth, you're burned. Nobody knows where the leak is, but it's somewhere in the Agency. I think I'd better just handle it, go get him quietly. The Russkies'll never know I was there."

"You want to do this *solo*? Are you nuts?"

"Yeah. It'll work better."

She shook her head. "I don't think I can get Dorsey and Rance to go along. If Cerberus is in the wind, then he could get snagged by the Iranians, the Russians . . . whoever. He'll break and spill everything. All the hacker holes Cerberus has opened will close. It's the worst possible outcome."

"Yeah, I know. But he's not in the wind. He's going to be executing the egress plan we set up eight years ago. If *I* go get him and bring him home, you can give him his own office over at Fort Meade and work with the NSA boys to bore shiny new hacker holes."

Meredith looked down at her shoes and shook her head. She swallowed. "John, this is too big. Way too big. We can't just rely on you to do this on your own. We need a SAC team on this. Stakes are too high."

SAC—Special Activities Center—was the new acronym for Dale's old group, the covert paramilitary arm of CIA.

"I agree," he said, "except you guys are burned. You saw the listening equipment the Spetz team set up on my property. They listened to you and me."

"Yeah, but we recovered the audio files."

"Maybe. We don't know what got transmitted off before I got them."

Meredith nodded hesitantly.

"Look," he said, putting his arm around her. "No offense, but I think we have to assume that anything associated with this op that comes through HQS is vulnerable. If you make this anything but back-channel, it'll lead the Russians right to Cerb. Then not only will they fix all their problems overnight, but we'll also lose the benefit of someone that knows their systems."

She nodded again. "Where's his facility? We can just send in some B-2s and crater the whole fucking place."

"Guess what."

"What?"

"Cerb won't tell me," he said. "It's like he knows us too well. He's feeding me info, but just enough to guarantee I get him out. Like the egress. I don't know when exactly he's leaving. Won't tell me. Just says to be ready. Says if we don't do it, he fucks over the whole program for good."

"What about his family?"

"He hasn't been that specific. I think he's worried we would grab the family and use them as leverage to stay where he is."

"Manipulative fucker," she said. "You guys are perfect for each other. You know, by the way, that the Agency can read your correspondence through the Baramar site."

"Nah," said Dale. "Not anymore. I set up a different protocol to head that off. It was actually Cerb's idea."

She shook her head. "Sounds like he's running you."

"Nah, he's okay. He's just in over his head. He wants out. We've been promising it to him for years. He's calling our bluff and using his leverage."

"Why does he trust you?"

"My winning charm?" Dale shrugged. "Must have been something I said back when we were in Canada. Or maybe he knows I'm dog shit at the Agency and I have a reason to distrust it as much as he does. When I go meet him, I'll ask him."

She flicked some rain off the arm of her suit jacket. "So—if I'm sworn to secrecy—what are you asking me to even do with all this non-information?"

"I'm going to need stuff," Dale said. "I need you to get me the right equipment, maintain my aliases, my credos, all of that shit. You know how it works. You know my favorite drop boxes."

"Some of the finest toilets in the third world. Literal shitholes."

"Yeah, I'll let you know which ones to use when I need them." He paused, squaring off to face her. "But, Meth, you're the only one I trust—you can't share plans with anyone. I mean it. I'm counting on you."

"Well, I'm going to have to share plans with someone if I'm stocking up C-4 for you all over the UAE."

"You'll make a cover story, Meth." Dale grinned. "There's no better handler than you."

A gust of wind slanted the rain toward their faces. Meredith dipped the umbrella like a shield. "So, without compromising your tactical position," she asked, her voice echoing off the nylon, "can you tell me what you're going to do now?"

"Sure. I'm going over to Annapolis to visit our daughter." He glanced at his watch. "I need to leave now, in fact."

"Oh, yeah? Does Grace know that or are you going to sneak up on her too?"

"Of course she knows. I call her all the time, reporting in. That's how we do it." He nudged Meredith with his elbow, goading her.

She thought of Grace's letter, the one she'd delivered to John's cabin several weeks back. "Right. I suppose you guys have your comms protocols. I never needed one since I was always home with her, dealing with her shit."

"Meth . . ." He turned his head just enough to meet her eye.

"Never mind." She glanced away. "What then? What's after Grace?"

"Dinner usually." Dale smiled.

She didn't return it. "Seriously, John, what's next?"

"I just told you. Going back to work." He leaned forward and unexpectedly kissed her cheek. He raised a hand to caress the hair near her ear, holding her face close to his. "I may be dark for a while. If I don't see you, Meth . . ."

She grabbed his hand, squeezed it, and pulled him close. "You'll see me. But be careful. Lean on me when you have to. Okay?"

He nodded, let go of her hand, and backed a few feet into the woods. He waved briefly before disappearing behind a thicket.

After the briefing, Dorsey asked Meredith to leave. He wanted to speak with Rance alone.

Since she'd already gotten what she wanted, she was more than happy to flee the SCIF and get to work.

After the SCIF door closed again, Dorsey looked at his head of Counterproliferation. "Well, Ed, what do you think?" He pushed his rolled sleeves past his elbows.

Rance crossed his legs, relaxing. Whenever Meredith left the room, he could feel the tension lift. He shook his head. "Letting Dale go get our asset on his own? Without a supporting SAC team? I think you know what I think."

"You don't trust Dale."

"Of course not."

Dorsey nodded. "At least he's back on side. Not easy after what we did to him."

"What he did to himself, you mean."

Dorsey grunted. "I know you don't like Meredith. But you have to admit, she did a good job bringing him back. At least now we have a play."

"A risky one," Rance said, staring at his bent knee.

"I'm asking you, Ed." Dorsey leaned over his elbows on the table. "Can you at least back off of the Dales long enough to let them give it a shot? Can you find your way to supporting this?"

Rance crossed his arms and composed his thoughts. "You do understand that this is all falling under my division. She's a hothead. And if it's up to me, I don't trust Dale. If you're saying it's up to you, then fine. It's your call. But I don't want this to . . ."

"Come back, bite you in the ass, fuck your career?"

Rance shrugged. "Things like that *do* happen around here."

"Right. They do." Dorsey turned to a credenza behind him. He'd stacked his leather-bound portfolio, an iPad, and a handful of red-striped classified files there. He brought the stack to the table. "Listen," he said, "I need to show you something."

Rance leaned forward. He was thinking Dorsey had been good enough to create a memo, absolving him of responsibility for this crazy Dale mission.

But instead, the deputy director fired up his iPad and turned it toward Rance. It was a wide-screen photo. Rance recognized the Four Seasons bar. He recognized himself. Genevieve.

Dorsey swiped through a half dozen photos, saying nothing. There was Rance talking to her. There he was walking away arm in arm with her. There they were kissing at the elevator bank. There he was, grabbing her ass beneath her skirt.

"Look," Dorsey said solemnly, tapping the iPad's power button, "since Meredith got burned, I've had the CI guys looking after everyone involved with Active Archer. That includes you."

Rance was speechless. "Jeff, I . . ."

"It's a matter of safety," he continued. "We know the Russians are onto us somehow. I need to counter it, protect my people, et cetera."

"You don't think *I'm* the leak, do you? You think I burned Meredith?" Rance said loudly, indignant. "You think I'm *bent*?"

Dorsey held out his hands, palms down. "*Whoa*, not saying that."

"Then what are you saying?"

"That you need to be careful." He tapped the iPad with his finger. "I don't know who *she* is, but I do know what I'm looking at."

"It's my business."

"It's a vulnerability. You did a background check on her?"

"Yes," Rance said. He had done one. But not the official kind that Dorsey meant.

The boss leaned far back in his chair, looking Rance in the eye. He laced his fingers behind his head. "You know, Ed, if we were a couple of execs over at Raytheon, I'd agree with you. This would be none of my business. But we're not. We operate differently. I can't have one of my top guys exposed like this. If I've uncovered it, you can bet the Russians have too. You'll probably be blackmailed before the year's out."

Rance thought of his wife and three boys. He grabbed the iPad and swiped through the photos, slowly shaking his head while his boss looked on. The silence in the SCIF was like a physical thing.

Finally, he looked up, meeting the deputy director's eye. "Jeff, I'll take care of it." He pointed at the photo of Genevieve. "She's gone. Over."

"Good man," Dorsey said, leaning forward, his elbows back on the table. "Enough said. But just to be safe, I'm going to ask you to get over to Europe for a few weeks. I think it would be good to break up our patterns."

"What about Archer?"

"You said yourself Meredith's got it. Keep an eye on her from afar. But I'm asking you, give her some leeway."

Driving back to his wife that afternoon, Rance replayed the conversation a half dozen times in his mind, agonizing over the fact he'd been caught. But Dorsey had made him a fair deal. He could give up Genevieve. It would suck, but he could do it. The unexpectedly positive turn was that he could now officially distance himself from Archer, per Dorsey's request. Fine with him. It was just a matter of time before the Dales fucked it all up.

CHAPTER 19

YURI KUZNETSOV SAT AT A STARBUCKS ON THE NORTH SIDE OF LUBY-
anka Square, nursing a Venti black coffee, trying to keep his head upright. He massaged his bald scalp with his fingers, trying to shake off a
splitting headache. He wore the same blue suit he'd traveled in, rumpled
now, his tie loosened, collar stretched open. He was trying like hell to
get some air.

Somewhere under the pounding jackhammer in his head, he dimly
remembered a saying he'd heard used by an American CIA officer once:
No good deed goes unpunished.

It seemed a fitting tribute to his current predicament, though the
Russian translation—*Ni odno dobroye delo ne ostayetsya beznakazannym*—
lacked the same sense of irony. In the Russia where Yuri had been raised,
good deeds, bad deeds, innocent deeds—any deeds were subject to
punishment.

He looked out at the gray skies of central Moscow, noting the snow
blowing between buildings, the wind harassing shoppers. This was the
touristy core of upscale downtown now. Around the corner from this
Starbucks stood a cavernous Nike store. The Lubyanka, home throughout the decades to the KGB and now FSB, sat just across the street—five
stories of crushing masonry that took up half a city block.

To Russians of Yuri's generation, the very name Lubyanka evoked
tremors, and with good reason. It had served as the clearinghouse for
terror of Russian civilians since Stalin. A mountain of gray stone and
yellow stucco, it stood as a perverse monument to despotism. Juxtapos-

ing it with the happy distractions of modern American retail was a Russian version of irony, he thought dimly.

He tried again unsuccessfully to piece together the events of the last twenty-four hours. He'd thought the coffee would help. Maybe it was helping. There were now at least parts that were perfectly clear, others opaque as tar.

It had started in Lebanon. He'd driven down from Damascus with Putov. After a day there, he'd caught the direct Aeroflot to Moscow. The plane had been deserted and he'd stretched languidly across three seats. He remembered zipping through customs at Sheremtyevo and coming out on the street, stunned by the cold.

A man had met him there.

That's right! He thought now, the fog lifting barely.

A balding redheaded man in a long leather jacket. Yuri had followed because the man had identified himself as FSB, state security. He'd escorted Yuri into the rear of a Renault, landing next to another FSB man in the backseat.

He remembered being told he simply had to answer a few questions at the Lubyanka, after which he could be on his way to his actual meeting over at Yasenevo. He recalled being pissed off, but also, as a lifelong foot soldier in the Russo–Soviet system, compliant.

Things were coming back to him now.

They'd given him a medical exam. They'd weighed him, taken his blood pressure and temperature. Then a young doctor had given him a shot. After that, things had gotten weird.

Thinking about it in the safety of the Starbucks, he yawned and downed more coffee. He knew now what the shot had been: scopolamine, hyoscine, a drug that blocked the responses of the nervous system. With the right dosage, it served as both a truth serum and an amnesiac. The Russian security services had been quietly using it for years.

But to do it to one of its own? Thank God he had nothing to hide, he thought. Suppose he had? He shuddered over the cup. *Lubyanka.*

He vaguely recalled an indeterminate period of questioning. At some point he remembered stumbling under the arms of two strong men who clumsily deposited him in a room with a cot and a locked door. He'd awoken in complete darkness but had no idea where he was, how he'd gotten there, what time it was. They'd taken his wristwatch. He'd slept some more. For exactly how long, he didn't know.

Trying to remember the interrogation now had that slippery quality of piecing together the elements of a fever dream. He couldn't quite be sure any of it had actually happened, could he? The career intelligence officer in him told him it had; but if someone had told him it was all a figment of his imagination, he probably would have accepted it. He could recall bits of emotion, feeling something. He'd been angry, indignant. But for the life of him, he couldn't remember what they'd been asking him or why.

Finally, harsh white lights had come on in the locked room and they'd provided a sandwich with some water. As though they'd mildly inconvenienced him, a uniformed FSB officer and a doctor then thanked him for "volunteering" for the interview and made him sign a one-page legal sheet as a condition of his freedom. Moments later he was out on the street, jacket in hand, tie in pocket, eyes blinking at the falling snow.

And now here he sat in a Starbucks, wondering why the hell all that had happened.

A good-looking blue-eyed blonde in a turtleneck under a fur coat came into the Starbucks with an enormous striped shopping bag on her arm. A blast of cold air followed her, ruffling Yuri's napkin. After ordering, the thirtyish woman took off the coat, showed off her chest, and installed herself a few feet away.

That was at least one thing he missed about Moscow, Yuri thought, rubbing his head. Perhaps the *only* thing. Women like her sure as shit didn't exist in Damascus. He thought about shifting his seat to catch a peek at this otherworldly creature, but his head hurt too much to bother.

After downing his coffee and a large wedge of carrot cake, he stepped into the freezing cold, looking for a secure spot to use his phone, out of sight of Lubyanka. He took a left on Kuznetsky, passing more shops, looking for shelter from the wind. Finally, he found a vacant retail storefront with an alley to the side. He stepped into it and called Putov through the encrypted mobile app.

"How's Beirut?" he asked, his voice rasping.

"A little hot," said Putov. "There are no sheep in the fields today."

Yuri nodded, rubbing the back of his head, still trying to chase away the headache.

Putov had just given him the code that their surveillance had still come up empty. He'd sent his deputy to Lebanon to watch for any sign of Kasem, the Quds Force operator he'd tipped about the Iranian leak. Though on a secure line, they still spoke in code because they assumed that some Russian security agency was listening to them. *Probably those murderous bastards a quarter mile away in the Lubyanka,* he thought.

"You're sure? No sheep at all?"

"No, none."

Though he'd tipped off the Quds man, Yuri had yet to see any significant reaction from the Iranians that would help establish the connection to the CIA.

He felt like he was losing time. Russian teams had been sent into various Iranian facilities and the trip to the half-completed Bushehr reactor was still on. But he'd lost the Zoloto link on the American network. He didn't know why. The information had simply dried up for some reason. It was as though the whole thing had just gone away.

"All right," Yuri said finally.

He rubbed his eyes and yawned, shaking off the cold. He considered telling Putov about the FSB pickup he'd endured here in Moscow, but decided against it. For all Yuri knew, Putov might have orchestrated it. And besides, the bastards were likely listening to him right now.

He simply said, "Any other messages?"

"Just that Colonel Niskorov confirmed your meeting for this afternoon at Yasenevo," said Putov. "Where are you staying, by the way? Down at Yasenevo or up in the city?"

"Yasenevo. The usual fleabag, Gostevoy Dom," Yuri said.

"Well, for whatever reason, they don't want you to take a cab to headquarters. You're to call this number and ask for a ride. I'll text it to you."

After the call Yuri looked at the number. The fact that his boss, Niskorov, had called Putov with instructions was interesting. It meant that the colonel was aware of Yuri's night in hell at the Lubyanka. Not exactly the reception he was looking for on returning home. He made the call and waited.

After several minutes, a white Lada Largus emblazoned with a taxi logo pulled up. Yuri suspected a fake brand. Sure enough, when Yuri entered the backseat, the driver turned to him and flashed SVR credos. At least he wasn't FSB—a marked improvement.

As the car pulled away from the curb, Yuri saw the good-looking blonde from Starbucks exit the Nike store, bags still on her arm, heels clicking down the sidewalk. Despite the burden, she walked with the tall, confident poise of a runway model.

Maybe being back in Moscow wouldn't be so bad, now that he was free of the FSB scum. He rubbed his head and lit a cigarette.

He arrived a little after noon at SVR HQ, without the benefit of getting to a hotel room to freshen up. He entered the lobby and endured a frisk, a metal detector, and a confiscation of his phone for the second time in twenty-four hours. Moments later he was on his way up the elevator and standing in front of his boss, Colonel Vladimir Niskorov.

Yuri came to slovenly attention. He had a two-day beard and a suit that looked like it had been crammed into a pillowcase.

"Ah, *tovarisch*, it's good to see you," said the colonel, seated behind his desk. "You look . . ." The older man stopped and eyed his subordinate. "Well, let's just say you look none the worse for wear."

He was in his sixties with swept-back white hair. He wore a black suit beneath perpetually half-lidded pale gray eyes.

"A lot of wear, sir," Yuri answered. His knees were unsteady. He found a chair and sat.

The office was modern—glassy, steely, brightly colored. It looked like a tech start-up. The new Russia.

Yuri glanced at his boss. "I presume you know I was a guest at the Lubyanka last night?"

"Yes," said the colonel.

He was writing something. The half-masted eyes remained fixed on his desk blotter. A bookshelf clock clicked behind him.

"I don't suppose you could tell me why, sir?" asked Yuri.

Before the colonel could answer, an older woman in a cardigan and woolen skirt arrived, carrying a tea service. She spread it on the table next to Yuri. It seemed to take her forever to fill the glass cups and arrange them.

When she'd finally gone, Niskorov looked up from his papers. He came from behind his desk and seated himself in the chair across from Yuri. He took another ten seconds to cross his long legs and smooth his trousers. The clock ticked.

"Well," he finally said, "I suppose I would say that you are something of a victim of your own success, Major. You're not the first officer to have been given such a . . . greeting."

No good deed . . . , thought Yuri. "What have I done of late that has been particularly successful?"

The colonel settled into his chair and touched the cup to his lips. He blew on it. "Your tip about the American operation in Iran." He sipped.

Yuri nodded once and waited to hear more. Evidently, the colonel had nothing to add. "Thank you," Yuri said unevenly.

"Yes," answered the colonel. "But unfortunately, now we think the Americans have taken countermeasures, changed the nature of their operation." He repeated the blow-and-sip sequence. "The S people are worried about security. Something happened."

The S people meant the spies in Directorate S, the illegals. The branch for nonofficial-cover operatives like Zoloto. By contrast, Yuri and Niskorov worked for Directorate PR, the branch that gathered political intelligence from embassies under diplomatic cover.

Yuri said, "I was corroborating what I knew from Dubai with the S source operating in America. The source was called—"

"Zoloto," said the colonel, sipping. He waited three clock ticks before continuing. His half-lidded eyes met Yuri's. "We are talking about the same thing. Zoloto is now off-line. Compromised, apparently."

Yuri's mind was nearly back to full strength. It dawned on him why FSB had picked him up, drugged him, interrogated him. He leaned forward, put his head in his hands, and sighed.

Looking up at his boss, he said, "They think I'm a mole?"

"I'm afraid it could not be discounted."

He leaned back in his chair, expecting to feel anger. But the drugs in his system were offering an oozy calm. "I suppose the fact that I'm sitting here now shows I passed. Am I clear now?"

"I saw the report." The colonel nodded curtly. "And yes, you are here now. Good to see you handling it with such poise."

"You may thank the scopolamine."

The colonel winced. "For what it's worth, Major, I do apologize. It was not my idea."

Yuri nodded. He drank his tea. "So the entire summons back . . . it was just a trick to test whether I was some kind of leak that somehow ruined an S team operation."

"Yes."

Yuri sat in silence for a moment, listening to the clock. "What should I do now? May I go back to Damascus?"

The colonel shrugged. "I suppose you may. There's a chance the S people may want to talk to you. But that's up to them. As far as I'm concerned, you should get back to your post."

A few minutes later, he was back out front to catch another fake cab to the nearby Gostevoy Dom Hotel. His plan was to immediately get into a hot shower and go to bed, then hightail it out of here.

He'd deal with logistics tomorrow. He'd arrange for the first flight out of Moscow, not even caring where it landed. Any city in Europe would suffice. He could find his way to Damascus from there. He just wanted to get as far away from the Lubyanka as possible.

A different driver arrived in the fake taxi and flashed SVR credentials. He was young and fit with short military hair, rolled-up sleeves under a down vest, and a tattooed forearm. He jumped out of the cab and opened the back door for Yuri.

He said, "I'm to take you to Hotel Baltschug."

"I *wish*," Yuri said, cramming himself with his bag into the backseat. "I'm staying at the Gostevoy Dom just over there, *pozhalsta*."

The driver looked at him and flashed a brief smile. "I was told, *tovarisch*, that as a gesture of appreciation and to make up for some of the inconveniences of your trip, you have been upgraded to a room at the Baltschug on behalf of SVR." He shut the door and slid behind the wheel.

Yuri thought about it for all of two seconds. The Baltschug was a glorious five-star hotel on the Moscow River. He might even stay an extra day to sleep off this miserable scopolamine hangover.

He said, *"Da. Ochen horosho."*

The room did not disappoint. There was a sweeping view of the river and a bed the size of a tennis court. He took a scalding shower, ate a double serving of room service pizza, and slugged two straight vodkas from the minibar. After drawing the thick blackout curtains, he turned in before the sun had even gone down, snoring under a pillow.

Two hours later, a knife was at his throat.

The SVR driver from the fake taxi was straddled over his body, holding him by the neck, jamming the point of the blade under Yuri's chin. When he opened his eyes, the driver hit him in the jaw with the butt end of a flashlight. The driver then flipped him over on the bed and squashed his face into the mattress.

Yuri attempted a scream, but it went harmlessly into the mattress. He could barely breathe. His hands were ratcheted painfully behind his back. He felt rope tighten around his wrists. He started kicking, bucking, doing anything he could to frantically get the man off his back. Nothing worked. He felt his ankles being tied. A gag went around his mouth; his hair was pulled as the assailant roughly tightened it.

He was flipped onto his back, helpless. The bright light was in his eyes. He now heard someone else in the room. They were talking. It was a woman.

The man dragged Yuri's head toward the foot of the bed. He felt himself being rolled, tilted down, faceup. The man had suspended Yuri upside down, holding him in place by his belt. Yuri stared at the ceiling. The flashlight was in his eyes. The gag was removed and he started to scream, but just as quickly the man covered his mouth with a meaty hand.

Thrashing, Yuri tried to bite it. The man punched him hard in the side of the head. A towel went over his mouth and nose, ratcheted down tight. The woman was now on the bed at his feet, raising them, tying his ankles to the headboard. Moments later they inserted an ironing board under his back. He heard the screech of duct tape binding his knees to the board.

Once he was secured, she hopped off the bed. She returned with a pitcher of water and stood over Yuri's face.

She poured water from the pitcher over the towel across Yuri's mouth and nose. His vision blurred. He coughed. The man held his head in place, straight ahead. Yuri felt himself drowning, panicking, wildly flopping his whole body as the water streamed into his nose and mouth through the towel.

The water stopped. The towel was removed. Yuri gasped. Air had never tasted so sweet. But the bright flashlight beam stayed in his eyes.

"How do you know Meredith Morris-Dale?" the woman said, her voice hot and close in his ear. "Answer very carefully. If you lie, you drown."

Yuri wheezed as the towel came up. He spit a gob of water into the air. *"Fuck you!"* he managed to scream. The mouthful of water fell back and splattered on his forehead.

The man put the towel back over his mouth. Water poured from the pitcher for five, ten, fifteen seconds. His heart was exploding in his chest. He was sure he was going to die this time. The towel came off again.

"How did you come across her name?" asked the woman. Her Russian was perfect, native. Perhaps from the western part of the country, St. Petersburg, maybe slightly Latvian.

Yuri struggled to answer. He tried to choke out the question: *who are you?* But he'd hesitated a moment too long. The towel went back over his face.

She had another pitcher waiting. The water poured again. Ten excruciating seconds. "Answer the question," the woman said. "Why did you submit her for surveillance?"

Yuri was gasping, coughing. The man slapped him and held him in place. The woman walked away, toward the bathroom. He could hear her filling the pitchers in the sink. He caught a glimpse of her. It was the beautiful blonde from the street. She was still wearing the white turtleneck, but her skirt and heels had been replaced by blue jeans and black boots.

"Please," he said, coughing. "Give me one moment to . . ." He burst into a coughing fit.

The man slapped him across the mouth. "Answer, *tovarisch.*"

"*Da, da.* Let me answer! You're S people? You know I was already questioned at the Lub—"

The towel was back. Yuri cried out, shutting his eyes. They held the water back.

"Do not ask us questions or you'll die this time," the woman said. "How did you come in contact with Morris-Dale?"

The towel came off. He was allowed to answer. "I know you're S Directorate people." He coughed. "I would never betray my country. I would never say anything to CIA. You must understand this!"

The man slapped him.

Yuri grunted. He tasted blood in his mouth. *"All right!"* he screamed desperately. "I'm PR Directorate based in Damascus. We coordinated a snatch about a month ago for a weapons buyer. The buyer turned out to be a CIA asset. I had pictures of the Morris-Dale woman, who led the CIA team. I asked for the tasking on the intel net. A surveillance order went out, a *Krasniy Odin.* That's all I really knew."

"You're lying," said the woman.

The towel came back. She started pouring the water again. Five seconds.

Yuri was desperate when the towel came off. "You must believe me," he said when he'd been given another chance. "Or just kill me. It is the God's honest truth. I don't know anything else. Look at the FSB records in the Lubyanka."

"Are you FSB?"

"What? No! I hate FSB. I'm SVR, same as you. PR Directorate." Yuri saw the woman raising the water. *"I fucking swear!"* he screamed. "What do I have to do to prove it!"

Suddenly his ankles were thrust off the bed. He was jerked upright. He coughed out more water, breathing hard.

The woman knelt before him, looking him in the eye. "You're coming with us," she said. "We'll verify your identity and your story. If it checks, we'll talk about what we're going to do next. If it doesn't, your corpse will be floating in the Moscow River by sunrise. *Vy ponimayete?*"

"Yes," Yuri said, "I understand. I want to get her as bad as you do."

"I doubt it," she said. "Do you know who I am?"

Scared to answer, Yuri shook his head.

She grabbed him by the back of his head, yanking his hair. "I'm Zoloto," said Maria Borbova. "You got two of my men killed, you idiot."

CHAPTER 20

IN THE PRIVACY OF AN ASCENDING ELEVATOR CAR, KASEM KAHLIDI RAN his hand along the underside of his chin. It itched. His beard had grown to a half inch, and while it was shorter than those of the rest of the *pasdaran* with whom he now traveled, he was beginning to look the part. But he hated the beard.

Occupational hazard, he told himself, noticing his face in the panel glass, adjusting the belt buckle of his green uniform. He shrugged off the thought.

The Quds man was accustomed to living a double life. He'd spent much of his career abroad equipping various Shia groups with the means to thrive. As an educated man who'd worn multiple skins, he'd eventually found the one that fit him best. It just so happened that it wasn't this.

Far from it. He vastly preferred the fictitious life he'd fashioned for himself as the president of a large ex-im firm in Beirut. That freedom to live the legend was why he enjoyed being a Quds man, the most prestigious arm of the national security apparatus. In this young republic, he saw it as his way to the top.

Quds, or Jerusalem, Force was named for the Israeli city the *pasdaran* intended to liberate. Their vision was to restore her to the Shia realm alongside her sisters: Mecca, Medina, Najaf. Quds was the covert special forces arm of IRGC, built up by General Soleimani. Until he'd been killed in the American drone strike, the general had been on his way up, a future president.

Kasem had navigated his career to be near the great man, eventually becoming his top weapons procurer. Most of the time this meant buying arms on the black market for untraceable use by Hezbollah. Over time, it had grown to include multiple international operations—Syria, Afghanistan, Iraq.

As president of his fictitious company, he had a closetful of Armanis in each of his four apartments in Europe. At each he maintained a car, a driver, and a ready stable of girlfriends. *This* had been the life to which he'd become accustomed—a long way from the Spartan *pasdar* he pretended to be now.

The elevator doors opened. He stepped out and walked the ten yards to his apartment door. Here he paused and ran his hand along the top left of the jamb, feeling carefully with his fingertips. He'd placed a piece of transparent tape at the crease between the jamb and the door, a routine he followed wherever he was staying.

The seal was broken.

Genuinely surprised, he backed up, retreating to a corner. He dropped to a knee, steadying himself with a deep breath. He wondered—could the Russians be monitoring him? The Russian embassy with its large, expansive garden was only three-quarters of a mile from here. Could that fat little Yuri Kuznetsov have set up surveillance on him? That would have been brazen.

Kasem fished through his shoulder bag for his nine-millimeter Browning service pistol. He withdrew it from its holster and crept to the door.

In a crouch, he waited, listening, the pistol at his side. There were no unusual sounds in the hallway, just the clunk of the elevator operating somewhere behind him. He slowly advanced to the door and pressed his ear against it. Inside the apartment, he could hear the clank of dishes, the hiss of the tap.

Kasra.

Relieved, he jammed his pistol in the rear of his waistband.

Opening the door, he was enveloped by the pleasant smell of roasting lamb. He looked across the white marble floor toward the kitchen and the bright view of the snowy Zagros, jagged against a pink sky. Kasra hadn't yet heard him.

He paused to admire her silhouette. She was the same age as him, no longer youthful. But more alluring now than the twentysomething girl he'd once known.

She caught him in the reflection and turned. "You're earlier than I thought you'd be." She turned, smiled, spread her arms, indicating the mess in the kitchen. "Surprise!"

He wore a black beret on his head with a lieutenant colonel's insignia. He liked it canted to the left in the style of the French. He smiled through his beard. "How'd you get in?"

"I think your doorman is sweet on me. When I showed up with a bag of groceries, he took pity."

He nodded. "How could he not be sweet on you?" He took note that the doorman might be a problem. But putting it aside, he said, "Let me get out of this uniform."

He walked sideways to his bedroom, careful to face front so she wouldn't see the pistol.

Reemerging a few minutes later in an open, untucked shirt over blue jeans, he snuck up behind her, embracing her as she worked.

"I'm not sure I can get used to the feeling of that beard on my neck," she said. She raised an arm behind her, pulling his head in close.

"Come now," he said. "I think you've found it acceptable when applied to other parts of your body."

She wriggled out of the grasp. "You're the worst." She poured a glass of cabernet. "By the way, I don't know where on earth you managed to get all of this wonderful stuff. But keep it up."

"France," he said, examining the label. "Just don't ask how I get it *here.*"

He poured a glass for himself. Mushrooms and vegetables were frying on the range. He leaned over the pan.

"May I add a bit to this?"

She nodded. He poured wine into the mushrooms.

"In France they use it in everything. I love it."

After dinner, they sat on his sofa finishing the bottle, bare feet touching. She was telling him about her day. She was a nurse with the gynecology practice at the nearby Akhtar Hospital, only a few blocks from his apartment.

She paused, pointed to the rising moon. "Come on," she said. "Let's look at it on the balcony." She pulled him to his feet.

This apartment in Tehran's first district, Elahieh, was a luxury, out of character for a *pasdar*. But worth it. They'd grown up together in the leafy Nakhvajan District, just to the northeast, in relative wealth. Her father had been a chemist with an oil company. His, an electrical engineer.

Her parents had emigrated to Germany when she was still studying medicine. By then she'd fallen in love, a contemporary who went on to complete his residency in a London hospital, a common destination for Iranian medical professionals. But Kasra had stayed behind, picking up work in the hospitals of Tehran, specializing in obstetrics, which she saw as sorely lacking in her home country. She'd carved out a life for herself, assuming her man would one day return. He never did.

After admiring the balcony view, they retreated to the sofa, a second bottle of red. She was fully at home now, going on about work, lazily intertwining legs as they reclined. When she'd finished discussing a girl who'd been recovering from a broken arm, she looked at him. "Your turn."

"For what?"

"To tell me about *your* day. That's how this is supposed to work."

He shifted on his hip. "I'm but a humble soldier in the Imam's service."

"Humble. You." She laughed. "Tell me, please, about the Guardsman that lives in a District One penthouse, sipping wine with a nonbeliever like me."

He shrugged.

"Seriously, Kasem," she said, her eyes hardening. "You must be able to share something. I'm not an enemy of the state."

He angled his head at her. "If you're trying to out me, you're making a big mistake." He smiled, deflecting.

She touched the scar that protruded from his collarbone to his sternum. "You can change what you wear, but you can't change who you are."

She pressed on the raised pink skin. "This is about four millimeters from your jugular. You know that, right?" It wasn't the first time she'd tried to get him to talk about it. She was looking at him intensely. He found it unnerving.

He felt the need to say something about it, for once. Touching his own finger to the wound, he said, "Bloody but unbowed, as the saying goes."

"What saying?"

He switched to English. "The line from *Invictus*."

She replied in accented English of her own. "Wine, poetry, mystery. You think you know a way to a girl's heart. But I can see right through you. I know who you really are. Don't forget that, Kasem *jon*." She nudged him again, harder this time. "Tell me about that scar. I'm asking. Seriously."

He put his glass on the coffee table and stood, gently pulling her up to meet him. Wrapping his arms around her, he kissed her, then spoke softly into her ear, reciting in English:

> *In the fell clutch of circumstance*
> *I have not winced nor cried aloud.*
> *Under the bludgeonings of chance*
> *My head is bloody, but unbowed.*

She pulled back from him and held his face in her hands.

"Incorruptible," she said. She stood on her toes and kissed him on the collarbone, right on the scar. "One day you'll tell me."

The following morning he was back at MOIS HQ, center city, near the airport. The commute from First District was maddening, taking him more than an hour.

He leaned forward over a capacious desk, looking at a stack of forty personnel files that stood to one side. He sighed.

Unlike his work setting up shell corporations in European capitals, this was the kind of analytical slog he'd managed to avoid. He considered himself a man of action, of charisma, of urbanity, not some desk jockey who had to sort through data. This was MOIS work.

He'd thought it would be easy. Since he'd begun this mission of rooting out a suspected mole based on the tip from Kuznetsov, he'd thought he'd uncover it in a matter of days and emerge the hero. He'd already imagined the laurels for the discovery of the mole. He'd envisioned how the powerful stroke would put him at the top of Quds.

But so far, he'd turned up nothing. The scientific summit with the Russians in Bushehr was only a week or two away. If ever there was a critical time in which to have a breakthrough, this was it.

He'd had the records pulled for every military and civilian scientist associated with *Zaqqum*, Iran's national nuclear project. *Zaqqum* spanned multiple facilities. There was the heavy water reactor at Arak, the partially completed Russian reactor at Bushehr, the former underground enrichment facility at Natanz, the reconstituted enrichment facility deep under Tabriz.

Throughout this entire national enterprise, there were thousands of workers involved, both civilian and military. Since Kuznetsov had referenced the leak, Kasem had reasoned that the most likely source would be where the Russians were now working. How else would they have detected one?

There were Russians working at Bushehr, Arak, and the secret facility at Tabriz, accounting for some three hundred technicians, all of whom were sequestered under guarded living conditions. As Colonel Maloof had said, all the workers associated with *Zaqqum* had been painstakingly vetted. It seemed airtight.

He placed his hand at the top of the stack of files. *Needle meet haystack.*

He spent the rest of the day looking over the backgrounds of the associated civilians. Much of the work was manual since the Iranian database files were woefully inadequate. Maloof had assigned three young MOIS officers to Kasem. He'd been having them chase down various details related to each of the civilians, following up with phone calls, verifying records. One by one they'd been clearing the technical workers, perhaps ten per day.

Toward five o'clock, as the shadows began to lengthen, he heard the *azan*. Brothers of the IRGC stopped what they were doing and knelt on their *namaz* rugs, facing Mecca.

Kasem joined them, clearing a spot by his desk. He knelt toward the holy city, west of Iran, and thought about the distance between himself and Saudi Arabia, across the Persian Gulf.

He thought about the crucial upcoming summit at Bushehr, a city on the Gulf.

He thought of Kuznetsov.

The *azan* chanted on; he remained prostrate, thinking. What if, he thought, he simply beat the daylights out of the SVR man, forcing him into a more forthcoming attitude? He'd been close to doing it the last time he'd seen him in Lebanon, but the Russian had wisely brought along reinforcements.

It might be different if Kasem could catch him by surprise. Through his association with Hezbollah, he had an extensive network of cutouts that could take care of the dirty work.

The *azan* ended. He stood and walked to the window.

He looked out at the MOIS compound, his mind elsewhere. An IRGC Mi-8 helicopter was lifting off from the heliport. A Russian-built helicopter screaming to gain altitude. The Russians had recently provided the IRGC with thirty of the helos, a goodwill gesture in order to buttress Iran's fleet of aging American UH-1 Hueys. He started thinking about Kuznetsov again.

Yes. Hezbollah. That would do it.

He retrieved his cell phone and made a call.

CHAPTER 21

THE MORNING SUN REFLECTING OFF THE THAMES OFFERED LITTLE comfort to the thousands of Londoners making their way across the walkway on Blackfriars Bridge. A snapping breeze had blown the stubborn mists out to sea, revealing a rare sunny vista of St. Paul's Cathedral. But it also knifed right through the woolen layers of pink-faced commuters on their way to work.

Among them, Genevieve Lund, née Maria Borbova, aka Zoloto, strode with purpose, blond hair spilling over a black scarf. Like the rest of the Londoners pressed between the rails, she huddled through the raw air. It was a two-mile trip from her Bankside apartment in the south to her Farringdon office on the north side of the river.

While it was cold, she thoroughly enjoyed these morning commutes. A winter in London was nothing compared to a winter in Moscow. She did her best thinking while walking on this bridge, just as she was thinking now.

As the breeze turned her forehead numb, the Directorate S officer pondered her course, now that her formerly dependable CIA source, Ed Rance, had gone silent.

Pointedly so. On her last trip to DC, she'd followed through with the usual text flirtations. He had responded that he wasn't available— hadn't even bothered to invent an excuse. How cliché.

She'd consoled herself that she knew his lusting weaknesses. Knew them all too well. Knew it was probably just guilt, the wife, the sons, the usual banal melodramas. She'd been expecting to hear from him at any moment.

But now, three weeks on, her confidence ebbed. Could it be the blown op at John Dale's property? Could American counterintelligence have mobilized, detecting her relationship with him, outing her? She'd run over her operational security practices. She'd been sure she was solid. But now . . .

Like a jilted schoolgirl, she was suddenly desperate to hear from this man that she so utterly disliked.

Her office at 4 Snow Hill Road took up the third floor of a nineteenth-century brick building that had once been a Victorian warehouse. The old red building, ornamented with white balustraded balconies and pedimented windows, stood like a soldier in ranks amid others of similar dominion.

She took the stairs to the third floor and entered suite three by punching a code on a cypher lock. Once inside, she unwrapped her scarf, removed her coat, and stood looking at a two-way mirror. Above it was a sign that read: RECEPTION, STOKE PARK INSURANCE, LONDON. PLEASE SIGN IN. A table held a telephone and a logbook. She dialed. A reinforced fire door buzzed and clicked open.

The other side revealed a floor that stretched all the way to windows overlooking the street. Shades had been drawn and the office was dim, save for lights hunched on the five desks spaced haphazardly across the carpet as though they'd just been dropped off by a moving crew.

Between them, strewn without any particular order, lay heavy black shipping cases, big as coffins, locked by thick silver buckles. Snaking between these were power cables duct-taped to the floor. A wide table ran along one wall with stacks of electronic equipment. A printer hummed, spitting out pages.

Two men sat at their desks, typing on laptops. One of them looked up at Maria and nodded as she made her way to her workstation.

"*Dobre utra.* You're in early," Oleg said.

He wore a gray suit with a white shirt open at the collar. He was the Spetsnaz Alpha operator who'd helped Maria interrogate Kuznetsov in

Moscow. He'd been assigned to her as the paramilitary lead, her number two.

"Good morning." She dropped her coat on the floor next to her desk and sat down. She turned back to him. "*Pozhalsta*, can I get a look at the message boards? Anything good from Yasenevo?"

"*Da.*"

He picked up the clipboard with its thick stack of dispatches. Most of them were administrative, having to do with the mundane details of managing SVR stations around the world.

But there was a certain gleam in his eye. He tapped the top of the stack as he set it on her desk. "Third or fourth down. A direct message from the Beirut embassy. Your friend Kuznetsov."

Maria grunted and picked up the clipboard. On her walk across the bridge, she'd thought of Kuznetsov. She'd been rough on the PR man. At the time she'd thought him a snitch, blowing her Rance operation.

She'd nearly killed him in that hotel before Oleg pulled her back. Thank God he had, she thought now, looking at Kuznetsov's message, her mouth curling. The little major might yet be worth something.

His report, filed from the Russian consulate in Beirut, noted that he'd established an international surveillance operation for John Dale and his ex-wife, Meredith Morris-Dale. After corroborating the intelligence taken from Rance, the recorded conversations at John Dale's property, and the bioweapons dealer picked up in the Dubai operation some weeks back who'd since met his demise, the Russians were convinced the Dales were at the center of a plot to infiltrate the Iran–Russia nuclear collaboration.

According to Yuri's message, steeped in SVR bureaucratese, they would now have a detection net in place ready to catch either of them entering the Middle Eastern area of operations.

She had to admire the nature of the trap. The major had attached images of the Dales to the records of real criminals wanted by the Russian government, along with a note that the suspects were likely to be using false credentials. He'd uploaded the doctored records with the Dales' photos to the Interpol database in Lyon.

Following proper diplomatic channels, he'd tasked Interpol to issue a Red Notice for the criminals in the doctored records, effectively an arrest warrant with an allowance for extradition back to Russia. With Interpol's one hundred member countries, it meant the Dales were screwed.

It wouldn't matter if they traveled under an alias, which they almost certainly would. Nearly all border points around the world used cameras. Their images would instantly be compared to the Lyon data center's facial recognition software.

Better still, she saw, Yuri's Red Notice was silent. It asked that the Interpol member country only *notify* the Russian police force of the entry—not make an actual arrest. It would allow SVR to roll up whatever operation the Dales were running before it got started.

Maria flipped the page. More messages from Yasenevo—most of them repeats of tasking orders for intelligence on American informants in Iran.

Right. She rotated her head in a circular motion. *If only Rance would call.*

The intelligence tasking orders were coming more regularly now, more urgently. In another week, a high-level delegation led by the minister of energy would be traveling to Bushehr to celebrate renewed cooperation on the reactor and secretly to negotiate continued collaboration on yellowcake processing, maybe even cruise missiles as a delivery vehicle. It was a high-profile public meeting designed to build political pressure against the Israelis and the Americans, who'd begun making noise about it.

When Maria finished reading, she set the boards aside.

Oleg slid in a wheeled chair toward her. "You like?"

She nodded. "A good net. First step anyway."

"Good thing we didn't kill him, eh?" He grinned.

She looked at him coldly. "I only hope Leo and Vasily would agree."

"We'll get Dale," he said. "As soon as he pops up, we're ready to roll."

She nodded. "I want a twenty-four-seven going on here."

"We know. I've split the team into six-hour shifts. We're actively monitoring the net, real time."

"Who was on last night?"

"Ochenko. But, boss—remember what we talked about?"

She thought about their conversation from the night before. The Spetsnaz men were eager to get out of the office and get in some proficiency work. She'd had them cooped up here for over a week now.

"You mean the training?" she asked.

"Yes."

"Show me the watch bill. If I'm convinced we're covered, then yes, we can go."

"You'll be convinced," he said. "I'll call Scotland Station."

He was right. By lunchtime, she'd become comfortable that they'd established a competent watch profile and agreed to Oleg's trip. She'd leave two men at the operations center and accompany the other three to the training grounds. Privately she knew she could use some small-arms refresh work.

By one in the afternoon they'd loaded their large heavy shipping crates into two vans and driven to Stapleford, a private airport just to the northeast of London, conveniently situated near the M25 freeway. There, they transferred their equipment and themselves into two Sikorsky S-76 helicopters, each chartered by the fictitious insurance company, crewed by on-call SVR pilots who were billeted permanently in London.

By three thirty the SVR team landed on a wide green lawn at Pickston, just to the northwest of Perth, site of a large Scottish hunting estate that was legally owned by the insurance company. All of them, the four SVR operatives and four aircrewmen, spent the night in the estate's moldy stone house, eating the meager rations they'd brought with them.

The caretaker of the estate hadn't been given notice and very little had been prepared. In the freezing Highlands, it seemed to take hours for the house to finally warm up to the point that they could get some sleep.

The next morning, her team completed a five-mile run through mossy woods. She was careful to keep her satellite phone close, just in case she should hear anything from the London watch station—or even better, Rance. But nothing came.

The real purpose of the trip opened up by midmorning, just as the sun was chasing away the freezing fog. In a fallow field less than a quarter mile from the house, Oleg had spread an array of weapons including four snub-nosed silent pistols for close-in covert work, four standard AK-12 assault rifles, and most exciting to the group, two of the new A-545 compact machine guns.

Oleg set up targets tacked to hay bales at various distances, the longest of which was over five hundred yards away. The sound of gunfire was nothing unusual in this remote, hunting-obsessed part of the country.

Around four forty-five, the sun turned orange and hid in the trees. Maria was chilled to her bones, and she hoped the old man who ran the estate had somehow succeeded in warming up the drafty old house.

The satphone on her hip buzzed. Oleg was lying prone, clattering off rounds from the extra-loud AK-12.

With one finger in her ear and the other to the phone, she stepped on the back of his thigh and yelled, *"Cease fire! Cease fire!"*

It was Dmitry, the Spetz operator on watch in London. "We have a message from Beirut Station," he said. "A hit on the Red Notice. Ninety-eight percent probability. The man—John Dale."

"Already? Where?"

"Mumbai."

She ran her free hand through her hair, which was stringy from dried sweat. Oleg got up and stood beside her, listening.

"Mumbai? As in Bombay? India?" she said. "You sure?"

"Chhatrapati International. Mumbai's main airport. Traveling under the name Reza Shariati. Canadian passport."

"An Iranian name," she said. She looked at Oleg, who shrugged. Into the phone, she said, "Canadian passport? You're sure? Diplomatic or civilian?"

"Civilian. I have a digital copy of it right here. It's him."

She smiled for the first time in days. "We'll be back in London in two hours."

Overhearing this, the team around her started folding their rifle stocks.

"Oh and one more thing," she said into the phone. "Patch me through to Beirut Station. I want to speak to Major Kuznetsov personally."

"Da, da, da," Yuri said to the beautiful blond Directorate S officer he still only knew as Zoloto.

She was as demanding on the phone as she was in person. She'd already asked fifty questions to ensure the facial recognition ping on John Dale was legit. It was getting old.

"The net will stay up," he said for the tenth time. "I'll have Mumbai Station conduct a diplomatic meeting with the Indian Police Service. As you say, I'll call them now. Yes, of course *now*."

He turned toward Putov and rolled his eyes. They were sitting on a white sofa, looking out at the lights of Beirut from a fifth-floor suite in the Olympic Hotel. Putov was smoking and smiling. It was a little after eight p.m.

"Da. Da. Da." Yuri rolled his eyes again. He hung up and placed the phone on the coffee table, shaking his head. "Bitch hung up on me," he grumbled. "Remind me to send a message to the Mumbai consulate *in the morning*."

"Not now?" asked Putov.

"No. Fuck her. After what she did to me in Moscow, you think I'm going to let her spoil my only good night in Beirut?"

Putov shook his head, commiserating. Changing the subject, he said, "We need to go, boss. The show starts in a half hour. Car's downstairs." He tapped his watch.

Yuri stood and checked himself in the foyer's mirror. Mostly bald at the top, he'd used some hair gel to move his side hair around. He re-tucked his shirt into his jeans and turned in profile, sucking in his gut. He thought he might have lost some weight on the torturous trip to Moscow.

"All right," he said, smoothing his hand along his chest. He faced Putov. "How do I look?"

Putov stood, grinning. "*I'd* fuck you, boss."

Yuri laughed. Good old Putov. The SVR major twisted into the shoulder holster carrying his small Udav nine mil. He threw a linen sport jacket over that and checked himself in the mirror one more time.

They took the elevator to the lobby and climbed into the back of a black Mercedes with an embassy driver. The car barreled through the hotel security gate and picked up speed as it merged onto Général de Gaulle Avenue, then east into city traffic, aiming for the Sodeco neighborhood.

They were on their way to Dalida Bar, one of Beirut's belly-dancing clubs. In the back of the Mercedes, they smoked and sipped from mini-bar vodkas. Yuri told the story again about how the FSB had rounded him up and drugged him and how Niskorov hadn't even given a shit. What a boss. This led to commiseration about life in the SVR that lasted through two more mini vodka bottles.

In the dark, neither they nor the embassy driver noticed the white minivan that followed them turn for turn as the city traffic thickened.

Thirty minutes later, Yuri was in heaven, having forgotten all about that bitch Zoloto and that bastard Colonel Niskorov. As Middle Eastern music vibrated the walls, three plump belly dancers writhed around his padded chair. Now and then he reached out to clumsily grope them, laughing with such force, he had a hard time catching his breath through his smoke-scarred lungs.

A half bottle of Jameson into the party, a particular dancer caught his eye. He couldn't stop focusing on her. With a more serious nod to Putov, a word was put in to the club's manager. The next thing he knew, the girl was pulling him by the arm up some rickety steps to a window-less second-floor room.

Once in the garish den, the raven-haired, henna-painted girl started kissing and undressing him, pressing her bare, overperfumed midriff against his stomach.

He wobbled drunkenly. She killed the ceiling lamp. A string of red Christmas lights hanging from one cracked plaster wall to the other provided just enough illumination to make things interesting. Their hands roamed over each other and Yuri unbuttoned his shirt.

Sensitive to the weapon around his shoulders, he pushed the girl off and unsheathed the pistol, sliding it under the mattress. She looked curiously at him, which made him feel interesting. He was, after all, a genuine Russian spy about to bed a beautiful woman in an exotic location. Overcome with whiskey-fueled confidence, he smiled as he unwound from his shoulder holster and dropped his shirt to the floor.

She kissed him as he lay on the bed, her hand wandering to his belt, which she began to unhitch, opening his pants. But just as he was beginning to enjoy things, she stopped. Placing her mouth over his ear to be heard over the pulsing music, she said in bad French that she'd be right back, that she needed to change.

The scent of her perfume, the warmth of her breath, the undulating depression of the mattress under her body weight, all made Yuri exceptionally agreeable. He nodded eagerly.

He placed his hands behind the stained pillow under his head and relaxed, crossing his legs, fantasizing about how the next hour would unfold. He closed his eyes, taking it all in. Propelled by alcohol, over-stimulated senses, and a raging imagination, he reclined on the dirty mattress of the squalid, pulsating room like a man balanced perfectly at the top of the world.

But then the door opened and a bearded man walked in, a pistol at his side.

Yuri leaned up on an elbow, confused, thinking it must be Putov. But the man was on him quickly, flipping him over, trying to secure his wrists. He was young, tall, strong. Yuri screamed but couldn't be heard over the music. He bucked wildly, panicking at the thought of again being bound at the mercy of an assailant. A second man appeared. Yuri vaguely heard them shouting to each other in guttural Arabic. The newcomer was grabbing Yuri's ankles, trying to lasso him with a plastic cord.

In the melee to zip-tie his wrists and ankles, the SVR major flailed wildly, careening off the bed. One of the men punched him in the jaw and his head snapped sideways. But the momentum of the punch carried the attacker off-balance.

Prone, Yuri kicked the other man in the ankles, toppling him onto the Russian's lap. As the fallen man lashed out, grappling for Yuri's throat, the Russian slid his hand under the mattress and found the pistol he'd stashed when he was undressing. He managed to free it, aim it, and squeeze off a shot that flew directly into the bearded man's jaw, blowing a portion of his whiskered chin to the far wall in a Rorschach blot of black blood.

The second man stared at the shattered head of his accomplice. Terrified, he raised a pistol of his own and fired, striking the shirtless Major Yuri Kuznetsov in the chest, knocking him hard against the bed. Yuri slumped to the floor, clutching his wound, gasping.

The music continued pumping, and the second bearded man met with a third at the doorway. This time they succeeded in zip-tying the Russian major, but it was to no purpose. He'd gone limp.

CHAPTER 22

JOHN DALE STOOD IN THE LOBBY OF MUMBAI'S TAJ LANDS END HOTEL, sweating in a suit at one in the morning, trying to check in. With dark skin, a thick beard, and shoulder-length hair slicked by pomade, he looked about the same as any number of other traveling businessmen in the area at that time of night—rumpled, tired, and grumpy.

The hotel clerk looked at his passport, thumbing through it carefully in search of Dale's entry stamp. It was the kind of unwanted scrutiny from a minor figure that drove him crazy when on mission. He took a deep breath to still himself and readjusted the open collar of his shirt, just to give his hands something to do.

"It's a bit smudged," said the twenty-five-year-old Indian clerk. "I can't see the date."

The handsome young Indian boy pulled the passport close to his eyes, studying the page with the precision of a gemologist. His shirt was two sizes too large and his necktie hung loosely.

"Let me check with someone. Just a moment, sir," he said.

Before Dale could react, the kid darted through a door behind the desk. Dale balled his fists, counting to ten. He'd now lost sight of the crucial passport, a rookie mistake if ever there was one. India's immigration systems were notoriously confused. The ability to fall through the cracks was one of the reasons he'd readily picked this country as an egress point for his agents. How ironic that it might be the thing that would turn around and screw him.

He looked around the lobby. For one in the morning, it was surprisingly busy. There were dozens of people checking in. A handful of them looked like foreign business travelers, but there were a number of breezy, well-heeled Indians who appeared to be on vacation wandering around the lobby, looking in the windows of the closed shops or parking themselves at the lobby bar.

That all seemed a bit weird to Dale, but whatever. Stuck out here on the peninsula by the sea, the Taj Lands End had a reputation for catering to the Bollywood film industry and all the groupies just such a place would attract. The clerk had mentioned that the Australian national cricket team was in town. He'd also said with a sly little wink that if Dale kept his eye out, he might catch a glimpse of an Indian film starlet. Whoever the girl was, her seven-syllable name went right by Dale. He'd pretended to understand just to stay unremarkable.

In truth, he cared not a whit about any of this. As he saw it, Mumbai was disorganized, choked with traffic, stuffed with people, and hopelessly inept at basic infrastructure. These were the aspects that made it an ideal country for a rendezvous with an agent looking to come in.

At least that was how it had been five years ago, thought Dale, the last time he'd been there. As he stood there waiting for the boy, studying the wealthy clientele, he wondered if he'd made a grave error. Along with the acceleration of the global tech industry, India had been booming. Most of the world's software developers seemed to come from here. With all that talent, maybe they were a little more organized now. Maybe they'd gotten their act together.

He quietly surveyed the revolving front door, thinking about what he'd do if he had to make a run for it. He knew reasonably well how to disappear here, which wasn't that hard; but admittedly, it had been a while.

He cared only about holing up in this hotel for as long as it took to establish the rendezvous with Cerberus. As soon as he got the word, he'd deliver the prized agent to the CIA station at the American consulate just upriver. With that done, he'd board his Air India flight to Delhi, then Air France to Paris, then Delta home to Seattle as a free man. Then he'd really be done with the Agency. They would no longer have a hold on him. That was the deal he'd worked out with Dorsey in order to execute this thing.

Just how long he'd be staying here at the Taj, he couldn't say. Cerberus had told Dale only to come to India, stay at the Taj, and wait for further word. Dale had been about to call bullshit on the whole thing, but Cerberus wasn't giving him much of a choice. Their sparse communications continued through the intermediary of a reconfigured digital drop box on Baramar support servers. The last time Cerberus had checked in was a week ago to leave this message to come to this very spot.

It wasn't a total surprise. Dale had known from the start he'd be headed to India for Cerberus. It was all part of the egress plan they'd worked out years ago. India was Iran's largest oil market and home to the world's second-largest concentration of Shia Muslims. Better still, the majority of those Muslims were *Ithna Asharis*, black-turbaned believers in the messianic Twelfth Imam, just like the most devout Iranian Shias. It was, in short, a good country to pull something like this off because the Iranians were generally not suspicious of travel there.

Dale's original egress ruse was that Cerberus would pose as a visiting lecturer and somehow wangle himself a trip. But it was supposed to be Delhi, not Mumbai. The meet was supposed to be in the grand old city at a hotel close to the American embassy. That way Dale could bundle him up under American protection quickly, the way it was supposed to be done. This Mumbai angle was a curveball.

The kid with the loose collar returned. He had a manager with him who wore a mustache and a badly tailored blazer. He looked like the first kid's slightly older brother.

"Sir, did you come in directly from the airport?" asked the older brother.

"Yes," said Dale.

"Taxicab?"

Dale shifted on his feet. It had been a steamy ninety degrees and the cab lacked air-conditioning. He could feel sweat running down his lower back, the sensation he most associated with this country.

"Yes, taxi," he said tersely. "Does it matter?"

The big brother shook his head, studying the passport hard. He muttered an incoherent apology. Dale started thinking about ripping the booklet out of his hand and bailing. Why the hell had Cerberus asked him to come to such a meticulous high-end place? Terrible idea.

The two kids looked up at Dale with wide, dewy eyes. It suddenly struck the American what was going on. He reached into his breast pocket and retrieved a wad of pink rupees. He said, "Here, let me show you the stamp myself." He took the passport, folded a half inch of bills into it, and handed it back.

"Ah, I see," said the manager, his face lighting up. "I think we have it now." He smiled. "Enjoy your stay, sir."

Rusty, Dale thought to himself. *Fucking rusty.*

Once in his room, he drew the curtains, bolted the door, and began to unpack his large roller bag. Traveling commercially, he had no weapon, but he did have a cache of implements for other exigencies: a coil of climbing rope, a red-lensed flashlight, binoculars, a trauma kit. He hadn't been exactly sure what might be in store, so he'd planned as he would have done years ago on any other extract mission.

Dead tired after the long flights, he changed out of his suit and into a pair of cargo pants. Over these he draped an Indian dhoti shirt that draped halfway down his thighs, covering the bulky pockets. He changed socks and slipped into a pair of hot-weather hiking boots. He ran some water through his dyed black hair and mussed it up. Diluting the pomade made his hair greasy. It hung in strands.

Inspecting himself in the full-length mirror, he felt he could pass as a local, if not exactly a native. Good enough. There were foreigners everywhere in this town of twenty-odd million and a good many of them spoke English, the official unifying language of India.

He sat on the bed and fired up his iPad. He considered whether to leave a message for Meth, but then thought better of it. He'd need her help to get Cerberus into the consulate. But the way Dale saw it, communicating with her now would just expose him to risk. Though he trusted her to keep quiet, she'd still need help from the Agency to get things ready. Someone else would eventually know what was up.

Yawning, he checked the Baramar servers to see if there was a message from Cerberus. With a sense of dread, he saw an empty in-box. *Bullshit,* he thought, angry with himself. There he was, old, rusty, making stupid rookie mistakes—and waiting like a witless imbecile on the asset he was supposed to be handling.

He shut the iPad down. The room had two queens. *Enough of the lazy mistakes,* he chided himself. He mussed up one of the beds, propping up some pillows under the covers to make a reasonable semblance of a sleeping body. He took the blankets and pillows from the other bed and carved out a niche for himself in the closet with his backpack as a pillow. He killed the lights, slid into the closet, and shifted to his side, fully clothed. If anyone came through the door, he'd have at least a few seconds of surprise on his side.

He started thinking about a weapon. *Maybe it would be worth the risk to ping Meth,* he thought. She could at least set him up with a pistol.

Uncomfortable, he flipped onto his back and checked his watch. *This sucks,* he thought. He wanted to go home.

A bright shaft of light pierced the crack between the curtains. Jet lag and the darkness of the room had Dale waking late. As soon as he'd shaken off the kinks of a rough night on the floor, he checked his messages again. Same result. Another demand from Meth, nothing from Cerberus. *Fuck.*

To make the most of his time, he spent the day on a recon of the city, ensuring he'd be familiar with at least the various twisting alleyways that led to the US consulate, just five miles up the River Mithi. He raided the room's expensive snack bar for a lame breakfast, checked his appearance in the mirror again, and set out for the streets.

Carrying nothing more than his Canadian passport and a thick clutch of rupees, he performed an SDR through the city streets before eventually finding his way to a local bus line. In the city's infamous choking traffic, it took close to an hour to cover the easy distance to the US consulate. No good. As soon as he had word from Cerberus, he'd invest in a motorcycle for a faster option. The little two-wheelers were everywhere, sometimes teetering through the roiling streets with a whole family on board. They seemed like the easiest way to snake through traffic and blend in.

Then he rethought it. Cerberus would almost certainly have his wife with him. He wasn't sure about the daughter. Dale looked out the dirty bus window at the crowded street. The bus was stuck, as usual, idling amid the chaos of an intersection. There was zero order to any of it—a wonder anyone got anywhere around there. Cars, motorcycles, scooters, pedestrians, street vendors, all of them wandered around like there were no rules at all. It looked like a depressing version of Carnival.

He studied the traffic, looking for multipassenger alternatives. *Maybe one of these crappy little three-wheeler delivery vans,* he thought to himself. That would probably do it. He figured he could wheedle one away from its owner easily enough by throwing down the equivalent of about two hundred bucks.

Toward late afternoon, exasperated by the heat, snarled logistics, and the general discomfort of waiting, he retreated to the Taj. As he entered the lobby smeared with the dust of the city, the uniformed bellman shot him a condescending look. Dale was happy to see that, reasoning that his disguise must have been at least somewhat effective.

Later, holed up in his room, he snacked on some energy bars and sucked down water. He went through the routine of checking his covert communications setup through his iPad. There were two more messages from Meth, pissed off, as usual, that he hadn't checked in.

They were really heating up now. He was a pretty good judge of her limits, and he sensed she was nearing the redline. Woe betide the poor schlub within the blast radius of Meth when she went off. The twelve thousand miles of planet between Dale and his ex-wife wouldn't be enough.

Occupational hazard, Dale thought.

For all Meth's brilliance as an intelligence officer, she had a blind spot when it came to the rhythm of fieldwork. Her idea for handling a deployed nonofficial-cover, NOC, officer had always been to check in regularly, at standard intervals, ensuring safety. *Leveraging HQS resources,* she'd called it, employing the corporate speak currently in vogue. Dale saw that kind of micromanagement as a nuisance at best, downright suicidal at worst.

He checked the Baramar site. Nothing from Cerberus.

Screw this, he said to himself.

Tactically speaking, this entire thing was whacked. He'd made enough mistakes. He needed to get sharp. The last thing he was going to do was sit here in a fancy hotel at the behest of an asset who, for all he knew, was already compromised. He loaded up his backpack with tactical gear, more energy bars, and a couple of bottles of water. He stepped out of the room and headed to the elevators.

Six miles away in the humid Mumbai dusk, a beefy Russian Mi-8 twin-engine helicopter of the Indian Air Force (IAF) settled onto its landing struts on the lawn of the Russian embassy. As the whining turbines slowed, four men with thick arms in short sleeves exited, ducking the spinning blades, carrying long ballistic nylon cases. Behind them walked a blonde, wearing black hiking pants and a black T-shirt and carrying a heavy green rucksack. A moment or two after the group departed, the helo spun up and lumbered aloft into the gathering dark, leaving nothing but the fading drumbeat of its rotors behind.

The five passengers made their way through a double-wide door and down a set of stairs to a concrete hallway that led to a concrete room. It was the basement of the Russian consulate, part armory, part troop garrison. Here they unloaded most of their gear and took turns using the lavatories to wash up.

One by one they made their way back upstairs, where they gathered in an anteroom. A plainclothesman in his early thirties greeted them with subservient courtesy. Wearing a golf shirt tucked into khaki pants, he was Captain Akirov, a Directorate PR SVR officer working under diplomatic cover in Mumbai. Maria and the team of Alpha operators merely nodded at his intro, staying mute.

"You will sleep here?" asked Akirov to fill the silence.

Mumbai was a backwater SVR post. He'd been shocked when the Foreign Ministry had called earlier in the day. They'd asked a favor of Indian Defense and would be landing a Russian cargo jet at an IAF base just north in Gandhi National Park. The crew was then to hitch a ride via IAF helo there to the consulate to pick up "technical updates." If asked, the cover was that they were here to help service IAF MiG-29s.

Akirov knew they were anything but a maintenance crew. He'd heard stories of S Directorate Alpha teams and he was pretty sure he was looking at one now.

It was after the consulate's regular business hours. Other than a few uniformed FSB officers standing guard out front, Akirov was the only one there. He leaned into a mini fridge and pulled out bottles of water for each of them.

"Can I prepare the cots in the armory?" he asked.

Settling into rolling desk chairs scattered around the main office, the Spetsnaz commandos looked at Maria to do the talking while they accepted the water.

"*Spasibo,*" Maria said, slugging some water down. "We'll repack and stay in the city somewhere. But for now I need to see the message boards."

Akirov nodded and left. While she waited, she checked her Android tablet's encrypted in-box. The other men started looking through their phones.

Maria sighed over her tablet. Nothing from Rance. Still hard to believe. She ran a hand over her hair. It could do with a wash. They'd been traveling for more than twenty hours.

The boards consisted of a thick three-ring binder of diplomatic traffic. Maria scanned through the book hastily, fagged out by jet lag and annoyed with Rance. She gulped more water and felt the impatient eyes of the team on her as she flipped through the stack of paper. She knew they were tired, but she wasn't about to let anyone turn in until she had an update on Dale.

There was no formal message from Beirut or Damascus Station. Kuznetsov had let her down. She wasn't surprised. She thought all PR

Directorate people were lazy bureaucrats who would eventually fall short on a mission.

A half inch farther into the stack, she came across something interesting. Reading along with her finger to make sure she had it right, she suddenly sat up in her chair. It was a redirected message from her own watch station in London, two hours old. Scanning through the lengthy communications headers that preceded the actual text, she saw that it was a second hit on the Reza Shariati passport that had come in from Interpol. *Dale.*

"*Govno!*" she exclaimed. She turned to her team, eyes wide. "He's over at a hotel called Taj Lands End."

Oleg nodded. He put down his water, picked up his phone. He thumbed at the screen. "It's over by the ocean, ten clicks. Still as Reza?"

"Yes. Same Canadian passport. It came in through their nightly immigration batch traffic. Hotels report passports here." She stood, flipping the binder closed. Hearing the commotion, Akirov returned. She turned toward the SVR captain. "I need a six-passenger van and some city maps. Good ones."

Akirov nodded, glad to have something to do. "Yes, *gospozha*. I'll have something waiting for you in the morning."

Maria shook her head. "*Nyet. Now*, Captain."

Dale put a handful of rupees down on the counter at the Basti Backpackers Hotel, a ten-dollar-a-night hostel in the center of the sprawling city. It was a run-down three-story building sandwiched between two apartment buildings that were even worse. Whatever the building codes for this part of India were, no one was bothering to follow them.

A mangy brown dog brushed insistently at Dale's leg as he waited for the clerk to count up his money.

"Okay, sir," said the withered old man. If he weighed a pound over one ten, Dale would have been shocked. With a wizened little arm, the old man extended the key. "Second floor, room eight."

Dale hefted his backpack over his shoulders and nudged the dog with his foot. It groaned and shuffled off, pausing to urinate on the sidewalk just outside the door. Dale stepped over the puddle and started up the outdoor stairs, sweating.

Two Western girls in flip-flops passed as they descended the stairs. They were tatted and braided, dressed like hippies. Dale thought he heard some German, maybe Dutch. Though he looked away, the girls seemed to stare at him—and not in a pleasant male-female way.

Oh, I get it, he thought. They saw him as a creepy older guy preying on a youth hostel. Whatever.

Room 8 was a far cry from the Taj. Dale shut the dented metal door and barricaded the jiggling knob with a grimy chair. He sat on the creaking twin bed, listening, looking at the walls, taking in his surroundings. The sun had gone down but he'd deliberately left the lights off. He didn't need them; yellow street light permeated the room.

The walls were covered in stained flowery paper and travel posters of more bucolic Indian scenes. There was a vintage seventies portable TV with rabbit ears. Above that was a window with a view that went directly into the dilapidated building next door. There was bamboo scaffolding between the buildings, common throughout this area. Dale wondered if that was a matter of renovation or a sad attempt at structural support. On the positive side, he thought he could dive out the window and climb down if need be.

Let's hope it doesn't come to that, he told himself, checking his watch. He could hear televisions through the thin walls, at least five of them. They seemed to come from above, below, and next door. Game shows, apparently, screams and exclamations. *What a shithole.*

He scrunched up on the bed, feeling each individual spring under the thin mattress. He checked his messages on the iPad again.

Good news.

Cerberus had checked in. Meet tomorrow, four o'clock, exact location to be delivered one hour before the meeting. No word about the wife or daughter.

Well, thought Dale, *at least this mess is almost over with.*

He acknowledged the message to Cerberus and said he'd be there.

He also noted to himself that he might punch the guy in the mouth when they finally met face-to-face.

Almost over, he thought, spirits lifting.

Perhaps now he could answer Meth's desperate pleas for a check-in. Using the Agency covert communications app, he let her know he was in Mumbai. He asked that someone deliver a pistol to the back side of the toilet in the southeastern men's room of the Mumbai Central Railway. She could text him with the final location.

That ought to make her happy, he thought, *not an easy instinct for Meth. But this, by God, ought to do it.*

He told her to be ready to accept "the package" for delivery at the consulate tomorrow night around six p.m. local.

She'd better be fucking happy, he said to himself, trying to ignore the idiotic TV noise.

He shut down the iPad and checked his watch. He looked up at the ceiling and watched a cockroach take a stroll from one corner to a small hole near the ceiling, where it disappeared. The TV in the next room blared incomprehensibly. He heard a toilet flush somewhere down the hall.

Almost done. As they used to say in the Navy, he'd be home in "one day and a wake up."

CHAPTER 23

JEFF DORSEY WALKED DOWN THE MAIN HALL OF LANGLEY'S SEVENTH floor at a brisk pace. Along the way a few staffers approached to intercept him, hoping to catch a quick word or a signature. But the resolute steel in the eye of the head of Clandestine Services scared them all off.

Around two corners, past a bank of administrative assistants and a row of interior offices, Dorsey finally found the one with his intended nameplate: MEREDITH MORRIS-DALE, COUNTERPROLIFERATION DIVISION, MIDDLE EAST. He knocked twice and entered.

Meredith was at her desk speaking into a bulky encrypted STU-III telephone of Cold War vintage. She talked in clipped phrases and took notes with her free hand. "Right. Right. Okay. You'll call me when? Right."

She looked up at Dorsey and waved him to the chair before her desk. In so doing, she smiled charmingly.

She hung up. "Something I can help you with, sir?" she said to her boss's boss.

"I see you smiling, Meredith."

"Am I?"

"Spill it. Colson's been calling the director looking for an update on Active Archer. I'm on my way up there now." Scott Colson was the White House chief of staff, a notorious ballbuster. "There's a rumor you have something."

Meredith leaned forward in her chair. She couldn't suppress the grin. "You know, sir, this place is terrible at keeping secrets. What did you hear?"

"That your husband checked in."

"*Ex*-husband." The grin flattened.

"Whatever. The director wants me in his office in fifteen minutes."

She was just about to explain when there was another knock at the door. Rance wasn't about to let one of his subordinates go off script with the higher-ups. He'd heard about Dorsey's beeline down the hall.

"Oh, hey, Ed," said Dorsey, shifting his chair to make room in the cramped office.

Meredith nodded to Rance and he took the other chair. He was, as usual, immaculately turned out, while Dorsey had his tie askew and sleeves pushed up past his elbows. Odd couple. Rance would be leaving for Europe in a few days, per Dorsey's direction. He hadn't been paying as much attention to Archer, but he also couldn't stand being out of the loop.

"Okay," she said, leaning over her notepad. "That was chief of station Delhi."

"Delhi? That's Nick Reeves," said Rance. "Why would—"

Meredith cut him off. "Yeah, Nick Reeves. The short story is that John is bringing Cerberus into the Mumbai consulate."

"What the fuck's he doing in Mumbai?" asked Rance.

"When?" asked Dorsey.

She ignored Rance. "Should be early morning our time, four or five tomorrow."

Dorsey looked at his watch. "It's what, like a twelve-hour time difference between here and India?"

"Ten," said Rance.

"Okay," continued Dorsey. "So late afternoon, Mumbai time. Dale is just going to sashay into the consulate with our asset? That's it?"

"Actually, I think it will be our asset and his family," said Meredith.

"How?" asked Rance.

She said, "Reeves is sending a Navy helo over to Mumbai, on loan from Seventh Fleet. *Bonhomme Richard* Marine Expeditionary Unit is in the Bay of Bengal. We'll chopper Cerberus up to Delhi and get him into protection immediately."

"Right," said Dorsey. "Meredith, check with CENTCOM. Let's see if we can get clearance from the Indians for a C-17 to drop in and pick him up right there in Delhi. I want this fucker landing on an American base for debrief in the next twenty-four hours."

She took a note.

"Hold on, hold on," said Rance. "Given what we've been through with the Russians back here . . . how do we know this is all secure?"

"John hasn't picked up any surveillance," she said.

Rance glanced at his boss. "Ever been to Mumbai? It's nuts. Would be hard to detect surveillance over there. Should we send in a SAC team?"

Before Dorsey could answer, Meredith said, "Ed, you know the rules of this one. Low profile. High speed, low drag."

"Because John wants it that way," Rance mumbled.

Meredith shoved her notepad away. A pen rolled across her desk and dropped to the floor. "No. Because *I* want it that way."

"At the request of your husband," he shot back.

"*Ex*-husband, Ed. He's my case officer and I'm handling him—per your request, I might add. Or have we all forgotten about that? Are you really questioning my judgment here?"

Dorsey was sucking the inside of his cheek, listening and thinking. "It's not a bad idea, Meredith. A little extra protection never hurt."

"No, it's not a bad idea," she conceded. "But those aren't the rules of this one."

"Uh-huh," Rance muttered. "So let's see. We have no idea who Cerberus is, how Dale is communicating with him, or how he's going to come in. All of this in trust to an officer who . . ." He looked at Meredith and shut his mouth.

She glared back. "Finish that sentence, Ed. Tell me what John is."

"You know what I think."

"I want to hear you say it."

He glanced at Dorsey, who, after donning reading glasses, was now checking messages on his phone, staying quiet. "All right," Rance said. "He changed out there in Mosul. I was there. I saw it. He's just not one of us anymore."

Meredith turned toward the wall and shook her head. "Unbelievable," she scoffed.

"We've been over this," said Dorsey, looking up from his phone, the glasses hanging precariously at the end of his nose. "Do we have to relive it now, Ed?"

"Sir," said Rance, "it's just that here we are with the most important catch in recent memory. We can't lose Cerberus. And we're wholly dependent on someone that we pushed out precisely because we thought he was untrustworthy."

"*You* thought that," said Meredith. "And you fucking pushed it!"

"I did what I thought was right. I'd do it again. I saw what I saw, Meredith. He let an enemy fighter get up and walk away. He fucking *waved* at the guy. The whole thing's on drone footage. You want me to play the tape for you again? He's compromised!"

"*Jesus*, Ed! He was tortured by fucking ISIL! They took off a finger! Who knows what the hell was going on in his mind at that moment?"

"No one," said Rance. "That's just it. John won't debrief, won't tell us shit, will he? What else are we supposed to believe?"

Meredith turned away, resuming her stare at the wall.

"Enough," said Dorsey. He slipped his phone back in his pocket. The glasses came off. "I'm already late." After a quick appraising glance, he said, "Look. We all know the story. No sense in rehashing this. We've made our deal with Dale and I'm going to honor it. If he pulls this off, he gets a clean bill of health, no questions asked." He leveled a steady eye at each of them. "We all good here, team?"

Rance nodded hesitantly. Meredith continued staring at the wall.

Dorsey said, "The tactical question in the here and now is whether we think we need to bring a SAC team into Mumbai to make sure John's ass is covered." He turned toward Meredith. "You're his handler. You've spoken to him. It's your call."

"India's not a hostile country. I want it quiet," she said. "*That* was also part of the deal." She settled a cold eye on Rance.

Dorsey stood. "Okay. Then that's how we're going to play it." He buttoned the top of his collar and tightened his tie. "Wish me luck, you two. I'm on my way in to brief the director. Can't wait to tell him Cerberus is finally coming in."

Colonel Naser Maloof, the MOIS counterintelligence chief, didn't bother to knock on Kasem's door. The older man simply walked in, scraped a chair into place, and lit a cigarette. In a shallow display of courtesy, he offered the pack of Winstons to Kasem, who quickly waved it off.

The younger Quds officer was at his usual post, perched at his desk behind a pile of personnel files of the scientific workers spread across *Zaqqum*. He and his two junior lieutenants had come no closer to finding the leak that supposedly existed, based solely on the inference from Kuznetsov. They'd cleared more than two hundred people at this point, about halfway through the program.

As he saw it, there were two significant problems with the failure to find the breach. First, there was the leak itself, which might jeopardize the country's national effort. Second, and perhaps more important to him personally, was the threat posed by Maloof, manifesting now in the old man's smug posture. The colonel lounged at the foot of the desk, attempting to blow smoke rings.

He knows something, Kasem thought. *And it's not good.*

"The Russians . . . ," the colonel started contemplatively. He paused to let another botched smoke ring depart. "They're really crawling up our asses all of a sudden. Going crazy."

The younger Quds lieutenant colonel offered a shrug. "Should I know why?"

"Well," said the colonel, "apparently they think the Americans are cooking up something—some kind of plot. Probably to frame us at the

UN. You know how they are. With the Bushehr trip happening next week, the Russians want to hear from our Foreign Ministry that everything is airtight. Otherwise they might delay. As you might imagine, the Supreme Council does *not* want a delay."

"I see," said Kasem. He could feel his gut tightening.

The colonel smiled behind a blue cloud of smoke. "I'm not sure what to make of it since I'm not involved in *foreign* intelligence. Just our own internal security. But I thought maybe you could provide some insight into their thinking."

Kasem nodded, his face neutral. He guessed the glib colonel had maneuvered this in such a way as to deflect the inevitable screwup. If an American plot was detected, it would be the fault of the Quds lieutenant colonel who should have known about it in the first place.

The colonel tapped a finger on the stack. "We really should close this out before the Bushehr trip, no, Kasem *jon*? We wouldn't want Brigadier Salami to worry about some kind of *internal* issue." He stubbed out his cigarette and left the dirty butt in the ashtray on Kasem's desk.

For the rest of the day, Kasem didn't react, continuing to work diligently at his desk. Since the rest of the building worked for Maloof in one way or another, Kasem guessed he'd be watched carefully. Rather than offer fodder, he pushed his lieutenants hard, clearing files without a break, other than kneeling on his *namaz* to pray.

With one exception. At some point in the middle of the afternoon, balancing his phone on his lap below his desk, he sent a text to his Hezbollah contact in Beirut.

He left the office at six. The weather had deteriorated to a confused mix of sleet, hail, and snow, leading to multiple car accidents. As it was, Kasem hated the bus, pretending to live the life of a dedicated *pasdar*. It was downright demeaning.

But there was Kasra. He'd hoped to see her for dinner. The slow bus ride home got even worse when he read a text from her saying that she'd be working late at the hospital.

He ate dinner alone, checking his watch often, wondering when she would call. Later, dropping the dishes in the sink, he was happy to hear the phone finally ring. But when he picked it up, he saw a Beirut country code.

"Oui," he answered.

"Tu as une minute?" A man's voice, the sound of cars honking in the background.

"Ouay," Kasem said. He continued in French, "I need an update on the Russian. Did you get anything out of him yet? I need it soon."

"He's dead. This morning."

The Iranian squeezed his phone hard, his knuckles white. *"Dead?* What the hell are you talking about? What happened? How could you be so stupid?"

"Écoute!" said the Hezbollah operative, his voice rising over the sound of a truck racing by in the background. "Your Russian killed one of my men. The other had to fire to defend himself. There was more of a fight in the snatch than we'd been informed to expect. You think we're a hospital?"

Unbelievable, thought Kasem. He wondered now if Maloof had known somehow. Killing a Russian officer was a very, very big deal, a class A fuckup. "You're sure it was Kuznetsov?"

"Ouay. He had ID. It was him."

"Not just from what you heard from your men, but you yourself. You can verify this?"

"Ouay! I'm sure. I was there for part of the interrogation. There was another Russian too. Putov."

"And him?"

"Also dead."

"Fuck, Nabil!" Kasem yelled at his Hezbollah contact. "You killed *two* Russians? Do you know what this is going to mean? They're going to wipe us out of Syria, probably Lebanon too. They're going to come after you personally." *And me,* he thought.

"Yes, of course," said Nabil, the Hezbollah man. "It's why we had to kill the other guy. We couldn't have a witness. *Inshallah,* you understand."

Kasem put a hand to his forehead. He could scarcely believe what he was hearing. He struggled for something else to say. "Well—what did you get out of him before he died? Anything?"

"A name," said the man.

"What name?"

"They're looking for someone. His name is Reza Shariati—I couldn't quite make sense of the rest of it. We didn't have a Russian speaker, so we—"

"Who is this Reza?"

"I just told you, I don't know. The Kuznetsov character died fairly early on. His comrade Putov didn't seem to know as much. We really have only the name."

"Nabil, listen to me," said Kasem. "You need to bury this. Get rid of those bodies and make sure they *never* see the light of day. This can't come back to us."

"I'll take care of it."

"Don't call again. I'll be in touch when I need you. Bury this deep."

"I got it, *patron*. I got it."

Kasem looked past his reflection over the sink, out at the dark sky. Sleet had given way to snow, flurries bouncing off the glass. He could only imagine what the traffic would be like tomorrow. He poured himself a very full glass of red wine and sat at his counter, sick to his stomach.

The plan had simply been to rough Yuri up, get him to start talking, scare him a bit. Kasem hadn't even been sure it would work, but he knew Hezbollah thugs were good at scaring the wits out of anyone, even Russians. And to have killed that little shit Putov too. Disaster.

The Russians were going to come swarming. It was probably the real reason they were lighting fires at the Iranian Foreign Ministry ahead of the Bushehr trip.

But at least he had a name to work with. He seized his phone. He called one of his junior lieutenants, the one who was good with databases.

"I need you to go back to the office," he said into the mic.

The young officer hesitated before replying.

"Did I say something confusing, Lieutenant?"

"No, sir!" said the younger man, rattled.

"Get in there and trace a name for me. Reza Shariati. We need to find anyone in the program even associated with that name. All right? As soon as you have something, call me back. Tonight. This can't wait. Understand?"

He hung up and took a big gulp of cabernet.

Kasra texted a few minutes later. She was still coming, but later, not till ten.

Kasem acknowledged the message and opened up his laptop. He Googled Reza Shariati, a fairly common Iranian name. It seemed pointless, but he was bored and anxious. Google came up with scads of people, none of whom he could connect directly to an element of *Zaqqum*.

He was pouring his fourth glass of wine, emptying the bottle, when his lieutenant called back around nine forty-five.

"Did you get something?" he said, his tongue a little thick.

"Maybe, sir. I did find one instance. But I'm not sure if it's what you're looking for."

There was a knock at the door. *Kasra.*

"Wait. Hang on."

Kasem put his phone on mute, set it on the counter. He went to let her in. As she removed her damp coat, he saw she was still in blue surgical scrubs. He waved her in distractedly, told her he was on an important call.

"I need some of whatever you're drinking," she said. "Smells like you may be way ahead of me."

He opened another bottle, handed it to her, picked up his phone. Cupping it, he said to her, "I need to finish this in the other room. Give me one minute."

She nodded and found her way to the sofa with the wineglass in her hand. She kicked off her shoes.

Kasem went into his bedroom, shutting the door behind himself. He took the phone off mute and spoke softly. "All right, Lieutenant, what do you have?"

"Just this one thing, sir. I cross-checked the name against everyone in *Zaqqum*. There was nothing."

He fought the urge to hurl his phone against the wall.

"But," the lieutenant added quickly, "I also checked all of the cleared supplier companies and foreign contractors associated with *Zaqqum*. I checked their employees going back ten years, where I could find records anyway."

"And?"

"And one of the supplier companies, Baramar—"

"The reseller in Dubai."

"Yes, that one. Baramar had a contractor on file who left about seven years ago by the name of Reza Shariati. A Canadian citizen."

Canadian. Western. "What kind of work?"

"Computer systems."

"What else?"

"Nothing. I just have his title as 'Consultant, Information Systems.' He was on the payroll there for three years."

"Which facility uses Baramar the most?"

"Tabriz. It's mostly centrifuge equipment. Swiss made."

"Okay. Tomorrow morning we do the Tabriz files. Maybe even head up there for interviews. I want a complete scrub of anyone who has access to Baramar at Tabriz."

After hanging up, he went back to the kitchen, directly to his laptop. From her perch on the sofa, Kasra could see he was all business. She didn't bother to speak to him.

Hunched over the kitchen island, he started Googling again. He tried variations of the name, adding in "information technology," "Canadian," and other permutations. Nothing obvious came up.

Ten minutes on, Kasra sat at the stool across from him. Her glass was empty. "I wish you would tell me what's so important," she said. She poured another and handed it to him.

Absently, he thanked her and took a sip, setting the crystal down by the laptop. "One more sec," he said.

On a new tack, he opened up LinkedIn and entered the name Reza Shariati in the search field. A half second later, a stack of tiny professional thumbnail images stared back at him, all with that name. He looked down the list of their corresponding business titles. A third of the way down, his eye landed on one that read, "Independent Information Systems Consultant, Montreal."

He clicked the link. The public profile of Reza Shariati, Independent Information Systems Consultant, Montreal, filled his browser. There was a picture of a bearded man in a suit and tie staring back at him.

Kasem froze. Four seconds later he backed away from his computer, tripping over a barstool, eyes still glued to the screen.

Kasra hurried to him, steadying him with a hand on his back. She raised the other to his chin, forcing his eyes toward hers. "Kasem *jon*, you've gone pale. You look like you've seen a ghost."

He glanced at her, eyes twitching. His hand went to his neck, absently stroking the scar. He stared back at the computer screen. "Yes," he said weakly. "That's exactly what I've seen."

PART THREE
GONE

CHAPTER 24

Five Years Earlier

DALE ROLLED TO HIS SIDE AND SQUASHED A PILLOW OVER HIS HEAD, doing what he could to blot out the clattering growl of the big brown armored vehicles. Ungainly and top-heavy, buried under combat gear, they were headed out on evening patrol, trundling like a herd of elephants through Camp Ramadi, a secret forward operating base sixty miles west of Baghdad.

The late-afternoon temperature bounced off ninety-six. Done inflicting its damage for the day, the sun widened and squatted on the brown hills, partially blotted out by the dust rising from the vehicles.

Dale looked at his watch and sighed. He'd slept for a total of two hours. His olive T-shirt stained with sweat, he stood and watched the patrol leave, happy to see the sun making its exit. This sunset was special—supposed to be his last one in Iraq. It couldn't have come soon enough.

He breathed the stale air and fanned himself with a three-month-old magazine. The hooch was air-conditioned but subject to frequent power outages, for whatever reason. He'd never gotten the temperature below eighty during the day when he was supposed to sleep. The Army, which officially maintained the FOB, seemed to lack the electrical prowess to keep things running in the walled-off corner where Dale lived, the collective barracks of the men and women called OGAs.

OGA, Other Government Agency in American defense speak, the

amorphous nomenclature for Americans on the payroll of a federal agency other than the military. It was mostly CIA, sprinkled with FBI, DEA, and defense contractors who came to town now and then, usually to join interrogations of new detainees. They wore no insignia and they went by nicknames. Dale's was Gramps.

His little slice of OGA land was at the northwesternmost corner, which put it extremely close to the staging area for the massive Army patrol trucks called MRAPs, a hopeful acronym for Mine Resistant, Ambush Protected. Their hulking diesels rattled on through most of the day as they came and went. When they weren't running, they were being pulled apart by overworked, hearing-impaired maintenance chiefs who shouted at one another.

Dale didn't mind too much that he'd missed out on the sleep. He was expecting to catch a helo to Camp Victory for a final chop of his orders, and then on to Baghdad Airport for a flight home. He'd sleep then. The helo was supposed to come for him after chow and the cargo plane was supposed to leave "the sandbox" around midnight.

He only wished it could have been under better circumstances.

Working in a special task force under the administrative command of Ed Rance, deputy Baghdad chief of station, Dale's SAD paramilitary team had been tasked to root out the command structure of the Islamic State of Iraq and the Levant (ISIL). The big prize was their commander, Abu Bakr al-Baghdadi; but they'd have settled for any battlefield commander, working their way up the line.

The op was called Broadsword. Its AOR, Area of Responsibility, was northern and western Iraq, unofficially extending into Syria. This fractured landmass was rife with ethnic Kurds who'd been pushing for an independent Kurdistan for a century, pissing off the Iraqis, Turks, Syrians, and Iranians along the way.

The Kurds were the good guys in America's fight against ISIL. For their part, the Kurds saw the ISIL expansionists as the latest obstacle to a sovereign Kurdistan. Rance's simplified way to run Broadsword was to brutalize whomever the Kurds told him to. To the Kurds, American sanction for knocking off ISIL was a beautiful thing.

Following the guidance of Kurd commanders, Rance had given his SAD team orders to go hard, snatching suspected ISIL sympathizers indiscriminately for violent interrogations, usually at the hands of rebel Kurds to keep it legal. If a few detainees happened to die in custody, well, that was the price of war.

Dale thought the whole thing misguided at best, criminal at worst. They'd snatched and interrogated hundreds. But their success rate for finding actual leads on ISIL commanders was depressingly low. More and more, he felt like the leader of a Kurdish-driven death squad.

As lead sniper, he was almost always on overwatch, a couple hundred yards off, covering the team as they cleared houses and rounded up suspects. Most of the time he didn't need to shoot. Every now and then, he did. ISIL was big on throwing themselves at adversaries with suicide tactics, wearing S-vests or simply hugging bombs to their chests. Dale had killed dozens of would-be martyrs in his efforts to protect his team.

At thirty-nine, the Gramps moniker fit. Most of his compatriots were in their early thirties, ex–Special Forces. But in their line of work, five years' age difference was a lifetime.

Given his age and mission, the team tended to look to him for leadership. They seemed to like his quiet opinion on matters tactical, strategic, and ethical. There were many beer-soaked philosophical discussions after mission debriefs. Dale had made no secret of his discomfort with Rance's tactics.

So much so that the onetime Eagle Scout and Naval officer decided to write a letter to the Agency's inspector general. Word of it leaked to the team. Now, two weeks later, he was being sent home early, supposedly because the Agency wanted him back at Langley for a stint on the analytical side.

He'd gotten the hook.

But he didn't care. It meant he could finally get away from Rance, perhaps press his claim of unjust tactics with the IG directly. Even if it meant the end of his CIA career, he wasn't sure it mattered. He'd done his bit. He'd said what needed saying.

Still, he worried about the blowback on his wife, Meth. She was something of a rising star at Langley. It wouldn't help her to be known as the wife of a rat.

But that was for another time. For now all he had to do was get home.

Just as the sun was setting, he muscled his big black bag onto his back and looked around his hooch. The plywood walls, the thin mattress, the knocked-together bookshelves had been home for almost eight months. His final act was to pluck a snapshot of himself, Meth, and Grace off the wall. He folded it into his wallet. Like hauling down the post flag.

The guys gave him something of a send-off in the chow hall. A lot of jokes about his age, inferring he was headed to a retirement community in Langley. They brought out a case of Ensure, mixed it with rum, toasted him with it—old-man eggnog they called it. They gifted him a wrapped package of Depends undergarments.

Beneath, there was sadness. Dale had been a rare voice of maturity, the guy with the judgment behind the scope. While others had qualms about their role in Broadsword, he'd been the one to say something. And for that, he was going home.

After dinner, he caught a ride in a Humvee over to the dirt airfield, where he sat with a couple of buck sergeants, waiting for his ride. Before long a black-and-gray MH-60 Blackhawk circled the pad, flared, and landed amid an ear-shattering hurricane of dust.

Dale had been expecting a regular Army UH-60 Blackhawk. The helo that landed was the armed-up variant used by the Army's Special Ops Aviation Regiment (SOAR), a real mission bird. Bristling with guns, it had a long refueling boom and a knobby nose for terrain-following radar. A crewman stepped out of the cargo door and helped down a man with foppish red-blond hair and baggy civilian clothes. Ed Rance.

Dale's instinct was to turn away, avoid eye contact, simply hide as Rance headed off into camp. But before he could evade, the deputy Baghdad chief of station walked directly up to him, offered a hand.

"I see I caught you," Rance said, shouting over the screech of the chopper's turbines, the wind blowing his hair around. He smiled, pumped Dale's hand.

A hunchbacked Humvee pulled up and squealed to a halt. It belonged to the Army lieutenant colonel who commanded the FOB. A young corporal hopped out with a flashlight. He swept it over Rance's and Dale's faces.

"Which one of you is Mr. Jones?"

"Me," said Rance, flashing a laminated credential around his neck.

"The colonel's waiting, sir. Come with me."

Rance looked at Dale, who was leaning against a squat auxiliary power unit the size of a lawn mower. He hadn't budged.

"Come on," said Rance. "I need you to come with me. This one is very hot."

Dale continued slouching. Over the whine of the helo's turbines, he said, "Sorry, Mr. Jones. I'm on the next flight out. I think you know that."

Rance tapped the breast pocket of his safari jacket. "New orders. You've got one more op."

About five hours later, Dale was in that same SOAR MH-60 flying through the dark. He was wearing his lightweight black combat fatigues, body armor, and combat vest.

Protruding from the vest were four pouches of twenty-round magazines for his Mk 12 SPR sniper rifle along with four mags for the Glock on his hip. He wore a black webbed helmet with NVGs tipped up and a boom mic over his mouth. His face was marked up with camo paint. The rifle lay across his knees.

He could see stars through the open cargo door. Dale's crew was headed north, to a little village called Jurn, just south of Mosul, a hundred eighty miles north of Ramadi. To either side and across from him were the other five members of his SAD crew, the same guys who'd given him a farewell only a few hours before. The door kickers were similarly clad but more heavily decked in flash-bang grenades, glow sticks, modified M-4s.

After in-flight refueling from a C-130, the helo dropped air and stuck close to the hills. In the clear night's quarter moon, Dale could see silvery earth sliding by as they banked side to side in preemptive defense. *Must be getting close,* he thought. The one good thing was that the night air whipping through the cabin offered relief from the heat. Pretty much everything else about it sucked.

Rance had arrived at the base with the kind of pregnant arrogance that signaled something very good for his career was about to happen. He'd briefed the team in a rush, deferring often to the Special Forces Army colonel who would offer air support.

According to Rance, a teenage Yazidi girl had stumbled exhausted and bleeding into Mosul yesterday. She'd told some Kurds she'd escaped from the home of an old bearded man who'd repeatedly raped her along with other hostages. One of them, the teenager said, was a brown-haired American girl who went by the name Kayla.

Kayla Mueller was an American aid worker who had gone missing in Iraq some months earlier. For a while, it seemed every unit in Iraq had been on a mission to find her. Rumors had been rampant that she was in captivity with the ISIL thugs, but real intel had been hard to come by and the search had gradually waned. To have a Yazidi girl come and say she'd been in a house with her hours before, calling her by name, seemed too good to be true.

But the girl's story did sync with corroborating SIGINT data. Supposedly Kayla Mueller was being held by the main ISIL financier, Abu Sayyaf. He was known to have owned a home in Mosul. Confirmation bias aside, this one was just too good to pass up. They needed to send in a team to check it out ASAP.

This type of op was usually for DEVGRU special operators: regular military, not CIA. But as the colonel had explained, it was all happening too fast. The tip had just come in and the information was highly perishable. The girl had said that her captors moved between houses frequently.

DEVGRU was already on task in Western Iraq near the Syrian border. Rance's Broadsword team was the next best thing. The SAD team would raid the suspected house and see if they could rescue Kayla and snatch Sayyaf. If it all turned out for naught, no harm, no foul. It was worth the risk.

A mile from the serpentine Tigris, the town was tiny, more like an outpost on the desert frontier. There were about five buildings, one of which was supposedly the house. The plan was to drop the team, execute the snatch, then swoop in to pick everyone up. Normally they'd have to line up Apaches for air support, but there weren't any on such short notice.

They decided to go ahead anyway. Drone footage had shown the place was dead quiet. Speed and surprise trumped deliberation.

They dropped Dale first, a half mile from the target, flying in low behind a hill to stay stealthy. He was to provide overwatch from the top of the rocky ridge, about two hundred yards' elevation. The thick nylon hawser flopped out and Dale fast-roped down, hitting the dirt and taking cover.

When the helo was gone and all seemed quiet, he removed his clear ski goggles and flipped down his night vision. He trotted up the hill. The dirt was firm, vegetation scraggly.

He found a spot with a good view, a nice little clearing between a boulder and a shrub. He set up the SPR's tripod and pulled his long-distance IR spotting scope from his vest. He took a good look at the house. All seemed quiet.

"Gramps has eyes on target," he said into the mic. A series of clicks came in response.

Five minutes later he heard the whop-whop of the rotors from across the little valley. The MH-60 had come in low and fast from the opposite direction. It flared steeply over the suspected house, its gas-turbine engines screaming for power. The rope dropped. The team slid.

All hell broke loose.

Right next to the dark house, a pair of obscured truck-mounted DShK "dushka" heavy machine guns opened up through camo netting, belching six-foot flames, firing right into Dale's team point-blank. The flare of RPGs tore straight into the hovering bird, which was now yanking back wildly, twisting in a mad effort to get out.

Two RPGs missed and flew harmlessly into the night. A couple others struck home. The Blackhawk took direct hits in the main fuselage, just aft the cargo door, and the tail rotor. At that low altitude, the bird spun two and a half times, flames licking from its engine nacelles, the turbines making an unearthly sound. It struck dirt and exploded.

Horrified, Dale watched the scene unfold from his hide. The crash formed a white-hot plume in his IR scope. The sound of the disaster hit him a second or two later. He heard the boom echo off the ridge, once, twice. Enemy soldiers were already picking over the remains of his team, shooting the wounded. All five of them now lay dead on the ground.

The whole thing had been a setup.

He constrained his breathing, ready to start picking them off. At the same time, he called out his position on the net, asking for extraction, reporting what he'd seen. After the one-second sat delay, the CP at Ramadi answered back that ISR, the drone hovering somewhere far above, had eyes on troops coming up the hill behind Dale fast. He needed to get out of there. Now.

A heartbeat later he heard a bullet zing and ricochet near his head. Then another and another.

Only one way he could go: forward. He picked up his rifle and ran for his life, leaping off the ridge.

The next three days were a blur. He'd crept in among rocks, lying like a lizard, sweating, pissing himself, just plain breathing. But his hunters were everywhere. They found him dehydrated and bleeding, suffering from lacerations and a concussion. He was delusional.

They dug him out and slapped him around. He'd told himself that when they finally came, he'd fight to the end, squeeze off a couple rounds from the Glock and take a couple with him. But when they actually pulled him free, he was hallucinating incoherently, in the late stages of heatstroke, near dead from dehydration. He couldn't stand up.

His next memory was of a truck and a river. He'd ended up in the water—the Tigris, he'd realize later. They'd let him drink and bathe. Dale soaked it up with the animalistic sensation of life reentering his body. He'd been stripped naked and they held on to his arms and legs. But the water got him thinking again. Fight to the end. Never surrender.

He struggled to get loose and run away. They laughed at his weakness and slapped him around. He sustained a hard kick to the ribs. Not long after regaining his senses, he was bound and tossed in the back of the pickup, two men beside him with AKs.

He spent two days in a cage, a zoo animal. Men in black turbans would walk by and spit on him, shove sticks through the bars to poke him. A couple adolescents flipped his cage over for fun, rolling him in a stew of his own bodily waste.

Sometimes they'd drag the cage into the sun and let him roast alive, stark naked. Others, they'd drag him into the rock recesses of a cold cave to let him shiver. They fed him a bowl of rice once a day, every now and then a bottle of water.

On the third day, another white Toyota pickup arrived. A new black-turbaned man stepped out. He spoke English with an authoritative air; a guy behind him set up a camcorder on a tripod.

They dressed Dale in a long filthy shirt and told him to confess his crimes before the camera. He was given a paragraph to read, scrawled carefully in capital letters on a torn sheet of notepaper, like some preschooler had written it. When he refused, he was beaten. The cycle repeated. He knew from his training that it was only a matter of time before he'd break. He was shoved back into his cage, deep within the rocks, bruised and bleeding, delirious. He hadn't broken yet.

For two days they seemed to forget about him. He lay shivering in the dark in his long shirt, accepting the rice and the water whenever he could. The interlude was just long enough that he began to recover a little, to think straight.

They came for him again. He'd torn a bit of fabric from the shirt and wadded it up, then rolled it in blood and dirt to make it hard. This time, when they opened up the cage and dragged him out, he jammed the wadded fabric into the catch of the cage's open lock.

Video man was back. He sat at a table like a judge. It was a sweltering-hot day and Dale just stood there, blinking in the sun. They made him sit in a chair, facing the judge across the table. They told him they'd found him guilty of crimes against Islam, said it in careful English. They brought out his right hand, held it down. They sawed off his pinkie with a Ka-Bar while he watched, videotaping the whole thing as he screamed.

For two more days he lay in his cage, nursing the mutilated hand, wrapping a tourniquet on the stub with strands from the shirt. He felt hollowed out. Nothing mattered anymore. He'd either escape or die trying. He had nothing to lose.

On the third day after he'd been cut, video man came back. He'd brought a new prisoner with him in a Toyota SUV.

Leaving Dale in his cage, the terrorists put the new man through a similar ordeal. Dale could hear him screaming, refusing to read the "confession." Dale was surprised to hear one of them speaking to the new man in Farsi, a language Dale understood since his mother had spoken it to him as a boy.

They were brutal to the new man. Asking him to confess for committing crimes against Allah. But like Dale, the man wouldn't do it. He was beaten ruthlessly. Dale was glad they had someone else to torment. For now they'd at least forgotten about him.

Later that day, they shoved a second cage into the cave. He couldn't see it, but he could hear the metal clanging against the rocks. He could hear the door opening and the Farsi-speaking man being shoved inside. The man was moaning, muttering incoherently.

The next day they came for the new prisoner and put him through the same routine. Afterward, he was dragged back into the cage near Dale. He was quieter this time.

When Dale was relatively sure no one could hear, he called out to the new man. "Hey—who are you?" he said in Farsi, his voice dry and cracking.

The man didn't answer for several minutes. Dale asked again.

Finally, the man responded, surprisingly, in British-accented English. "You speak Farsi like an American," he said between labored breaths.

Dale could hardly believe it. That little bit of an English accent felt hopeful somehow. "British? SAS? Pilot? How'd you get here?"

"I didn't answer their questions," the man said. He let out a sick, jarring laugh that turned into a groan. "Why should I answer yours?"

Dale cradled his wounded hand against his breast. "I don't know," he answered. "Something to do before we die."

The man on the other side of the rock laughed in his grotesque way. Then he fell silent. Dale heard him sobbing. He tried to get him to speak again, but he wouldn't.

That night, Dale went to work on one of the bars of his cage. It was rusty. He thought that if he could pry loose a piece of rust that was strong enough, he might be able to wedge it into the lock where he'd already lodged his balled-up fabric. He hoped it would be just enough to free the hasp.

He spent the entire night trying to get a piece loose. Just before dawn, he had something he thought might work. But it was still too dark to try to do anything.

The next day video man was back. Dale heard them come for the Farsi-speaking Englishman. Overhearing bits of the Farsi exchange, Dale guessed they were putting him through the mock trial sentencing.

Now that there was daylight poking through the rocks, Dale went to work with his sliver of rust. After several attempts, he got it to work. The metal poked the fabric and slid the catch just enough for him to be able to open the cage.

This is it, he thought. *Die trying.*

He slid from the cage and crawled across the dirt, his long ragged shirt trailing behind him. As he neared the cave edge, he was blinded by daylight. He paused to let his eyes adjust.

Video man was off to the right, making a speech in front of the camera. Four black-clad men stood around the table, looking into the camera behind him. Rifles leaned against a banner on the table that said something in Arabic.

For the first time, Dale got a look at his cave mate. He was bearded, dark skinned, Middle Eastern. He was clothed in the same kind of long shirt that Dale wore. A man stood behind him with an AK pointed at his back, just as they'd done to Dale.

Hidden by boulders, Dale lay prostrate, watching the proceedings, wondering what to do. The answer came before his eyes in the form of sandals. A man apparently sent to check on him rounded the corner, ducking into the cave. He had an AK slung around his back. As he ducked to make it between the two boulders that marked the entrance, he almost tripped over Dale.

No decision to be made. Dale grabbed the man by the turban and yanked him to the ground, throwing him into a choke hold. They struggled, but Dale had the angle. He squeezed as hard as he could, then heard the man's thorax break, jamming his fist in the man's mouth to keep him quiet. The terrorist kicked and struggled. Eventually, he stopped. Dale continued squeezing until he saw the final twitch.

As soon as the other man was still, Dale robbed him of his sandals, pulled the AK free from his lifeless body, checked the curved magazine. Full.

If he exited the cave, he'd be in full view of the handful of terrorists who were out there conducting their kangaroo court. But he didn't care. He was going to kill every last one of them. He cared more about killing than surviving.

Die trying.

Dale took the filthy black turban off the dead man's head and tied it around his own, obscuring most of his face. It smelled of sweat and garlic.

He crawled out of the cave, sticking to one side to remain unseen as long as possible. In what he assumed would be the last moment of his life, he lay still, taking in the scene.

His fellow captive was leaning forward, head on the table. Two black-turbaned men held him in place. A third carried a serrated carving knife in one hand, a machete in the other. They were going to cut the prisoner's head off on camera.

Dale saw the knife touch the man's neck as the speaker's voice rose in some kind of speech. The captive screamed crazily.

Dale rose to his knee in a classic infantry position. He chose the knife-wielding head cutter as his first target, blasting the man with a three-round burst to the shoulder blades. He shot the man holding the prisoner to the left, catching him in the head. Four other ISIL terrorists reached instantly for their rifles, which were leaning against the table as props for the video production.

Dale whipped a ragged volley across the lot, felling two instantly. Others crawled, wounded, trying to get to cover. Dale walked right up and blew their heads off point-blank, screaming as he pulled the trigger. Their heads exploded like smashed watermelons.

The rage-fueled burst drained the magazine. He picked up a fresh AK, checked its mag. Full.

He dropped to his stomach and swept for targets: no one left except for the man at the table, tied to his chair, whimpering and crying. He was bleeding at the neck from the initial cut. Looked bad. Dale got up and ran to him. The knife was still in the grasp of the dead man at their feet. He pried it loose and cut the captive's hands and legs free.

"Here," Dale said in Farsi, removing the turban from his own head. "You're cut, but I don't think it's that bad—just a surface wound. Wrap your neck with this. You're going to be okay." He didn't really think so.

The man looked at Dale with quivering red eyes. His face was streaked with blood, tears, snot. On closer inspection, Dale could see that the cut was long but shallow. Arteries hadn't been severed, but it was messy. The guy might have a chance.

Dale pulled him to his feet. The wounded man stumbled against him, whimpering.

"We have to get out of here," Dale continued, holding the other man's face up, looking into his bloodred eyes. "Just focus on that. Hear me? We have to run. Now. Focus!"

Stumbling, they headed toward a copse of vegetation. The Tigris. They crouched in some reeds on the bank. Voices of villagers, the high pitch of women and children, not too far away. Dale and the other prisoner drank as much as they could. Then Dale checked the man's wound, much cleaner now.

"Think it's going to be okay if we can get you some stitches in the next couple hours. Just keep that bandage on tight." Dale made a tight wrap around the man's shoulder.

"What about your hand?" the man said to Dale, looking at the bloody stump of his finger.

The tourniquet had come loose in the water, revealing a glimpse of bare bone. Dale nodded and tore a new strip of cloth from his shirt to rewrap the wound.

After another minute, Dale said, "I say we swim."

The man nodded.

They went out to the center of the river and floated, still as a couple of logs, moving steadily south with the slow current, only their noses and mouths above water.

When they'd made it a few miles downriver, stopping occasionally to hide in the shadows of the bank or walk in the shallows, Dale pulled the man to shore.

"Kurdish territory. Safe to walk here."

They walked along the muddy bank until late afternoon. Toward sunset they moved to the road. Focused only on getting away, they didn't speak.

At dusk they encountered a Kurdish patrol driving American vehicles. Dale hailed it and identified himself. Their commander spoke broken English. He was skeptical at first, but he'd been working regularly with Americans and Dale knew exactly how to talk to him.

Dale promised to call in some air support for their mission if they would let him use their radio. It was an American PRC-152, supplied by the Green Berets helping to train the unit.

Dale walked free of them, giving himself ten yards of privacy. He called up the American net. Using code, he found the tactical operations center at Ramadi and identified himself as Gramps, the Fallen Eagle. He could hear the shock of the watch officer on the other end. They would send a SAR helo to pick him up. Dale identified a nearby hill as an LZ, about a mile's hike away.

He returned to the Kurdish platoon and gave the radio back. He told the commander that air support was on the way, but that Dale and his companion had to be moving on. The commander was grateful. He handed them a pack of beef jerky.

Dale and the man walked on, toward the hill, eating the meat.

The sound of a low-flying Blackhawk beat up against the hills, just as the sun was setting.

"That's our ride," Dale said.

The man hesitated. It was the first time he'd spoken in hours. "I can't get on an American helicopter."

"It's not going to be a problem," said Dale.

"Yes, it is," the man said. "I'm not British. I'm Iranian."

"I figured," Dale said. "You speak Farsi like an Iranian." He attempted a modest smile.

"You rescued your enemy."

Dale blinked. "We're both fighting ISIL."

Holding the cloth to his neck, the man said, "You know how it is."

Dale nodded. "Yeah."

The man offered his hand. Dale shook it. They were both so weak, they nearly fell into each other. The man brought his other hand over Dale's in a two-handed grasp, leaning, letting his bandage go loose.

"Thank you for saving my life," he said in his British-accented English, staring into Dale's eyes, swaying.

After a few seconds, he released Dale's hand and turned, swaddling up again in the bandage. He started hurrying down the hill, holding the turban to his neck, moving clumsily. When he was a dozen yards away, he looked back with a final wave.

Dale returned it.

The Blackhawk crested the hill.

CHAPTER 25

OBSCURED BY THE CROWD, NONE OF MUMBAI'S CENTRAL RAILWAY STA-
tion's grand colonial marble floor was visible. Dale shouldered his way
through the tightly packed bodies with impatience, which the rest of the
travelers seemed to lack. He bumped into more than one slow walker
and found himself repeatedly apologizing, though few of them even
seemed to notice.

Sliding his forearm over the gray head of a short old woman, he
checked his watch, three o'clock: time to receive the message from Cerberus that would determine the meeting location.

It had been a hell of a day, having already taken him two hours to
cross the sprawling town to get to the station. On finally arriving, he'd
burned another fifteen minutes finding the men's room and toilet indicated in Meth's message.

There, sunk in the rusty water of the tank, wrapped in plastic, he'd
retrieved a Glock 17 with four full magazines taped to the barrel, now
reassuringly stowed in his backpack. But he'd also worried that whomever the Agency had sent to deposit it might be surveilling him now.
The last thing he wanted after all of this trouble was to pick up a tail,
even a nominally friendly one.

To shake it, he'd performed a lengthy SDR by buying a train ticket,
hopping in and out of several overstuffed passenger cars, then reversing
course through the station. He hadn't seen anything suspicious, but just
about anyone could have found cover in that bustling crowd.

Now, a little after three, he broke free of the station and found himself in an equally busy market lined by vendors in plywood stalls offering everything from food to electronics. Wandering up and down the aisles, he happened upon a knife merchant where he bought a six-inch blade with a leather-wrapped handle for the equivalent of ten bucks.

A few stalls down, he purchased another dhoti tunic and a khaki ball cap, thinking they might come in handy as a change of clothes. Last, he picked up an old-fashioned Zippo lighter with a tiger on it whose stripes had letters spelling B-O-M-B-A-Y. He bought that just because he thought it was cool.

He carved a niche of space for himself in a gap between stalls and removed his backpack, stuffing his things inside. He sat on the roots of a rubber tree and scanned the crowd, looking for a tail. When it felt safe, he retrieved his phone.

There it was. Cerberus had left his message. At last. They were to meet for the pickup in room 2501 of the Taj Lands End. Since Dale was a guest of the Taj himself, he knew the room number referred to the second tower, fifth floor.

Interesting, he thought.

He wondered if Cerberus had been at the Taj this entire time, quietly observing Dale. Thinking about it, he shook his head sorrowfully. One more insult to his professionalism.

But that was okay, he consoled himself. He was almost retired for good now. At the thought of his normal life, he snapped a picture of the colorful market under the high palm trees with his phone. He thought it might make a decent painting one day.

The Taj was about five miles from the market, not a long trip. But before he could get over there to set up, he had a few more things to figure out.

He strapped on his backpack and entered the crowd. He wandered up and down the busy street of quibbling merchants, scanning over the heads of the crowd. Eventually he found what he was looking for.

The vendor was selling *paan,* an Indian street food consisting of herbs and sweets wrapped in a betel leaf. Dale wasn't interested in *paan*. He was interested in the yellow three-wheeled truck the vendor had parked next to the stall.

He walked up to the vehicle and inspected it. It was old and dented. Its blunt, scratched-up nose was draped with taffeta flowers on a string. A rusty but intact cargo area was covered with a stained canvas tarp. Good enough.

He stood in line for the *paan*. When it was his turn, he asked about the truck. A middle-aged man with a potbelly emerged from the booth, sensing opportunity. He was the vehicle's owner and he spoke very good English.

It cost Dale six hundred American dollars when the bargaining was finished, probably twice what the vehicle was worth. He'd have paid five times as much.

Officially called an auto rickshaw, he drove his ungainly vehicle through the tangled streets, checking his phone frequently. It had begun to rain and the pockmarked streets oozed mud. He was happy to see the little yellow three-wheeler didn't leak.

He parked it on the narrow street that stood between the Taj and a concrete boardwalk that ran along the high black rocks of the seashore. From here he had a good view of the Taj's second tower, the one where he was supposed to meet Cerberus. The rain had thinned the crowd on the boardwalk; but since it was Mumbai, there was still a crowd.

Dale switched off the truck's engine and sat waiting and watching. Looking up at the small balconies of the hotel, he wondered which of the rooms might be 2501. But he was soon distracted as he was enveloped by pedestrians on all sides. The people strolling around him paid him no heed. Perfect.

Between the walkers, he caught glimpses of the heaving sea beneath the rainy white sky. The tide had gone out. Several fifteen-foot canoes sat listing on the sand. Since the day's catch was processed right there on the street, the whole place smelled of offal.

Satisfied he was unobserved, he studied Google Maps on his phone. He memorized the route he would take to the consulate, noting landmarks and detours in case he needed them. His plan was to have Cerberus and his family squeeze into the modest cargo bed and huddle beneath the tarp for their ride to freedom.

Pleased with this simple exfil plan, he dug out the Glock and seated home a magazine. With a round chambered, he shoved the pistol in his waistband and stuck the spare mags in a cargo pocket on his thigh. In the other pocket, he jammed his new knife. Tossing on his backpack, he left the little truck and walked up the street toward the Taj.

The condescending doorman looked away as he entered, remembering him but not approving of him.

"I think I have him," Oleg said into his Bluetooth.

He was sitting at a table covered in beer steins with two other Spetz operatives. They were at the lobby bar, which had two tiers of seating. Oleg and his team were on the upper, close to the taps.

"Description?" asked Maria.

She was out of sight around the corner, covering the elevators, pretending to window-shop. They'd been at it all day, shifting positions, coming and going. There had been no sign of Dale. They were beginning to think they'd missed him, though he hadn't popped up anywhere else on the Interpol feed.

Oleg glanced down at the picture of Dale that he kept on his phone. He compared it to the man coming through the lobby.

"It's him," he said quietly in English. "He's coming your way, toward the elevators. He's in a dirty tan Indian peasant shirt, wearing a black backpack. He looks darker than the surveillance photos. Bearded."

"Got it," Maria said. "I'll tail him to his room."

She touched her phone, hanging it up, and hovered near the elevator bank.

Dale walked across the lobby's tiled floor, aware that people were looking at him. He knew he looked rough—that had been the idea. But he didn't like that it attracted attention here in the Taj.

His eyes ran over the lobby. Other than rude glances here and there, things looked normal. There were perhaps fifty or sixty people either walking around the shops or sitting at the tiered bar. He noticed three fit white guys drinking beer up by the counter.

One seemed to glance at him, but only briefly, not unlike some of the others. Dale didn't like the idea of a military-age male checking him out, but he let it go. He remembered the Taj had a reputation for hosting cricket teams, the national obsession. The Aussies were in town, according to a promotional sign for the match in the lobby. The three men were wearing Aussie team colors and polo shirts. Those guys could have been either players or fans, he told himself.

As a precaution, he ducked down to tie his shoe, looking at the beer-drinking Aussies in the reflection of a shopwindow. One of them was looking his way, but not obviously. He seemed to be on the phone. *Probably paranoid,* he told himself. He stood up and continued through the lobby.

When he made it to the elevator bank, there was a good-looking blonde hanging around one of the fashion shops, hovering just inside, close to the entrance to the store. Dale couldn't help but notice; she was a rare beauty. Her hair was swept back and up. She was tall and slender with flawless makeup. Statuesque, her posture was set off pleasantly in a pants suit that looked expensive.

But she was alone, which seemed odd. And there was something about her shoes. She wore more functional shoes than he would have expected. That didn't quite fit unless she worked here somehow. Yet she was looking at merchandise, shopping for overpriced sportswear, not working.

When he pressed the up button on the wall between the elevator doors, he could see through the reflection in the black glass surround that she was now standing a few paces behind him.

He turned and glanced at her, sure to keep his face neutral, trying to look past her toward the lobby. She smiled at him. *Wow. Gorgeous.*

He didn't like it. It was off. A woman like her would never smile at a guy like him: smeared, smelly, unkempt, shifty.

He glanced at his watch and made a gesture as though he'd just remembered something. He turned back toward the lobby and walked away.

He heard the elevator bell. The blonde continued into it, walking through the open doors. Once he saw them close, he circled back and found a heavy push door that led to the concrete stairs.

Five floors to go. He decided to run them.

Maria rode the elevator to the second floor. She'd lost communications with Oleg when she was in the elevator. She called him immediately when she stepped out.

"I think he got spooked," she said, irritated with herself. Why had she smiled at him? *Stupid.* "He ducked away from the elevators when I got on. Do you have him?"

"He didn't come back this way," said Oleg. "It's the only exit."

"Right. You stay there. He must have gone for the stairs. Make sure Dmitry has eyes on the street out front. Is the drone up?"

"Yes. He said he's got an aerial of all four sides. If Dale comes out, we'll see him. You think he made you?"

"I don't know," she said, running toward the stairwell. "I couldn't tell. But why else would he peel off like that?"

"Perhaps a standard evasion route. Anyway, we'll keep the exit covered here and the street watched by the drone. It'll be all right. At least we know he's in the building."

Maria stood listening in the stairwell landing. She could hear footsteps somewhere above her, running upward. She paused for two seconds just to take it in. The runner made a lot of noise. She thought she could hear the sound of what might have been a backpack shuffling up and down. Then the runner went through a door and everything went quiet.

Dale.

Thinking of what he'd done to Vasily and Leo six weeks back, she started running up the stairs after him. He had a lead of at least three floors. She couldn't be sure, but she guessed he'd gone out of the stairwell on the fifth. In case she was wrong, she decided to hold back calling Oleg. She should positively ID Dale first; if she was wrong and sent the team into the stairs, she risked losing her target through the lobby exit.

The plan had been to take him in his room and, just as she'd done to Kuznetsov, torture him into the truth of his mission. But Kuznetsov was a soft little bureaucrat. Dale was a veteran CIA operative. She and her men had packed significant firepower.

However it went down, Dale was a dead man. Since all of this was taking place in a neutral country where they were all working in non-official cover, a kill was well within the rules.

Dale was near positive the blonde was bad news. When he made it to the fourth floor, he sprinted down the hall, found the stairwell on the opposite end of the building and climbed it to the fifth floor. The room was at the other end of it.

He thought of his first brush with surveillance on this op. It had been Russian, back at his home. The blonde could have been a Russian; the Aussies at the bar could have been Russian. It fit with what he knew of their tactics. If they were indeed on his ass, he'd at least have to evade long enough to get to Cerberus and figure something else out.

He made it to the door, puffing hard, and pounded with his fist. He heard the same door he'd just used from the stairwell click open at the far end of the carpeted hall. But at the same time, the door to room 2501 opened.

A well-dressed dark-haired woman in her mid-fifties stood in the hotel room threshold. She wore a black skirt, a purplish blouse, and a patterned scarf around her neck. He entered and immediately shut the door as quietly as he could. Before saying anything to the woman in the room, he threw the bolt and pressed his eye to the peephole. He could see nothing. But that didn't mean much.

He turned to her. "I presume you're Mrs. . . ."

"Rahimi," she said, offering her hand. "I'm Nadia Rahimi." She spoke halting English.

Rahimi. Dale finally had a name. But no Cerberus. He looked past her, alarmed to see an empty room. There was only one suitcase. "Where is your husband?"

"He's not here. He told me to know your identity before I say."

What the fuck is this? Dale turned back to the peephole. Still nothing in the hall. "What? Where is he, lady?"

"He not here. He say I know you identity . . ." Her hands smoothed her skirt. She took a deep breath and switched to Farsi. "I'm supposed to ask you a verification question: what drugs do I take?"

Dale stood there blinking. He sat on the bed and put his head in his hands. He answered in English. "Your husband is seriously not here? Where is he?"

She had a deep voice for a woman. She tried her English again. "He serious that I know you—"

"Shit, lady!" Dale stood up. "I don't really remember."

He took a deep breath, switched back to Farsi. It would take all day in broken English.

"The medicine was for multiple sclerosis. You've had it for at least five years. I think we changed it a couple of times as it got better. . . . We . . ." He ran his hands through his long hair, exasperated, his Farsi rusty. Back to English. "We don't have time for this shit. We're in danger."

"Okay," she said, her voice tightening, seeing the evident distress on his face. "We go."

The room phone rang. "Don't pick that up!" he yelled at her. "I need to speak to your husband now. Where is he?"

"Iran," she said. She reached into her purse. The phone continued to ring. She added in Farsi, "He said he would be coming when he was ready. He said to give you this."

A sealed envelope. Dale tore it open. A few sentences in English on a single folded page and a USB stick. The page said:

Mr. Reza,

Meet my wife, Nadia. When she is safe, I will leave Iran, but not before. You are to get her to America and prove to me that she is not in danger and that she has full protected-residency status. You at least owe me this. On the USB stick, I have devised some code you can use to communicate with me. But I will not respond to anything else until I see that she is safe. In the meantime, I have closed off access to the SCADA systems to your people. I will reopen them only when I know she is safe, not before. I trust you to deliver her. I have told her that you are to be trusted. I will be in touch in the future with another package that you will find very valuable, much better than my previous work. It will end everything. Thank you.

The room's phone finally stopped ringing. Dale shoved the USB stick into a cargo pocket. He loosed his backpack from his shoulders and dug out the tiger Zippo. He went to the sink and lit the letter on fire. While it burned, he walked past the woman and approached the large sliding-glass window at the other end of the room, then threw the curtains open. There was a view of the sea, the boardwalk, the swirl of people walking. He could see his little yellow truck parked down below, parting the steady stream.

"You look a little scruffier than the picture he gave me," the woman said in Farsi, attempting to put this strange man at ease. "But I still recognize you. You are Persian? You have a good Persian name and you speak our language. What do we do now?"

He ignored her, thinking through his options. There weren't many. He was stuck in this room. He thought the best thing might just be to spend a few hours holed up here and then sneak out later somehow, as long as he could get past those Russians. From his fifth-floor view, he studied the driveways that led up to the hotel from the boardwalk, wondering if there was a way to access them unseen.

As he looked, a black object the size of a basketball moved sideways across the window from his left to his right in a buzzing blur.

He leapt back.

The black object swung back and stalled into a swaying hover just outside the room.

Dale threw the curtains closed.

"What is *that*?" the woman asked. The buzz outside the window was steady and loud.

"Drone. We have to get out of here. Now."

CHAPTER 26

THERE WAS A KNOCK AT THE DOOR. DALE RAN TO IT AND LOOKED THROUGH the peephole. The buzzing drone had moved off but the phone was still ringing. Whoever was knocking was keeping out of sight.

"Hotel security," a male voice said on the other side of the door.

Dale ignored it and hurried back toward the bed. "Give me your bag," he said. He spoke in Farsi to make sure Nadia Rahimi understood.

She gestured to a large roller bag sitting vertically near the minibar.

Dale hoisted it onto the king bed and threw it open. He turned it over and dumped out the contents. "Do you have a belt?" he asked, sifting through the bag. "Like a big strong one?"

"Yes, I suppose. It's . . ." She pointed.

He found a wide leather belt, the type to be worn with jeans. He also found a long shawl and tossed it toward her. "Hang on to this. You may need it later."

He found some athletic shoes and a pair of yoga pants. "And these."

The knocking at the door continued.

Dale said, "Put the pants and the sneakers on. Right now. Keep the belt around your waist, a little loose but buckled. Okay?"

The knock intensified on the door. She gaped at him.

"Right fucking now! *Do it.*"

She disappeared into the bathroom and hurriedly changed while Dale started emptying the contents of his backpack.

When she was back, he said, "Your cosmetics, where are they? I don't see them here."

"I have a makeup bag in the bathroom that I . . ."

Dale dashed past her, found the case in the bathroom, and returned to dump it on the bed. He also had a Kleenex box, a wad of bath towels, and a roll of toilet paper. He threw all of it on the bed in a messy pile.

He turned to her and said, "Keep the curtains closed and stand over there, that side of the window against the wall. Do exactly as I tell you and we'll live to tell about this. Question me or hesitate and we are both going to die today. Do I make myself clear?"

There was a loud slamming noise against the door.

Fuck.

It was a breach. Some kind of battering ram or sledgehammer trying to bust the hinges right off. Dale had never been on the inside of this before. He was used to being the one kicking in doors.

Hunched over the bed, he picked up Nadia's can of hair spray. He applied it to wads of toilet paper and Kleenex. He poured a six-ounce bottle of nail polish remover across the paper. He picked the mess up and made a pile of it in front of the door, with the hair spray can standing in the center. The steady slamming thumps were still coming a few feet away. Dale guessed he had fifteen to thirty seconds before the attackers broke through.

He pulled the bathroom and closet doors, which, when opened together, covered the width of the room's entryway, blocking it, isolating the small entry from the rest of the room. He took what was remaining of the nail polish remover and poured it in a circular pattern on the entry carpet near the door. The liquid shone in a small ring around the piled-up Kleenex.

He went to the other side of the two doors, the main part of the room. Before he pulled the two doors together again, he bundled up another wad of paper and lit it with the Zippo. He tossed the flaming paper on the pile. He pulled the doors together to wall off the entry. He pulled a zip tie from his backpack and used it to hold the doors together.

He took note of the room's fire sprinkler system, wadding towels at the top of the two open doors to separate the entry from the rest of the room. There was no sprinkler on the entry side. Once he felt he had it about right, he shoved Nadia out of the way and muscled a desk sideways into the entry to backstop the two wedged doors.

A burning odor filled the room. He hit the room's speakerphone button on the nightstand, got a dial tone and then the front desk.

"Yes, Mrs. Rahimi, how can I help you?" answered the receptionist, her English accent lilting pleasantly.

With smoke creeping into the room, Dale said slowly and deliberately, "I am from the Islamic State. I have a bomb and am going to blow up this hotel and everyone in it. You have five minutes to evacuate."

He hung up and pulled a coil of black-and-yellow-striped climbing rope from his bag, along with a tangled set of metal hooks and carabiners.

The rising fumes from the chemical burn made Nadia cough. He ran a knot through a carabiner and looped it around the edge of the heavy bed frame, through Nadia's belt, then his own. He spent ten seconds tying it all together, arranging the rope. He put his backpack around his back, tightened the straps, and turned toward the window, with Nadia close behind him. Back at the burning entryway, he could hear the doorjamb beginning to crack and splinter.

He spread the curtains. The drone wasn't there now. He opened the sliding-glass doors and felt a rush of humid sea air.

There was a loud bang at the entryway. The can of aerosol hair spray had finally blown. Flames were leaping at the edges of his little barricade and black smoke was hovering near the ceiling, now pouring out of the open doors over his head. He heard the ringing bell of the fire alarm and the hiss of the sprinkler. His delaying tactic wouldn't last long now.

He saw the two open doors that had formed his barricade break apart. Through the flames he caught a quick glance of a man's head. One of the "Aussies" from the bar. His instinct had been right. The man was forced to turn away from the leaping flames.

Tethered to Nadia, Dale shoved her to the balcony, squashing her against the railing. He'd threaded the rope through his legs and across a few carabiners to form a crude Swiss seat. He'd bound her to him, wrapping her belt and torso. Wearing gloves, he pushed her hard into the railing.

"Climb over *now!*" he shouted, jostling her against the railing.

She screamed. He didn't care. He grabbed her by the shirt and belt, violently hoisting her over the railing while she continued screaming. Her weight took him with her. They were in free fall for about ten feet before the king bed slid all the way to the edge of the room and arrested them with a jerk. Dale and the woman dangled thirty feet above the ground, looking up at the smoke coming out of the room somewhere above them.

Grunting, he used his legs to push against the white stucco of the building. He released more line, dropping them another five feet. Pushing out again, he swung onto another room's balcony on the second floor. He was out of rope and they were still too high to sustain a fall to the pavement below.

Dangling like a marionette, he used his feet to maneuver, finally hooking a balcony railing with his ankle. Flexing his hamstrings, he pulled them closer to the building and pushed Nadia over the railing. He released his last few feet of line and they fell in a heap on the concrete balcony, gasping. He'd landed on top of her. She was crying, muttering something, her makeup a smeared mess. He undid her belt and pulled her to her feet.

"You're okay," he said, shaking her by the shoulders. "Just keep listening to me and we're going to live through this."

The glass door in front of them was locked. Dale pulled the Glock from his pants and took aim at the glass.

"Going to be loud," he said.

He shattered the glass with five rounds in a circular pattern, followed by a poke from his elbow. Ducking to avoid the falling shards, he made it into the room. Nadia followed.

She was horrified but compliant. Whoever her husband was, he must have told her something about his business.

A steady stream of guests was flowing through the wide-open front doors. As they ran out, a fire-alarm bell clanged insistently, echoing off the tile floors. A few of the maroon-jacketed dark-skinned hotel staff were waving the guests on, hurrying them outside. A police van rolled up, lights blazing. Two heavily armed cops fought against the rush of people to enter the building.

Maria remained standing near the bar, watching them leave. Oleg's voice crackled in her ear. "We're through the door but the room's on fire. He went out the window, but we couldn't see much," he said.

"Anything in the room worth getting?" she asked.

"I can't tell. Fire's keeping us out. We can't get past the entryway."

"Dmitry, what do you have?" she asked one of the other Spetz men. He was in the parking lot, set up in their white minivan, operating the drone.

"He must have come out on a rope. I lost him for a few seconds in the smoke, but the rope is still there. It stopped near the second floor."

"Stay on it," Maria said. "Oleg, get the team back to the lobby. He has to be coming out here with this swarm of people."

Shortly after she spoke, one of the maroon-jacketed men came and grabbed her elbow, pulling her toward the exit. She jerked free and glared at him. He moved on to someone else.

Dale took a quick scan of the second-floor room they'd entered to see if there was anything he could use. An open suitcase on the bed. Male clothing. He went to the closet. There was a midlength raincoat.

"Here," he said to Nadia, removing his backpack and holding it to her. "You put this on for now."

She shouldered into the backpack, sobbing. He tightened down the straps. With the loss of the climbing rope, the pack was significantly lighter, less bulky. Dale unzipped it and removed his ball cap, which he then tightened over his head. He untied the long green shawl from

Nadia's waist, cut a hole through the center of it, and draped it over her, pushing her head through the hole. He arranged the shawl over the backpack, pushing against the fabric here and there, knotting the shawl at the back of the bag.

"I want you to walk behind me, hunched over, okay? Tie your scarf over your head like you would in Iran."

She nodded and did as asked.

Dale put the blue nylon raincoat on. It was three sizes too large, which was fine with him. He tightened his ball cap again and glanced at himself in the mirror. Before leaving the room, he shoved his Glock into his waistband.

There was a steady stream of guests descending the stairs. Dale and Nadia joined in the swell, the hotel's warning Klaxons and ringing bells echoing off the walls.

"Stay hunched," Dale kept saying to Nadia as they moved down the steps. He stole a few quick glances at the nervous people shuffling around him.

When they were in the lobby, a cop was waving his arms, directing them toward the door. There were flashing lights outside. From beneath the brim of his hat, Dale's eyes shifted around the lobby. All was movement toward the door, except for the cops. Then he saw a blond head. She was over by the bar, staring intently into the crush of people, the only civilian standing still.

Dale looked back at the floor and pulled Nadia close to him. *"Hunch!"* he said through clenched teeth, squeezing her arm. "Very important. Make yourself short."

A few seconds later they were through the door, among a milling crowd in the parking lot. Dale kept her moving toward the west end of it, aiming for a gate on the far side that went to the boardwalk. Under the raincoat, the heat was insufferable.

He shuffled her through the maze of parked cars. He didn't have too much farther to go before he made it to his little three-wheeler truck.

"Anything?" Maria said into her earpiece, her rising voice indicating a growing unease. "They haven't come through the lobby. Dmitry, is there another exit?"

"Yes," Dmitri, the drone operator, said. "I can see one in the back, the kitchen. But so far no sign of our target."

"What can you see in the front?"

"It's a huge crowd. Cops everywhere," he said, watching the aerial view in his laptop screen. He was sitting in the front passenger seat of the white minivan they'd borrowed from the consulate. Via the laptop, he made small adjustments to the drone above him. "I parked it at a higher altitude so the cops wouldn't notice. But they probably will soon."

Oleg said, "We're coming down the stairwell now. We'll set up a cordon outside in the parking lot."

The drone operator slunk down as two people approached his car. They were weaving through the other parked cars, apparently on their way to the back gate of the parking lot. After they'd moved on, he looked at them again. The Spetz operator noted the man's ill-fitting raincoat in the oppressive heat. There was something wrong with the way the woman's back was shaped. Together, they looked downright weird. He caught a glimpse of Dale's face.

"Hang on," Dmitry said over the net. "I think I may have him. Was he with someone?"

"Don't know," said Oleg.

"Well, he is now," the drone operator said.

Meredith had commandeered one of the watch stations on the second floor at HQS. She and her team of two deputies had maintained a twelve-hour vigil, waiting to hear anything from John. She was on her fourth cup of coffee, feeling queasy, struggling to stay awake. She decided she'd better eat something. She cracked open the wrapped sandwich from the Agency cafeteria she'd been saving—room-temperature tuna. Gross but better than nothing.

Three televisions over her head were set to all-news cable channels, on mute. Scattered around the cold, windowless room were a handful of desks, phones, and laptops. She'd been there since four in the morning and it was now approaching seven. She knew John was supposed to meet Cerberus somewhere in Mumbai about now. But she'd heard nothing from him, as usual.

"That was Captain Collins from the Marine Air Wing on *Bonhomme Richard*," said Rick Desmond from the desk on the far side of the room.

"And?"

"The Osprey they sent just refueled at the IAF base near Mumbai. The crew's standing by."

"Good," Meredith said.

"The thing is . . . ," Desmond added.

"Fuck," she groaned, swallowing some of the tuna salad. "What now?"

"He says they'll only hang out for another half hour or so. They're concerned about crew rest. He said if it goes much longer, they're shutting down and getting some rack time."

"Bullshit," she said. "Your Captain Collins has no idea what we have in store for him."

By that, she meant that she would rain holy administrative hell down on the poor USMC captain's head from the DC halls of power.

She'd been busy greasing the wheels of this exfil and no lowly captain was about to get in her way. As promised, Dorsey had gotten the director to say something to the Secretaries of Defense and State for a little help, just in case she and her staff ran into issues. And of course, they'd run into issues. The American national security establishment was the world's largest bureaucracy, dictated primarily by inertia, as all such bureaucracies are.

But Dorsey had delivered. Like magic, the Indians had agreed to let an American aircraft enter Indian airspace. Already in the Gulf of Oman, the Marines moved the Second Marine Expeditionary Unit (MEU) farther to the east.

Its flagship was the *Bonhomme Richard*, a small aircraft carrier de-signed for ground support with an air wing of helicopters and jump jets. When within range, *Bonhomme* had detached an MV-22 Osprey tilt-rotor aircraft to an IAF base near Mumbai. The long-range vertical-takeoff and -landing bird had arrived within the last hour.

Desmond was about to respond to Meredith. He suddenly paused, distracted by the TV. He studied the other TV over Meredith's head.

"Huh," the thirty-year-old analyst said.

"What," Meredith replied irritably.

"Look at this." He pointed to the TVs.

Meredith backed from her desk to get a better view. She picked up the remote and turned up the volume on one of them. She was looking at a head-on view of the Hotel Taj Lands End in Mumbai. Smoke was pouring from a window on one side of the building. The chyron be-neath the picture read, "Breaking: Terror Plot at Mumbai Hotel." She listened to the anchor describing what they knew so far: a bomb threat from ISIS, a fire, an evacuation. All three TVs were going to the live feed.

John.

"Call that captain back," she barked at Desmond. "Tell him to get that Osprey to the consulate. *Now!*"

"Do I follow?" asked Dmitry, sitting in the van. "They're almost to the gate."

"No," Maria said quickly.

He could tell by her voice that she was already running toward him on her way out of the building.

She continued. "We need you focused on the drone. Follow them that way." She ordered the team out to the van immediately. "We're coming to you," she said before signing off.

Dmitry maneuvered the drone to get a wider view of the walkway by the sea. There was a huge crowd there now: some who'd come to watch the calamity at the hotel, others part of the swarm of evacuees heading in the other direction. Amid the swirling pack, he had a hard time picking out his target. But then he saw them, steadily maneuvering through the crowd toward a small parked vehicle.

Moments later the Alpha team was at the side of the van, crawling in. Oleg maneuvered himself behind the wheel. Maria was right behind him.

"They just entered that vehicle," he said, angling his laptop so they could see it.

"Where is this?" asked Maria. "Where physically?"

"Over there, through the gate. There's a walkway and then that's them."

"Drive," she said to Oleg.

CHAPTER 27

DALE ARRIVED AT THE THREE-WHEELED YELLOW AUTO RICKSHAW AND shoved Nadia in the back. "Stay as low as you can," he said in Farsi. "We're going to be all right. I'm getting you to the US consulate now."

She nodded, terrified. He took his backpack from her and tossed it on the front seat. The truck started with the key turn and he put it in gear, moving forward slowly, impeded by the throng of people walking all around him.

He laid on the rickshaw's meager horn and decided the anemic squeal wasn't worth it. *Screw it*. Around there people must have to dodge those things all the time. He sped up, seeing the whites of panicked eyes and flashes of anger on faces as he nudged a few people with his hood.

Finally, he broke free onto a small curving frontage road. It was supposed to lead to another that would double back south and then toward a major thoroughfare that would head upriver and east to the consulate. He got the rickety three-wheeler up to twenty mph, pleased with the distance he was now putting between himself and the Taj. But it didn't last long.

He screeched to a halt in gridlocked traffic.

The cops had set up a roadblock. Dale had known the police response to the call he'd made to the front desk would be swift. Back in 2008, real terrorists had invaded the larger Taj Hotel in central Mumbai, killing thirty-one people. The Taj Lands End was a sister property on the water, but the association would be inescapable for the entire Indian populace, especially the Indian Police Service.

He was forced to turn left to get away from the blockade, which would take an hour to get through. He leaned over his shoulder to check on Mrs. Rahimi.

"Ma'am," he shouted over the whining clatter of the two-cylinder engine, "you okay?" He hit a pothole before jumping a curb. He saw her bounce off the bed's rusty metal.

She glanced up at him with a combination of anger and alarm. "I have no idea what is happening," she said. "Who was trying to break into the room?"

Dale was busy dodging pedestrians, occasionally nudging the narrow vehicle onto the sidewalk to get around them. He was averaging about ten miles per hour. The consulate was four miles away.

"To keep you safe, I won't go into details. But your husband has been doing important work to keep peace in the world. I'm not sure how much he told you. I was supposed to meet him along with you and your daughter to get everyone to safety. The people trying to break in back there have other ideas."

She nodded as she repositioned herself on the metal. They banged along for another thirty seconds.

Dale eventually looked over his shoulder and asked, "Why are you here alone?"

"I'm just following Zana's instructions," she said.

"I guess that makes two of us. But where's your daughter?"

"You know about Sahar?"

"I didn't know her name. Or yours. But your husband and I have been communicating for years. He told me he had a daughter. I was expecting to see the whole family for this trip out."

"My daughter died tragically in January," she said over the revving engine as Dale jumped another curb.

Processing this, he was silent for a few seconds, busy. "Sorry. Hold on."

He veered the truck across an intersection and headed into oncoming traffic. Mumbai's chaotic streets had turned into something of an advantage. Several vehicles honked and swerved out of his way. He wasn't sure he was on the right road anymore, but he knew if he kept moving east, he'd eventually run into a river, which would then lead to the consulate.

"You say she died tragically," he said, glancing over his shoulder at her once he'd found some freedom on the road. "I'm very sorry for your loss. Can I ask what happened?"

"She was on the plane that they took down. The airliner in Tehran. She was on her way back to Canada. A student."

Dale was looking straight ahead. After a few seconds, he realized the significance of what she'd said. "Plane crash? You mean the Ukrainian jet the Iranians shot down by mistake?"

"Yes. I was there. I saw the whole thing from the ground."

Dale nodded, considering what Nadia had said. That had been about when Meredith had come out to his house. At least he had Nadia talking now. "What's your husband's full name?"

"I'm not sure I'm allowed to tell you. I thought you would know."

"Ma'am, look around you right now. Do you really think that matters? My mission is to get you and him back to the US safely."

She bounced off the cargo bed again with a yelp. He mumbled an apology and went back to driving.

Half a minute passed before she answered. "His name is Zana Rahimi. He said he met you when you were a student in Montreal. You don't remember him?"

"Well," Dale said, "he didn't contact me until years later. He never told me who he was. He wanted to protect you and your daughter, of course. He's very clever."

"Yes. He's a nuclear physicist who became a computer scientist."

"Where did he work?"

"At first in Tehran at a research facility. But then a few years ago, he started on some kind of government mission. It was somewhere in the northwest. He was allowed home only on scheduled breaks. You'll bring him, yes?"

"Is he there now?"

"I think so. He was home for Sahar's funeral. There were guards watching him. He told me about this trip to India and I started preparing. He was careful not to speak to me after that—for my safety, he said. I had no idea what I was in for."

"Me either," said Dale.

"How will you get him out now?" she asked. "Did he give instructions in the letter?"

Dale veered across another intersection and onto a wobbly bridge. They were crossing over the delta of the Mithi River. There was a larger road ahead that would follow it to the northeast. Once he merged with it, he'd be one turn away from the consulate. But as usual, it was packed with cars that were barely moving. He could see police vehicles streaming the other direction, their blaring sirens making things worse.

"It would seem that your husband thinks it would be safer for you to get out first. Sounds like he used your daughter's mourning period as a reason for you to get out of the country."

"Yes," she said. "I was supposed to go to a yoga retreat."

"Right. But I'm guessing that your husband is attached to some pretty important work right now and isn't permitted to leave."

"I don't know."

"Right. Anyway, I'm sure he has a plan."

"And what is your plan, Mr. Reza? Where are you taking me?"

"Another few miles up the road and we'll be at the US consulate. From there it will be easy. But I want you to stay down, just to be sure. As you saw, there are some people out there that would like to get to you before we get you back to the US."

She nodded. "Do you think—"

Before she could finish the question, two noisy metallic clanks interrupted her. An ingot of metal tore loose and rattled around the bed. A hole appeared in the small tailgate. She screamed.

"Climb up front!" Dale yelled at her.

With his free hand he seized her shirt and pulled her forward. With the other he veered across the street.

"They're shooting at us?"

"Yes."

He turned up a narrow alleyway, clearing it by only a few feet to either side. It widened with sidewalks after a hundred feet. They were lined with people, dogs, buildings covered in bamboo scaffolding. He looked back through the mirror.

"Down!" he shouted.

A white minivan had attempted to make the turn to follow, but it wouldn't fit. It sat at an angle, stuck at a pinch point between protrusions of the bamboo walls. Dale saw a muzzle flash. The bullet hit the low tailgate again, scattering more metal. He guessed the Russians were trying to take out his tiny tires, a tough shot. He could also see that he had the advantage in the smaller vehicle.

He turned right down another narrow alley, back toward the river, thinking he was home free. There was daylight ahead. Through another dark cluster of ghettos, he could see rows of government buildings on a spacious boulevard. But frustratingly, there was a maze of crossing streets to get through first. He told Nadia to lie flat and did what he could to reassure her. He punched a button on his phone.

Meredith's personal cell phone rang. She was at her desk watching the news. Her team had been on and off with the Marine Air Wing and the State Department. She was way, way out on a limb with the brass at this point.

She looked at her phone and saw it was John.

"Hey," she answered, her voice hushed. She left the ops room and leaned against a wall in the hallway, looking for privacy.

"Meth, I got some problems here," he said immediately, shouting over the clattering engine.

"We're not on a secure line."

"Yeah, I know."

She could barely hear his voice over the noise. "I've been watching the news," she said. "Do you have him?"

"Sort of," he said.

Sort of? Before she could tear his head off, he kept talking.

"I've got a situation here, Meth." There was a loud bang as his vehicle jumped a curb. "The op was burned. Same kind of guys that were at my house. They're on our ass right now."

"Fuck. Just give me the tactical details." She was standing up straight, squashing the phone to her ear, struggling to hear him.

"There's a team of shooters behind us. They attempted a snatch at the meet. Suffice to say they really don't want us to get to our destination. We're going to be coming in real hot. Tell them to look for a yellow delivery truck, one of those shitty little three-wheeler things they have here. Can you make sure they know that? I'm basically going to be charging the gate."

"John, wait. Things are pretty tense there right now. You can't ram the gate. They think there are Islamic terrorists on the loose. They're on lockdown. I assume that was you."

"Yeah," he said. "Sorry. I needed something drastic. You have to make it work, Meth. I'm sorry."

She swallowed. "Don't worry about it. I'll figure it out. How far out?"

"Five mikes."

"Just get there, John," she said. "We'll be ready. Just get there."

"I will." He hung up.

Dale pushed his phone back into a cargo pocket. He checked on his passenger. He saw another alley with daylight between the buildings. Beyond it there was what looked like a riverbank. He turned and caught a brief view of busier streets up ahead. A white minivan waited at one of the intersections.

"What the *fuck!*" he yelled aloud.

There was no way they could have followed him. There was no way they could have anticipated he would be poking out here. Even if they knew he was headed to the consulate, it faced the other direction.

Reluctantly, he turned away from the river, back into the maze of little twisting alleys. At the next corner, there was some space between the buildings. He paused for a moment, leaning out his open window, craning his neck to look up at the sky.

That was when he saw the drone.

"Son of a bitch," he said. "Thought so."

It was the same annoying black aerial robot he'd seen back at his hotel room. If it stayed aloft, he was screwed.

"Right turn," Dmitry said.

"I can't," Oleg shot back. "Too narrow."

Maria was behind them, looking at an old-fashioned paper map. "Skip this street," she said. "Is he still going south?"

"Yes," said Dmitry, studying his laptop screen. The yellow three-wheeled truck with the dirty white canvas back was at its center. "See him here? He seems like he's trying to get to the road by the river. But he'll be blocked."

"I don't see him," Maria said, leaning forward.

The minivan hit a bump and all of them lurched for a moment.

Recovering, she looked at the laptop. "Where'd he go?"

Dmitry zoomed in. "He was here . . ." His fingers swept over the keyboard. "He's under this bridge somewhere."

"You need to see what he's doing."

Dmitry nodded.

She put a hand on the driver's shoulder. "Oleg, turn right up here. That will put us a block behind him."

"If we can't see him, maybe he's ditched the vehicle? Could he be proceeding on foot?"

"It's why we need to get the drone low enough to see under the bridge." She paused, looking at the map. "We're in embassy row. I think he's making for the US consulate here." She pointed to a spot on the laptop.

"Right," Oleg said. "Makes sense."

"Get that drone down there," she said.

Dale had pulled the vehicle up onto a curb beneath the two-lane bridge. The bridge was about twenty feet off the ground. It was crowded with pedestrians, motorbikes, and the occasional three-wheeled rickshaw. Below, where Dale had parked, the alley seemed to be a sort of driveway for residences. Dozens of older citizens squatted on the ground or sat in low chairs near small door stoops. A handful of motorcycles went by now and then. By Mumbai standards, it was downright quiet.

After cautioning Nadia to remain still and low in the back of the truck, Dale got out and stood in the alcove of a doorway under the bridge. An old man across the street sat watching him, saying nothing, as though this kind of thing happened every day.

Dale put a fresh mag in his Glock and held it at his side. Even this didn't seem to bother the old man.

There was a buzzing sound echoing off the buildings. Dale pressed his back against the door, listening. It got louder, louder, louder still.

Now.

He stepped from the threshold and saw the little quad copter moving toward the yellow truck. It was twenty yards away, hovering ten feet off the ground, trying to get a view under the bridge. Dale raised his arms in a three-point shooter's stance.

Aiming at the drone's center, he started firing. About half of the shots rang true. The first knocked the drone sideways. It recovered and turned toward him, its camera angling toward Dale. The next hit it square in the face. It started to fly higher. Dale put five or six more rounds into its belly until the Glock's slide locked open.

The drone went silent. Its rotors froze. It plummeted toward the earth with all the aerodynamic aplomb of a flying set of car keys. Dale walked over to the electronic carcass in the street, which lay twitching and humming. He stamped the remaining life out of it with his bootheel.

"We lost visual," Dmitry said, stating the obvious.

He'd watched the man in the ball cap aiming a pistol for just a moment before his screen went to fuzz. He closed his laptop.

Maria looked at the map. "Shit. Our only chance to cut him off is to circle back here and come up from the south."

"We could put Pyotr and Vlad over here," Oleg said. "If they sprinted on foot, they might be able to gain a firing position on this street. Then we drive up from the south to surround them."

Maria nodded. "Right." She turned to the two Spetz operatives in the backseat. "You hear that?"

She explained the plan to them again, using the map. They got out of the van and checked some radio equipment. Moments later they were trotting up the street, sniper rifles slung across their backs.

Dale headed north. The consulate was frustratingly close now. If he had been on the raised freeway up above, this would have been a piece of cake. Instead he'd been busy down there in the alleys, avoiding the Russians in the minivan.

But he was pretty sure the Russians were fucked now. He'd taken out their eyes and he had this goofy little vehicle that was pretty useful for ducking in and out of alleyways. He jammed the accelerator to the floor, picking up speed, jumping a curb here and there in his attempt to break out to a bigger road.

That was when there was a loud bang under the hood. The rickshaw sputtered out.

"Oh, come *on*!" Dale shouted, attempting to restart it. Exasperated, he slammed the dash with his fist. "Piece of *shit*!"

Nadia knew what was happening. She looked on, worried. Two or three curious Indian civilian men in their mid-twenties wandered up to them as the man behind the wheel beat the tar out of the dashboard.

They wore long rags and smiled knowingly. Nothing like seeing someone lose his mind over one of these poorly made pieces of junk.

Dale didn't have time for this.

He hopped out of the rickshaw and pulled Nadia free. Another curious kid on a small motorcycle had stopped. The new kid stood grinning with the other guys. Dale didn't know what was so damn funny.

They stopped smiling when he raised the Glock at them. He gestured toward the kid on the motorcycle, but leveled the weapon at the whole gang to make sure no one got any ideas.

"Off," Dale said. "I need the bike. You guys can have the truck. The keys are sitting in it."

It didn't matter whether the men understood English or not. They understood the Glock. They backed up. The kid got off his motorbike. Dale reached in a cargo pocket and took out a handful of rupees. He had no idea how much money it was—could have been twenty bucks or two hundred. He stuffed it in the shirt of the motorbike kid. He gestured for them to get farther back. Nadia climbed on the seat behind him, hugging him tight.

He put the bike in gear and started toward the river road.

Up ahead in the daylight, he saw something truly beautiful. A massive tilt-rotor Osprey aircraft had slowed over a building, which Dale thought might be the US consulate. Its engines were at an angle as it moved from horizontal flight to vertical.

In the otherwise unworldly hash of the Mumbai slums, it was nothing short of a big, glorious haze-gray apparition. He could see a gunner in the cargo door, God bless him.

Nice work, Meth.

He slowed the bike for a second, tapping Nadia's knee. He pointed at the magnificent aircraft. "That's us," he said, surprising himself with a surge of pride.

Mission fucking accomplished, he thought.

She nodded. For the first time, he saw some relief in her eyes. Dale gunned the bike and approached the river road. When he saw a way to get up on the road via a concrete walkway, he stopped and dialed his phone.

"Yeah," Meth said after the first ring.

"An Osprey?" Dale said, grinning in spite of himself. "Nice, Meth!"

"It took some doing. You have no idea."

"Listen," he said. "Change of plans. We're coming in on a motorcycle. It's red. I'm wearing a blue baseball hat. My passenger is a woman in a green shawl."

"Wait. What? What do you mean, a woman in a green shawl?"

"It's a long story. Just have the Marines ready at the gate. We're coming in hot."

He hung up. He knew she'd be pissed. She'd get over it.

Maria checked in with her two operatives set up on a bridge up ahead. She'd directed the minivan to head up to the north and circle back. Theoretically, they were on both sides of the building now, one north, one south. The minivan was perched at the turn just before the consulate driveway. She saw the enormous Osprey aircraft slowing into a slow-moving hover. Only the Americans flew the Osprey.

The radio crackled. "I have a guy in a blue ball cap and the woman in the green shawl coming up the road on a motorcycle," he said. "What do you want me to do?"

Maria straightened. "It has to be them. Can you get a shot at one of the tires?"

"We're on a bridge over the freeway. Yeah, maybe."

"Do it."

Dale saw some dust rise up in front of him. At the same time, a chunk of asphalt bounced up and ricocheted painfully off his knee, tearing the fabric of his pants. Without even thinking about it, he veered the motorcycle to the right, weaving behind a city bus. He pulled over and prodded Nadia off. He laid the bike down. He could hear the giant Osprey moving to a hover over the consulate. There was a bridge up ahead before the driveway to the building. Shooters. He dragged the bike into an alley; he lay flat on the ground next to Nadia. He'd have to call Meth back. She answered before he even heard a ringtone.

"Meth—we got snipers now, the real deal. Need some help from that Osprey," he said.

"Do you have Cerberus or not?"

"I have his wife. It's a little complicated. He sent her in first. We have to take care of her or he's not coming out."

He realized Nadia was staring at him with wide eyes, but had no time or inclination to protect her sensibilities.

He heard Meredith curse on the other side of the world.

"First thing's first," he said. "I'll get him. In the meantime, I got two shooters on a bridge between me and the consulate. They're wearing light blue polo shirts—cricket jerseys, actually. And . . . hold on." He studied the road ahead. He saw the white minivan parked. "There's also a white minivan just outside the entryway to the consulate. It's a hostile. I need those Marines to nail it or we're not coming in and this whole thing falls apart."

"We can't just shoot up India's largest city, John. That's not the ROE."

"Fire if fired upon, right? Well, I've been fired upon. I'm on the home team here."

Meredith was thinking how this would certainly ruin what was left of her already flagging career. "Even so, they're in the middle of a terrorist lockdown. We're going to scare them to death. This is just—"

"Sounds like the perfect cover story. You nail these fuckers, then tell the Indians they're the bad guys from the hotel. It's halfway true. You'll just need a little time to stage it."

Twelve thousand miles away, leaning against the hallway wall, Meredith considered what he was saying. Impossibly, she thought it was actually a pretty good idea. She allowed herself a very deep sigh.

"Okay," she said. "Bridge outside the consulate, two shooters and a white minivan nearby. I'll see what I can do. We have the air wing on the other line."

Maria was shouting at her fire team, trying to get confirmation of whether Dale's bike had been hit or not. They couldn't tell. He'd taken it off the road. As she spoke, she was watching the big Osprey, which seemed to have broken its hover. It rose about two hundred feet higher and started rotating on its axis. Its nose tilted menacingly as its engines angled forward in a roar.

Toward her.

"Oh, shit," she said. She looked ahead to the narrow alleyways of the ghetto she'd just raced out of. "Head to those buildings. Now! We need cover!"

Oleg slammed the accelerator down and the van leapt over a median. A dozen yards before they were in the safety of an alley, Dmitry screamed. A fifty-caliber bullet from the Osprey's door gunner had come ripping through the roof and entered his thigh. A second one put a hole between him and Oleg. A third shattered the window by Oleg's ear. One second later they were in the alleyway, in cover. The van had slammed into a building, wrecked.

Through her earpiece she heard her shooters reporting on the Osprey. They were running for it. Then nothing. She leapt out of the crumpled van and walked back to the street. The Osprey was hovering over the driveway to the consulate. She saw a man on a motorcycle with a woman clinging to his back speed up the drive toward a line of Marine guards. They let him through and the gate closed.

CHAPTER 28

"NA ZDROVIE!" SHOUTED NIKITA, ZANA'S SCIENTIFIC ESCORT FROM Russia.

He sat at the head of the table of eight intermingled Russian and Iranian scientists, the shot glass poised in his hand. He waited drunkenly for the rest of them around the table to raise their own glasses in salute. In keeping with their religious abstention, the Iranians were drinking apple juice. The Russians didn't care.

"Ochen horosho!" Nikita roared with approval when he saw that the Russians had downed their shots. He turned his glass over on the table, pleased with himself.

Javad, Zana's boss, forced an awkward smile. He stood formally to address the delegation. "I may not drink vodka, but I can and will toast us all for completing phase one of the project. *Inshallah*, may phase two be just weeks away."

One of the other Iranian scientists spoke Russian. He translated for the table. It was good enough for the Russians to pour themselves more vodka. Javad sat down again, smiling while they drank.

Zana downed his share of apple juice and checked his watch. It was getting on toward midnight. He wanted more than anything for these obnoxious Slavs to get tired and let him go off to his room.

They were all finally in Bushehr, staying near the beach at a single-story forty-room hotel called the Parvaz. On more pleasant occasions, it was considered a hotel for family vacations. But the Energy Ministry had chartered the whole thing for the visiting bigwigs from Russia and their counterparts.

Tomorrow they were to take the political leaders from Iran and Russia on a tour of the nuclear power plant a few miles down the road. The Russians had brought media with them. The idea was to show the deep cooperation between the peoples of Iran and Russia toward a successful, nuclear-powered future.

While the Americans might howl about it at the UN, raging on about violations of the NPT, the rest of the world would see the placid politicians and earnest scientists in league together at this sunny seaside town, working on civilian energy. As a side benefit, the Russians considered it a coup de main to be in bed with the Iranians ahead of the Chinese. The more publicity, the better.

After the ceremony, while the media feasted on a PR tour of the plant, the delegation was to peel off and receive a briefing on yellowcake enrichment.

Zana had thought he'd be long gone by now. In accordance with the bereavement leave he'd been afforded since his daughter's death, he'd asked to travel to India with his wife. His superiors had denied the request, but granted it for his wife. The commander felt that with the Bushehr summit on the horizon, it was simply too risky to spare anyone from the Tabriz working group.

Rather, the commander had generously suggested that Zana should join them on the Bushehr trip. The commander thought the change of scenery, the sun, the sea, the professional stimulation would all do his senior enrichment scientist some good. Besides, he should celebrate now that the enrichment issues appeared to be fixed. So here Zana sat, looking at the drunk Russians and the bored Iranians, drinking his apple juice.

Javad leaned into him. His smile was gone—no need to be charming to his own team. "Zana, you're ready for tomorrow?"

An opening, the scientist realized, that could lead to a hasty exit if played correctly. "Javad *jon*, if you don't mind, I think it better if I get back to my room to do work on the presentation. I'm not comfortable with some of the figures."

Javad nodded, grunted. "Probably a good idea. We need to make it look good for tomorrow."

After the millions they'd poured into the secret complex, Zana's area, centrifugal enrichment, had finally begun to come through. With the help of the Russians, the Iranians believed they'd finally produced a small quantity of HEU. More was on the way. Self-sufficiency in nuclear weapons development, the ultimate dream of the Twelvers, was finally within reach.

"You have my word, sir," said Zana. He got up to leave.

Nikita raised another vodka glass toward him and said something indecipherable in slurring Russian. Zana smiled, bowed, and made his way out of the hotel restaurant.

His room was midway down the single-story building. He walked through a pleasant beachfront arcade, listening to the gentle lapping surf of the Persian Gulf just over the sand dunes. It was coal dark out over the water. Bugs bounced against the outdoor phosphorous lights. Two uniformed Guardsmen were leaning against the wall near his room, casting long shadows.

"Going to bed?" one of them asked as Zana prepared to unlock the door.

"I wish," he responded, shaking his head. "I have some work to do." They nodded at him. The *pasdaran* were generally sympathetic to him. He was the nice scientist whose daughter had been killed in the Ukrainian Air disaster.

Safe in his room, he opened his laptop and looked over the presentation materials, making tweaks. Over a forty-minute period, he could hear doors opening and closing down the outdoor arcade as his colleagues made their way back to their rooms.

When all seemed settled, he opened a VPN on a cellular connection and navigated to the Baramar site. He clicked on the designated word on the hidden site and saw a file pop up. He downloaded it. To the uninitiated it looked like electronic gibberish.

He removed the USB stick from the hidden slot in his pocket and inserted it in the laptop. He dragged the file over to an executable on the USB. The electronic gibberish converted itself into English.

His pulse quickened when he saw the message from Reza.

Mr. Rahimi—

May I call you Zana? I finally know your name. Nadia is safe. She is back in Virginia and our people have made her comfortable. I will upload a second file with a message from her and a photo as proof. I've held up my end of the bargain. I need you to hold up yours. Let me know the plan. Our people are very worried since they've lost visibility—I doubt you have much time once the regime realizes she is gone.

Despite the warning at the close of the message, he sighed with relief. He smiled so widely that his cheeks hurt. Nadia was safe. Reza Shariati, whoever he really was, had managed to come through for him against all odds. His instincts about the man he'd observed so long ago in Montreal had been right.

He opened the second file. It was from Nadia; she'd managed to write it in English.

Zana jon,

It is very nice here and the people are very good. You do not need to worry about me. Instead I am worried about you. Please come as soon as you can. We are very concerned for your safety. The people here think you are a hero. Please come back to me soon. Do it for me. Do it for Sahar. When will you come? Mr. Reza swears he will protect you. The woman in this picture is his wife. He is a good man, as are you. Love.

There was Nadia, standing on the Mall with the Washington Monument in the background, smiling. A lean, serious-looking brunette stood next to her. Together they held a copy of the *Washington Post* newspaper in front of them to show the date. Zooming in, Zana saw that it was only yesterday.

He sat back on the bed, thinking.

Nadia's planned sabbatical to the yoga retreat in India was scheduled to last a month. Unless the MOIS men had someone spying on her, then he still had time to bring his plans into effect. He looked at the bedside clock and listened. All was quiet beyond the door. The Russians were finally sleeping off their alcohol. Now was as good a time as any to compose a response. He typed his message.

Mr. Reza,

Thank you for taking care of Nadia. She has been through a lot. You are a man of your word. I am also a man of mine. I need one more week to take care of a few things. I will contact you then.

The next morning, he rose early. He nodded to the two Guardsmen posted outside the rooms and asked if they would mind if he walked on the beach. An apricot dawn glowed over the dusty sea. As he thought of Nadia tucked safely away in America, it filled him with hope.

At ten they boarded a bus for the twenty-minute drive south to the reactor, where they would host the meeting. Four armed Guardsmen sat in the back, acting as security. The four Russians sat up front while the Iranian scientists hovered in the middle. They were very familiar with this seating arrangement. They'd ridden the comfortable coach bus all nine hundred miles south from Tabriz in a marathon of driving.

Except for the uniformed Guardsmen, the Iranians were dressed in shirts and ties. Due to the rising heat of Bushehr, they had been allowed to leave their suit jackets behind.

As they approached the facility, Zana noted the truck-mounted SAMs parked in revetments on either side of the road, dug into the sand, angled toward the sky. The soldiers manning them seemed busy this morning. Diesel smoke poured from the generators at the command trailers that connected them. Considering their deadly purpose and the trigger-happy fools who commanded them, Zana turned away, looking back toward the sea, thinking of Sahar. They were all part of the machine that had murdered her.

When the coach arrived at the security gates for the reactor, Zana had expected to see the long black cars of government ministers waiting for them. But the parking lot was filled with IRGC men in uniforms scurrying about with preoccupied military resolve. The bus was waved toward a side gate, where it sat idling, waiting. A guard told the driver to park there until further notice and keep everyone on board. The driver shut down the engine, which killed the air-conditioning.

Up front, the Russians were sweating, hungover, impatient. One of them threw open a window and complained to the interpreter.

The interpreter turned to Javad, the most senior-ranking scientist and a major in the IRGC. "Mr. Paskarov asks what this is all about. He's worried we'll be late for the meeting."

Javad nodded. "Tell him I'll find out."

He got up and exited the van. Before long, Zana could see that Javad was in discussion with other Guardsmen, who then waved him into a small building that Zana took to be the military command post for the garrison charged with guarding the nuclear reactor.

Ten minutes on, Javad emerged, his face stern. He addressed the ten passengers spread across the bus, the interpreter at his side.

"Brothers," he said in Farsi while the interpreter echoed him in Russian, "the meeting has been postponed. We have received credible information of a threat from the Americans. For our own safety, we are to return to Tabriz immediately. We are all considered to be in secure lockdown from this point forward. No one leaves the bus without an escort."

Six hundred miles north in Tehran, Kasem sat at his desk in the MOIS office building near the airport disguised as the Iranian Meteorological

Center. A young Guardsman knocked on his door and said that Colonel Maloof was looking for him.

Kasem had expected the summons. For the past week, he'd been working with his lieutenants on leaks that might trace back to Reza Shariati, the name he'd picked up from his Hezbollah men when they'd foolishly taken down Yuri Kuznetsov and his deputy.

The search hadn't been easy. The one link they had to work from was the equipment reseller based in Dubai called Baramar. Reza, whom Kasem knew to be a US operative, had worked for Baramar as a consultant. Baramar's equipment had primarily ended up at the Tabriz site. It stood to reason that if there was some kind of leak in the entire *Zaqqum* enterprise, it would be there in Tabriz, connected to Baramar and Reza Shariati.

But over the years, hundreds of workers had come and gone through Tabriz. Many had been in contact in one form or another with Baramar. Still, there were only about fifty who had been given IT access to Baramar directly, and of those, only about ten were still active in the *Zaqqum* program.

One way or the other, Kasem knew that if he didn't plug the leak, the colonel was going to find a way to burn him. He reluctantly made the trip down the hall.

The creases in the colonel's uniform seemed extra sharp this morning. The old man had trimmed his beard and slicked his hair.

He must be expecting a big day with the brass, thought the Quds man.

"All right, Kasem *jon,*" the colonel started. Kasem took a seat across from his desk. "I've been in touch with the Tabriz garrison."

"Have all ten been confined to the base so I can interview them?"

"I gave the base commander the names."

"And?"

"Some of the senior scientists on your list are in Bushehr at the program summit meeting."

"If you'll give me the helicopter, I could be there in a few hours."

"No," said the colonel. "The summit has been canceled."

"What? Why?"

The colonel's eyes narrowed. "Do you remember when I told you the Russians were getting nervous?"

"Yes."

"Well, something's happened. The Russian ambassador seems to think we have a major espionage problem. They suspect the Americans have a mole. One of their men was getting close to exposing it. But he's been eliminated, apparently."

Kasem froze. He thought about the blowback of Kuznetsov and Putov dying at the hands of Hezbollah . . . his hands. If the Russians pulled out, he might find himself in Evin Prison before nightfall.

"Well," Kasem said, swallowing, "that is unfortunate."

"Yes, it *is*." An edge in the old man's voice. "Perhaps as the counter-intelligence service, we ought to know what *the hell* is happening!" He balled his fist and bounced it off the desk.

Kasem noted the display. Something about it rang hollow. The colonel was acting, setting the blame trap that would eventually snare the Quds man. Predictable.

"I agree, sir," he said coolly. "Let me get to those ten men. I'll find our mole."

The colonel eyed him warily. If a counterintelligence problem screwed up the oil-for-nukes deal with Russia, heads were going to roll.

"All right," the senior man finally said. "I've told the base commander to sequester your ten technicians. You can interview them tomorrow."

"Sir, with respect, given the urgency, I should think I need to get up there today."

"Two of the men you want—Major Javad Mirzadeh and Dr. Zana Rahimi—are driving back. It will take them all day."

"May I suggest, sir, that they fly? I should interview them right away if I'm to uncover this plot quickly."

The colonel paused. "Who was your original source for all of this, Colonel Kahlidi?"

Kasem stared at him, unblinking. "You know I can't tell you that, sir."

"Hezbollah, I'm guessing."

Kasem felt a chill. "I can't say, sir. You understand."

The MOIS counterintelligence chief acquiesced with a nod. "I'll tell them to fly the technicians up to Tabriz to save time, as you suggest. You can have the helicopter to meet them there. This investigation is all on you now."

Back at his Bushehr hotel room by the sea, Zana threw cold water on his face and took several deep breaths. He'd sweated through his undershirt.

Before packing up, he decided he'd better change into a fresh one. He needed to look calm. Javad had given them five minutes to pack up and get moving. The bus was already idling.

Five minutes. It seemed like just enough time to do what he had to do. He pushed the window curtains back an inch and saw the Guardsmen a few doors away. Probably enough time.

It could be now or never. Some cold recess of his mind told him it might be his last few minutes of freedom. He would have liked to have gotten another message to Nadia. But there wouldn't be time. He had to prioritize.

He powered up the laptop and found the cellular-data connection. Jumping through the hoops of authentication took another minute. He removed the USB from his pocket and prepared to upload the script he'd devised.

Just as he got to the appropriate page and inserted the USB, there was an insistent knock on his door. The Guardsmen. On this slow connection, the upload would take too long. They would soon grow impatient, which, with the bus idling a few yards away, wouldn't work.

He'd have to figure out how to upload the script on the long ride back to Tabriz. Even if the mobile connection was slow, the drive was long. It had to get done.

He opened the door, his bags over his shoulders.

"Doctor," the Guardsman said. "Major Mirzadeh wants to see you in the lobby. *Now*, sir."

"All right, all right. I'm ready. Let's go."

Javad watched them approaching through the big picture window that looked out on the parking lot. His IRGC-issue duffel was at his feet. The bus was idling nearby, its diesel clacking away.

"I'm ready," Zana said as he approached. "Shall we get on the bus?"

"You're the last one," Javad said, taking a long rude look at Zana. "What took you so long?"

"I've always been a slow packer."

The bus revved up. In a cloud of blue exhaust, it began to pull away from the lot, entering the road, leaving them behind.

"We aren't taking the bus?" Zana asked. "I don't understand."

"The base commander has called you and me back immediately. We've got a plane instead."

Zana's heart skipped. "Just you and me?"

"Yes, and our two Guardsmen friends. We split the security detail between the bus and us. Commander's orders."

"Do we know why?"

Javad didn't answer. He picked up his bag.

A hotel van pulled up. They got in for the short ride to the Bushehr Airport two miles away.

CHAPTER 29

WHAT AN ODYSSEY, DALE THOUGHT TO HIMSELF, WALKING ACROSS THE bone-dry, wind-whipped, sun-scorched tarmac of Turkey's Erzurum Airport. Total travel time had been over twenty-three hours, involving a Kuwait Airways flight into Kuwait City, then Turkish Air to Istanbul, then finally a beat-up turboprop to this Podunk field.

He donned his Ray-Bans and squinted against the unrelenting brightness of the concrete. Another prop plane was spinning up somewhere down the line, crushing his ears. The smell of aviation gas burned his nose. It was acrid and harsh, but then, it probably smelled better than he did.

He'd found a quickie tailor in Mumbai to produce the light gray suit he was wearing. He'd actually been pretty proud of it on his business-class flight out of India, thinking he could use a suit like this. Back then it had looked appropriate for the French oil executive whose identity he'd now assumed.

But after he'd sweated in airplane seats for twenty-some hours, it was starting to grab in all the wrong places. He really needed to find that hotel room.

For a mere fifty bucks a night, the Otel Zade was actually a pretty nice place. It was a damn sight better than that shithole hostel in Mumbai. It was certainly better than the even shittier hostel he'd stayed in after getting Mrs. Rahimi safely off to the USS *Bonhomme Richard* as the first leg of her long journey back to DC.

After tipping his Turkish driver generously—he wasn't exactly sure how many liras there were to the dollar—he left his bag with the bell-man and went for a walk around the block. Tired as he was, he knew the right thing was to conduct an SDR for an hour or so before check-ing in. He'd had a tail since day one of this op, and he wasn't about to start letting his guard down now.

He'd been to Turkey many times over the course of his former ca-reer. But he'd always been down in the extreme south of the country, near the Iraqi border, for his adventures in Kurdistan as part of Broad-sword. He'd never been up here in the eastern province, close to the Iranian border.

He liked what he saw. Erzurum, as it turned out, was a pretty sweet gig. Surrounded by sunny green hills, it was an ancient Anatolian city that had been bandied back and forth between the Persian, Roman, and Armenian empires for a couple thousand years. At five thousand feet on this clear day, the thin air was cool, the sun hot. The mountains in east-ern Washington were like this; it gave him a brief flash of homesickness.

The city of Erzurum's defining feature was a hulking madrasa built in the thirteenth century with twin minarets and Byzantine arches. Dale walked around the thick walls of the citadel, gawking like any other tourist.

He took a few pictures, thinking that its pink spires glowing against the smooth green hills would make an interesting painting, particularly if he could capture some of the lined brown Turkish faces he saw. One could read a lot into those faces.

He scanned the crowd through his phone's viewfinder, seeing no one particularly suspicious, just the serious Turkish men and women. And Russian tourists. That was unnerving, but given the proximity to Russia, unavoidable.

He rounded the corner, doubled back, found a market where he bought a bag of oranges, and kept his eye open for a tail. Nothing. He went back to his hotel room, feeling reasonably secure. He knew the best way to lose surveillants was simply to bore them to death and he thought he'd done a pretty good job of that today. He made up his makeshift bed in the closet, bolted the door, put his devices on chargers, and drew the curtains. He slept for four hours.

After treating himself to a meal in the hotel restaurant, black Turkish coffee, and a couple of oranges, he finally felt fresh enough to handle the call he was so dreading. Meredith was going to rip him to shreds. His list of offenses was long and distinguished.

For starters, he'd ducked out of the consulate in Mumbai as quickly as he'd gone in. Everyone, Meredith included, had thought Dale would be on that Osprey heading out to sea and the safety of an American warship.

But while he needed to get Nadia Rahimi off to safety, he knew she wasn't the real prize. The mission to nab Cerberus was far from over. The last thing he wanted was to get himself folded fully into the CIA's clutching embrace, only to have them compromise him again somehow and then send him back out into harm's way. *Fuck that.*

What was more, Dale was an experienced Navy man. He knew that once aboard a ship at sea, he'd be trapped. His only way off would be at the mercy of the captain. Dale couldn't imagine anything worse than being sequestered on that ship, enduring annoying questions via satellite video feeds from clowns like Rance.

No way. That was another reason he'd fled that consulate. He'd rather face the banged-up Russians than a self-righteously empowered Rance.

Besides, he'd been burned twice on this op now. There was something wrong somewhere back at Langley. He continued to trust only Meredith. Even with her, he felt safe enough to drizzle out only tiny bits of information, lest someone somewhere down the line piece together what he was up to. He couldn't afford that kind of lapse. It continued to drive her nuts, but that was the deal.

He dialed his phone, utilizing the secure app.

She picked up on the fourth ring. He heard a tone as her app also went secure. He realized it was only five in the morning her time. Oh, well. He apologized.

"It's all right," she said. She sounded alert and fresh. "I'm getting ready for my run."

"Are you . . . alone?" Dale was never quite sure how to ask what Meredith was up to these days in the romance department. Jealousies aside, he needed to know for security reasons.

"*Yes*, John. I'm alone."

"Cool. Thanks. How is Mrs. R?" he asked.

"We've got her set up in a safe house in McLean. She's been doing a lot of shopping and yoga. She keeps waiting for her husband to call, worrying."

"So that makes two of you, then."

"Nope."

Failing to find a rejoinder, Dale grunted. He parted the curtains and looked outside. The sun was beginning to set behind the hills. He heard bells somewhere in the city. It really was a charming place. Maybe he'd come back here one day, do some hunting in those hills. Or maybe painting. Both. At least divorce granted him that liberty.

"Anyway, Meth. As directed, I'm checking in to tell you I'm in place. Almost."

"Have you heard from Cerberus?"

"No," Dale said. "But I expect to. He can't possibly have much time and we've fulfilled our end of the bargain. You saw how she wrote him a nice letter."

"After the clusterfuck of getting her out, I'd be surprised if the Iranians don't already know something's up."

"Right. Let's hope not," he said.

"Not to mention, did you see that the Bushehr nuclear summit with Russia got called off?"

"No."

"Yeah," she went on. "It went from being a very noisy PR event to a very quiet cancellation. We're seeing the IRGC spin up air defense radars."

"Do we know why?" he asked.

"No."

"That's a hell of an intelligence agency you've got back there."

"Fuck off, John. Maybe someone knows at HQS, but I don't."

He laughed.

She continued, sounding more like her professional self. "I can only assume it has something to do with the Russians' extracurricular activity in Mumbai. They probably pulled the plug on Bushehr out of an abundance of caution, thinking we might have something. Anyway, it's gotten everyone's attention. The director is running Stalinesque purges, desperate to get some info. He's pretty focused on keeping Active Archer solid."

"Yeah, I figured. I'm working on that," said Dale. "At least you have half the package. Have you gotten any blowback from the Mumbai thing?"

"Not yet. The blonde you saw got away. Nobody else saw her. We recovered three dead guys, though. The two shooters on the bridge and another guy in the wrecked van. All three look like Spetz, as expected."

Dale said, "Yeah, had to be. I'm getting pretty tired of them screwing up the op. No blowback on you specifically? It was a gutsy call to give the shoot order."

"I'll be okay just as long as you can get our man. We played it like you said. Linked it to terrorists. The Russians, of course, have been in full denial. We'll quietly return the bodies to them. Shit happens."

"Nice."

"Right. So, John, this is starting to eat into my run time. What's up? What do you need to get this thing done?"

He yawned. The jet lag was creeping back in. "Well, first of all, I wanted to thank you for the new credos and the extra dough. Worked like a charm. I didn't get a second look coming into either K City or Istie. I think we can assume that Reza Shariati is compromised, so you may as well deactivate that old legend, for what it's worth."

"Yeah, I suppose so. I'm going to miss him—we had a lot of good times once."

In the ensuing three seconds of silence, Dale felt like he was supposed to say something. But he drew a blank.

"Anyway," she said, covering the delay, "I'm glad the new credos worked. You can thank our friends at DGSE for the French passport. What now?"

"Same as before," he said. "I need a weapon. And a ride."

"Do you know where yet?"

"Based on Mrs. R's info, I think our man is somewhere up in the Azerbaijan Province, maybe Tabriz. It fits. Anyway, even if he's still in Tehran, getting through from Turkey is my best bet."

"Okay. I go back a ways with the chief of station Istanbul. Pretty solid guy when it comes to Iranian ops."

She left out that she'd been dating the Istanbul chief of station off and on for the past six months. She'd seen him six weeks ago on one of his periodic trips back to Langley.

Dale left out that he knew as much through Grace. "Thanks," he said.

"What kind of ride are you thinking about?" she asked.

"There was a guy. We used him to get into Iraq. Smuggler. But it's been five years. I need you to find him and direct him east, not south."

"If it was five years ago, then he's probably not in it anymore," she said.

"There's always a guy. You know how it is."

He could hear her sighing. "I'll ask around."

"And, Meth . . ."

"Yes, John, *I know*. I have to keep it quiet."

"Right. Even with that Istanbul-chief-of-station guy. I always thought he was a bit of a douche, by the way." Before she could respond, he added, "Hey, speaking of douches—you're not going anywhere near Rance, are you?"

"Trying not to. I'm going back channel as much as possible. But he *is* my boss. Dorsey's on his ass, so he asks about you all the time."

"He's dirty, Meth. Keep your distance."

"Yeah, well, that's a little easier this week. He's in London."

"Why?"

"Some nonproliferation conference with MI-6 and DGSE. They're trying to figure out how to handle this Iranian thing. They're starting to think it's only a matter of weeks before the Iranians achieve breakout, at least on the low-grade uranium. I think they're really trying to figure out what to do if Active Archer folds up shop. With Cerberus off the radar, our techs can't get into the systems back there the way they used to. We're blind. The Russians are pumping in the 'cake. It's scary."

"Yeah, I know. Cerberus will be back online once I bring him in," Dale said. "He's going to come in for his wife."

"She's already pretty broken up about the daughter. I've been very reassuring when it comes to her husband. Don't make me a liar."

"I won't. Just get me a weapon and a ride. I'll get him. You know I will."

Javad had been particular about the seating arrangements. He'd asked Zana to sit up front, two rows behind the closed door of the cockpit. The aircraft was a Chinese-made Harbin Y-12, an ungainly high-winged dual-engine turboprop from the early eighties. The fourteen seats were in seven rows of two.

Feeling Javad's eyes on the back of his head, Zana slumped against the window, looking at the ground three thousand feet below. On this clear, sunny day, he watched the desert scrolling by. The landscape had gone from coastal sands to lowland scrub to high plains to the series of long, ascending ridges that would eventually scrunch up to form the western edge of the Zagros Mountains.

How he longed to be down there, free of this aircraft. Each ridge he passed seemed like one more step up the staircase to Tabriz, where he was sure he would be facing his doom.

For years, he'd done what he could to cover his tracks with the manipulation of the systems. But the Twelvers who ran *Zaqqum* had done it now. Between the Russians working through the Zippe centrifuges and a concentrated effort on forensic computing, they'd certainly figure out what he'd been doing.

He would be tried and executed as a traitor. But that was only if he lived through the torture he would surely face in Evin Prison first. That was how it always went. He would follow the path of his brother and the scores of other resisters over the years, both innocent and guilty. And thinking of the USB in his pocket, he knew that he'd only delayed them, not stopped them.

The one thing that gave him solace was that he had at least gotten Nadia out. They wouldn't be able to use her against him. Then of course there was Sahar. He stared down at the desert, trying to think only of his family, trying to convince himself that it had all been worth it, even if he had really only bought some time for the rest of the world.

He pressed a finger against the hard lump in his pocket, watching the desert scroll by. Unless . . . If there were just a way to get through the upload . . . it would be his final, lasting revenge. A bit of code to take down the whole array in one cascading fireball.

The Y-12 was amazingly slow. He wondered if they might be fighting a headwind. The crew said they would be cruising at a hundred eighty knots at best. He kept his eyes focused on some scraggly brown ridges up ahead. The airplane's engines were revving hard. It seemed to be straining into a climb.

He started to think about what he was going to say when they finally touched down in Tabriz. He could picture the scene. Most likely it would be the base commander, a few MOIS plainclothesmen, and one of the Russians. He supposed that one of the Russians must surely have found him out and said something. He supposed that was really why they had pulled out of the conference in Bushehr. It was all inevitable, like it had been for his brother.

The aircraft bucked with turbulence a few times as it attempted to gain altitude. Zana watched the ridge, wondering what it would feel like when he finally knew they had him figured out. Would he just admit it and accept his fate?

Probably so. He knew he was on his way to an execution either way. There would be no point of withstanding torture first. If he had only taken the time to upload the software the night before, then it wouldn't matter as much. If they had only just let him take that bus.

He felt the aircraft turning left, heading west. His view was to the south now. He felt the aircraft begin a slow descent. The engines became quieter. Zana wondered what was going on. Tabriz was still a few hundred miles to the northeast. He had yet to sight Lake Urmia, so he knew they were less than two-thirds of the way into their journey. The brown mountains of the foothills receded as the aircraft continued descending to the west.

The door to the cockpit opened and one of the uniformed IRGC pilots shouldered his way down the aisle. He didn't make eye contact with Zana. He seemed focused on Javad, the ranking officer. They had to shout at each other over the plane's engines to be heard.

"Strong headwinds," the copilot said, pointing outside. "We're going to have to set down and refuel."

"We have orders to be back immediately," Javad answered without hesitation.

"Fuel is fuel, sir. We won't make it as it is. There is a small airfield nearby. It won't take long."

Zana chanced a look back at them. Javad's brow was scrunched. He waved the pilot away with irritation, accepting the reality. He caught Zana looking at him and simply stared back. Zana turned his head toward the window.

Perhaps, he thought. Just perhaps there would be a chance that he could upload the software script while they were on the ground. He would need a few minutes of privacy and a reasonable network. Javad, while treating him like a criminal, had at least not yet taken his laptop.

After another ten minutes of descent, Zana saw the field as the transport went into the downwind leg of the pattern. It was little more than a long dirt strip with a few other light military aircraft parked around it. There was another Y-12 and an old American Huey helicopter fallen into rusted disrepair. He saw a single hangar building and a few parked cars.

Zana felt the wheels touch down and the jostle of the landing gear running over the dirt. The rollout took nearly the length of the dirt strip, but the pilots managed to bring the plane to a halt with a groan from the brakes. They turned and taxied toward the small hangar in a cloud of dust. Finally, the engines went silent and Zana watched the propeller in his window slow to a stop.

"Nobody moves," Javad announced when it was quiet enough to be heard. "This is just a brief refueling stop."

The pilots had opened their hatch and thrown open the larger fuselage door. Zana felt a wave of warm air flow into the plane. One of the pilots turned toward them.

"I'm sorry, sir, but everyone has to get off. Regulations. We can't refuel with passengers on board."

Zana glanced at Javad, expecting him to protest. He could see his boss wrestling with what to do. He was a slave to regulations and orders.

"Fine," he said at last. "Let's go. But everyone stays within a hundred feet of the plane with me."

Zana edged out of his seat and slung his laptop bag over his shoulder.

They deplaned and stood in the sun, the two Guardsmen, Zana, and Javad. The Guardsmen were intimidated by Javad and said nothing. Javad was apparently in no mood to speak to Zana, so the four of them just stood there, watching as a squat little fuel truck drove out from the hangar.

It was midday and the sun stood high, beating down on them with high-desert intensity. The wind that had caused them to have to refuel raked the airfield, stiffening the orange wind sock that stood at the junction of two dirt taxiways. Peeking inside the hangar, Zana saw a maintenance crew.

"I have to use the lavatory," Zana said. "May I go inside to find it?"

Javad was watching the fuel truck. He turned and looked Zana over.

One of the Guardsmen said, "I have to go too, sir."

"All right," Javad said irritably. "Stay together. We have orders not to separate."

Zana and the Guardsman walked briskly across the dirt taxiway into the dusty hangar. There were two maintenance men buried to the waist in the cowling of a single-engine propeller plane. The bouncy twang of Azerbaijani folk music creaked out of a radio. A long tool bench stood along the wall. The Guardsman asked one of the mechanics about a bathroom. He pointed to a corner on the opposite side of the hangar.

Given the pace and urgency of the Guardsman, Zana knew the younger man had to go first. He waved the guard inside the greasy bathroom, which had a single toilet and a sink. The Guardsman was grateful.

Zana looked at his phone. There were a couple bars of data signal here on the cellular network. If he could get a few minutes alone in this bathroom, he thought he might be okay. But as insurance, he thought it might be good to bar the door to make sure he wasn't interrupted. It seemed the only way.

He wandered toward a tool bench. There were some emergency kits—life vests, flares, rations—designed to be stowed in aircraft. They were stacked at one end. Toward the other were a set of screwdrivers and sockets on a black cloth strip about two feet long. Zana rolled the cloth around the tools and stuffed it into his laptop bag.

The bathroom door creaked open and the Guard came out. Zana glanced out at the daylight through the hangar bay doors. The fuel truck was there. The pilots were operating it, fastening the hose to a wing tank. Javad and the other Guardsman watched.

In the bathroom, Zana surveyed his options. The door had no lock. He would need to create some kind of stopper to keep it closed. He removed the lid to the toilet tank and looked inside. There was a rubber float. After choosing from the tools, he jammed two screwdrivers into the rubber float and carefully, quietly, wedged it under the door. He thought the friction of the rubber against the concrete floor would form a reasonable barrier.

He immediately opened his laptop and went through the sequence to establish a connection into the servers at Tabriz. He fumbled through his pocket with a shaking hand to remove the USB and began the upload. The connection was pitifully slow. He wasn't sure it would work at all. He waited.

Five minutes on, he knew he was in trouble. The data connection kept dropping, delaying the upload. He wondered if he should just leave his laptop behind, letting it upload while he returned to the plane. He could stash it somewhere behind the toilet. But the broken connections kept requiring him to reestablish it.

He heard the Guardsman knocking at his door. "The major is looking for us, sir. Time to go."

Zana insisted to the Guardsman through the door that he needed more time. Zana ignored the escalating entreaties to return. The knocking became insistent. The Guardsman went away. Zana thought he'd bought himself a few more minutes.

Then he heard Javad's voice. The jig was up.

"Dr. Rahimi, let's go," the major said forcefully.

Zana pleaded for more time, the laptop balanced on his knees.

The major would have none of it. There was a loud bang. The doorstop flew across the floor and the bathroom door burst open. Javad could hardly believe his eyes.

CHAPTER 30

ZANA COULD SAY NOTHING. HE SAT ON THE TOILET FULLY CLOTHED. IN his haste, he hadn't thought to advance the restroom ruse by undoing his pants. The laptop was open on his knees, hands poised over the keyboard. Javad stood in the doorway. The makeshift doorstop had skittered across the floor and landed at Zana's feet. So much for that.

The scientist's analytical mind instantly flipped to three possible actions: lie, destroy the laptop, or fight.

A heartbeat later, the calculus changed. Javad rushed toward Zana, reaching for the laptop. The little bathroom was so small that the door banged closed behind him. The major seized the computer by the screen, wrenching it free of Zana's hands. The hinge bent unnaturally as the scientist tugged back, gripping the keyboard tightly in an attempt to maintain control. The hinge snapped and the laptop came apart.

In the tug-of-war, his thoughts sank to darkness. He was a dead man. The software script hadn't uploaded. Javad would see what he'd been trying to do. Evin Prison wouldn't be brutal enough for what they would have in store for him. And worse, he had failed to get the deadly file in place. They would all be doomed now.

With a great final yank, he pulled the base of the computer. The USB came loose and flew into the toilet. As they both looked at the broken computer in shock, Zana shot out his heel in a savage kick to his boss's kneecap.

Javad's knee buckled. He stumbled back for a moment, then charged forward, freshly enraged. The IRGC major punched Zana once in the jaw with a swift jab. He followed the thrust by grabbing Zana by the collar, pulling him up, half strangling him.

Zana shrank back against the wall, wiggling out of the hold. His foot touched the doorstop at the base of the toilet. Struggling against the two-fisted clasp of his boss, he slumped to the toilet seat and reached toward the floor. In the struggle, the plunger was triggered and the toilet flushed.

So much for the USB. Nothing to lose now.

Zana found the handle of the long screwdriver he'd used to stiffen the rubber of the float.

Javad was yelling, spit flying from his mouth, teeth flashing close to Yasmin's eyes. *"Kha-en, kha-en!"* the major seethed. *Traitor, traitor!*

Ignoring him, Zana maneuvered the screwdriver with his fingers, twisting the long metal shaft out and up. With a solid grip on the dimpled plastic handle, he rammed the tool into the soft underside of Javad's chin, piercing it. He used the heel of his palm to bury the screwdriver to the hilt, driving it home with a savage grunt.

Blood spurted through Javad's teeth and nose as he attempted a scream. Without thinking, Zana shot a hand over the major's mouth, pressing him against the wall. He slid the shaft free, then reared back to shove it into Javad's throat. It went easily into the soft tissue, penetrating both larynx and esophagus in a single stab.

An embedded reptilian instinct had broken loose, causing Zana to thrust over and over, concentrating on the throat. Blood spurted down Javad's collar, flowing like warm oil down the scientist's attacking forearm. He continued tearing at the hole he'd created, destroying Javad's neck, transforming it to a bloody, fibrous gash.

His boss slumped to the floor, suffocating and bleeding to death, bubbles gurgling from his open wounds, his hands futilely attempting to hold his neck together. The scientist had removed the physical ability for the major to take a breath or make a sound.

Breathing shakily, Zana regained his senses. He released his grasp on the screwdriver and let it clatter to the floor. He looked at the remains of the laptop. It was in multiple pieces, smashed to bits. There was nothing on the hard drive he could use. Nothing particularly incriminating either. He'd kept his subterfuge on the USB. He simply picked up the mess and threw it in a trash can.

He glanced down at his dying boss, who was twitching, writhing. The sight brought a wave of nausea. He considered kneeling over the toilet and throwing up.

No time for that. Straddling the major, he opened the sink taps and splashed water on his arms and cheeks. He caught sight of himself in the mirror and looked away, burying his face in his wet hands. At fifty-two years of age, he'd thought any impulse for violence would have long been expunged. Not expunged, he realized now, just dormant.

He forced himself to take a deep breath. Right or wrong, he'd committed to a new path. He put what was left of the tools in an outer compartment of the bag. He wiped the screwdriver free of blood and dropped it on top.

He stepped over Javad, now nearly stilled, his throat gurgling. Doing his best to ignore the grisly sight, he pressed his ear against the grease-stained door, smoothing his shirt, composing himself. He looked down at his shirt, which was smeared with blood. He took it off and reversed it, putting it on inside out. He heard nothing strange on the other side of the door, just the typical sounds of aircraft maintenance: drills, clangs, the humming of the fuel truck's pump, the occasional voice.

With the continued delay, he'd thought one of the Guards might be right there. But he guessed that Javad would have sent them both back to monitor the plane.

He opened the door a crack. As he'd imagined, the Guards were both standing near the aircraft, looking for shade. A long, thick fuel hose with a bright metal clasp was hooked to the wing over their heads, snaking back to the fuel truck, glinting in the sun.

Zana wet a paper towel and wiped the soles of his feet free of blood. His mind had become distant, oddly objective. Javad was dead now.

There was a surreal quality to his thoughts. He now considered himself finished, on borrowed time, about to join Javad in whatever place he was in. There was nothing left to lose. Nothing.

The maintenance men were still digging into their aircraft cowling in the hangar, paying no mind to the IRGC visitors who had dropped into their dusty auxiliary field.

Zana walked the length of the tool bench toward them. He picked up one of the yellow survival packets and continued on, his laptop bag over his opposite shoulder. The movements of his body felt remote, like he was someone else.

On a hook over the tool bench, he saw a key ring with a long gray Toyota insignia and some other shorter keys. He quietly lifted and slid them into his pocket. Fifty feet beyond, the Guardsman who had accompanied Zana to the bathroom looked in his direction and waved. The scientist stopped and waved back, then stepped behind the door to stay out of sight. He looked carefully through the survival bag. He found what he'd been hoping for.

The Guardsmen were shuffling on their feet, talking and gesturing in the unconcerned way of young men, glancing up toward the hangar now and then. They hadn't bothered to look for Javad, which wasn't surprising. Zana could imagine they'd consider every minute free of the major as a reprieve.

Having surveyed the contents of the survival packet, he knelt briefly to put it on the ground halfway between the hangar and the fuel truck.

The hose wound twenty feet between the tanker and the aircraft wing. Zana walked toward the truck along the far side, shielded from the view of the Guardsmen and the aircrew.

Walking sideways to remain out of view, he reached into his shoulder bag and retrieved the screwdriver. He pressed his back against the humming truck, smelling the fuel that pumped from its swollen tank. He inspected the hose. It was old, sunbaked, frayed. With his bare fingers, Zana probed over the coils, looking for softness. He glanced back toward the aircraft and saw that he was still out of sight of the Guardsmen.

At a spot he deemed suitable, he jammed the flat screwdriver tip into the hose. It took several attempts, but he eventually broke through the old rubber. A jet of aviation fuel spurted free, arcing to the ground like blue urine.

Despite having created the breach, Zana stepped back, astonished with himself. He watched the fuel puddling in a dark stain on the tarmac; then he backed toward the hangar, replacing the screwdriver in his laptop bag. He'd now be in view of the Guardsmen, but it didn't seem to matter since they still seemed indifferent to Zana's absence. He bent down and picked up the survival packet he'd dropped to the tarmac a minute earlier.

He backed up several feet, almost to the threshold of the large hangar door, careful to remain out of sight. He rooted through the emergency gear. His hand passed over a rolled life vest, a flashlight, a can of water, and a whistle. Toward the bottom of the nylon container, he found the bulbous gun and its sealed pack of flares.

He'd never fired one before, but it seemed easy enough. Dropping the rest of the gear to the ground, he opened the blister pack, cocked the plastic gun open, and loaded a thick flare. With a wavering arm, he pointed the gun at the growing puddle of fuel beneath the truck. He breathed deeply to still himself. He pulled the trigger.

In his surreal state of mind, he could hardly process what happened next. He saw a glowing orange flash streak like a comet toward the truck. It hit the puddle and burst into an ethereal blue flame, running straight up the leaking hose.

Less than a second later, the truck exploded, leaping off its axles in a violent paroxysm of belching yellow fire. The tank separated from the chassis, which cartwheeled toward the runway, cloaked in black smoke. The large white tank collapsed to the ground and burst, spewing shards of metal, which slammed into the hangar doors behind him, high over his head.

A searing wave of heat knocked him off his feet, sending him backward into the hangar. He skidded across the smooth concrete as burning chunks of metal fell to the ground.

But he was unharmed. He heard the maintenance men shouting to one side. He saw to his amazement that the Y-12 was now also burning at the wing. The crewmen and the Guardsmen were running for their lives down the taxiway, blocked from the hangar by the flaming wreckage of the truck.

Zana scrambled to his feet, then ran into the hangar, past the maintenance men and smoking chunks of debris. His lungs burned. A sensation like rubbing alcohol singed his sinuses. Improbably, the laptop bag was still slung over his shoulder.

He found a set of double doors that went to a small office. Windows showed daylight. Across a few scattered desks, he saw another door secured by a dead bolt and guessed it would lead outside.

On the other side he found a parking lot and four vehicles baking in the sun. One of them was a white Toyota pickup, the favored truck of the IRGC. He heard another explosion somewhere behind him on the opposite side of the building. Turning briefly, he saw a black bubble of smoke floating skyward. *Unreal.*

He punched the unlock button on the Toyota key and saw a truck's headlights blink. He opened the Toyota's door, threw his laptop bag on the bench seat, and fired the engine. He settled behind the wheel and dropped the truck into gear. He drove through the open gate of the chain-link fence, skidding onto the dirt road, still in disbelief that he'd managed to do any of this: he, Zana, a mild-mannered fifty-two-year-old nuclear physics professor.

Dreamily, he sucked a deep draw of smoky air through his rasping throat and pressed the accelerator to the floor. He could see black smoke rising high in his rearview mirror. *Incredible.*

At another airfield three hundred miles to the northeast, Kasem bent under the spinning blades of an MI-8 helicopter. The late-afternoon sun stretched his shadow beneath the slowing rotors as he walked toward the waiting vehicle.

He closed the top button of his dark suit coat. He'd trimmed his beard and shined his shoes. There was nothing more imposing to a garrisoned military man, he knew, than a sharply turned-out civilian who seemed to have the sanction of high government office. For this reason, he'd cast aside his IRGC uniform in favor of the suit.

It was a short drive to Tabriz University. Kasem rode in the back of a Honda Accord with a young Guardsman driving up front. Passing through the gates, he surveyed the academic environs: manicured lawns and midcentury modern buildings stretched over a dozen acres. Clusters of male students walked between buildings, carrying books.

A half mile on, the driver made two turns toward an entrance. A striped wooden bar blocked the road. Kasem's driver said a few words to a Guardsman with a flashlight. The barrier rose.

They'd now entered a part of campus off-limits to students and operated by the Ministry of Defense. Officially an IRGC Army barracks charged with the local defense of Tabriz, this cordoned-off area was manned by olive-uniformed guards in black berets. High fencing and shrubbery kept it concealed from the rest of the school.

The garrison commander was in his mid-sixties. His long black beard had aged to frosty wisps. Kasem knew something about the old colonel, who'd been around long enough to have participated in the revolution forty-odd years earlier. He'd paid his dues intensely enough to have been awarded this sleepy post before he retired.

Putatively, he was in charge of the local defense of Tabriz. In truth, there were operational IRGC commanders spread around the city in charge of air defense and infantry. The colonel was effectively a high-ranking figurehead whose single duty was to make sure no one went down the elevator shafts that led to the underground enrichment labs. For that, he maintained a detail of forty Guardsmen and a staff of ten officers. Every now and then, some administrative trouble might emerge from the labs, but the *Zaqqum* scientists who worked below were judged a quiet, cooperative lot.

Kasem presented his credentials to the colonel, which included a letter from Colonel Maloof. The base commander looked the documents over, sitting imperiously at his desk, knowing he was probably powerless to comment. To save face for a meeting with the counterintelligence man from Tehran, he'd brought a young bearded captain with him, his aide-de-camp. The colonel left most of the talking to his subordinate.

"As you requested, sir," said the young captain to Kasem. He tapped a stack of folders on the desk. "These are the files of the ten men you asked to interview."

"Thank you," Kasem answered. "I have those files myself, back in Tehran. Are they assembled? I'd like to speak to them right away, one at a time."

"Yes, sir," said the captain. "All except two are waiting on the second floor." He pointed up, toward the ceiling.

"Which two?" asked Kasem.

The captain looked nervous. "As we informed Colonel Maloof, Dr. Zana Rahimi and Major Javad Mirzadeh were on the Bushehr delegation. They're still on their way back to Tabriz."

"Yes, I'm aware. But they should be here by now. I asked that their travel be expedited. We sent a plane. . . ."

The captain looked at his commander before continuing. The colonel stayed mute. "Yes, sir, we know. But they still haven't arrived. The plane is late."

Kasem looked at his watch. It was almost six. Maloof had pulled strings to have a plane sent down to Bushehr from Dezful in the early morning. The two scientists should have landed in Tabriz hours ago. He'd have to call back to Tehran and get connected to the IRGC Air Force officer who had somehow managed to botch this simple task. The plainclothes Quds lieutenant colonel rubbed his bearded chin. He crossed his legs and smoothed the gabardine of his trousers at the knee.

"Well, I'll find out why the plane is delayed. In the meantime, I can interview the others." He removed a notepad from the breast pocket of his suit. "While I'm here, I may as well ask you about our two delayed men."

The captain looked at his commander for guidance. A short nod gave him the signal to proceed. "Certainly, sir. What questions can we answer?"

"Let's start with Javad Mirzadeh."

"Ah, Javad," the colonel said, smiling. It was the first time he'd really spoken. His voice was raspy, that of a lifetime smoker. "A true *pasdar*."

"Indeed," answered Kasem, nodding, writing. "Can you tell me about his work here? His access?"

The colonel folded his hands over his belly, smiling slightly. "Major Mirzadeh is a senior scientist, but also an active officer in the Guards. Given his position, we've given him administrative and security duties over the scientists that work for him. He has . . . how many men?" He glanced toward his aide.

"Fourteen scientists, sir, including the two guest Russians here in Tabriz. They're the team that runs the lab protocols. He has a few more over in Natanz."

"He maintains the equipment?" asked Kasem. He circled Javad's name, thinking that his special leadership access would give him free rein for espionage.

"The major's group does it, sir," said the aide.

"And they work with the supplier company primarily. . . . Baramar? Out of Dubai?"

The colonel maintained his modest smile and nodded. "Perhaps not directly. I believe you're aware of the arrangement," he said.

Kasem nodded. It was understood that Baramar, while a legitimate reseller of technical equipment, worked through several front companies controlled by the Guards. "So not necessarily Baramar per se," Kasem corrected. "But rather through one of the front companies."

The colonel nodded.

"Still," Kasem continued, "given the technical nature of the work, they must occasionally have to interface with Baramar directly . . . or the manufacturers. They must have some kind of access for technical resources. No?"

"We give them access to technical servers, support, things of that nature," the captain said. "You are correct that that's necessary."

"And do you keep a log of the access?" asked Kasem.

"The IT group keeps a log of all access that leaves our network, yes. But we would have to go get it. We don't have it prepared."

"But do you know who would at least *have* the access? Who would need it?"

The colonel and his aide conferred in a brief sidebar. The younger man looked back toward Kasem and said, "At a minimum, it would probably be Dr. Rahimi. He maintains the equipment. He specifies the design. We'd expect Major Mirzadeh would have access as Dr. Rahimi's manager."

"So Dr. Rahimi primarily," Kasem said. He took another note. "A civilian educated in Canada."

"One of the most brilliant minds in all of *Zaqqum*," the colonel said. "A good man."

Kasem nodded. "Yes, based on his credentials, it would appear so. I've also noticed that he travels frequently to Tehran. You allow such trips?"

"Yes, many of our people travel home for family visits. In the case of Dr. Rahimi, he has a . . ."

The colonel looked at his aide before continuing. The captain started to say something but the colonel waved him off. The older man pursed his lips and sat back thoughtfully, hands clasped again across his midsection.

"Are you aware, Lieutenant Colonel Kahlidi, of the tragedy that befell Dr. Rahimi earlier this year?"

"Tragedy? No. What do you mean?"

"His daughter was on the Ukrainian airliner that was lost some months back. The one that . . ." He replaced the rest of the sentence with a wincing shrug.

"*Really,*" Kasem said, sparing the older man from having to finish the description. He was genuinely surprised. Kasem's team had missed this connection back in Tehran. "How did he handle that?"

"Like a *fedayee*." A devoted patriot.

"He didn't ask for a leave?"

"We granted him a leave to Tehran for mourning. It was brief. Too brief, perhaps, for such a thing."

"But he was escorted, I assume, per the security policies of *Zaqqum*?"

The colonel sighed. "He was, yes. Two Guardsmen stayed outside his home, day and night. There was nothing to report but the tragic grief of a family. He did ask me if he could take a trip to India with his wife. But with the importance of the lab, we denied it. He took it graciously. A *fedayee*, he cares about our mission here. He has been hard at work with the Russians since they've arrived, preparing for Bushehr. I'm told there was some kind of breakthrough recently."

Kasem wrote a note about the request for India. It was not uncommon for Iranians to take trips to the Shia mosques there. He was somewhat surprised it had been denied after the IRGC had killed his daughter.

"So he just came back here? He left his wife to deal with the grief? Other children?"

The colonel looked sympathetic. "As I said, we denied his travel. I did approve it for his wife, though, who seems to have some health problems. There are no other children. The thought of her being home alone to deal with this . . . It seemed the right thing to do." He shrugged. "I gave her the stamp. She's there now."

"I see," said Kasem. He closed his notebook, sliding it into his pocket. "As you can see by my line of questioning, I'm curious about anyone that had access to Baramar. Unfortunately, that sounds like the two men that are delayed. Can you at least get me the IT records now so I can look them over?"

The two IRGC officers huddled for a moment, discussing how they might do this. As they talked, Kasem felt the phone buzzing in his pocket. He pulled it free and looked at the screen. Maloof.

"Pardon me. It's Colonel Maloof calling," he said to the two officers.

He stepped into a hallway to take the call. He could see through the windows that the sun had gone down. The sky was purple. A few distant lights winked on a hillside.

"Something significant has happened," Maloof said immediately.

"What?"

"The plane with Rahimi and Mirzadeh landed at a remote field to refuel. Some small out-of-the-way training base called Saqqez. There was an accident."

Kasem took a few steps away from the office to ensure privacy. "What do you mean, accident? The plane crashed?"

"Worse. Sabotaged on the ground. There was an explosion."

"Have we . . ."

"I've sent a Guards' platoon to investigate. They've interviewed witnesses. We found Major Mirzadeh stabbed to death in a bathroom. Another Guardsman was killed in the explosion of the plane."

Shocked, Kasem leaned against the wall for support. "And Dr. Rahimi?"

"Missing."

Kasem leaned against the wall, his free hand cupping his forehead. "You're saying . . ."

"It looks that way."

"Okay." Kasem stood up straight. "I'm going to fly there right now and take tactical command of the search."

"Yes, you'd better, Kasem *jon*."

As Kasem wrapped up his meeting with the garrison commander and spat out orders for the flight crew to get ready for a trip to Saqqez, his phone rang again. One of his lieutenants. Annoyed, he answered curtly. He had things to do.

"I thought you should know right away," began the young officer.

"About Rahimi? I already know. Colonel Maloof just told me. I'm going to Saqqez now. I'm going to need you to—"

"Sir—no, not that. It's about the man you told me to track: Reza Shariati. I put a bulletin out through Interpol, like you said."

"And?"

"And . . . as it turns out, there's already a Red Notice out for that name."

"Really? By who?"

"Issued by the Russian Foreign Ministry," said the lieutenant.

"When?"

"About six weeks ago."

The leak. Kasem suddenly put it together. Kuznetsov had known about it. But he hadn't had the goods yet, so he kept things shadowy.

Reza Shariati, the fake contact at Baramar, was the CIA handler for Rahimi. It all fit. But Kasem wasn't sure what to do with any of the information yet.

"That's all you have?" he asked the lieutenant. "That's why you called?"

"Sir, there's more. The facial recognition system detected this man. Ninety-five percent probability."

"Here? You're saying he's here? In Iran?"

"No, sir. Turkey."

Then that's it, he thought. The man he knew as Reza, the man who'd mysteriously saved his life by the Tigris River, was coming to get his spy.

CHAPTER 31

MEREDITH WAS SLEEPING SOUNDLY, DREAMING NONSENSICALLY ABOUT her time at the Farm. Somehow John was there too, even though their training hadn't overlapped in the real world.

He seemed inexpressibly sad for some reason. Her dream was filled with the stress of trying to keep his spirits up while she missed required training briefings. The missed meetings were going to get her bilged out of the elite Clandestine Services program. John was being confoundingly dense, morose, unable or unwilling to comprehend that. Even in the otherworldliness of her dream, she could feel a buzzing sense of irritation.

There was a loud jangling noise. As she shook herself awake, it took two more trills before she realized what was happening.

She switched on a light and looked at the glowing smartphone screen on her nightstand: of all things, a cell call from the secure burner phone they'd given Nadia Rahimi. She forced herself to take a deep breath and run a hand through her tangled hair, pulling her mind out of the dream, back to reality. Once there, she felt even worse.

Nadia shouldn't have been calling. It was a flagrant violation of all the instructions and protocols Meredith had given the middle-aged Iranian woman, who was tucked into a safe house a few miles away in Arlington. But it was just shy of five in the morning. It must be important. Meredith answered gruffly.

"I've heard from Zana," Nadia said at once. Her voice was shaking, rushed.

"Okay." Still raw from the dream, Meredith's mind was slow to comprehend. She asked for Nadia to repeat what she'd said. On hearing it a second time, it clicked.

This was going to be bad.

Meredith had been hoping that John had gotten to the scientist by now and that the two of them were on their way out of the country. If Cerberus was calling directly, something must have gone very wrong.

"What is it? What did he say?"

"It was via text. He wouldn't tell me much. He just said that he is safe but that he wants to talk to you."

"Me?" She was sitting up now. "How does he even know about me?"

"I told him in my letter about you. I told him you are Mr. Reza's wife."

Meredith didn't bother to correct her. "All right, Nadia. I'm going to need his number. As soon as we're done, you'll text it to me. Got it?"

If nothing else, she'd need NSA to scramble the phone's geolocation, throw off any unwelcome surveillance.

"Yes. But I also already gave him your number. I don't know when he will be able to call. He only told me not to worry and that he would be in touch."

Goddamn it, Meredith thought. She absolutely hated this lack of control. But she needed to keep Mrs. Rahimi on ice.

"It's all right. At least we'll have a way to communicate now. I'll set something up with him. Just text me that number when we're done."

"Okay. I just wanted you to know first."

"Thanks, Nadia. You did fine. But remember what I said about not contacting me directly? You need to use the phone at the house and call the duty officer. Remember that talk?"

"Yes, I remember."

The older woman sounded deflated. Meredith would have to address that. Both Rahimis would be more cooperative if they remained hopeful.

"It'll be okay," Meredith said.

No, it won't, the veteran handler thought. Active Archer had seemed

cursed from the start, a cascading series of mishaps since that first briefing in Dorsey's office. She swallowed her irritation, concentrating on
the frightened woman on the line.

It took another three minutes of soothing before Meredith hung up.
Once the phone was back on the table, she pressed her palms to her
eyes. Why hadn't John checked in? She picked up her iPad, secured
her reading glasses on her nose, and looked through the messages in her
secure app, the way John was supposed to get to her. Nothing.

Inconsiderate prick.

The last she'd heard, John had met with Steve Chadwick, chief of
station Istanbul. If she needed to, she could check with Steve on John's
whereabouts—but she'd rather not. She was supposed to be the handler
for this op, and she didn't like showing that kind of incompetence. Besides, having dated for a few months, she and Steve had a complicated
relationship.

What a mess, she thought, sighing.

A run would have to be her therapy. She forced herself out of bed,
feeling uneasy, looking for her tights. Her phone chirped. Nadia had
texted the number. Meredith would deal with that in a minute.

The phone rang while she laced her shoes. She willed it to be John.
But it wasn't. Maddeningly, it was HQS, Langley. Just what she didn't
need right now. She coached herself to cool off, lest she say something
she'd regret.

"Morris-Dale," she answered, initiating the secure connection.

"Hey, Meredith, it's Desmond."

"Morning, Rick. What's up?"

"Something happened in Iran a few hours ago. Military communications are lighting up. Air defense radars are going nuts."

"The whole country?"

"The tactical activity is concentrated in the northwest . . . Azerbaijan
and Kurdistan provinces. Not too far from Tabriz."

Tabriz, she thought. John had said he thought Cerberus might be in
Tabriz. Desmond knew as much.

"There's more," her deputy said. "We have Echelon intercepts. IRGC commanders are ordering troops to a small airfield. It's basically a dirt strip, but the name keeps coming up in their conversations. It's called Saqqez. Seems to have been some kind of attack there or something. Some of the wilder IRGC guys are saying it's an American strike."

"Ha," she said mirthlessly, stretching a hamstring. "I wish. Can we get eyes over it?"

"Negative, no imagery. Too deep in-country and out of range of our current satellite paths. We can retask, but that'll take a while. It would be at the NCA level."

"Roger that. Okay. Any sign of John?"

"Not since he made contact with Istanbul two days ago."

She'd finished stretching by now. She was standing at her front window, looking out on a shining street. Rain—a perfect complement to her sinking mood.

John was supposed to be headed toward the Tabriz area. Not only was he silent, but the IRGC hornet's nest had been kicked. Not good. Not good at all. She was sick and tired of being in the dark, learning of everything thirdhand. She had half a mind to book a flight for Dubai to get back to her field team as soon as she hung up just so she could operate near the same miserable time zone.

The phone beeped twice in her ear while Desmond was giving more details about SIGINT activity. Another call was coming in through WhatsApp. There was no name, just a number that began with +98— Iranian country code—the same as what Nadia had just texted her.

"Rick, sorry. I have to take this. I'll be in as soon as I can."

She switched to the incoming line and took a quick breath. "Hello," she said.

"I think you know who I am," replied a male in heavily accented English. A heavy wind ruffled in the background, distorting his voice.

"Yes, I think I do. Your wife told me you might call," said Meredith.

"Something has happened," the man said.

Meredith was scrambling at the table by her unmade bed, looking for a way to take notes. She found a pen but no paper. All she had was a half-finished paperback, a guilty-pleasure bodice-ripping romance novel. She opened the back page and wrote down the name of the air-field Desmond had just given her: *Saqqez*. There was so much wrong with the way this was going down.

"Wait," she said to the man in the wind. "Before you go on, I need to make sure you are who I think you are. Okay?"

"Yes, okay. But please hurry."

"Fine. What's your wife's middle name?"

"Elaheh."

"What's her birthday?"

"July twenty-seventh."

"Okay. You passed. What's happening? Why are you calling?"

"You are Reza's wife?"

She paused a moment before answering. "Yes. But you must understand, this line isn't secure."

"I do understand. I have borrowed a phone. It is not my number."

"That's good. Keep it. But take out the SIM and power it down as soon as we're done. Only turn it on when safe and to check in with me every day at this same time if you can. Reza needs to meet you. I'm coordinating that. You understand?"

"Yes. But I am in hiding now. I've had to run for it. I've lost my way to communicate with him. That's why I'm calling you."

She took a note. That meant he'd lost access to the Baramar servers. John wouldn't be able to initiate communication with him. Meredith would have to be the go-between. "What do you want to tell him?"

"You mean, you don't know?"

The man sounded frustrated. She could hear him take a strained breath, an exasperated sigh.

"Do you understand, Mrs. Reza, what I have in my head?"

"No, tell me."

"Your access. *The* access. If anything happens to my wife—"

"Whoa." *The balls on this guy.* She realized what John had been dealing with. "Hold on, sir. Your wife is just fine. Nothing is going to happen to her. We're just trying to get you to safety now."

"I trust only Reza to do that. I do not know you."

"You called *me*," she reminded him. "I'm his . . . wife. You'll have to trust me."

Another gust of wind whipped through the phone. It sounded like a burst of static. He said, "I have to tell you something—now. Important."

"Okay. I'm listening."

"They've done it."

"Done what? Who?"

"The scientists. The thing you've been trying to prevent. Critical mass."

No! Meredith thought, reeling. She felt a cold stab in her gut. Her mouth opened and closed twice, saying nothing.

The Iranians had achieved breakout.

It was all for naught, the whole goddamned thing.

"You're sure?" she said weakly.

"Yes, they had help. I was compromised. Russians."

Russians. She thought of the surveillance, the roll up in Dubai, the Spetz Alpha teams tracking John. Had she been the thread they'd pulled to have it all unravel? Was her screwup on Sagebrush and subsequent unmasking the thing that finally, indirectly allowed the Iranians to achieve breakout? She felt sick. Angry. Hurt.

"Why do we need you?" she asked rudely. "What's in your head that's so important?"

"Everything. I can undo it."

She listened to the ruffling wind. "There's still hope to turn this around?"

"Yes. If you act quickly with the information I have. But you have to get me. Now."

Seriously, the balls on this guy, she thought again. But at least there seemed to be a chance. "We'll get you. *Reza* will get you."

"Tell me where I'm supposed to meet him."

"Hold on."

She reached for her iPad. She opened Google Maps and zoomed in on Iran. She checked the note she'd taken when speaking with Desmond. *Saqqez.*

She typed the name into the search bar. The description of a dusty city on a river popped up instantly. Kurdistan Province. One hundred twenty miles south of Tabriz, fifty miles east of the Iraqi border. She knew John was coming south through Turkey toward Tabriz. Where to have them meet? The IRGC would probably set up a cordon around Saqqez, given what Desmond had just told her. She knew she had to get Cerberus out of there.

Kurdistan Province. John had loads of experience with the Kurds. He certainly wouldn't appreciate that she was calling the shots, but an exfil through Iraq made the most sense for everyone, John included. She could surge military resources out of Baghdad if she needed to.

She needed to make the call. Now. Who knew if she would really get the chance to speak with him again? *Fuck it.*

She zoomed in on a village that she thought would work as a rendezvous. "Okay. I want you to make your way to, ah, a village called Alut. A-L-U-T. Did you hear me?"

"Yes." More wind through the phone.

"Commit it to memory. Now take out that SIM and do *not* try to contact your wife again. That was dangerous. If you do that, you endanger her and yourself. You check in with me only when safe, every twenty-four hours if you can. Do you understand me?"

"Yes, I understand you. But how will Reza find me?"

"For now just get to Alut. I'll give you further instructions on how to meet. Let me worry about that."

Let me worry about that, she repeated to herself, exhaling. She was certainly worrying now. She was the only one in the US who knew the Iranians had achieved breakout.

As Rance walked down the sidewalk with a barely suppressed grin on his face, the clouds parted. A rare London sun lit the imposing White-hall buildings a shade whiter.

A good sign, he thought.

He was glad he'd dismissed his driver and decided to walk to the tube. It gave him some time to think. Walking around cities had always done that for him, all the way back to his early days as a new buck spy posing as a foreign service officer in Buenos Aires almost thirty years ago.

He'd just finished a meeting with an MI-6 colleague in the Defence Ministry building and was now strolling past the busts of imperial Victorian conquerors with a feeling of kinship, just the inspiration he'd been looking for. The e-mailed summary he'd just digested on his phone had put him in this happy place. It told him that the director had called Dorsey into his office for a briefing on Archer. The director was not happy. Things were not good, not good at all. Archer was failing.

And there it was.

Once terrified that the great leaning shit pot known as Active Archer would canter and spill on him personally, Rance had now come to realize that the stain would miss him. What was more, if played deftly, there was even the possibility the stinking, spreading mess might sweep away the bevy of nuisances that had dogged his career going all the way back to his days as deputy Baghdad chief of station and the ridiculous accusations about his judgment during Broadsword. Then there was this latest reprimand from Dorsey about Genevieve. That would be gone with Dorsey himself.

How perfectly apt that would be, he thought now, passing through the security gates toward Trafalgar, walking along the crowded sidewalk, perfecting the political angles. All of it would be swept away with the tide.

Stopped at a traffic light, he watched a red double-decker strain through a turn.

There would be no escaping it for Dorsey now, he thought. As NCA had taken an interest in saving Archer, the head of Clandestine Services had stupidly stepped into the breach, owning it, blowing it, allowing the Iranians to achieve breakout.

Yet it was Dorsey who'd pushed to involve the Dales. It was Dorsey who'd removed John Dale's suspension. It was Dorsey who would have set in motion the chain of events that would lose Cerberus. Owned, owned, owned.

Idiot, Rance thought, rounding a corner, shouldering through a mass of tourists toward Charing Cross. He'd warned all of them about the foolishness of trusting John Dale, an untrustworthy wild card if ever there was one. Dorsey, signing his own death warrant, had even doubled down against Rance's advice, which, thanks to all of those meetings with General Counsel Sheffield, was quite formally on the record.

Moreover, Rance thought, his mind pleasurably aglow, there wouldn't even be guilt by association since Dorsey had removed Rance from the equation. Dorsey had instead sent him on this boondoggle to London to talk about the vulnerability of African rare-earth minerals with MI-6. As if that mattered now!

It had been meant as exile—no one cared about Africa, least of all him. Yet here it was. Far from exile, it had proven to be a lifeboat. Rance wouldn't even be in *town* when the ship of Archer finally sank.

A masterstroke, he thought, smiling, shuffling down the steps to the tube, pleased to be ducking into some shade. The long walk had quickened his pulse and dampened his forehead.

He inserted his ticket into the turnstile and descended the long, tiled subway stairs, roaring with echoes of fellow passengers and the rushing wind of trains. His mind plumbed in the murky depths of Archer outcomes, he headed in the wrong direction, toward the wrong platform. Suddenly aware, he doubled back on the stairway, moving against the crowd.

In doing so, he had a brief collision with a fellow traveler in his mid-twenties. He didn't think much of it, given the tightly packed crowd. The young man wore an Arsenal hoodie pulled over a shaved head. He grunted before dashing off in the other direction.

Clod, Rance thought. As far as he was concerned, no one under the age of forty had any manners anymore, even in London. Maybe he should have taken his Agency car after all, he thought.

But then Rance went back to congratulating himself. Hanging on a strap, jostling his way under the city streets toward his hotel, he praised his own handling of Meredith. Knowing as he had that the odds of

John Dale coming through were long, he'd given her all the leeway she could have possibly wished for.

It was Meredith's authorization that had torn up a city block in Mumbai only to emerge with the wife of the asset rather than the asset himself. It was Meredith who had insisted on keeping everything secret from Rance. In the sum total of events, Rance now realized that his hands were antiseptically clean in the disaster that would forever be associated with Archer. Game, set, match!

Exiting the tube and shouldering through shoppers on Oxford, surfing ever farther on his own celebratory wave, he decided to treat himself. He ducked into a tailor and looked at bolts of wool, wondering if he might be in town long enough to order a new suit.

Thinking that prospect over, he stood in front of a mirror, holding various shades of neckties to his face. In doing so, he didn't bother to notice the young man with the shaved head under the Arsenal hoodie who walked by the shopwindow.

The twenty-eight-year-old football fan was careful not to make eye contact with the man trying out ties in the window. He ducked into a pub across the street and took a seat near a window, watching Rance. He looked down just long enough to type out a text: *Made a stop. But think he's on his way to the Langham. Prob be there in ten.*

Sure enough, Rance concluded that he did deserve that suit. He made an appointment for a measuring tomorrow morning and then continued on his way across Oxford Circus.

By the time he crossed through the heavy leaded glass doors of the stately Langham Hotel, he was in high spirits, imagining himself in his new suit, commanding the Clandestine Services from Dorsey's office. The sun, the clothes, the self-immolation of Dorsey and the Dales, and the picturesque streets of London had produced a perfect cocktail of satisfactory flavors.

Just then, when it would have seemed that life could not possibly have gotten any sweeter, it suddenly did.

"Well, hello!" he said to Genevieve Lund.

He could scarcely believe his eyes. She was sitting in a chair in the lobby across from three other business executives. Her long legs were crossed. He caught a tantalizing glimpse of thigh under the short skirt of her business suit. When she stood to shake his hand in a display of appropriate commercial courtesy, his knees nearly gave.

Standing on her four-inch heels, she was an inch taller than him.

"Oh, my," she said, putting a hand to her breast.

It was a little after five. There was a mixed drink on the table next to her, something bright and fruity.

"Fancy meeting you here," she said with a knowing smile and a blush. She pumped his hand twice before letting it go.

"I must say, it is quite a coincidence," he murmured, dumbstruck.

She explained that she was at the Langham for a conference on international shipping. The three men with her all worked for her company, Stoke Park. He went through the perfunctory introductions. He forgot each of the men's names as soon as he heard them.

During the cocktail hour after the meeting, Genevieve started to relate a story. Her compatriots joined in, talking about something that had happened in the courtyard out back. As they recounted the incident and began to laugh, Rance felt her hand run down his back.

"Well," one of the men said, "we should probably get back to it."

Yes, they all agreed. Genevieve said she would be along in another minute. Suddenly, she and Rance were alone, standing face-to-face among a crowd of strangers.

She just looked at him. Her smile was gone, replaced with an icy feminine glare.

He was suddenly unnerved, awash in guilt, a pang of fear. He'd jilted her. He'd done it after Dorsey had called him on the carpet to tell him it had all been too risky. Rance had done his duty, ended his affair with Genevieve. But now here he stood. What could he do? It hadn't been his decision. Besides, thanks to Archer's failure, Dorsey was finished.

"I assume it had something to do with your wife," Genevieve said coldly, doing her best to play the part of the disappointed mistress.

"No, it wasn't that." He took her hand in his, deeply aroused by the pout of her perfectly shaped lips. "It was something else. . . . It had something to do with work. The hardest thing I—"

"Spare me." She looked away, dissatisfied, extending her lips farther.

"No, really," he said.

He caressed her fingers. He realized he would say just about anything now. Her peevishness was *such* a turn-on. The old tingle was back. And, he reminded himself, Dorsey was finished.

"Meet me for dinner tonight," he said.

A few hours later in an Italian restaurant four blocks away that Genevieve had called her favorite, Rance's phone rang. Putting down his pinot noir, he glanced at the screen. The call was coming in over the secure app.

Meredith. *Fuck.* There he was, having painstakingly repaired the damage in his relationship with Genevieve, on his way to a perfect ending to a perfect day, when none other than Meredith should call to screw it all up.

Rance thought about the time difference. It would be midday in DC now—prime working hours. Meredith hadn't called him since the botched Mumbai op, in which Dale had duped all of them by bringing in Cerberus's wife.

Rance had liked it that way. The less he heard from her these days, the better. Let her hang herself.

He looked at Genevieve, flashing the buzzing phone in front of her. "I'm sorry. I know this is rude, but I have to take this. It's work."

"As long as it isn't *her*," said Genevieve, puckering her artfully painted mouth.

"Well, it's *a* her," said Rance. "But not *the* her. Work."

He stood and made his way toward the entry, where he ducked down a hall.

"*What?*" he said, irritated.

Meredith was nonplussed by the tone. "Sorry, Ed. Am I . . . am I interrupting something?"

"Huh? No, not that. I'm at a dinner . . . the MI-6 thing. You know. Anyway, I assume it's something urgent."

"It is," Meredith said. "I'm getting ready for the Cerberus meet."

Shit, Rance thought. By now he'd figured that Cerberus was rotting away in some Iranian jail. The op still had a chance?

"And? Where is he? Does John have him?"

"No, not quite. But they're getting ready. I'm putting together the exfil."

"Where?"

She hesitated.

He clenched his free fist. It was back to the old excuse that John's whereabouts were to remain only between the ex-husband and his ex-wife handler. *God,* he was sick of these two. But he knew now they'd been outmaneuvered. The more they left him out of it, the deeper they dug their own graves. Fine.

"Never mind," he said, preempting her. "I know the drill. So why are you calling?"

"I need your authorization to go back to my team at Dubai Station. It's just too hard to control the op from back here."

"So Cerberus is still in Iran, then? You can admit that much to me, Meredith."

"Yes, Ed, he's still there. But we've got a good exfil shaping up."

"Fine," Rance said. He was watching Genevieve. She was giving him that come-hither look. "You have my authorization to do whatever you need to do," he said.

Walking back toward Genevieve, he asked himself how he should play it if Meredith and Dale actually managed to get Cerberus back. If she was somehow successful, he would need to maneuver himself to be able to share in the credit—if the asset even mattered at that point. He didn't think anything would come of it, but it was hard to say, an angle to be covered. The Dales could be surprising.

CHAPTER 32

"JOHN DALE IS HEADED TO IRAN," MARIA SAID INTO THE PHONE.

She was in the third-floor Stoke Park Insurance office in Farringdon. Just as soon as she could slither out from under Rance's sweating, heaving body to download the take from his phone, she'd returned here, anxious to call Oleg. It was three a.m.

She wanted a shower. She wanted to wash Rance off of her. But duty called. She'd arrived and immediately analyzed the audio file. It was good. Really good.

Oleg had been asleep. He was in Istanbul, where it was now five in the morning. "How do you know?" he asked.

She stayed silent, declining to answer.

Oleg knew what that meant—Zoloto had her ways. There was an unspoken agreement between the two professionals that they shouldn't discuss the tradecraft of their respective callings. It was one of the things they liked about each other.

He corrected himself. "Never mind. Sorry. *What* exactly do you know?"

"I picked up one end of a phone call from Meredith Morris-Dale. Before I tell you—any sign of Dale over there?"

The Interpol Red Notice had picked Dale up entering Istanbul. They knew he was under a French passport using the name Etienne Crochet, an executive with Shell Oil. As soon as the Red Notice came in, Maria had dispatched Oleg to Istanbul while she stayed to work Rance.

"Not since Erzurum. Either Turks are lazy about reporting travelers or he switched passports again. Do we know why he's going to Iran?"

"Now I do," she said, smoothing the hem of her skirt. "They have a spy. The code name they used is Cerberus. Apparently, Dale is on a mission to exfil him. The wife is going to run the op from Dubai. She's on her way there from the States. Apparently, she's his handler."

"Have you briefed Yasenevo yet?"

"Not yet."

She paused. When she'd gotten back to the office, her first thought had been to file the new intelligence in the SVR database, per the standard protocol. But she'd hesitated—hesitated because she wanted to test it with Oleg first.

He grunted over the phone. "It's your call. You want me to stay on here?"

She looked out the windows at the dark city. There was a low crescent moon on its way down, a few silver clouds gliding by the newer glassy buildings across the street. Far off in the other direction, there was a hint of purple dawn.

"Kuznetsov's Red Notice is still in effect for both of the Dales, right?"

"Yes."

"We know he's on his way to Iran and she's on her way to Dubai . . ."

She paused a moment, thinking, weighing what she was about to suggest carefully. She'd been trained to operate independently, to take the initiative however it presented itself. But there was a fine line between that and willful disobedience. She knew she should file the report with Yesenevo. But she had other ideas—and she was reasonably sure Oleg was an operative she could lean on.

"Oleg, why not just get in position and wait? We could snatch both of them ourselves."

"Without getting orders first?"

She looked around the dark office, a breath of vulnerability washing over her. She was almost certain FSB couldn't monitor them. Supposedly, SVR had encryption that was unknown even to the rest of the

Russian government. That was what they'd told her. But the two organizations were infamous for lying to each other.

"I *will* tell them," she said for the sake of the assumed monitors on the other end of the call. "But speed is important here. We can't afford a delay."

There was a long pause on the other end of the line. "You sure?" Oleg dragged out the words. He knew what she was thinking. He knew it perfectly well.

"Yes, I'm sure," she said, underlining her conviction. "They've taken down five of us, Oleg. Five. We need to get them. Both of them. This is hot pursuit. We need to act now."

"You're the boss. Besides, I've never been to Dubai."

Maria breathed deeply, swelling with relief. He was on board.

"She's mine," she said. "I'll be going to Dubai. I need you in Tehran."

He grunted. "I figured. I want him anyway. Fucker has killed four of my men, not to mention Kuznetsov."

"Can you handle him alone?"

"*Da.* Given the speed with which we'll want to do this, I'll have to. Besides, I can't take a whole Alpha team into an allied country, especially if we're not going to wait for HQ."

"Right."

"You sure it's Tehran?"

"No. Might be Bushehr. Wherever they've stashed Cerberus, their asset. If Cerberus had something to do with the Bushehr summit meeting, then maybe Dale's headed there. Wherever Dale lands, he'll pop on the Red Notice."

"Maybe not. Who knows how he's getting in? You think you can access any other sources that could help pin this down?"

"The best source will be Meredith Morris-Dale herself. Based on my intel, I know she's in contact with Cerberus. I'll use her to get to Dale. When you get Dale, you get that asset. I assume you still have access to scopolamine."

"I have a kit with me. I can't say I can be trusted to be gentle with Dale, though. It may take more than drugs."

Kasem hurried across the tarmac at the small Saqqez airfield to the churning helicopter. The closer he got, the more dust from the spinning rotors pelted him. He pulled the T-shirt he wore under his military blouse and tented it over his nose, straining for a breath of fresh air, instead getting a whiff of his own body odor. He took one final glance back at the young captain he'd left in charge, a company commander of the local Guards regiment. The captain waved at him.

In the greasy, noisy helicopter, a crewman helped Kasem to a seat. The Quds lieutenant colonel strapped in and placed the boom-mic headphones over his ears. He told the pilots he was ready to go and watched the lone crewman settle into his rear seat. The engines screeched, the blades whopped, the ground suddenly fell away. Kasem felt the helicopter pitch forward as it gained altitude, banking, corkscrewing up over the field in a wide right turn.

Looking through the open cargo door, he could see the burned-out hulk of the twin-engined Y-12 pushed to one side of the field, barely recognizable with one wing blown to bits. He could see the scorch marks on the taxiway where the plane had caught fire. There was an enormous brown streak where the fuel truck had exploded. Chunks of the chassis were still lying in the yellow grass. Farther down the runway, he saw the vehicles of the captain's Guards company spread around a tent, their temporary command post.

Over the internal communications system, he listened to the pilot radioing a clearance to the local IRGC commanders on the ground. Before long, he could see them too. A dirt road leading to a revetment of six SAMs dug into the scrub, surrounded by heavy trucks. As the helicopter flew farther, he could see the roadblocks, a heavy DShK machine gun set up behind sandbags. Every road that led to the city had at least a squad-strength patrol manning a barricade with a heavy machine gun.

Kasem squinted against the glare. Off in the distance, he could see the town of Saqqez itself. A dusty cluster of buildings and roads that stretched toward the river of the same name. A midsized city where the locals spoke Kurdish in their houses and Farsi in their schools. The valley stretched with the river into the inhospitable hills. Dr. Zana Rahimi was down in that city somewhere, Kasem thought. He had to be.

Under the jurisdiction of MOIS, the Quds officer had personally interviewed the witnesses and overseen the cordon that stretched around the city. He'd ordered the local police commanders to drop everything for a house-to-house search of the physicist.

But doubts were mounting. It had been three days.

Kasem watched the hills slide beneath the wheels of the helicopter, feeling the warm air rushing in. Was it possible? Could a by all accounts mild-mannered fifty-two-year-old physicist really have gotten out of the area somehow?

No, he concluded for the fortieth time that morning. *Not a chance.* Within a few hours of the explosion, they'd ordered air surveillance and troops onto the roads, fanning out for a hundred miles. Given the inhospitable landscape, there really wasn't anywhere to go, except for the town.

Unless the scientist had help. Kasem thought of Reza.

Now that the helicopter had leveled at a thousand feet, Kasem leaned back against the nylon cords of his seat. A blast of fresh air, cool, burst through the door. The ungainly aircraft bucked through turbulence. Another windy day. He gulped in the breeze, grateful for something that smelled better than aviation gas.

Looking out at the brown horizon, he was thinking again of the man he knew as Reza Shariati. He was sure that CIA was all over this now. Amazingly, the mysterious CIA operative who had spoken Farsi to him so long ago in Iraq had been on the Baramar payroll. It seemed inescapable that he'd been the link to Rahimi, their spy.

Too many pieces fit together for there to be any other explanation. Rahimi's wife had disappeared on a trip to Mumbai, just as the city had been shot up in a supposed terrorist incident. She was nowhere to be found now, surely in the embrace of the Americans.

Unfortunately, there were no loose ends to pull when it came to Rahimi. His parents were long dead. His brother—a supporter of Massoud Rajavi, the socialist sect leader who had rivaled Khomeini—had died in Evin Prison in the eighties. There were some more recent rumors that his daughter had been developing some ties with the radical student sect. Her boyfriend, Esfan, who'd also died on the Ukrainian airliner, had been on a watch list.

But so was half the country. Rahimi was too important to discard because of peripheral antigovernment associations. For decades his work had been exemplary, and though his file noted potential risks, it also documented the wife and daughter as insurance against any possible treason when Zana had been read into *Zaqqum*. They'd been his collateral, a requirement of everyone in the program. At the end of the day, Rahimi wasn't much different from any other scientist. Except for one thing: his daughter had been killed in the idiotic shoot down of the Ukrainian airliner by the IRGC.

Yes, Kasem thought, idly watching the clouds hunched over the distant mountain peaks, *it's CIA.* Whoever Reza Shariati really was, he was certainly in the middle of the whole thing. And if he was anything like the man Kasem had met years ago, he could well be down there right now orchestrating his agent's escape.

And what if Rahimi did slip through their net? What would it mean for Iran? The scientist knew everything about *Zaqqum*. He knew everything about the systems that ran it, the architecture, the design. He'd probably been in a position to sabotage their efforts for going on a dozen years now, ever since he'd returned with his doctorate from Montreal. The patch through Baramar had enabled the Americans to do whatever they would have wanted. God only knew what kind of malice they'd already planted.

It had all been right under their noses. When the Supreme Council learned of the scheme, it would be considered the greatest intelligence failure in the history of the republic. A *treasonous* failure. What would happen then?

Because Kasem had thought this through several times over the past few days, his mind fell into a familiar groove. It was better to think about success than failure, he reminded himself. If he, as the only officer with the complete picture, was able to capture Rahimi first and foil the plot, he would gain full credit. He would be a hero. He would almost certainly step into General Soleimani's vacant shoes, assuming leadership of Quds. It was a perfect golden opportunity, the chance of a lifetime.

But if the worst should happen . . . if Rahimi somehow got away into the clutches of CIA . . . how best to distance himself? There was only one answer. Kasem would have to find a way to pin it on Maloof. It was an internal security issue, after all.

Ever since Kuznetsov had hinted at the presence of an agent, Kasem had been positioning himself as someone who'd at least provided a warning. He'd been prudent, pulling MOIS in early. If MOIS failed to uncover the plot in time, well, then, that would be the fault of Colonel Maloof, wouldn't it? Kasem would position himself as the whistleblower who had been ignored.

Of course, Maloof would claim just the opposite. He would say that the failure to apprehend Rahimi had been Kasem's fault. He would say that he'd deputized Kasem, given him full authority to execute the operation. A failure.

Still. Kasem was a Quds man. He'd shown up as a volunteer with the best intentions.

There was, he considered, one fatal flaw. It was Kasem's link to Hezbollah that had killed Yuri Kuznetsov. That was the thing that had spooked the Russians, Maloof would say. That was the loose end. Kasem had fucked up, declared war on the Russians. The entire deal had crumbled because of his brazen stupidity.

The battering of the rotors had a hypnotic effect. *No,* he thought, closing his eyes. He would close off that avenue by getting to Rahimi first. He, Kasem Kahlidi, was the only man in the entire country who had the complete picture.

Once he foiled the plot, rounding up Rahimi and his handler, he'd be a hero to the Supreme Council. His first act on assuming leadership of Quds would be to have Colonel Naser Maloof jailed for incompetence. Let him shout out his protestations to the concrete walls of his prison cell until the end of his days.

Nearly drifting off, Kasem thought again about the face on the

LinkedIn profile. There was something chilling about it, as though he could feel the presence. He crossed his arms, warding off the sudden cold, thinking of it, remembering. He absently touched his neck. He sensed the man he knew as Reza was down there somewhere, orchestrating the whole thing. Kasem couldn't let that happen. There was just too much at stake.

He reached his office at dusk. Maloof was gone for the day, which was just as well. He was in no mood to spar with the wily MOIS commander.

One of his lieutenants was at his desk, running through lists of records from the Rahimis' cell phones.

"Anything?" Kasem asked, leaning against the door.

The young officer looked back at him, his face white in the glow of the desk lamp. "No, sir. Sorry. Nothing from either of their phones for two weeks. Hers went dark in Mumbai, his at Saqqez. Since then, nothing."

"Not surprising," Kasem said.

He pulled a folder from under his arm and approached the lieutenant's desk. He spread the folder, showing a print of the LinkedIn profile of Reza Shariati.

"We need to find this man," he said. "Find *him*, and we've got it all."

A few hours later, after leaving orders for the search for both Reza and Rahimi, Kasem slipped into the bed of his high-rise apartment in north Tehran. Kasra was already there, deep asleep. He knew she'd worked late at the hospital today and he was careful not to disturb her. She'd been staying in his place regularly now.

As he shut his eyes, he wondered if he'd done all he could. He believed he had. He expected he would hear something from one of the IRGC commanders out in Saqqez in the morning. He could well have Rahimi in custody by the end of tomorrow. And perhaps Reza. *Reza* . . .

He reached over and caressed Kasra's smooth forehead, brushing her hair back.

If it all fell apart, he thought, they would come for her too.

CHAPTER 33

THE ISTANBUL CHIEF OF STATION, STEVE CHADWICK, WAS STILL A DOUCHE, thought Dale.

After spending a half hour with the man in a café in Erzurum, Dale had been left wondering what in the world his ex-wife saw in the guy. Sure, he was fit and had high cheekbones. And yes, his mother's Armenian heritage had blessed him with a thick head of wavy dark hair and eyebrows that canted in variously suggestive directions; but other than that, Dale thought him a dandy, a paper pusher, a midlevel bureaucrat. One look and all Dale could think about was Chadwick's perfectly creased suit and his silky purple pocket square. What kind of CIA chief of station wears a *fucking pocket square?*

And why had Chadwick gone to all of the trouble to come down personally from Istanbul to Erzurum just to see Dale? Back in Dale's day, no self-respecting chief of station left the office to see a transient case officer. The guy said Meredith had asked him to do it, which only served to annoy Dale further. *This asshole just jumps at everything she says? He's that devoted to her?*

What was more, Chadwick had a way of using those expressive eyebrows to keep staring curiously at Dale, as though questioning why the man in front of him would have ever thrown over a woman like Meredith. He seemed to be wondering why the man in front of him would be skittering around the dusty mountains of Kurdistan at his age with some half-baked plan to get into Iran when he could be going home to a woman like Meredith instead. Didn't they have a daughter together? Wasn't he more or less retired? What was he doing here?

Dale had felt his ass puckering. For want of a more urbane response, he had an urge to take a swing at the guy.

And just who the hell did this douche think he was, criticizing Dale's plan anyway? He didn't know *jack shit* about the wizened old Kurdish trucker Dale used to employ to get into Syria. He didn't know *jack shit* about alternative covert routes into Iran. Chadwick said he'd always sent people through the regular public routes with better legends. *Better than this one,* he'd emphasized, tapping Dale's French passport, the one he'd picked up in Mumbai. Dale would never be able to pull off a surreptitious entry into Iran as a French oil exec, said Chadwick. Dale's suit wasn't good enough. His French wasn't good enough. He didn't really look the part.

What the fuck did all of that mean?

Chadwick had taken it upon himself to come up with new credos after consulting with Meredith. Dale was supposed to be a Turk now, with Persian ethnicity. His alias was an independent geologist coming down to consult with the mining school at Tabriz University after having done some work for Karzkak, a Turkish oil company on the Caspian that tended to shelter identities for the CIA. Well, that was fine with Dale. But he didn't like the idea of Meth and this guy discussing him— didn't like that one bit.

Jesus, he thought now, recalling that faint feeling of betrayal, smothering it. Was he actually jealous? He needed to get refocused on the mission in front of him. That was all that mattered.

Chadwick, for all of his metrosexual ways, had at least delivered the package that Dale had asked Meredith for. Slung over John's shoulders now was a cheap-looking Turkish-made rucksack with a number of CIA-designed hidden compartments in the lining containing the requisite exfil tools.

Specifically, a satphone, a new Glock 17, two hundred feet of paracord, a wad of cash, a knife, and the assorted tools Dale always tried to take with him on solo missions. Perhaps most important, an innocent-looking piece of shiny fabric sewn to the inside of a strap that would double as his IR reflector when he was finally hightailing it over the border into Iraq. That was the plan he'd worked out with Meth. The US friendlies on the Iraqi side of the border would be able to identify him with ISR from miles away. They'd give him air cover if he needed it. Hopefully he wouldn't.

The more incriminating items in the pack were concealed artfully in the lining, hidden from customs inspectors. The big open compartment held clothes with Turkish labels, including useful things for tramping around in the wilds: a bucket hat, a checkered kaffiyeh, climbing gloves, a blanket. There were also a couple of implements a mining consultant might have—a rock hammer, a hand trowel, a sifter, a chemical test kit. Dale hoped like hell that no ambitious inspector would ask him to demonstrate that test kit.

He looked up at the checkerboard-tiled train station in the small Kurdish city of Van. As promised, there was no security screening ahead of the train. That was at least one thing Chadwick had gotten right.

Having switched identities, Dale had borrowed a rental car from Chadwick and driven south from Erzurum to Tatvan, where he'd caught the old white ferry steamer across the lake to this picturesque city with its first-century castles.

He'd arrived on a Saturday. Iranian Rail service ran to Tabriz only on Mondays. With two nights to kill, he'd walked around the cobbled streets conducting SDRs and filling up on Turkish food in little restaurants where he could keep an eye on the door. He spoke to no one and kept a black ball cap pulled over his long brown hair. He wore a pair of thick twill khakis, a long black T-shirt, and a pair of desert hiking boots, courtesy of Chadwick. His beard was full, stretching down his neck, brown streaked with gray lines, some areas sun-bronzed.

Though Erzurum was a nice city, Dale liked Van better. There were fewer Russian tourists here, since the Russians hadn't been too hospitable to the Kurds in the Syrian war. The lack of visible Slavic faces, at least, was something of a relief.

But that didn't mean he'd let his guard down. The Russians, undoubtedly, were still out there somewhere. Though Dale couldn't quite put together the whole picture, he knew there'd been a breach. And for that reason, he'd have to keep Meth in the dark as much as possible, which she hated. *Tough shit,* he thought. As much as he trusted her personally, clearly she'd led the Russians straight to his own house, his mission.

But then there was the even scarier part: he couldn't pin it *all* on Meth and the Agency. There was something else going on.

He hadn't told a soul he was going to Mumbai until he was there in the city, a day before the meet. Either Meth was a Russian agent, which was ridiculous, or they were onto Dale personally. *He'd* become the magnet for them. But he couldn't figure out how.

Maybe the Agency had screwed up getting an old-timer like him. Maybe he'd been out of the game too long to know how it was done. But what could he do? He was in it now. Vigilance seemed his only defense. The old methods were really all he had.

Then there was the scale of the Russian operation to consider. It was wildly unusual to see an Alpha team operating with lethal impunity in the US. Waltzing into the Crimea and bullying sotted Ukrainians in the streets was one thing. But that Alpha team had been playing commando in little old Cle Elum, Washington, literally his backyard.

Then they'd shown up in Mumbai, twice as strong. What could unleash that kind of firepower? It had to have been a matter of desperation. Dale was no egghead foreign-affairs type, but he'd read enough to believe that Putin held on to power by barely keeping the petro economy afloat and stoking nationalism through jabs to the US.

Dale's working theory was that the Russians needed their oil-for-nukes deal to hold all of that fragile business together. They needed it as a strategic hedge against the Chinese and as a way to bully the Americans out of the Gulf. They needed to keep the flag-waving sliver of the populace happy by showing the Americans limping back to their own hemisphere.

Which meant that, most of all, they needed to stop Dale from coming in to fuck it all up for them.

He was relatively sure he'd given them the slip in Mumbai and he felt good about a clean entry to Turkey. But surely they'd have picked up a new piece of the puzzle with Nadia Rahimi's registration at the Taj. They'd know about Cerberus by now. Dale couldn't know what kind of relationship Russian SVR had with Iranian MOIS or, worse, Quds. But he figured the Russians would be waiting for him over there, somewhere across that border at the other end of those train tracks.

Shuffling through the station, he ratcheted his hat snugly over his forehead, thinking about his small but suddenly significant role in the world. While his part was scary, he felt a certain amount of masculine pride. Yeah, that was right: he, washed-up old John Dale from Cle Elum, Washington, was going to stick it to the Russians and the Iranians, and they couldn't figure out how to stop him. Who knew?

Nobody. Fucking nobody . . . as usual. He smiled at his own private joke.

Then he immediately cursed himself, running a hand over his mouth. A man grinning like an idiot deservedly attracted attention. Facial recognition systems were popping up everywhere, even in random little shitholes in the middle of nowhere. Like the Van train station.

Focus, Dale, focus. *No more rookie shit.*

He controlled his pace through the midsized terminal, shouldering his pack through the crowd of villagers, hiding behind his sunglasses. Van's historic origins were in evidence everywhere, right down to the leathery Kurds who hunched under the giant mechanical clock with sacks full of belongings heaped onto old porter carts. A rusty PA churned out incomprehensible announcements about train movements. Except for the way the locals kept their noses buried in their phones, Dale imagined the action in this station hadn't changed much since World War One. *Good.* That was how Dale liked it in the field.

The platform signs were digital, another grudging nod to modernity. But they were blinking on and off, dim in the blinking old bulbs of the station's ancient chandeliers. Dale had to raise his Ray-Bans long enough to study them. The signs were almost all in Turkish, which he couldn't make heads or tails of. But then he saw the one with Farsi subscripts. His route. He made his way toward it.

In the hour wait for the train, he bought a jug of water in a kiosk and clipped it to his pack. Then he settled on the floor to more or less disappear. Like everyone else, he looked at his phone. But he kept his eyes up behind his sunglasses, scanning for surveillants. Finally, the train arrived with a hiss, right where it was supposed to.

Before standing, he took a look at the long silver-and-white train with the red boot stripe. It was a journey of about seven hours to cover three hundred miles, which meant it was either painfully slow or would have some lengthy stops. According to the wall map, there'd be only two before they reached Tabriz—Kapikoy on the Turkish side and Razi just across the border. It was in Razi that Dale would see whether his credentials were really holding up. If they didn't, he was going to come back and revisit old Steve Chadwick one fine day. The douche.

Approaching the train, his empty jug of water clanking against the outside of his pack, he took one last pause before stepping over the gap. He looked up and down the length of the dozen cars. Entering Iran by rail was a new one for him. He wasn't too sure about it. But Chadwick had been confident. Hesitantly, Dale stepped into the narrow passage of the second-class car. Even more reluctantly, he put his pack on the luggage rack just aft of his assigned compartment, backing up slowly so he could keep an eye on it. His life depended on the contents of that pack.

His seat was one of six in the tight compartment. Before long three other passengers showed up: an old married couple who spoke a low Kurdish dialect and a serious-looking man in his thirties with a mustache worthy of Saddam Hussein. He wore a black suit with no tie and a white shirt buttoned all the way to the top. He had nothing but an attaché case for luggage. He was big for around here, shaped like a guy who knew his way around a weight room.

Dale stared out the window, trying to become as boring as possible, avoiding a direct glance at Saddam. But their eyes met briefly in the reflection of the window. He didn't like it. A bolt of concern shot through him. It was off—way off. He glanced toward his pack stowed about ten feet away. He considered getting up, grabbing it, and hopping off.

Fuck Chadwick, he thought. *Fuck this train and this buff Saddam character.*

He'd go find his old trucker contact and barter a way in over the roads, stuffed into a hidden compartment until dropped in the middle of nowhere the way it was supposed to be done . . . the way it used to be done. He reached one hand forward on an armrest, gripping it, just about to hoist himself up.

But then he heard the hiss of the doors, the electric hum of the train revving. He felt the jostle of movement as it eased away, slowly, easterly, back toward Iran.

Well, he thought, scrunching down into his clothes, *maybe it will be fine.*

Maybe.

For just the briefest moment, Kasem seemed to experience a sort of calm. Perhaps the physical act of praying, kneeling prostrate toward Mecca, was enough to achieve some sort of enlightenment, he thought, his face buried in the fibers of his *namaz.* His agnosticism aside, the physical act at least offered him a few moments of reflection, free from interruption. There seemed to be something to that.

Grateful for it, he pressed his cheek to the floor, his eyes wide open. The afternoon sun angled in through the slatted windows and painted stripes across the floor in front of him, marring the intricate pattern of the small rug. He noticed how it made the red and blue stand out in stark contrast, the shine of the worn wool, the intricacy of the tribal patterns. Then, involuntarily, the name of this particular tribal pattern popped into his head. It was called a Tabriz. Though he'd pressed his face to this rug perhaps a hundred times in the past month, he'd never thought about that before.

Tabriz, home of *Zaqqum*'s secret uranium-enrichment facility.

The time for peaceful self-reflection was over. He couldn't afford it. Still prostrate, he turned his head in either direction. The office was empty. The young officer who had been assigned to him had been summoned to another office for an urgent phone call. Kasem found himself alone in his mock prayer. Suddenly annoyed by the rug, he rose to his feet, brushed dust off his thighs, and returned to his desk. He had a lot to do.

Rahimi was in the wind. *Zaqqum* was fucked, throwing a special intensity on the political maneuvers.

Kasem's few recent encounters with Maloof had been brusque, at best, amounting to a recall of his temporarily assigned lieutenants, a denial of further use of the base helicopter, and a clumsily worded intonation that the Foreign Ministry had said the Russians were no longer satisfied, whatever that really meant.

Kasem knew the game, of course. Maloof was isolating him, setting him up for the inevitable fall. Had the circumstances been reversed, he would have been doing the same thing. Alas, they were not reversed.

The fact remained that one of their best scientists had flown the coop. The postmortem would reveal both a failure to cover the risk, a MOIS issue, as well as the failure to stop a potential CIA incursion, a Quds issue. More specifically, a Kasem issue. Because of the way Kasem had set himself up as the sole proprietor of this particular Quds enterprise, he had no one to blame but himself. Others in the government would quickly agree.

Unless he got Rahimi back—then *he* would have all the leverage. If only . . .

There'd been a few leads in the search. Under enhanced interrogation, a Saqqez market owner known to be sympathetic to the Kurds had admitted to slipping food to a man fitting Rahimi's description. The MOIS team on station had leveraged that info to obtain some blurry street video of a man who *might* have been Rahimi, walking alone, a phone pressed to his ear. With the precise time stamp and location, they were able to use cell-tower triangulation to narrow the list to about a hundred phones in use at the time. All of them were making domestic calls except one, which they suspected to have been Rahimi. But on tracing the number, they found it was to a WhatsApp server, a voice over IP data call that they couldn't penetrate. Since that sighting, the trail had gone cold.

Just as worrying as Rahimi's absence was the disappearance of Kasem's Hezbollah contacts in Beirut. Nabil, the man he'd tapped to round up Kuznetsov, had gone dark. Others who knew Nabil weren't answering. Kasem's carefully cultivated network seemed rolled up. That had never happened before. When he made a few more calls to Quds associates to see what was up, he was told there'd been a lot of foreign intelligence heat on the ground. Everyone had gone underground.

In the past, that had almost always meant Mossad. But no. This time, he was told, it was SVR.

Having worked with them for years in Syria, Kasem knew plenty about SVR. For what they lacked in subtlety, they accrued in persistence. Eventually they'd find Nabil, if they hadn't already. Nabil would talk, as everyone eventually must. The finger would be leveled at Kasem. It was as inevitable as the change of seasons; but like the weather, the timing might vary.

When, then?

He half expected to be arrested every morning that he arrived at the office. The Russians would accuse the Iranian government of murdering one of their intelligence officers. The Supreme Council would happily pay obeisance by sacrificing the rogue who had done it.

If it came to that, Kasem would die in Evin Prison. First, he'd be tortured by MOIS thugs who lived for that sort of thing. He had no stomach for it, but the stories he'd heard were sadistic—an obsession with mutilating male anatomy. After that nightmare, provided he lived through it, he'd be cast to the waiting mobs of prisoners, who would be more than happy to stick a shiv in the side of a hated Quds officer.

No, if he entered Evin, he would be leaving feetfirst. Rahimi must be recovered.

He leaned back in the chair behind his desk and closed his eyes, listening to the distant sounds of Tehran traffic coming in through the cracked window. He wanted to see Kasra. How many more nights would they have together? he wondered, inhaling deeply, sighing. He had come to think of himself as savoring them, cataloging each moment so that he might return to it one day. Worse, he'd been snatching secret glances at her pleasant face, wondering what hell he might have rendered upon her. Perhaps, he'd concluded more than once, he should break it off now for her own sake. It would be easy. He could just disappear, like he usually did. That was the paradoxically noble thing to do.

But then he'd never considered himself to be noble. And what was more, though unable to admit it to himself, he couldn't bring himself to do it.

His lieutenant stepped in, throwing the door wide, interrupting Kasem's dark reverie. There was something different about the way the lieutenant walked—a confidence, a swagger. An irreverence? *Dear God,* Kasem thought. *Et tu, Brute?*

"Good news," the young MOIS man said, somewhat short of breath.

Kasem was too cynical to get a rise out of this. His young officers were often overexcitable. He raised an inquisitive eyebrow.

"I think we found Shariati," the younger man said. "NAJA got an Interpol Red Notice. A hit on our man at a Turkish train station." NAJA was the Persian acronym for the Iranian National Police Force.

Kasem stood and leaned over his desk, his chin thrust forward. "And?"

"Facial recognition hit. Ninety-five percent probability."

The lieutenant put a folder on Kasem's desk. Kasem opened it. There was a black-and-white close-up of a face looking up toward the ceiling, a crowd behind him. It looked like an airport or a train station. There were sunglasses draped across the bill of a black ball cap pulled tightly down over long dark hair. A bearded man, a beard streaked with gray. Oddly enough, he seemed to be smiling.

Kasem recognized the eyes, the facial expression. There was no mistaking the memory.

He suddenly felt the need to move. He came out from behind his desk. "Where? How? What now? How did we get this from the Turks?"

The lieutenant pointed toward the blurred background of the image. "That, sir, is the train station in a small Turkish town called Van."

"Yes, I've heard of it."

"The route crosses the border at Razi and then goes on to Tehran. We have an immigration treaty that lets us share info with the Turks. The Interpol warning popped on both sides and the Turks alerted NAJA."

"Who put out the Red Notice?"

"Russia."

Kasem went pale. The Russians. They were looking for Reza too. That probably also meant they already knew everything about Rahimi. Had Kuznetsov known from the start?

Kasem's mind was racing so fast that he stumbled with what to do. *"Well?"* he finally blurted at the lieutenant, irritated with himself. "Say more, Lieutenant. Where did he go from there?"

"Sir . . . NAJA keeps a presence in the station. An undercover officer was alerted and initiated surveillance. They're both on the train. Right now."

"You're saying that we have Reza Shariati on a train that's headed here to Tehran with a NAJA undercover officer tailing him? Has it crossed into Iran yet?"

"No, just left the Van station."

"How far out?"

"Seven hours to Tehran."

"*Inshallah.* Get back on the phone with NAJA. Have their man shadow him. Under no circumstances is he to let the man out of his sight. He'll lead us right to Rahimi. Do you understand me?"

CHAPTER 34

HER TEMPERATURE STILL ELEVATED FROM THE MORNING RUN, MEREdith arrived at the office sweating through the powder she'd applied to her forehead. She'd deal with that later, she told herself, as she had a pile of work to get through first. She hurried through the usual batch of e-mails and then turned to the operational planning.

The details were slowly falling into place.

Starting with Chadwick, the Istanbul chief of station, who'd called just as she was going to bed the night before. He'd met with John in Turkey. He'd set John up with fresh credentials and gotten him the tools he'd need for the extract. He'd come up with an infil plan for Iran, which happened to be via train. According to Chadwick, John now had a weapon, a satphone, and an infrared reflector to use as identification when he approached the Iraqi border. All he needed now was a way to get to the exact meeting site. John would have to improvise all of that, of course—but that was what John did.

Clearly expecting a hearty thanks, Chadwick had then let the conversation wander into the personal. He'd asked about her, how she was, how Grace was, other details of her life that she'd shared previously over too many glasses of wine. Meredith detected it for what it was and became instantly guarded. She liked Chadwick but not that much.

Still, she needed him, so she did her duty. *Wow, Steve, you're the best. Simply amazing job, thank you.* She stopped just shy of saying, *I owe you one.* She believed a woman should *never* say that to a man.

Whatever the cost, it was one more step to getting John home safely.

Grace had been calling in during her limited free time at the Academy, asking where her father was. Though her mother had remained mute, Grace seemed to know that Meredith knew. It rankled them equally, but for opposite reasons.

John was in place almost, but she couldn't be sure about Cerberus. His WhatsApp check-ins had been almost as sporadic as John's. At least she'd gotten NSA to spoof the phone's IP address in order to throw off any monitors, in case the IRGC had gotten some kind of read on him. For all of the gaps in Cerberus's assigned check-ins, she was at least confident they were secure. There was that.

In the few times she and Cerberus had been in contact, Meredith had relayed that the meet was to take place at a small sheep farm close to the border near a town called Alut. It was a Kurdish village in far-western Iran near the Iraqi border. Not knowing how Cerberus would get there, Meredith had relayed a smattering of geocoords, prominent landmarks, and the equivalent of Google Maps directions. In four more days, Cerberus, Rahimi, was to present himself in that farm field, night after night, between the hours of midnight and four. She'd sent the same rendezvous plan on to John via his satphone through the secure app, though, typical of him, she had yet to receive an acknowledgment.

Provided her case officer and her asset didn't get themselves arrested, she thought she'd done all she could do.

And yet . . .

Last night, just after the call with Chadwick confirming John's whereabouts, she'd lain awake, unable to still her ever-waggling feet. Illogically, the knowledge of John's position had ramped her anxiety. She trusted Chadwick as much as she could trust anyone. Nevertheless, his knowing where John was meant that someone else was privy to operational details, a premise that kept her sheets knotted for the better part of three hours.

Her only comfort, a cold one, was that John himself had appeared for the meeting with Chadwick, voluntarily. He could act accordingly to save his operational integrity, using his own judgment. It would be John's call, as it had to be in the field.

But she felt miserable about shifting the responsibility.

Something was definitely rotten in Denmark or, more specifically, Langley. She'd been burned in Dubai several weeks back, which inexorably had led to the Russians tracking her to Washington State. But how had they found John in Mumbai? Not even *she* had known he was going to be in Mumbai until he was there reporting in for help. Only a day had passed between his message to her and the eventual meeting. The Russians couldn't have reacted that quickly—could they?

As Meredith lay there in bed with her shaking feet, her mind had bloomed with possible faults. Could Cerberus actually be some kind of Russian double? It was, after all, peculiar the way the man had set up the meet in Mumbai, swapping out his wife. Was he leading John right into a trap of Iranian design? But the utterly gullible innocence of Nadia Rahimi and the real-world death of Sahar, their daughter, seemed to discount that possibility. Nadia Rahimi was no spy and her husband was clearly devoted to her. And what would have been the point? Just to take out a recently retired case officer? That didn't sync. It was John leading them toward something, not the other way around.

And how was that happening?

Could SVR have some kind of tracker on John? Unlikely. He was as paranoid as they came and barely communicated. Even when he did, it was always through the secure app on a fresh burner. If that channel was compromised, then the whole agency was compromised. When it came to communicating, John was solitary as a clam.

As the moon crept across the night sky, she'd thought about others who knew something about Archer. Her deputy, Rick Desmond, came to mind. But while Desmond knew the most about the operational details, Meredith knew the most about Desmond. After she'd been burned, the CI team had given her a secret report on Desmond, since he reported to her.

Other than Meredith learning that he was gay—surprising enough—his life was clean. The CI team had surveilled him for weeks, monitored all of his communications, and the result was that Desmond was spotless. The fact that he was gay didn't matter. It wasn't like the early days of the Agency when that was a target for blackmail. Desmond hadn't tried to hide his sexuality out of the office. Meredith simply hadn't bothered to get to know him. That probably said more about her than him, she concluded, chiding her own management shortcomings.

Whatever. Can't do everything.

That left General Counsel Sheffield, Rance, and Dorsey. Sheffield knew about the op, but he was removed from the tactical details. Even if Sheffield was dirty, there wasn't much he would be able to do without raising a forest of red flags. As for Dorsey, he was simply too earnest about pulling Cerberus in. Meredith knew how to read people, knew how to detect liars. If acting, Dorsey was turning in a Tom Hanks–level performance. No way.

Rance.

He'd always been a calculating ass, and God knew she didn't trust him. But Rance had always acted with one goal in mind: the betterment of his career. That, unfortunately for the rest of the Agency, had been going just fine as it was, partly *because* of his utter lack of conviction. Depending on how a particular meeting was going, she'd seen him shift positions faster than a senator with sinking poll numbers. If there was one consistency about Rance, it was his inconsistency.

Lying in the dark with nothing better to do than let her mind roam, Meredith *supposed* she could think of an instance where Rance might sabotage Archer just to pin a failure on Dorsey. But Rance was just as likely to jump out in front of the parade and take credit for Archer if it went well, which it damn well might. Now that she thought about it, she realized Rance was in a fine position for either outcome. Typical.

And yet . . .

Rance had kept her awake for an hour all by himself. There was something about the way he'd been acting. He'd been drinking a lot. She'd seen the hangovers, the pallor, the headaches. He'd also been leaving the office in a hurry over the past few months. She'd almost detected a certain laziness about his work, which was new. Up until now Rance had been one of those guys who practically slept in the office. He'd always had the uncommon ability to merge a suicidal work ethic with a nose for realistic intelligence ops. He might have been a world-class brownnoser, but still, he'd risen to be the head of Counterproliferation because he knew what the hell he was doing. So why did he seem pissed off every time she called in with an update?

Did that sound like the work of a man who was anxious to gather a bunch of info and pass it along to the bad guys? Strangely, he barely seemed to care at all, except when he got the chance to remind everyone that John was some sort of shaky turncoat. If the Russians knew how to track John, and Rance was one of them, then he should have been *promoting* John as the critical actor in the whole thing.

Ugh, she'd thought around three a.m. This job was enough to drive one mad. She tried to think about something else, anything else.

It didn't work. Maybe it wasn't an inside leak at all. Maybe the Russians were just fucking good. Of course they were, she'd finally concluded at four, rolling to her stomach, thinking about that blonde John had encountered in Mumbai.

That was the last thought Meredith had before she'd finally drifted off, managing to grab a fitful hour before her alarm had thrust her into her running shoes.

Now, sitting at her desk, using her phone's selfie camera to examine her makeup in the brutal fluorescence of her windowless office, she found herself wondering again about the Russians, specifically the blonde. Meredith wished she'd seen a picture of her, but John hadn't ever been in a position to get one. He'd been too busy dodging sniper fire. But still, he'd noticed enough of her to describe her as *striking, a knockout, an eleven.* Meredith noted the sweat shining across a few wrinkles in her brow.

An eleven? Fucking John. Leave it to him to piss her off with that description.

Her mood continued to sink over the next hour. She'd heard from neither Rahimi nor her ex-husband. How either of them was progressing toward the rendezvous, she couldn't say. Meanwhile Rance had texted, asking for an update and then—classic Rance—had sent her repeated callbacks to voice mail. In her role as handler, that left her with the one concrete task she could accomplish for the morning: logistics.

At least Desmond was reliable. They were in a small SCIF, the one on the first floor near the cafeteria that was relatively easy to schedule because it was so awkwardly placed.

"All right," he began. His laptop was hooked up to a large TV monitor that was bolted to the wall. "This is a digitally colorized image of the rendezvous point in Alut off the low-earth-orbit satellite we tasked. And here's our farm."

He ran the cursor over a patch of green earth in the otherwise barren hilly landscape. The imagery was good enough for them to be able to identify individual fence posts, strands of barbed wire.

Meredith could even see that a few of the sheep had been sheared. But she already knew this farm well. She'd been the one to propose it in the first place.

"Right," she said, reminding him of this. "What more have we learned?"

He cleared his throat. "SIGINT confirms there've been no phone calls in the area, no radio transmissions. The farmer or rancher or shepherd or whatever you'd call a guy like that seems to live over here." He dropped his cursor down the length of the image. "It's about a half mile."

"Family members? Houseguests?"

"We've seen a wife hanging laundry. That's about it. I think they're pretty old."

"How does our farmer get up to that pasture up there?" She pointed at the screen.

"He has a small pickup down at the house. Takes this dirt road. Keeps the truck in this little barn, ah, here." The cursor moved to indicate a small shed-style roof.

"Can someone drive up to the pasture without being seen at the house?"

Desmond shrugged. "Maybe. You can see where the road passes by. But there's a depression here, sort of a little wadi. We suspect that could mask some sound. Do you think Dale or Cerberus will be arriving in a car?"

"No idea. But this is a long walk from anything else, so it can't be discounted. What's this road here?" Meredith pointed to a ribbon of dirt about a half mile from the property.

"That's the border road. There's no way around it. It goes the whole way more or less, running north-south."

"What kind of patrols?"

"Every two hours or so, a lone vehicle comes through, a white IRGC Toyota pickup. It alternates northern and southern directions, so we assess he comes up to this dead end, turns around, and comes back."

"*Assess?* Why aren't we sure?"

"Because it's too close a view for this quality of imagery from a LEO bird. You think it matters?"

LEO meant "low earth orbit." For a satellite to get image quality this good, it had to fly low, which meant a narrow field of view.

"I suppose not," she said.

But as soon as the words left her mouth, she wondered if she would come to regret them. Intelligence failures were infamous for overlooked, seemingly innocuous assumptions.

She let it go. Time was of the essence. Information was never perfect and the die was already cast. She couldn't change the rendezvous point now even if she wanted to. Who knew when she'd be back in touch with John?

"Okay," she said after asking a few more questions. "Tell me about our strike plan."

"Right. We'll put a drone on-site at the appointed hour, assisting a DEVGRU package that will be on standby here at FOB Hammer. That's the closest base to the Iranian border we can use."

"What's the flying time between there and the border for the DEVGRU team?"

Desmond switched to a high-res map view of the area. He measured the distance with his cursor from the village of Alut in Iran back to the secret military base in eastern Iraq. "I'd say about twenty minutes."

"Not ideal."

"No."

She considered the distance for a few moments, studying the map. It seemed unlikely that John would come tearing across a hill with bullets flying over his back. He was way too cautious for that. If anything went awry, it would be well before he got there, she thought. But . . .

She said, "I guess we can have them in a holding pattern over here as soon as we know our assets are in the area. They know about the friendly IR reflector—we've worked that out already?"

"Yup. All set. The drone will catch it." He circled a spot on the map with the cursor. "When the helo gets close enough, it will have eyes as well. Should be clean."

She nodded. Seemed straightforward. The farm field was a good LZ too. Provided both her men arrived on-site intact.

"One thing, though," Desmond said. "DOD has been pretty clear they're not going to enter Iranian airspace or territory. So they won't land in that field like we wanted. John has to get across that border road."

"Good Christ," Meredith muttered, dropping her forehead into a cupped hand. "When did they tell you this?"

"Yesterday."

"Sometimes I wonder why we even have a fucking military," she said, sighing.

Desmond waited until the storm had passed. She shuddered briefly, shaking it off, looking up.

"Okay. How bad is the walk?"

Desmond switched back to the imagery. "In the overhead view, it looks easy enough. Climb this barbed-wire fence, cross the border road, descend into this gully, and you're in Iraq. Home safe."

"Yeah," she said. "On the picture it looks easy."

She could hear John's voice in her head. How many times had she heard him going on and on about the lack of consideration from mission planners for the little things? She thought about it for another ten seconds.

"Rick, who at DOD said they wouldn't enter airspace? Was that CENTCOM himself?"

"No, it was his J-2. Admiral Miller."

"What did he say exactly?"

"Something like . . . for instant action in the heat of battle, he said he'd need the order to come from an SES Level Five CIA officer, on-site."

Meredith cursed whoever Admiral Miller was. This kind of bureaucracy was the thing she hated most. She happened to be one level below the crucial SES level. She was a GS-15, the equivalent of a military full colonel. The level up from her, SES, had all the real trust of the US government. She'd have to get Rance to be on-site, but he'd probably go wobbly right when it mattered.

Before heading next door to lunch, she zigzagged her way to the basement office for travel. She wanted to get to Cerberus and John as soon as she could, personally. Given the knowledge of the Iranian nuclear breakout, she considered every moment precious. She planned to debrief Cerberus right there in Iraq on the spot, then keep grilling him on the plane all the way home. His days of manipulating the CIA were going to be over, by God.

But CIA officers of her rank didn't simply waltz onto US combat bases in Iraq. It took days of numbing paperwork to get cleared to go up to the FOB. While she waited, Meredith figured she'd preposition herself in Doha, capital of Qatar, to be near CENTCOM. That way she could easily hitch a ride on a military aircraft up to the base as soon as her orders came through.

Consequently, she'd be traveling under nonofficial cover (NOC) via civilian means. After an hour's work, the Agency travel desk had set her up with a flight plan, a secure driver, and a hotel, all to be used under one of her favorite cover identities, Maggie O'Dea, an Irish-American international management consultant who specialized in the oil industry. Meredith liked posing as Maggie because she got to wear a red wig and green contacts. She thought she looked particularly good as a ginger—John had always thought so anyway.

An eleven. Bastard.

Just off the elevator, on her way back to her desk, Rance called. Anxious to get it over with, she ducked into a copy room. It was the end of his day in London. As usual, he seemed in a hurry.

He began without preamble. "What's the situation on Archer? We a go? Still using Alut for a border crossing into Iraq? Anything new?"

The directness of the questions struck her cold. She'd lain in bed not seven hours ago, wondering about this man. Was she really prepared to give him intimate details of the operation days ahead of time? But how could she not? He was the boss. Eventually he'd have them.

She needed a minute to think. "Hey, Ed—I'm sorry. You caught me in the ladies'. I'm not alone. . . . Can you give me just one second? Hold on."

"Oh, I . . ."

That ought to leave him thinking, she thought.

She put him on mute and bit the inside of her cheek, her arms crossed as she leaned against a paper shredder the size of a foosball table. What could she do?

She took the phone off mute and heard her voice quaver. "Okay, sorry. I can talk now," she said.

"Meredith, I sincerely apologize. I didn't realize you—"

"Don't worry about it," she cut him off. "I'm heading over to Doha tonight. We're still planning the meet—haven't finalized the details."

"But it's still Alut, right?"

Well, she supposed, he already knew that much. "Yes," she confirmed.

"Have we set up military? What base?"

She realized that withholding information was going to be challenging, if not impossible. Rance was the head of Counterproliferation, the ultimate owner of the entire op.

"Yes," she said, her anxiety climbing. "We've set up a DEVGRU team out of FOB Hammer."

He would need to approve that, so it was just a matter of time before he'd know.

"Any sign of John since he entered Turkey? What about Cerberus?"

"No," she said. "Nothing on either of them. John's MIA, as usual."

She'd just lied openly to her boss. Egregiously. She'd better tell Chadwick to keep his mouth shut.

"Okay," said Rance. "I want to be there too, on-site at FOB whenever it's called. I'll meet you in Doha in, what, three days? Friday?"

"Yes."

Well, she thought, at least she'd have an SES Level Five officer to authorize action into Iran if necessary.

"You flying civilian NOC or military?"

"I'm going NOC. Going to stay in town at the Doha W until the DOD details come in."

"Nicer than staying on base. See you there."

After she hung up, she retraced her steps to the travel office. The same guy who had just taken her orders for Doha stood up to greet her.

"Change of plans," she said immediately, flashing her ID again. "Cancel Doha for me. I'm going to Dubai instead."

If Rance was the leak, she'd need to actively duck him. She'd rather run John directly out of Dubai with her team than be sitting under Rance's watchful eye.

CHAPTER 35

RANCE HUNG UP, SLIPPED HIS PHONE BACK INTO HIS JACKET POCKET, and stepped into the old iron elevator of London's Langham Hotel. The call to Meredith was his final duty before meeting Genevieve for dinner and then, God willing, heading right back up to his suite for some fun.

He'd ditched the rest of his colleagues back at the MOD building in Whitehall and taken the secure car service back to his hotel, feigning a headache. He was the only Agency person staying at the Langham—he'd made damn sure of that. He didn't need any whispers of his liaisons making it back to his wife—or, worse, Dorsey.

He found the high-ceilinged, marble Victorian lobby bar and ordered a bourbon. It was all of four fifteen in the afternoon, but why not? That was how he and Genevieve did things.

London's milky white daylight had a sparkling quality when viewed through the leaded-glass doors of the grand old Langham. Especially when Genevieve stood in front of them.

"*There* you are," she said, glowing, running her hands over his shoulders, touching his chest. She was still dressed in business attire, which, for her, meant heels stacked high and skirts hemmed short.

"Where do you want to eat tonight?" Rance asked, smiling, arranging her usual seat.

He noticed the perfect shape of her thigh as it stretched across the oval of the leathery barstool. How he admired the shape of that leg.

Just then his phone buzzed. He reluctantly tore his eyes away to glance at the screen. His assistant calling, probably to help arrange his travel to Doha.

He suppressed a fresh wave of irritation. For heaven's sake, he'd shot her an e-mail with all the necessary details not ten minutes ago. Why the hell was she calling him? He thought about sending her off to voice mail. But then again, he wanted an interruption-free evening.

He made his quick apologies to Genevieve and stepped into an alcove to take the call. Sure enough, it was a simple confirmation of his plans. He was back at the bar in under a minute.

"Where were we?" he asked, sliding his hand across the smooth knee.

She leaned in close, a touch of gin on her breath. "I'm just *so sorry* to have to tell you this, darling, but I'm going to be short on time tonight. No dinner for me, poor girl. A business trip just came up. I'm off to Tokyo on a midnight red-eye. BA. Haven't even *packed* yet, if you can believe it. Probably just go there with the clothes on my *back*. Can we just finish this drink and rush up to the room to make the most of our time?" She squeezed his arm.

Dear God, Rance thought to himself, face flushed, *could this relationship get any better?* He slugged down what was left of his drink and giddily offered his elbow.

Less than an hour later, she exited the elevator on her way out of the hotel. Her face was grave as she thought about the vial of tranquilizer she'd dumped in his drink when Rance turned away to speak to his secretary. It was the heaviest dose she'd ever tried.

But worth it.

Twenty-two hundred miles to the southeast, John Dale stared at his hands. They hadn't yet started to shake.

That was about the only thing going well.

Except for the ominous suited man with the Saddam Hussein mustache, the first two hours of the rail trip had been uneventful as they neared the last stop in Turkey, a small city called Kapikoy.

Still, by then, Dale had made the decision that he'd be getting off. He wasn't comfortable entering Iran via the Iranian National Rail service—not with this serious creature lurking next to him. If he was indeed a tail, Dale figured he'd be able to lose him if he stepped off unexpectedly.

Then things had gotten worse.

While he pretended to lose himself in a Farsi newspaper he'd picked up in Van, Dale had kept his eye on the man, who sat an empty seat away, to Dale's left. Twice the man had gotten up when his phone rang. Both times Dale could see him through the reflection of a far window. But standing in the free space between cars, the man didn't speak through the phone. He just responded to the message by thumb-typing. Not good. The man was so concerned with whatever texted communication he was getting that he wasn't comfortable reading it in front of Dale.

As they approached Kapikoy, Dale already pictured how he'd snag his pack and disappear into the Turkish town. After losing the tail, he'd wait a day or two to figure out some other route into Iran. Meth's message had said there would be a four-day window over in Alut to meet Cerberus. He still had plenty of time.

But instead of slowing as it approached Kapikoy, the train had sped up. A number of passengers looked at one another, confused. The conductor announced over the PA that, unfortunately, the Kapikoy station would be closed to eastbound traffic due to unforeseen construction problems. Passengers wishing to depart could get off at the *next* available stop and double back, free of charge.

The next available stop was in Iran.

There it is, Dale thought.

Looking at his steady hands, examining his stubbed pinkie, he surmised what it really meant. The Russians knew about Cerberus based on the lead they'd picked up in Mumbai from Mrs. Rahimi. The Russians had managed to stay on Dale somehow, and they were giving the Iranians a heads-up. The man next to him was almost surely a MOIS officer, maybe Quds, though his disguise seemed too thin for that.

That left Dale with exactly one option: leap off the train. But how to do that with his adversary right next to him?

A trace of gray twilight spread across the dark, featureless desert outside the windows, a handful of lights winking in the distance. He'd be able to figure out a way forward if he could get to a little town of some sort. And at least he'd have the cover of darkness to work with.

Most of all, though, he needed to make sure he got his bag. It was his lifeline. Not only did it have his weapons and survival gear; it also had the IR reflector and the satphone. Without those, he had no way of completing the mission.

The train had Wi-Fi and a weak cell signal. Dale checked his phone as a muffled clackety-clack rattled on around him. Shifting to his right against the bulkhead to conceal his phone from mustache man, he studied Google Maps. They'd just crossed the Iranian border. They were now headed toward Razi, the official Iranian port of entry, moving along at about forty miles per hour.

That was, what? Ten minutes?

He slipped his phone back into a cargo pocket, smiled at the old Kurdish couple across from him, and stood up. For good measure, he asked them in very slow Farsi if they knew which way the restroom was, since he'd seen them get up a few times. The old man jerked a thumb that indicated it was over near the baggage area, the space between the cars.

As Dale moved out of the compartment, the suspicious man leaned his knees sideways, letting him pass. Dale attempted a glimpse down the man's jacket toward his belt for something incriminating.

He found it: the hint of a black nylon strap running across a rib.

A hint, but Dale knew what it was—a shoulder holster. As he kept moving toward the passageway, he braced himself, waiting for the man to react.

Nothing happened.

Dale walked a few feet forward toward the luggage area, eyeing his bag. It was under another, stuffed into the chrome rails of a rack. But he'd be able to jerk it free pretty easily. The only person who could see him as he stood in the empty space between the cars, right near the small restroom door, was the mustached man.

In the privacy of the bathroom, Dale considered his options. The Glock was in his bag. He had to get to it, but how to do that without tipping mustache man? He thought quietly for a few moments to come up with something.

He removed his shirt and splashed water on his face, soaking his beard, wetting his hair. He ripped a small cloth towel free of the hand dryer and ran it under the tiny tap, like a washcloth. He opened the door, conspicuously facing the suspicious man, shirtless, wiping down his armpits.

Mustache man watched Dale, though he pretended not to. His eyes darted toward either side of the car and then back down to his lap. Dale continued to mime a sponge bath and then dropped to his knees, pulling his bag free, as though looking for a fresh shirt. The man didn't get up, but Dale noticed that he'd pulled his feet beneath him, ready to spring.

Dale yanked his pack into the bathroom with him, setting it on the sink, shutting the door. The restroom was reasonably large, big enough for Dale to set the bag on the sink and riffle through it. First, he found his Glock and shoved it in his belt, cold and oily against his skin. Then he put his shirt back on, leaving it untucked. Finally, he found some minty gum and threw it in his mouth, chewing furiously.

The train made a loud crashing sound. They'd just entered a tunnel and the echoes of the squealing steel wheels created a racket. He could feel the shift in air pressure in his ears. Shadows strobed at the crack of the door.

He took the liter water jug off its carabiner on the pack. He drank down what was left of the water and stuffed the empty plastic bottle into a little spot above the mirror within easy reach. He tore off a bit of gum to make sure it wouldn't bounce free.

That accomplished, he opened his phone's camera app. He shoved the bottom of the phone into an outer pocket of his bag so that it stood up on its end with at least half the screen still visible to him.

With his hat pulled low over damp hair, Dale stepped out of the bathroom, back into the area between cars where they kept the luggage. Before he shut the door, he took the remainder of his gum and jammed it in the door latch to make sure it wouldn't lock, though the eye-level bolt was still thrown. To an outsider it would look like the bathroom was occupied. Dale tested the door, staying out of sight. It worked. He stepped forward into the luggage area, now fully clothed, his ersatz toilet completed.

Through the window reflection, he saw the suited man watching, leaning forward, his hands ready to move. Dale calmly put his pack on the top rack with his back to the man. He subtly arranged his bag so that the exposed phone's camera faced aft, into the passenger compartment. He made a show of closing up zippers, as any other traveler might.

Once the bag was in place, Dale stepped into the passageway. But instead of turning back toward his own compartment, he went forward—out of sight of the suited man.

The train burst forth out of the tunnel with a blast of air pressure. Dale turned the corner into the passageway of the next car, walking unsteadily against the sway of the tracks. After he'd made it to the next car, he entered a passenger compartment, turned, and pressed his back to the bulkhead.

His position meant he had to invade the space of some other passengers, but there was at least a vacant seat to work with. As Dale made himself flat against the wall, teetering with the rhythm of the train, the old Kurdish travelers looked up at him like he was nuts.

Dale ignored them. Through the reflection of an opposite window, he could see his phone, which was propped just so on his bag on the opposite bulkhead. Like a two-stage bank shot, the window reflection gave him a view of the screen, which then gave him a view of the suited man via the camera. He watched mustache man get up. When he came closer toward the space between the cars, the man's hand went into his coat. He pulled out a short-barreled pistol, a Beretta from the looks of it. Wishing to look unarmed, the man kept his arm bent, the hand with the gun just inside his suit jacket.

All right, thought Dale. *Threat confirmed. Right hand.*

When he saw the man come abeam of the bathroom door, Dale spun on his heel around the bulkhead and leapt. He was springing into a disarming maneuver he'd been taught years ago, back at the Farm. Carried forward by his falling momentum in a right-knee lunge, Dale clamped his hands on the barrel and twisted. The Beretta dropped.

Propelled by gravity, Dale kept going, then shot up with the force of his own sprung leg, bringing the man's wrist with him. He ratcheted his victim's forearm into an ungainly twist, turning his hand in the wrong direction behind his back. Dale was now behind the man.

Instead of stopping there, as taught back at the Farm, Dale kept pulling, breaking the man's arm, possibly his wrist. He felt a crack, heard the man's gasp, a low growl. Needing to shut him up immediately, Dale stunned him with an immediate jab to back of his head. He then balled his fist and reached around to shove it in the man's mouth. With his other hand, he pulled the lavatory door open and threw him in, stepping in behind. The entire episode occurred in under three seconds, out of view of other passengers.

Once in the lavatory, the man regained some of his senses and fought back. He bit Dale's hand, ripped at his face, left a nasty scratch across his cheek. He tried a kick to Dale's crotch, which partially connected. Dale felt the sickening tug of stung testicles in his gut. He ignored it.

The man was an inch taller than Dale and strong as a bull. He bucked Dale off, slamming him into the bulkhead. He threw an elbow back that took Dale's wind. It was just enough of a letup that the man broke free, turned, punched Dale in the face.

Jesus, Dale thought, his head stinging senselessly. *This isn't going well.*

Out of instinct, Dale hit back, landing a solid jab to the bridge of the other man's thick nose. The man gasped. Dale thrust mustache man's head down and smashed him with his rising knee, another shock to the big man's nose.

The big Iranian threw Dale off, smashing him into the mirror, which cracked. He swung his burly arm and missed, hitting the wall. With his other hand, he was going for his gun, but he had little room to maneuver. Dale pushed him backward against the wall, trapping the man's arm. With a little more space freed behind him now, Dale reached to pull the Glock free of his own waistband.

He swung the butt of it against the big guy's mouth, drawing blood. He did it again and then grabbed the empty water jug from the spot by the mirror where he'd left it. He aimed his pistol through the bottle's mouth and fired, putting a bullet through the man's crown. It passed all the way through, embedding itself in the vinyl bulkhead.

The big man spasmed once with a flail of his arm and then crashed awkwardly against the wall, limp as a sack of seeds. The bottle had done its job as a makeshift silencer. While the shot had been deafening in the confines of the cloistered bathroom, Dale was confident it had been sufficiently masked against the loud ambient noise of the rolling train.

That was way too fucking close, he thought, breathing hard. Some blood had spattered up on his shirt, but because the shirt was black, it didn't matter much. More gore was visible on the wall behind the toilet and the cut on his cheek was shiny. Dale went through the man's pockets as his inert head rolled from side to side. He took a moment for himself to splash water on his face, removing blood. He glimpsed his own eye in the mirror.

The adrenaline had surged. His hands were shaking now. He forced himself to breathe deeply, pushing out what he could. He'd come very close to getting himself captured, likely killed. He went back to searching the body.

The gun was gone from the man's holster. Dale remembered it lay just outside the door. He'd have to hide that quickly. He riffled further and found a black wallet, which he threw in his cargo pocket. Then he found the phone, a cheap Android.

Now that he knew the Iranians were onto him, he needed intel desperately. He stabbed the power button on the phone to light it up. Password locked. But there was an animated red arrow pointing down toward a silver circle at the bottom of the phone, a ring about the size of a dime.

Fingerprint sensor. Bingo.

Feeling ghoulish and shaking badly, Dale held the dead man's stubby right index finger up to the phone. It opened. He went to the messages. He scrolled through with a trembling hand. Though the writing was in Farsi, Dale didn't understand much of it, either because his language skills were too primitive or because the Iranians were using some kind of intraservice jargon. But after a lot of confusing headers, the last message read: *Do not lose sight of suspect. Officers stationed for intercept at Razi.*

Razi was the first Iranian point of entry fifteen miles farther down the track.

The previous message was full of gibberish, but there was an attachment. Dale opened it. It wasn't the best quality, but he recognized himself. It was from the Van train station. There he stood, looking up toward the terminal signs with his black ball cap and the sunglasses on the visor. He'd been smiling.

God, what an idiot, he thought.

The shaking got worse; he noticed his own rapid breathing. The dead man slumped farther down, sliding in a pool of his own blood. Could there be others on the train? The phone didn't indicate that, but Dale couldn't discount the possibility. He had to get out of here now.

He had one last idea.

He looked through the sent messages. There was one from about a half hour back. *Suspect sighted. Surveillance initiated on train.* Others of a similar style. They'd started before he was even on the train, still back at the station.

On the dead man's phone, Dale composed a message to send back to the headquarters of whatever organization this guy had worked for. He wrote: *Have suspect in custody. Do not stop train at Razi as suspect may have ambush planned there. Go direct to Tehran. Repeat, do NOT stop train at Razi. Ambush.* He had no idea if it would work.

He hit send, saw that the message went, and shoved the phone back into the man's pocket.

He washed up as best he could and exited the bathroom, making sure the OCCUPIED sign was still displayed, held in place by the gum. He scanned the floor and saw the man's Beretta. He shoved it deep into some suitcases, since he didn't want the extra weight. He pulled his pack free and slung it over his shoulders, ratcheting down the straps. He then checked his pockets to make sure they were secure. He pulled his hat down tight and moved aft, walking between cars to the back of the train, nodding politely to the civilians who looked up at him from their seats. He hoped he wasn't covered in blood. He'd done his best to clean up. He stuffed his hands in his pockets to hide the shaking.

He made it to the last car. He'd thought it might be empty. No such luck. There was another luggage compartment, like the one he'd used up forward. On this one, however, there were no passengers behind it and none facing it.

Dale stepped into it and examined the double train doors that would serve as the regular exit between the cars. Above it was an emergency-exit window that he could kick free. But he was sure that if he did that, the engineers would get an alarm and stop the train. He needed something else. Looking up at the ceiling, he saw a hatch with a padlock through a hasp. It would have to do.

He bent to one side to look out the windows. The train was curving now, arcing to the right. Dale could see lights up ahead. That would most likely be the town of Razi, he thought. That was where the Iranians would be waiting for him—unless his message had actually worked.

He wasn't about to take the chance. To give himself a shield from the other passengers, he piled up a few roller bags, stacking them as a barrier. Then, when no one was looking, he aimed his pistol at the lock, through the water jug.

This was old-school stuff. At the Farm, the instructors had taught him once how to shoot a lock so that it came apart. Thank God they had. Dale pressed the barrel and the jug at the correct angle at the lock over his head. He fired. The lock broke into pieces.

He put his pistol back in his pocket and started restacking the bags, slamming them loudly, trying to make a similar sound. A few passengers had turned to look to see what all the noise was about. They saw that it was just the sloppy guy with the long hair and the baseball hat rearranging the luggage. He mimed an apology, and after a while, they all looked away.

Dale studied the hatch above him. He needed a foot or two more of height to work on it. He stepped onto a particularly beefy roller bag and put himself in a reasonable position. He threw the handle. The hatch opened an inch and then, grabbing the rushing air, slammed back with frightening speed, like a sprung mousetrap. If Dale had had his hand anywhere near the hinge, he would have lost another finger.

Cool evening air rushed by the open vent and a few stars shone through the aperture. He could envision jumping up, hooking an elbow, and getting through it to the roof of the train. But not with his pack on; it was too narrow for that. He had reached a point of no return. Again.

He took off his pack and jammed it up through the hole. The air caught it. Off his lifeline went, skittering somewhere into the night. Dale jumped up, hooked his elbow, and wriggled onto the roof of the train, which was moving at about forty miles per hour.

It was harder than he had thought it would be, but he was up there, lying on his stomach, facing forward, his T-shirt whipping across his back. It was horrendously loud both from the rush of the wind and screech of the wheels. He wanted to replace the hatch, but against this wind, it wasn't easy. Yet it had to get done. It was just too obvious any other way. He wriggled to his side and forced the hatch up. It came down with a heavy clang.

He took a quick look around at the gray blur of land whizzing by. To the left, there seemed to be an incline, a bank. To the right, the ground went downhill. He reasoned that the incline would be the shorter fall. The wind ripped the ball cap from his head and sent it flying into the night.

Wither thou goest . . . , he thought.

He rose on one sore knee and peered out, thinking about how much jumping off the train was going to hurt. He was already in pain from the kick to the groin and the punch to the face. He didn't have the luxury of searching for a soft landing. He'd just have to get lucky. But he'd always been lucky. Sort of.

CHAPTER 36

KASEM HAD REGAINED USE OF THE HELICOPTER, DESPITE MALOOF'S edict to stay away from it. Things had happened fast in the night while the old man slept. The national order from the Supreme Council to find the murderer of a NAJA officer had given Kasem the license he needed. Maloof couldn't very well stand in his way now, not with that kind of scrutiny.

When the train had arrived at Tehran in the wee hours of the morning, Kasem had been there with his lieutenants and a thick cadre of armed NAJA officers. The Iranian National Rail train, which had skipped all of its stops until arriving at the capital, was kept sealed as officers searched car by car. Eventually, after finding the dead officer with the bullet through his head, the NAJA men had taken each and every one of the passengers into the station for questioning by the busload. Only Kasem knew it would be a massive waste of time. He kept that knowledge to himself.

It was dawn in Saqqez. The sun was rising toward an overcast, hues of gold light cast beneath a gray ceiling. Kasem was the only passenger. Over the internal microphone, he directed the helo's crew to land on the dusty soccer field of a secondary school on the outskirts of town.

The captain of the local IRGC garrison who had been charged with the search met him there. He drove Kasem to their operational center, updating him along the way. Kasem kept signaling his comprehension, but struggled to pay close attention. He couldn't stop thinking of Kasra.

He'd gotten ahold of her before boarding the helo. She'd been in a deep sleep, but the tone of his voice caused the fog to lift quickly.

Without much time, he'd gotten right to the point. Given his position in the security apparatus, he was relatively sure their communication was secure. He'd done a secret internal search for any record of surveillance on Kasra and, thankfully, come up empty. He'd gone to great lengths to conceal their relationship. But who knew if he'd actually succeeded?

"Get to your aunt's house up north," he'd said when he was sure she was really awake. "Right away. Tell them you're sick at work, but tell no one where you're going. Tell no one about us. Get a different phone. Use cash—make sure no one can follow you in your travels. Stay with your aunt until you hear from me." He realized how crazy he must have sounded.

"Kasem, you're out of your head. What's going on?"

"Kasra, *azizam*, you know who I am. You know *what* I am. You must. Believe me when I tell you, you need to go. Today. Please, Kasra, my *azizam*, please."

The pleading went this way for a while. Eventually she relented, nominally at least. She'd grown up in a police state where she'd seen others rounded up by the police, only to disappear. Though she didn't yet understand the circumstances, she understood the stakes. But a part of him worried she might not have taken him seriously enough. He'd texted again before the helo soared out of range over Tehran, assuring her that he was completely sincere, a matter of life and death. She hadn't replied immediately, and then he'd lost the cell service as the aircraft rose above the cell towers. The entire flight west, he'd wondered what she must have been thinking of him.

But on landing in Saqqez when the signal came back, his phone had buzzed with a reply. He was relieved to see it was from a different number, a new one. The message said: *I will go.* A surge of relief had washed over him as he slipped his phone back into the cargo pocket of his IRGC uniform trousers. Now as he rode along in the Toyota four-by-four, he couldn't stop thinking about her, worrying about her passage to her aunt's home on the Caspian. But the young officer in charge of the search wouldn't shut up.

Still talking, the captain produced a steaming mug of tea for Kasem, who wore an IRGC lieutenant colonel's uniform. They were in a portable classroom, a trailer, close to the soccer field. It was pleasantly heated with forced air. The school had been closed, momentarily taken over by the IRGC with no explanation to the staff or students. Maps were pinned to the wall. A few white Toyota pickups were parked outside amid a jungle of radio antennae and a few towed heavy machine guns on trailers. The captain had cleared the room of the enlisted men to brief the lieutenant colonel who'd arrived from Tehran.

Kasem listened now, setting aside thoughts of Kasra. Her safety was linked directly to his mission.

The search had been exhaustive. Except for the one suspected surveillance photo, they'd come up empty for the past few days. But they had their suspicions. This was Iranian Kurdistan. The people weren't always cooperative here, at least without coercion, according to the captain. The search might take a little longer, but they'd eventually get their man. They'd just have to be a little harsher, like in the old days.

Kasem took it all in, calculating what he thought might happen. The man he knew as Reza would be here soon; of that, he was dead certain. Reza would find Rahimi. Together they would escape from the country. Unless Kasem outwitted them. It had to happen—or Maloof would win.

As the captain went on with more detail than Kasem cared for, the Quds officer studied the map. They would attempt to cross the border, he thought, into Iraq. The Americans had Iraq as a permanent base now. It seemed obvious that they would go that way, slip in under the protective dome of US military might.

Without relaying any of his reasoning to the earnest IRGC captain, Kasem explained the reason for his visit. He removed a folder with both the LinkedIn and Van train station photos of Reza Shariati.

"This man will be in the search area. He will be attempting to meet with Rahimi and move them southwest, somewhere down here toward the border."

Kasem stood and sketched the approach to Saqqez from the northeast, from Tehran.

"Set up a cordon around here," he told the captain, tracing an arc to one side of the city. "You can find him as he enters, if he hasn't already. And we'll need to beef up security patrols all along this border road. I suspect he will try to lead Rahimi into Iraq."

A mile southwest of Saqqez, where the roads turned to dirt or vanished altogether, three men warily watched the approach of the MI-8 Hip helicopter circling the town. They were up high with a good vantage over the city, crossing a ridgeline, moving slowly over the jagged rocks, twelve witless sheep bleating around them.

The men wore long draping shirts and checkered scarves to ward against flying grit. The lead man gripped a battle-scarred AK-47 and signaled for the other two to dive under the brush. If they were spotted from the air, the sheep would have to serve as their cover, again. But that was okay with Zoran, their forty-six-year-old leader. He'd been playing this game for a long time.

The helicopter slowed and descended, over near the school. It raised a large cloud of dust that swirled away like a mini tornado. The leader gave the men the all clear. They reappeared and continued on their way.

Zoran was the local commander of the militia of the Democratic Party of Iranian Kurdistan, the PDKI. He'd spent five years of his life executing guerrilla raids against the IRGC to little effect, until he'd given up altogether for want of other volunteers.

It hadn't always been this way. There'd been a time when the separatist Iranian Kurds had had international support, as they did in northern Iraq and Turkey. At the PDKI's peak, he'd commanded thirty men. But the Americans had since sold them out. As a quiet concession of a 2014 nuclear nonproliferation deal, the Americans had officially declared the PDKI a terrorist organization. Zoran had found *that* rich with irony.

Under the threat of an emboldened Iranian government, his militia band had shrunk. Predictably, the IRGC had stalked them, scaring them farther into the hills, running for their lives. Even courageous Zoran himself had gone underground, returning to his life as a jute farmer, forgetting about the cause, burying his trusty old Kalashnikov.

But when the IRGC had descended on the town a few weeks ago, one of his former compatriots, a farmer like himself, had come to him. He'd urged Zoran to leave, to go hide in the hills, like back in 2014. The IRGC's burgeoning presence—blocking the roads, inhabiting the schools—surely meant a new offensive on the PDKI. It was just a matter of time before they'd arrive on Zoran's doorstep.

For what?

Zoran failed to see the connection. They were hardly a militia anymore. They hadn't had a meeting in five years. They'd effectively declared defeat.

But then he'd seen the helicopters for himself. He'd seen the weapons towed through the streets, the soldiers questioning villagers in a house-to-house search. That hadn't happened since the days before the American sellout.

Whatever was causing it, Zoran saw it as the recruitment opportunity of a lifetime. He'd put out the word that he was looking for men quick. They'd take to the hills and defend themselves. Whatever the hated IRGC had in store from them, rest assured, he'd told his contacts, they'd be in the hills waiting for a chance to strike back.

As word had gone out, something odd had come back. There was a rumor, fourth- or fifth-hand, that there was a man hiding among them. He might be a high-ranking member of the Iranian Defense Ministry. Though shadowy and vague, he seemed like a man on the run looking for help.

Zoran and his men had found him sleeping on a door stoop, playing the part of beggar. It didn't fit. He looked like a Persian. When they'd roughed him up, but not too much, he'd told them a story. It had taken a while, but Zoran believed him now. There was something noble about the gentleman with the ragged beard and aquiline nose.

The gentleman had confessed that he was looking to defect across the border, that he was on the run from the IRGC. Among other things, he'd said he was looking to tell the Americans the true story of the Iranian policy toward the Kurds. Based on the way he spoke, the things he knew, Zoran assessed him as educated, worldly, a man who could testify as to the wrongheadedness of the American policy. The man admitted that he'd had a brother who had died in Evin Prison back in the eighties. He'd been a supporter of Rajavi, the socialist revolutionary.

Those were sufficient bona fides for Zoran. Under the nose of the searching IRGC, he and his men had taken the gentleman in, given him the burner phone he had asked for. He needed it to get in touch with the Americans, he'd said. Zoran was delighted to have a mission again. Farming jute was not all it was cracked up to be for a man like him.

"Get me to Alut," the man had insisted after his second phone call on the burner. "Get me there safely and I will personally fix everything with the Americans."

They had ninety kilometers to go.

CHAPTER 37

THE THIRTEEN-HOUR FLIGHT FROM DULLES TO DUBAI HAD BEEN SOME-
thing of an endurance test. Meredith had eschewed the movies, filet
mignon, and French wine in favor of long blank stares out the window
and a steady stream of Perrier. Maggie O'Dea was doing well with her
consultancy; she could afford riding business class on Emirates Air. But
Meredith Morris-Dale couldn't abide it. She barely ate or slept.

When the fuselage door finally opened, she gathered her things.
Her hair was red, eyes green. She wore her favorite Lululemons under a
button-down linen shirt and atop running shoes. Despite the exhaustion, a glance through her phone showed the concealer she'd applied on
initial descent was doing its job. A mere hint of depression under the
eyes, lipstick redder than the way she usually wore it. But that was Maggie's style, not hers.

On the long walk toward immigration, wearing a backpack and
dragging her specially equipped roller, she checked her phones. One
was buzzing with messages from HQS. She skipped it, opting for the
phone she used as her link to John. But she was disappointed.

The HQS messages sounded urgent. Before leaving the airport, she
ducked into the expansive Emirates lounge, found a relatively quiet
spot, and called Desmond. It was midnight back in DC, but answering
at all hours went with the job.

"The Iranians are spinning up," Desmond said after they'd authenticated securely. "DIA is reporting activity that they're starting to call a
war footing."

"Great," Meredith said, sighing. "That's really helpful." She ran a hand over her wig to make sure it hadn't come loose on the flight. "What specifically?"

"Air defense radars active, lot of chatter between command centers."

"Maybe IRGC thinks we're coming in."

"Sounds like it."

"You know what I'm going to ask next," she said.

"No word from Cerberus. Assume it's the same on your end?"

"Yeah. Nothing—Cerberus or John."

They talked for another ten minutes about the operational plan to get both men out. As she was about to go, he said, "Hey, Meredith, one more thing."

"Go."

"I know I'm analyst nobody, but if we're really this close to an escalation with Iran, no one's going to want to start a war by entering hostile airspace."

She'd been thinking the same thing.

It took another half hour to get through immigration. Meredith slid Maggie O'Dea's US passport under the glass and faced the camera. The UAE customs officer seemed to take a while with his computer. But eventually, he waved her on without saying a word.

For an additional forty minutes, she performed an SDR through the terminal, taking long pauses in secluded spaces, carefully watching the exiting stream of passengers. She was looking for the Russians, a beautiful blonde in particular. An eleven.

Finally outside on the curb, she gulped in the humid Gulf air and blinked at the sun reflecting off the modern architecture. She looked due north, across the narrow channel of the Gulf, toward Iran, just eighty miles away. She noted the line of overcast over there, orange in the morning light.

Oleg had been driving all night. He gripped the wheel of the rickety little Nissan Sentra and shook off a yawn, moving down the two-lane highway at the speed limit, a hundred kph. Though he was studiously obeying the law, he really had no other choice since he was already near the Nissan's top speed. Its misaligned wheels and overtaxed engine had been shaking him for the better part of six hours. At least the sun was up now, he thought, glimpsing the brown hills, the brightening overcast.

He was following Zoloto's orders. As instructed, he'd been staying in Tehran, waiting for Dale. The diplomatic team in the Tehran consulate knew who he was and had set him up with an office and access to the facilities. They knew better than to ask what he was doing there.

He'd caught the Red Notice on Dale at the consulate and waited for details from the local PR Division SVR group, which was monitoring the Iranian response. The PR men had provided a copy of Dale's photo from the Van train station. Oleg had studied it carefully, noting the clothes, the disguise, Dale's luggage.

He'd been amazed that Dale seemed to be smiling, looking up at the camera. On seeing the photo, Oleg had reflexively grinned. A gesture of respect among professionals.

The Iranians had been surging NAJA all along the train tracks, ready to nab Dale, whom, based on the Interpol feed, they considered a dangerous Russian criminal with a bogus Turkish passport. It was determined that they'd eventually get him in Tehran, no stops along the way. They let the Russians know the arrest would be going down a little after midnight. Oleg seriously doubted that, but waited around just in case.

By two a.m., it had been declared a bust.

Now Oleg was driving toward Alut, where Zoloto had said the meet between Dale and Rahimi would take place. Oleg had set out in the middle of the night with this borrowed consulate car. He'd asked for something rugged, maybe a Land Cruiser.

Nope. Though they'd had the best of intentions, the Sentra was the best the consulate could do on such short notice. The good news was that the diplomatic plates would get him through any roadblocks, the PR men had said.

Oleg was skeptical. Stuffed in the trunk were an AK-12, a Dragunov sniper rifle, and assorted tactical gear. He'd dyed his hair a darker color. He'd been growing out his beard, bronzing his face with long sessions under the sun. The plan was for him to look like Dale. He and Zoloto thought he might fool Dr. Rahimi into walking right up to him, provided Oleg had the exact details of the meet.

His satphone rang. He pressed it to his ear, angling his head so the antenna had a straight shot at the sky.

"Any sign?" asked Maria.

"They missed him in Tehran."

"As expected," she said. "How long until you're in Alut?"

"Couple hours. Making good progress. How's Doha?"

"Bad," Maria answered. "She's not here."

Oleg knew not to ask too many questions. But he needed information on the meet. "She didn't show? How will I know where to go?"

"We just got a new Red Notice. She's in Dubai."

"Huh," Oleg said. "What do you think that means?"

"Probably that the asset I've been using up until now is compromised."

Oleg rattled on in the Sentra, noting the distance to the next town on a road sign. He needed to get gas and take a leak, maybe pick up some food.

"So what now, then?" he asked. "How do we get the info on the meet?"

"I'm on my way to Dubai now."

CHAPTER 38

DALE SLUMPED IN THE BACK CORNER OF THE DUSTY LITTLE CAFÉ. HE'D indulged in a thick Turkish breakfast of eggs, tomatoes, spicy sausage, and pita. It was a departure from his steady traveling diet of protein bars and water. But he'd been starving.

He'd walked, or more accurately limped, for the past few hours. After jumping from the train's last car and smacking his knees against the embankment, he'd had to walk a half mile back before finding his backpack. With that lifeline recovered, he'd retreated into some low hills, putting a few miles between himself and the tracks. Heading generally south, he'd navigated toward the lights of a small town, then napped in the hollow of a windbreak with a good tactical egress route. Before the sun came up, he'd entered town. At the back of a gas station with no surveillance cameras, he'd found a hose and taken a very long drink, washed himself up.

He'd changed his clothes and tied his hair back in a short ponytail. His ball cap was long gone, but that was just as well. He'd considered altering his face by shaving his beard, since his legend was now blown. But he wanted to fit in with the locals, who tended toward facial hair. Though a little old for it, Dale now opted for the drifter-backpacker look.

He'd been dragging out his time in the café. It was the kind of roadhouse that might see twenty customers across two meal services, getting by on revenues of perhaps a hundred bucks a day. There'd been only a few patrons this morning. A single hustling kid shifted between grill, tables, and cash register.

Dale had been delighted to find it, a sleepy little hole in the wall where he might recover some energy.

A potential interloper had come in about a half hour back. At first Dale thought he was going to be trouble; then he'd reconsidered.

The new kid had short hair and a goatee. He was about twenty-five and had that nervous, twitching quality of someone up to no good. When he'd come in, the boy who ran the place had simply nodded from across the grill. Goatee had taken a look around, noted Dale, and parked himself at a table like it was his office. He'd been there ever since, drinking Turkish coffee from a tiny cup, answering his frequently ringing phone in a voice too low to be heard.

The bell on the door rang and another young Iranian walked in. He was dressed like a construction worker: beefy boots, orange sweatshirt. He and Goatee went out in the parking lot, out of sight. Dale heard the muffled sound of a car door, maybe a trunk. Then the bell dinged again as Goatee came back. He had another call three minutes later.

Dale had a theory: Goatee was a drug dealer and he was allowed to work his table in the open for a cut to Grill Boy. His supply probably came from across the border in Turkey, making the café a uniquely valuable location. God knew the restaurant needed the money. The food was only so-so.

The kid in charge came to clear the table. Dale ordered coffee to drag his stay out a little longer. He could also use the caffeine.

Google Maps said he needed to cover more than three hundred miles to get down to Alut. He had three days to get there. It wasn't going to happen on foot. He wondered if Goatee might be up for a quick buck.

With the Glock in the small of his back, Dale approached his table. The proprietor was washing dishes now. It was just the two of them during a momentary pause between cell calls.

"I need a ride," Dale said after a polite greeting in his accented Farsi.

Like the entrepreneur that he was, Goatee appraised Dale. His eye lingered on the CIA man's face, probably noting the scratches that ran from below his left eye to the top of his beard.

"I'm not Uber," the kid said. "We don't have that around here."

His phone rang again. The kid looked at it, pressed a button to silence it, set it down.

Okay, Dale thought. *He's at least up for a negotiation.*

"Precisely why I need a ride," Dale replied.

"Where you from, old-timer?"

Old-timer? "Canada. Just doing some trekking. I need to meet some friends down south. I've got money."

The magic words. The kid leaned back. They talked about a price. Dale started low; the kid jacked him high. When it got high enough, the kid asked Dale to prove he'd be able to pay. Dale held up a fistful of rials. Goatee nodded, disappeared behind the counter. Dale could hear him talking things over with the cook in the kitchen, but he couldn't make out what they were saying.

Goatee came back and said no. He needed more money. He said there were a lot of police about. Not that they were doing anything illegal, but there might be roadblocks. NAJA did that sometimes. To get around them would cost extra. Dale promised more and threw in the sweetener of a 50 percent down payment.

A few minutes later, he was in the front passenger seat of an '89 Peugeot bouncing over a gravel road. The low growl of the tires, the hazy gray daylight, and the long sleepless night put him in a lull. He knew he couldn't afford that.

He reached into a pocket and found a tin of Altoids. Buried inside, he located one of his pills, an amphetamine. He threw it in his mouth with some mints, slugging it down with the bottle of water he'd bought at the diner. A few minutes later, he was wide-awake with fresh breath. He kept one eye on the kid, one eye on the road.

Goatee shifted his glance sideways. He smiled at Dale.

Whether from jet lag, the extra gravity of bad news, or low blood sugar, Meredith was beginning to slump in her seat. More than anything, she wanted to cast aside all vanity, bend forward, and lay her head down like a preschooler at nap time. But her team was giving her the latest on Iran.

Having yet to check in to her hotel, she was still in yoga pants, running shoes, and a linen shirt. They were in the featureless Formica conference room on the third floor of a featureless Dubai office building. The sign on the locked door at the foyer declared it as suite 301, Fuse International Partners, a consulting company with a wholly fictitious set of books submitted to the IRS every year for good measure. The firm's managing director, Maggie O'Dea, was in town. Business was not good; Maggie was not happy.

The Iranians were continuing to ramp up their military posture. Planes had been fueled on tarmacs. Naval ship boilers had been fired. Troop leaves had been canceled. The intelligence signs were plain. Yet they were also lacking, since no one knew the status of the nascent Iranian nuclear capability.

The man who could provide some answers was supposed to be on his way in. The DEVGRU commandos who were to help the exfil were in place up in eastern Iraq at FOB Hammer. They'd taken one practice run toward the border, just to check the timing and the terrain. They had a Reaper drone quietly surveying the landscape from the Iraqi side, bulking up useful intel.

But CENTCOM was getting cold feet. Meredith had had to get on the phone to soothe some colonel up there in charge of operations. That was bad enough. It got much worse when Rance called.

She'd been tempted to send him to voice mail. But she knew it would only make things worse. She steeled herself and stepped into the hall. No need for the team to witness this. She tightened her abs, waiting for the gut punch.

Rance's salvo was both intense and voluminous. Just what in the fuck was she doing in Dubai when she was supposed to meet him there at the W in Doha? Where the hell were her husband and Cerberus?

Why didn't Rance have the details of the meet yet? Didn't she know that CENTCOM himself had escalated to Dorsey? Just WTF kind of op was this?

Meredith absorbed the words like arrows, wincing now and then at some of the harsher language. But callused by years of practice, she was armored up for this kind of thing. Profanity? Check. Indignation? Roger. Condescension? In spades. The one-way conversation had so far met all of her expectations of the Significant Male Tantrum.

After Hurricane Rance had blown itself out, she stayed quiet for five long seconds, nothing but a hiss on the line between them. She clenched her toes, enduring the calculated silence.

"Well?" Rance finally shouted at her. That was her cue—the invitation to speak.

"Ed, you're right," she began. "My behavior has been inexcusable." Step one in the playbook: ensure the male felt vindicated. "I should have been able to handle all of this without any of your involvement." On to step two: stroking the aggrieved ego. "I really look up to you and it feels terrible to have let you down." Finally, the crucial third step: feigned sacrifice. "If you were to ask me to resign right now, I'd fully understand. Really."

They both knew *that* wasn't going to happen. Like it or not, Meredith was the one and only link to John, who was the one and only link to Cerberus. Cerberus was perhaps the only person in the world who could help them with the Iranian conundrum.

She heard Rance sigh, two hundred miles away.

"All right," he said. Another breath. "Let's not overreact. No need to get crazy. I guess I'm here anyway. So what now?"

This would be tricky. She needed things to sound positive, while still keeping him at arm's length. She still wasn't willing to risk details that might be compromised. Not when they were this close to the end. She briefed him on what CENTCOM had done so far, the practice sortie, the Reaper drone.

She added, "Tomorrow night's the first night that Cerberus should be at Alut. He'll ping us as soon as he's on-site. Just as soon as my DOD orders clear, I'm headed up to Hammer, and I will personally brief the DEVGRU team."

"All right," Rance said. "But I want you up at Hammer tonight. Just in case your husband is early."

"I don't have orders from DOD yet."

"Fuck that. I'll get them," he said, boasting. "Expect a bird to pick you up in the next couple of hours."

Though Rance thought he had that kind of juice, she doubted it. DOD was impenetrable. Then again, Rance could be surprisingly effective when he wanted to be.

Hours later, after the sun had set, when she'd begun to think her flight to Hammer might not materialize until morning, she trudged to her hotel. She bade her team goodbye and caught a cab to the Marriott.

She couldn't stop thinking about John. In one sense she expected his bias toward silence. On the other, she thought something was off. To calm herself, she called Grace from the back of her cab. But it was the middle of the day back in Annapolis. Grace was off doing naval things.

The lobby was busy. It seemed to take forever to check in. But finally, she had her room and the key card to a very high floor, thirty-some stories up. It was a long walk through the lobby to the express elevators. Meredith wished it weren't. She felt weak.

Just as the elevator doors were closing, an Emirates Air flight attendant thrust out a hand to make them reopen. She got in the car next to Meredith, muttering a thank-you with a vaguely English accent. She stood on the other side of an overweight Arab businessman.

For less than a second, Meredith wondered why the default thank-you had been in English. She let it go. Everyone spoke English. The Arab got off at the first express stop, the twentieth floor. It was just the two women now.

Meredith had admired the uniform of the flight attendants during the flight over from the other side of the world—desert tan fitted skirt and jacket, charming red hat with dark veil. As the elevator resumed its climb skyward, the flight attendant fiddled with a makeup kit.

For God's sake, why? Meredith wondered, looking at the flight attendant from the reflection of the number pad. The woman was beautiful, as were most of the handpicked flight attendants of the chauvinistic Middle Eastern airlines. Beautiful. *An eleven.*

Meredith became suddenly uncomfortable. She reached forward to hit the number of a different floor. She thought through the location of the Glock she'd picked up at the office. It was in her handbag. She moved her fingers toward the clasp.

The blonde suddenly spun toward her. There was something in her hand. It looked like a pen. While Meredith reached for her gun, the blonde jabbed her in the jaw, snapping back her chin. Before she knew what was happening, Meredith felt a terrible sting in her neck.

The CIA officer raised an arm in a defensive maneuver and tried to kick the woman in the knees. But her limbs felt suddenly weighted. While her mind churned through five things she should have been doing to neutralize the threat, her body wouldn't listen. Powerless, she sank to a crouch on the elevator floor while the blonde zip-tied her wrists.

CHAPTER 39

OLEG HAD PUSHED THE OLD SENTRA ALL THE WAY TO THIS DUSTY
brown village called Alut. He could see a cluster of dark buildings in the
moonlight. Few of them had lights. He'd arrived well after dusk, around
ten, sought out concealment, and prepared to sleep. He'd taken down
some of the food he'd brought with him and slugged down the water.
He'd need to be careful with that, he thought, as he wasn't sure how
long he'd have to be here.

He hoped it would all be quick. He was low on food and gas. Whatever went down in the next twenty-four hours, he wasn't sure how he
was going to get back to Tehran. The Nissan had an eighth of a tank and
the last gas station had been forty miles back.

He'd passed by the station because he didn't like the heat he'd seen
on the highway. Better to duck down to the random gravel tracks in the
dark whenever he could, following his handheld GPS as he picked his
way forward. No sense in taking additional risks with the Iranian police. His Dragunov sniper rifle was in the trunk alongside an AK-12.
His GSh-18 nine-mil sidearm was under the seat, just in case he couldn't
talk his way past a nosy cop.

His satphone buzzed on the seat next to him. He angled its antenna
out the window and threw an earbud in before answering.

"I've got the details," Maria said.

"Horosho," he said. It was astonishing the kinds of things Zoloto
could pull off.

"Where are you now?" she asked him in a monotone.

Oleg recognized when she was in mission mode. "I'm on the outskirts of the town," he replied. "Not much here. A few small houses, more like farms and ranches."

"I have the coordinates for the rendezvous. Ready?"

Still connected by the earbud, he put the satphone on the car's roof to keep the signal. He groped for a pen, scrawled the numbers on his forearm, white in the moonlight.

"Hang on while I validate," he said.

He typed the digits into the GPS. There was total silence on the line as Maria waited.

"It checks," he said. "About a half mile from where I am right now. When?"

"She's set up a rendezvous window over a couple nights, beginning tomorrow, between midnight and four. Once they link up, a Special Forces team will come in for the egress. But she doesn't have a pos on either Dale or Rahimi. Neither of them has been in touch with her for a few days."

"She doesn't know how Dale and Rahimi are approaching? Vehicle? Direction? Anything?"

"No, nothing. Believe me, I would have gotten it out of her."

"What about military? Could the egress team already be in-country somewhere with ground assets? Could some of them be with Dale already?"

"No. Dale's alone. The plan is for the commando team to come in from the west. Iraq."

Oleg nodded. That was how he would have set it up too, given the circumstances.

"What's she like?" he asked.

"Compliant."

Dale was on his third amphetamine pill. He hated relying on them, but he didn't see that he had a choice. Especially now.

His driver, Goatee, whose given name was Jamil, was starting to fade. They'd made good progress until an hour back. Things were slower now.

Up on the highway they'd seen an increasing police presence. They were on the back roads, which didn't go in a straight line. Occasionally Dale had noticed the blinking anti-collision lights of low-flying aircraft. Once he'd even heard the crackling thunder of a fighter jet soaring by.

As they'd approached a small city called Saqqez just after dusk, they'd seen a genuine blockade in the distance. Expecting to see the blue-striped vehicles of NAJA, Dale had instead witnessed the green-and-tan military vehicles of the IRGC. Jamil had gotten extra twitchy then. So had Dale.

To keep him focused, Dale had offered an extra incentive of more money, given the unexpected challenges. That had woken the tired kid up for a while, but now he was insisting on a stop. He'd said he would need reinforcements to get through all the cops.

He had a friend in town who could set them up with supplies and help with a better route through Saqqez. By supplies, Dale assumed the kid meant drugs, most likely coke.

Dale went along with it. While he could have just stolen the car, he thought traveling with the kid would be good cover in case they were pulled over. And maybe Jamil's friend really would know how to navigate through the town.

They were waiting on a corrugated dirt road. The kid's head was starting to droop. Dale figured there was no real harm in letting him sleep. He wanted to check his satphone for any updates from Meth, but he didn't want to chance that with the kid next to him.

A pair of headlights appeared over a rise, then a silvery cloud of moon-lit dust, then a dented white Suzuki Samurai of Reagan-administration vintage.

Jamil woke up and smiled. "Finally," he said, opening the door. He stretched.

Samurai and Jamil met up with a complicated handclasp. Dale watched them through the windshield, backlit by the Suzuki's head-lights. They were both grinning. The new guy was shaggy—long hair tied in waxen dreadlocks and a beard that met up with his chest hair. If Iran had a Rastafarian culture, this kid had found it. Jamil waved to Dale to come on out.

There was some small talk. Rasta wanted to know who he was. Dale made up a story, but he got the feeling that Rasta had other things on his mind. He clearly wasn't listening. Jamil told his friend to get "the stuff." Rasta went around the back side of the Suzuki and opened the little tailgate.

He came back with an old revolver.

He was pointing it at Dale.

"Let's just see how much money you have, Canada," Jamil said, smiling. The kid was wide-awake now.

Dale had wondered if flashing all those rials might lead to trouble. Now he knew.

Dale started reasoning with them. He said they could have the money. He just wanted the ride. Jamil replied with something along the lines of: no, this was as far as they were going; money please.

Dale shrugged. "Okay," he said, "let me get it out of my pocket."

Hopped up on uppers as he was, Dale was hyperalert. The Glock flew out of his waistband with practiced ease. Though he really didn't want to kill anyone, moralizing at the open end of a gun barrel often proved fatal.

Dale put two bullets through Rasta's chest before either kid understood what had happened.

The revolver fell to the road as Rasta fell back, the sounds of the automatic pistol echoing off the hills. Jamil's eyes went wide. He went for the fallen weapon, diving to the dirt.

Oh, Jamil, Dale thought with the slightest flicker of regret. *Why'd you do that?*

He shot the kid in the thigh, just above the knee, shattering the femur. Jamil rolled over, screaming, clutching the wound. Dale heard a helicopter in the distance, reminding him that he didn't need this kind of nonsense.

In between agonizing sobs, Jamil started pleading for his life. It worked. Dale couldn't just kill this defenseless grifter. He tore a strip from Rasta's filthy shirt. He knelt to tie a tourniquet on the kid's leg. Jamil, to his credit, sat up and tried to attack Dale, clutching at his eyes. One last gasp. Poor kid.

Dale hit him hard twice in the face. The second blow sent the kid's head to the dirt. He was unconscious, most likely because he was also going into shock, Dale thought. He finished tying the tourniquet, careful to avoid staining his own pants with the kid's blood.

Alone in the moonlight now, with only the distant sounds of helicopters and the wind racing across the scrub, Dale searched the two cars. The Samurai had a full tank of gas and piles of stinking clothes. It was as though Rasta had lived in there. There was a smudged jug of water but no food, nothing else of value.

Between the aging Peugeot and the ridiculous Suzuki, Dale opted for the latter. It seemed a better fit for his drifter getup. It also had four-wheel drive.

He dragged Jamil over to his Peugeot and laid him to one side. He took the sedan's keys and threw them into the desert. Then he found the old revolver. On snapping open the barrel, he saw that it had all of three bullets. Pathetic. Dale took them out of the gun and scattered them in the brush. Then he tossed the old pistol in the other direction.

Well, Dale thought as he drove off in the straining Samurai, at least he had his own ride now. One step closer to getting out of that shithole. And the kid had a chance, sort of.

He stopped and took a look at the coordinates he'd gotten from Meth a few days ago. The GPS said eighty clicks to go. They'd be slow ones, dodging the IRGC and all that; but he'd get there.

Kasem had spent an uncomfortable night on a makeshift cot at the school in Saqqez. He was personally supervising the search now. The prior day, he'd joined the helicopter crew on flights that went up and down the roads, looking for anything unusual. They'd come up empty.

When Kasem was back on the ground, the captain had told him of some rumors that elements of the old PDKI, the Kurdish freedom fighters, were getting back together in the hills. But Kasem had no interest in pursuing that. The man he was looking for was no guerrilla and the PDKI was probably just reacting to the heavy IRGC presence. He'd redirected the searching IRGC garrison to the border areas.

The sound of the helicopter spinning up on the soccer field woke him around midnight. He'd heard that Maloof was still furious that Kasem had defied his orders and taken the aircraft west. As he listened to the turbines whining, he thought about running out to the field, trying to stop them. But he didn't think it would work. They knew whom they really worked for.

He was even more worried now without the helicopter. His authority seemed to be slipping away. He sat up. Sleep would be impossible. He scraped together the implements for tea and checked his phone for messages.

Nothing from Kasra. As he plugged in the electric kettle, he rationalized that maybe it was a good thing. Perhaps it was because she was incommunicado on the westbound flight across the Med. Inshallah, *let that be true,* he thought, wondering at his unexpected nod to Islam.

Farther down the list was a message from one of his lieutenants in Tehran. Kasem called him back.

The last time they'd spoken, Kasem had asked for a check with the IRGC Air Force on any American military presence on the Iraqi border. If he'd already missed Rahimi outside of Saqqez, perhaps he could catch them at the border. He needed to narrow the search.

"Got your message," Kasem started, dropping a dry tea bag into a cup. He'd ordered the young officer to be ready at all hours.

"I hope you're having a good evening, sir."

If there was one thing Kasem disliked about his young lieutenant, it was his sycophancy. *"Well?"* he said, annoyance rising.

"Sir—one of our patrol aircraft picked up an American drone on radar. It was following an orbit close to the border. They said they'd never seen one that far north before."

"Don't you think the Americans might have increased surveillance because of all of our military maneuvers? I can't even sleep for all the jet noise."

"Yes, sir. I said the same thing. But they said they've seen the American response to exercises before. There are a lot of drones up. But this area is a new one—near the border."

Kasem thought it over. The kettle had come up to temperature. He turned it off and poured.

The obsequious lieutenant became uncomfortable with the silence. "You said to concentrate on the border, sir," he said.

"I did. It's interesting. Anything else?" He stirred his tea.

"Yes, sir. The Air Defense Force monitors American flights in the area, constantly looking for cruise missile attacks—that's how they picked up the drone. Usually there aren't manned aircraft. But yesterday early-warning radars detected a helicopter. It came up a few miles shy of the border and turned around. I don't know if that matters."

"Did it land?"

"No, sir."

Kasem sipped the scalding tea. He asked for the coordinates of the drone and helicopter pings, wrote them all down, hung up.

Alone in the classroom, he plotted the coordinates with a pencil on the chart taped to the chalkboard, stood back, and looked at the lines. The north and south points of the drone orbit came in tangent to a small jut of Iranian land that reached into Iraq like a short peninsula. The helicopter path neared it as well, perpendicular to the drone track. The two pencil lines looked like a sideways T. It was only a hundred clicks south of where he was now. The closest village was a little hamlet called Alut.

Because Kasem had conducted exfil operations himself, his intuition fired: favorable terrain, easily traversed on foot or in a Jeep; friendly Iranian Kurdistan, where the locals might not mind. Most telling, the shape of the border would allow the Americans to set up defenses on three sides without technically entering Iranian airspace. He should have noticed that before.

He pulled the map from the chalkboard and folded it to a rectangle that exposed the area around his own pencil marks. He went and found the captain, who'd been asleep in a nearby tent. He rudely shook the young officer awake.

"I need someone to drive me down to this area," he said. "Right now."

CHAPTER 40

IMMACULATELY CLAD IN HER TAILORED EMIRATES AIR UNIFORM, MARIA thanked the young bellhop near the revolving front doors for bringing in her enormous rolling equipment case with the Emirates Air markings. It was one in the morning and there was no one else around the Marriott's front entrance, save for a few cabbies smoking in the breezeway.

Feeling chatty, the bellhop commented that the case was much lighter than it looked. Predictably, he then flirted with Maria, saying something suggestive about how he might bring it up to her room himself.

Her steely blue eyes shot him a cold look that made him shrink behind his desk. She rolled the big black case back toward the elevator, her heels clicking on the marble floor.

There wasn't much time. By morning, Maria assumed, the CIA would declare Morris-Dale MIA and be there with guns drawn. The plan had been to dope her up with scopolamine, get quick information on the meet, then spirit the CIA woman away in the large rolling case for further interrogation. After that, none of it would matter. She'd leave Morris-Dale's body in a dumpster.

But things hadn't gone smoothly. Maria had overestimated Morris-Dale's size and overdosed the tranquilizer. It was supposed to immobilize her, make her malleable—not knock her out. As it was, it'd been a struggle to get her down a public hallway and into Maria's room.

Fortunately, passersby respected the striking flight attendant's uniform. With Maria's perfect composure and erect bearing, other guests simply parted so the two women could pass, accepting the idea that it was someone in authority aiding a distraught civilian.

Once they were in the room, it'd taken an hour before Morris-Dale became lively enough for the scopolamine. But it had finally worked. Under the influence, the CIA woman had eventually detailed the plan for the exfil, albeit blearily. Then she'd gone completely slack, passing out. Now she was securely bound and locked away, sleeping it off.

If Maria could keep her sedated, she'd dump her in the case and wheel her to the rented van, then take her to a leased office where a more intense interrogation could unfold. She wanted more details about Rahimi, wanted to know more about the CIA network across the region. But she knew she needed to be careful with the drugs. She didn't want the CIA woman to die before spilling all of her secrets.

Thirty floors up, Meredith came awake. She was lying on her side, a sheet of duct tape over her mouth. She was groggy, her head splitting, confused. The blockage in her mouth caused her to strain for air. She started to hyperventilate.

She shifted to her side and shuddered, struggling for lucidity. In doing so, she methodically cataloged one dreadful fact after another. Her hands were bound behind her with a zip tie. Her ankles as well. The red wig had been ripped from her head.

These realizations caused her adrenaline to surge. She felt her heart rate racing, her breath going faster, out of control. She had the sudden urge to vomit.

She'd been trained for situations like this. She started to tell herself not to panic, though she was already there. She inhaled shakily, commanding her stomach to settle, her hands to remain still. She had to think—had to get her body under control. That was what they'd always said back at the Farm.

Use the facts. Start from the beginning. How'd she get here? She remembered the blonde and the elevator, but that was about it.

She took in her surroundings. She was in a closet. A trickle of light came through the crack under the door. Patterned hotel room carpet— her hotel room, she realized. She could see the wheels of her suitcase over by the bed. The bracket where the iron should have been was empty. There were no hangers on the rail. It was all stripped.

Though she couldn't remember much, she knew what it meant. If she didn't get out of this, she wouldn't live to see another sunrise. The trainers had always said that if your abductors moved you to a different location, you were dead.

She bent her knees and rolled side to side, testing the space. She realized she was in her socks. Her shoes had been removed. So had her linen shirt. She wore only her stretchy yoga pants and the tank top that had been under her shirt, a running bra under that.

There seemed to be no one else in the room, but she dared not make a sound. Focused on her breathing, she did her best to think, to take stock of things and develop a plan, like she was supposed to. It was clear she'd been searched and stripped into what she wore now. But she wondered if that really included everything.

She said a silent prayer to herself, thinking of Grace. She also thought of John, remembering the whole reason she was in this city, this room, this predicament. Whatever happened, she thought, they would be okay. Then she thought of John again. He was still in the wild, depending on her. Maybe he wouldn't be okay.

She thought further, doing everything she could to focus. There was a chance she had a way out of this. But only if whoever had searched her had missed something. It would be her best shot. Irrationally, she paused before checking for it. If it wasn't there, she didn't know what she would do. Probably die.

When she was finally ready, she quietly turned toward her other side, rocking deliberately back and forth against the floor, ignoring the impulse to cry. But then she felt the pressure on her thigh she'd been hoping to feel. Though she'd been deliberately controlling her emotions, she let out a small involuntary gulp of excitement under the duct tape.

When Meredith was traveling through public airports undercover, she was unable to carry a pistol. But that didn't mean she was defenseless; she carried things that escaped scrutiny with airport security. In the rails of her suitcase handle was a concealed knife, sheathed in lead. In her pocket she always kept a health insurance identification card. *That* pocket, the small flush one on the thigh of her svelte yoga pants.

She could feel it there. It was slightly thicker than a regular laminated ID card, about the size of a magnetized security pass. When properly manipulated, it separated to expose a razor blade.

Meredith breathed deeply again. Its presence let her thoughts flow more easily, a ray of hope. She sat up in the dark, her bound ankles out in front of her, her arms clasped behind her back. She could do this, she told herself.

She exhaled fully and sat on her hands. Flexible from countless hours in yoga studios, she bent at the waist, sliding her wrists along the backs of her thighs.

Yes. She *would* do this.

She took one more deep breath before completely deflating and bending almost in half. An inch at a time, she scooted her bound wrists under her butt, her thighs, her knees. She was so far forward that she felt her shoulders separating. With one more exhalation and back-breaking stretch, she retracted her bound ankles and, with a final grunt, slipped her wrists under her heels. She now had her bound hands in front of her.

Anxious with this first physical success, she reminded herself to control her breathing. She paused to listen. Still no sound from the other side of the door.

She slid her manacled wrists along her thigh and withdrew the ID card. She put one end of the card in her teeth, squeezed both sides with her thumbs, and pulled. It separated. She now had a razor in her hands. She bent forward and sawed her ankles free first, then held the blunt end of the razor in her teeth while she moved her wrists in a sawing motion to cut the plastic zip tie.

But just as she freed her hands, she heard an alarming beep. A lock turned. The room's main door opened.

Meredith froze. She could see shadows of movement beneath the door. The person was coming toward the closet. Meredith silently propped herself on one knee. There'd only be one shot at this. One.

When the closet door slid open, Meredith saw the hat and veil of an Emirates flight attendant. The CIA officer sprang up and forward with a slash of the razor. She was aiming for the flight attendant's jugular. But still disoriented from the drugs, she missed.

The blonde was quick. She stepped back and kicked Meredith, sending her into a wall. She followed this with a punch to the ribs, another to the side of her head. Meredith saw stars, felt the wind coming out of her. The blonde was turning, reaching for something under her coat.

Expecting a gun, Meredith dropped to the floor and lunged for the blonde's ankles. She connected the blade to the rear of a bare left leg, just above a patent leather shoe. Meredith ripped the blade savagely across the Achilles tendon, then ran it straight up the exposed calf.

The blonde gasped and stumbled, but stayed upright somehow. She had a syringe in her hand. She landed it in Meredith's shoulder blade but had to let go as she twisted away. It stayed hanging on Meredith's back for a moment before falling free.

Meredith roared in anger, swinging the blade out and up as she rose from her crouch. This time it swept thickly across the meat of the blonde's neck.

The Russian's blue eyes widened. She made a ragged wailing noise that turned into a groan. She brought her hands to her throat, backing away, a look of disbelief on her face.

The gash in her neck was only a few inches wide. But it was enough. Her blood sluiced through her fingers. The animalistic growl she'd been making sputtered into a gurgle.

Shaking and out of breath, Meredith took a step back, ready to strike again, watching, her breath heaving.

But she wouldn't need to.

The blonde's lovely painted mouth opened and closed rhythmically as she grappled with the wound. Slowly, the life drained from those beautiful blue eyes.

A few minutes later, her lungs gasping hoarsely, Meredith forced herself to think about the mission. She searched the blonde but found little, other than the unmarked vial of drugs and a locked phone. The Russian's tradecraft had been too sharp for anything else incriminating, other than the large empty roller case, big enough for a body. Meredith had a good sense that it had been fitted for her. She supposed the drugs were to keep her tranquilized until she could be renditioned to God knew where.

Eventually Meredith recovered her own phone, which had been buried in the blonde's bag. Turning it on, she took a photo of the dead woman's face. She would need that.

Slumping, she sat in a chair and fought off the urge to simply deflate, to cry, to fall to pieces as she thought about what she'd just been through. Thinking now of John, she steeled herself, looking at the dead woman in front of her. She thought about what to do next, the implications of all this. It brought a wave of anger forward, focusing her.

Not an eleven now, she thought.

CHAPTER 41

TWENTY-SEVEN HOURS LATER, MEREDITH SAT IN THE DARK AT A PLY-wood table, watching the gray-green feed from the drone on an overhead monitor. It was dark and cold there in the operational nerve center of FOB Hammer. Serious men and women in green uniforms crouched over scopes, speaking to one another in low voices. They used a mystifying jargon of acronyms that she had a hard time following. It was all the more difficult because her mind was still not quite right.

A flight surgeon had taken pity on her and given her a quilted Nomex flight jacket. A Marine first lieutenant had donated an MRE—Meal, Ready to Eat—to take down right after she'd landed. She was at least warm and well-fed now, thanks to her military hosts.

But her eyes were sunken with exhaustion, her mouth puckered with worry. She'd discarded Maggie O'Dea's wig in favor of an efficient ponytail. A thick layer of makeup covered the emerging bruises. She knew she looked like hell and didn't much care.

She still hadn't heard from John. But watching the drone feed, she could at least see that he was in place now. In the white-hot blur of IR, he lay in a sniper's position a few hundred yards from the sheep pen across the border in Iran, which they'd all started calling "the corral." She had no idea how John had managed to get there or procure the rifle in his arms, but that was the kind of thing he was good at.

She stared at the screen, at him, willing some kind of telepathic communication. She wished desperately that they could speak for real, even for a few seconds. But he'd been ignoring the messages. Seeing him there, vulnerable, far away, she was willing to excuse his silence—for once.

She strained at the image to better understand his real status. Hurt? In danger? In contact with the asset? In the blurry projection of IR, she could see only the vague white shape of a man lying on his stomach.

He wasn't wearing the IR reflector. But NSA had received intercepts that the IRGC was conducting a manhunt across Iranian Kurdistan—yet with no mention of Alut. With that kind of heat, Meredith assured all of them that John could have lost all of his gear in his surely perilous journey down from Turkey. Plans in the field with officers like John were all about improvisation. The man lying there had to be John, IR reflector or no.

A wider view from the side-scan video of the drone had revealed a compact Nissan Sentra parked alongside the road a few miles up. Its engine was still glowing white, though faintly. The official assessment was that John had probably left it there and snuck up on the ranch via a wide, circuitous route, extra cautious, as he was known to be. He must've done it during the day, before the drone had arrived on station.

The drone had arrived only a few minutes earlier, since every second on the wrong side of the border invited a shoot down from the IRGC Air Defense Force. Planned mission time over target was a max of sixty minutes, as long as they didn't detect fighters heading toward it.

But since their man was there, the military operations team thought the hour would be enough. The modest car, the stealthy approach, the sniper's tactical hide—all of it smacked of John. They'd looked to Meredith for confirmation of identity and she'd given it. A rumor in the ranks said she was the wife. If anyone should know, it'd be her.

Now, whenever the drone shifted to show that white blob of a human form, Meredith felt a weary surge of tentative satisfaction. She'd almost gotten John home. She'd almost given Grace her father back. Almost. If only goddamned Cerberus would show so she could call it a wrap. Then she'd deal with the dead Russian operative in her hotel room. Then she'd deal with Rance.

Every now and then she glanced over at his red-blond head. Rance was near the door, speaking with the DEVGRU CO as though he were one of the boys, a tough guy. He wore a khaki vest with cargo pockets and pressed olive pants of heavy twill. She wondered what that hard-bitten Navy captain would do to Rance if he understood what she really knew of Rance.

Or *thought* she knew, she reminded herself, ever the intelligence professional. She went back to staring at the image of John. What did she really know about Rance?

The presentation of evidence against him was damning at a circum-stantial level.

Rance had called her, angry that she was in Dubai, not Doha. He'd said he would send a helicopter to get her out of there, up to Hammer. Yet in the ensuing interlude, quite the opposite had happened. She'd been ruthlessly attacked by the blond Russian operative, the same one who'd gone after John in Mumbai. Coincidence? No way. Verdict? Guilty.

But beyond a reasonable doubt?

If Rance really was a willing accomplice, an active agent of the SVR, then he was hiding it well. He'd shown no real surprise when she'd ar-rived at the dusty airfield. He'd mumbled an apology about the delay in the transport, true to form. All of his usual foibles were there: the fussi-ness about the operational details, the crankiness about John.

But he was also focused now, free of the distractions that had seemed to plague him over the past few months. Since Meredith had jumped out of the helo from Dubai, Rance had been quick to drill her for de-tails. He seemed fully in command, impressively efficient at getting the DEVGRU team briefed up. None of that fit with someone running a side agenda.

It was all very confusing. If he'd really known about the blonde's mission, he should have been shocked to see Meredith. Even now, slouch-ing against the wooden wall, his posture showed nothing unusual.

He certainly couldn't have known the blonde was dead now. No one knew except Meredith. After killing her, she'd pulled the bloody body into the bathtub, containing the leaky mess, covering it with a bedsheet. She'd also covered the floor stains with bath towels, as though it even mattered. She'd done it only so she wouldn't have to look at them.

Meredith had done a quick scan for intelligence, an SSE, surveying the blonde's luggage. There was a phone, locked, and no sign of a weapon. The clothing in the bag was a well-ordered array of fashion with English brands, a spare Emirates uniform, some frilly underwear. There was a makeup kit with expensive French labels. The big empty equipment case had stenciled Emirates serial numbers on it.

That was a nice touch, Meredith thought. *A little too nice.*

The SVR assassin had overlooked one small lapse in her concealment. Two small clear vials of liquid in the makeup case, presumably the drugs the blonde had been using on Meredith, had tiny Cyrillic markings on the bottom. There could be no mistaking it. The blonde was SVR.

Meredith had then sat up all night in the very closet that had acted as her initial prison, her phones blinking in front of her, the Glock across her knees. She'd reasoned that if the blonde had help, it would be coming through the door. She'd be ready.

She'd thought about calling CIA ops for reinforcements, but then reconsidered. If it was as bad as she thought, then there was no way she was going to tip off Rance.

Besides, even if Rance *wasn't* the spy she believed he might be, she knew what his reaction would be. Meredith would be declared radioactive again, burned, a careless fool for going back to Dubai as a NOC officer. She'd be pulled off the op right before the critical meet. She sure as shit wouldn't be sitting here in this operations center, watching the drone feed, confirming John's presence.

She'd made her decision. She'd keep her mouth shut in defense of the mission. That was the most important thing, for now.

But she was still conflicted. After all, what was *her* role in jeopardizing the mission? Given the memory gap, unconsciousness, and searing headache, she now suspected she might have been injected with some kind of truth serum—sodium pentothal, scopolamine, or some other concoction SVR had cooked up. Had she revealed something to the blonde? Her official assessment was that the risk was slight. Anything she'd said to the Russian assassin had surely died with her.

Around three a.m., when her phone had rung with orders to Hammer, she'd cleaned up, gathered her wares, and left the room with a do-not-disturb sign on the door. Boy, would housekeeping be surprised when they finally entered with a master key.

The aftermath would be an agency disaster. But she'd deal with the fallout later. The important thing was that Meredith was here now, looking at John in that gray-green monitor.

The on-deck SEAL team was a mere hundred meters away from where she sat, suited up in combat gear, slumped around a fueled-up helo. The plan was to launch once John and Cerberus started heading toward the border, not a moment before. They figured it would take John about a half hour to cross over on foot, the same amount of time it would take to fly the SEALs there.

A rising murmur among the soldiers suddenly caught Meredith's attention.

One of the Air Force noncoms saw it first, said something aloud, alerted the others. He used a laser pointer on the monitor. The drone zoomed in.

Two men, white with heat in IR, were coming up the road toward the corral. One of them carried an object. Another view revealed the telltale shape of an AK-47.

"Tighten up on the man with the rifle!" the DEVGRU CO barked.

CHAPTER 42

ZANA RAHIMI WAS DEAD TIRED, FREEZING COLD, AND NEARLY OUT OF his head with thirst. Zoran, the iron-limbed man who had become his guide, had almost carried him for the last twenty kilometers.

And it was only Zoran with Zana now. The others who had started off with them were long gone. They'd vanished days ago when the IRGC patrols had thickened along the roads. Only Zoran had remained loyal to the mission to get the older gentleman south to the Americans.

It was Zoran's idea to approach the farmhouse first. He knew how to talk to the villagers around here, he said. He also understood the limits of a man's endurance. If they didn't get some help right away, he believed, then the older gentleman from Tehran might die. What good would that be? The Americans needed to understand how badly they'd underestimated the mullahs' cruelty to the Kurds.

The conversation lasted for about fifteen minutes. The farmer listened, nodded, stood back by the dim light of the clapboard porch. His aging wife provided some water and cold beans left over from dinner. Zana wolfed it all down right there on the porch.

With niceties exchanged, Zana checked his watch. He apologized and told them that he needed to be up in their pasture now. He was tired and liked to sleep under the stars. The old couple thought it an odd thing to do, since they'd offered a bed. But Zana and Zoran insisted.

They walked the last half mile to the pasture in the dark. When they finally arrived, they piled up some cut weeds along a bank and crouched, waiting.

Oleg watched the two of them approach. He was on a bluff, set back from the pasture by about two hundred yards. His head was covered with a black-checkered kaffiyeh, his face darkened with dirt. He was lying on his stomach, looking through the IR scope of the Dragunov, his nine millimeter strapped to the back of his thigh. The AK-12 was within arm's reach, shoved against a scraggly bush.

He'd been lying there for nearly the entire day. In the old lament of the sniper, he'd had almost nothing to eat and been forced to piss himself twice. He wanted desperately to get up and stretch. But now it was game time and he dared not move a muscle.

He watched the two men coming up the trail toward the pasture. One of them was surely Rahimi, he thought. The weaker one, presumably the scientist, walked slowly. The stronger of them carried a Kalashnikov. Oleg zeroed in on the armed man, thinking it was probably Dale.

But then, even through the IR scope, he could see that it wasn't. The beard was too long, the posture off—this man was thicker than Dale.

Oleg thought about shooting the armed man anyway. He could take him down, then move to scoop up Rahimi.

But that would spook Dale if he was out there somewhere. Oleg wasn't going to retreat without knowing John Dale was dead. He decided to wait.

A half mile away, Dale pulled the Suzuki Samurai into a ditch. He wasn't sure what to expect up ahead, but he certainly wasn't going to come driving up to it without a solid reconnaissance effort.

It was nearly midnight. The moon, hidden by overcast, had done him the courtesy of providing some ambient light. He threw his pack on the hood of the Suzuki and went to work in the silvery light.

First, he removed the bag's back plate. After straining with the clever assembly for a minute, he then removed his shirt.

The rigid liner that had formed the frame of the bag was made of Kevlar. Dale used Velcro straps from the bag's outer straps to position the Kevlar over his chest before throwing on a thicker khaki shirt. He then tore the flexible IR reflector from the bag's handle and shoved it in a cargo pocket. He was supposed to put it on his shoulder once he sighted Cerberus. That was the way it was supposed to go.

Once ready, pistol in hand, he did a final check of the GPS. He looked at the hill in the moonlight. Things were quiet. Thank God.

He was almost home. For good.

CHAPTER 43

THINGS HAD GOTTEN CHAOTIC IN THE OPS CENTER AT HAMMER. THE drone operators were zoomed in on the two men walking up the hill, one of them with an AK. The armed one seemed to be helping the other man along. They asked Meredith, "Could that be Cerberus?"

She needed to be sure. She asked for a short digital video clip of the weaker man to be sent to her phone. While waiting for it, she called Desmond and explained.

She zapped the video over ten thousand miles of ether to a CIA server. Desmond called back five minutes later. The wife, Nadia, said it was Cerberus. Nadia had been horrified by her husband's diminished state, Desmond said.

Meredith couldn't have cared less. Of greater concern was John's response: lying there with the sniper rifle. Why wasn't he approaching Cerberus? Why wasn't he communicating with him somehow?

Damned if Meredith knew. She bit the inside of her cheek. John was going to get himself killed if he didn't let them know what was going on. Then again, she could surmise why her ex-husband hadn't seemed to move. The man with the AK was a wild card. John would simply perceive the threat and wait.

Every officer in the Hammer ops center wanted to know what AK man was doing there. They kept asking Meredith, as though she were pulling the strings from afar. Her only response was a suggestion that they launch—get the DEVGRU SEAL team in the air now, just as a backup. It was clear that all of the players had arrived on the field.

"No," Rance said, overriding her. Not until they knew what was happening. No one wanted to start a war. As previously discussed, John needed to get his man to the border first. That was the deal. No one wanted to start a war, Rance said again.

Dale climbed to a bluff with a reasonable view of the fenced pasture. He paused to scan it with an IR scope cleverly disguised as a flashlight.

What he saw shocked him: two men huddled to one side, crouching. One of them had a rifle, the unmistakable outline of a banana clip. An AK.

Dale looked closely, zooming in. In the strange, inverted, photo-negative light of the scope, he focused on the unarmed man's face.

Meth had provided him with a photo of Rahimi, obtained through the wife. Straining against the eyepiece, Dale thought he was looking at the man. He said a silent prayer of thanks. *Cerberus—at last.*

But who was the man with the Kalashnikov?

Dale studied the mystery man as best as he could. It was clear that he and Rahimi trusted each other. The man was dressed in the ragamuffin style of a mujahideen fighter. He was no IRGC regular.

Given Rahimi's trust in the armed man, Dale decided it was going to be okay. Whoever the man was, he must've aided Rahimi in getting there. That made sense. It was no easy hump crossing the last ten miles to get to this remote little farm.

But Dale was still cautious. He advanced toward the corral in a tactical crouch, moving slowly, pausing now and then to sweep for threats with the IR scope.

CHAPTER 44

"WE'VE GOT ANOTHER MAN!" SHOUTED THE AIR FORCE SERGEANT IN the ops center. The drone feed shifted slightly to show a man coming forward in a crouch, moving carefully.

They all swarmed around Meredith again. She stood, ignoring them, walking from behind her table, approaching the monitor. There was something about the way this newcomer walked, the way his knees rose and fell, the flicker of his free hand beside his hip. She had to be right about this.

"That's John!" she shouted, looking back toward Rance and the SEAL captain. She quickly remembered her protocol. "That's our case officer. That's our guy. We need to protect *that* guy!" She slapped the bottom of the monitor with her pointing hand.

"I thought you said the sniper guy was John," said the frustrated Air Force lieutenant colonel in charge of the drones.

Meredith admitted she'd been wrong. It had been hard to tell. But this new guy—that was him; that was their officer. The colonel rolled his eyes.

A chorus of voices asked if she was sure, noted the gravity if she was wrong. They needed a PID, positive ID, not this wishy-washy might-be stuff. Meredith felt a rising sense of frustration with all of them. Yes, she was motherfucking goddamned sure. Of course she was. She'd been married to the man. Did they think she didn't know who the hell he was? Then, gaining control of herself, she added that she was extra certain because he was moving now, making him easier to recognize.

"Confirm PID," she said with grim finality, swallowing hard.

When Rance asked her one more time if she was sure from across the room, she nearly pulled her sidearm from her hip to shoot him. Then she fought off the impulse. *Keep it together.*

"Yes, I know that's him," she announced again across the room, her eyes steady on John's screen, watching him advance slowly. But then she glanced at the other monitor, the one zoomed in on the unknown contact they'd previously thought was John.

"Oh, shit. *Look!*" she cried, willing all of them to see the same thing.

"We need to launch!" she shouted.

The grizzled SEAL captain scowled at her, startled. He said something about taking it easy.

She cut him off. "Can't you see that sniper? He's moving! He's aiming at our officer! We need to fucking *go!*"

Oleg couldn't believe his luck. He saw the new man approaching. The stealthy crouch forward and the studied use of concealment suggested he was a skilled operator. On focusing further through the scope, Oleg saw that it was Dale. He recognized the face. Finally.

Not smiling now, are you, Dale?

The Spetsnaz Alpha sniper shifted the long barrel of the Dragunov, putting the CIA man in the center of the scope's reticle. He paused to think through the slight wind drift, the distance. He exhaled slowly, squeezed the trigger. He fired.

CHAPTER 45

ZANA AND ZORAN WERE CONFUSED.

They'd heard the loud echo of the shot. Zoran, who was trained in the ways of war, had seen the brief yellow spark of the rifle.

"Did you expect that?" Zoran asked the older gentleman. "It sounded like a rifle. The shot came from over there." He pointed.

"No," Zana said, bending forward in fear. "Was he shooting at us?"

"No, not at us," answered Zoran, seemingly unfazed. "It went off that way, I think, based on the way I saw the muzzle flash."

Zana pulled Zoran down low, cowering. "All I can think," the scientist whispered, "is that it's Reza, the man I'm supposed to meet. Maybe a signal?"

"Did they say anything about a signal?"

"No."

"It could be IRGC, then."

"If it was IRGC, they would have come and arrested us first," said Zana. "There'd be jeeps and helicopters everywhere. It has to be Reza. Maybe you should fire that thing once up in the air to let him know we're here?"

"No. Whoever it is might think we're the enemy."

"Well, then let's just walk to the center of the pasture, like we're supposed to. I'm sure the Americans will have some way to see us in the dark."

"Yes, I suppose so," said Zoran.

The veteran guerrilla fighter stood first. They walked forward, toward the pasture's center. As they got close, Zana heard another rifle shot. It sounded closer than before, louder. Then he heard a thudding crack two feet from his ear.

Zoran took the bullet in the head and fell back, the AK skittering to the dirt beside him. It took a few beats for Zana to understand what had happened. Then he saw that Zoran's head was virtually gone, like it had just vanished.

Panicking, the scientist ran back to the tall grass that surrounded the pasture, then dove into a copse of weeds.

When he'd finally gathered his wits, he thought that maybe it was Reza. Maybe the CIA man had perceived Zoran as an enemy after all. The shot had gone so cleanly at Zoran, not at him.

After thinking it over, Zana thought it plausible. It had almost certainly been a tragic mistake. He now thought that it made more sense to come out and show himself as unarmed, ready to meet. But he felt sick for poor Zoran, the iron-limbed man.

A hundred yards away, Dale had risen to his hands and knees, gasping. The sniper's bullet had nicked the armor plate over his abdomen at an angle, breaking some ribs. Dale had been springing from a crouch, crossing a dry creek bed with a leap when it hit.

Jumping that creek bed had probably saved his life, he thought, gasping at the searing sting in his gut. The bullet had probably been aimed at his head. Instead, it hit as a glancing blow, smack in the middle of the Kevlar.

Now he scrunched up against the bank, panting, trying to fight off the pain. There was no blood. The wound hurt, but he wasn't out of the fight yet.

He had to get control of this. He had to know what was going on up there in the corral. If he didn't, he was a dead man.

Then he heard the second shot.

Fuck, he thought. Whoever was up there shooting had probably just killed Cerberus. The whole thing was a bust. *Fuck!* He forced himself to breathe deeply, told himself to calm down, to assess the tactical situation. Right now he had to worry about his own ass.

It had come from that bluff up there, about two hundred yards over. It had to have been the same guy who had gotten him in the breastplate. Now he was pinned down under the bastard.

He remembered the IR reflector in his pocket. Moving slowly, painfully, he shifted to get it out. He attached it to his shoulder with Velcro. Maybe, just maybe, there was an armed American drone up there in the night sky with a Hellfire. Maybe somebody watching would have the good sense to plaster that bastard sniper on the bluff.

He was half right.

Meredith had yanked Rance into the DEVGRU CO's tiny plywood side office, which had been carved out of a corner of the ops center. They were alone in the six-foot-square space, jammed against the CO's makeshift desk, which was scattered with yellow legal pads and Post-it Notes. Meredith stood before Rance, glowering, her arms crossed tightly to smother a heaving sickness working its way up her gut.

"You need to order the launch. *Now*," she said. Her voice had an uneven quality. Her mouth was dry.

Rance looked at her piteously. "You're the one who said it was John out there, Meredith. If you were right, then you have to accept that he's gone." Rance tried to take on a consoling, fatherly look. "I know it's tough, but the facts are the facts. I'm sorry."

She had no time for his attempt. "He was moving, Ed, crawling. He may be hit, but he's alive. For God's sake, it's a twenty-minute flight right across the border. We can get him *and* Cerberus. This can all be okay! What the fuck is wrong with you?"

"And the sniper? We've been *had*, Meredith. Face it. I'm sorry about John. I really am, but we can't rush into the middle of an ambush. This isn't a video game."

"Do we not have a fucking SEAL team standing right over there?

404

Do you think they can't handle a sniper? We've got ISR and enough firepower to create a swath of flame from here to Tehran. Let's *go*!"

"No," he said flatly. "My official order is no. I'm sorry."

He put a consoling hand on her forearm. She jerked free of him, disgusted.

He said, "Meredith, I know you're in pain right now. But even you can't deny that there's something wrong with the op. It's compromised. Rushing into it with guns blazing would be a mistake. We can't risk a war over it."

This idiot in front of her, the crazed assassin, John, the botched op . . . it all was suddenly too much. She clenched her eyes shut, raised a hand to pinch the skin at the bridge of her nose, bit a cheek. She had to think of something—now.

Rance looked on, silent, watching her.

She expelled a rushed breath. She recrossed her arms to steady herself. *No.* She was *not* going to let this happen.

Rance's last few words rang through her head like a bell. *Compromised? Oh, yeah, it sure has been,* she thought. She'd been waiting to say anything about this, wanting to get John to safety first. But now what did it matter? She was out of options.

She pulled out her phone, opened an app. "Who's *she*, Ed?"

It was the photo of the blonde. Her throat was cut, smeared with blood. The cold blue eyes stared vacantly. The made-up face was framed by the patterned carpet of a hotel room. Meredith watched Rance carefully as he comprehended it.

"What's this . . . ?" he started. "What do you think . . . ?"

His mouth went slack, his face turned ashen. He groped for something to say.

She knew beyond a shadow of a doubt then. The leak had been Rance.

"You're *fucked*," she said. "I killed that bitch in my hotel room twenty-four hours ago. She came to hit me. Same Russian whore that went after John in Mumbai. But I fucking got her. Didn't plan on that, did you? How'd *that* happen, Ed?"

Visibly deflating, Rance sat down in the CO's desk chair, his head in his hands, hair spiking through his fingers. Just on the other side of the plywood wall, the operations team was still at work. Meredith could hear a military voice now and then, but otherwise she was alone with Rance.

She persisted. "Who is she, Ed? Huh? I'd guess SVR Directorate S, wouldn't you? You want to tell me now or do you want to explain to the SEAL team out there that you're a *fucking traitor?*"

"No."

"Fuck you. *Traitor.*"

"I'm no traitor."

"What, then?"

"I'm—"

She cut him off. "I don't know what you are. But you know what else? I don't have time for this shit. You're going to give the order to launch that team. Right now."

"Meredith, no. No matter what you think this is . . . I can explain it. It's not what you think. I still can't start a war. *We* can't. There's clearly been a compromise. It's bigger than—"

"I'm tired of hearing that, Ed. I think you already *did* start a war. Give the order."

"No."

Standing over him, she let one hand fall to her side, resting it on the Glock's grip. But the hand stopped there. "We both know I'm in charge of this op now, *traitor.*"

Rance closed his eyes, shaking his head. His throat moved as he swallowed before he spoke. "It was an affair, Meredith. That's all you need to know. I'm not a traitor. But I was stupid. She must have been . . ."

His eyes opened. They danced back and forth as though searching for something.

"Give the order. Tell them to launch," Meredith said. She kept her hand resting on the grip. *"Do it."*

"I can't do that. It would be wrong."

"Do you want me to get Dorsey on the line right now to clear up the chain of command?"

Rance didn't move. Meredith put her phone on the desk, hit a button, put it on speaker.

A watch officer at Langley answered. "This is Meredith Morris-Dale for a FLASH message to—"

"Stop," Rance said to her. "Hang up."

Meredith hung up. "Your turn. Give the order. *Do it!*"

"All right," he said weakly, raising a hand. "Okay, okay."

He found a legal pad in a corner of the DEVGRU CO's desk. Grabbed a pen, started writing.

"Wait. *What?*" she blurted. "I don't need it in writing, asshole. I just need you to give DEVGRU the order. We don't have *time* for this!"

Rance shook his head, continued writing. "It'll only take a second. Here. Sign this."

Meredith looked at the note. It was a one-liner specifying that she was taking full tactical command of the Active Archer op.

Fucking Rance, she thought as she scrawled her name under it. *Has to cover his ass right up to the end.*

Rance countersigned, saying, "Dorsey already knew about her—the woman that I . . . that you . . . killed." He glanced up at her. Some color had returned to his face. "You've got command now, Meredith. But just know that I was a target of SVR, same as you. It's all part of the same compromised op. And that's why I wouldn't give the order now. Know that much."

She held up a hand and turned away. She didn't need to hear the rest of it.

He went on from the CO's desk chair anyway. "And keep in mind, Meredith, the leak started with SVR exposing *you* when *you* botched Sagebrush in Dubai. It was through *you* that SVR must have eventually gotten to me. I may have been compromised, but it all started with *you.* When we get back, I'll be opening up an IG investigation into all of this and—"

407

"Go fuck yourself, Ed," she said over her shoulder, halfway through the door.

It took her thirty-five seconds to find the DEVGRU CO and drag him into his own office. The Navy SEAL captain was shocked at the sudden authorization to cross the border, utterly astonished when the lady spook said she wanted to go along for the ride.

That was a bridge too far. The CO pushed back. He wasn't about to let a nonoperator get on that helo. This wasn't some kind of PR tour. There was going to be a firefight, for Chrissakes. He appealed to Rance for help, but the senior CIA man simply shrugged and deferred to the woman.

Faced down by both of them, the grizzled Special Forces CO began to weaken. This was a CIA op and that was their guy up there on the screen. Besides, one look at the feisty brunette with the Glock on her hip told him she was probably going to kill somebody if she didn't get her way. Maybe even him.

The CO gave the order.

They weighed her down with a heavily armored combat vest. They tightened a helmet over her hair and asked if she wanted an M-4. No, she said, she was good to go. Now get the fuck going.

The senior chief in charge assigned a bearded boatswain's mate they called Tex to look after her. Sure enough, Tex had a Texas-flag patch on the front of his combat vest. It was hard to see because it was otherwise covered with hand grenades.

Tex took a look at Meredith and nodded to her. Roughly, he grabbed her by the arm and strapped her in with a grunt. He seemed to be of the opinion that the Navy was always asking him to do ridiculous things. To him, this was all very weird, but par for the course, so not really a problem. Situation Normal: All Fucked Up.

Now they were rushing over the landscape, which whizzed by in a monochrome gray. Meredith started to feel airsick. That MRE might have been a bad idea. But she wasn't about to puke in front of this crew.

Oleg rose from his hide. He left the sniper rifle where it was and picked up his AK-12. He readjusted the pistol on his leg and cinched down the strap, securing it for the run he had ahead of him. It would take him a few minutes to cover the distance to the corral and snatch Rahimi. He dashed forward, grateful for the opportunity to finally unkink his legs.

He'd nailed Dale in the chest—of that, he was sure. He'd seen him fly backward into the ditch. Nobody could have survived that; then again, Dale was a lucky son of a bitch. After nabbing Rahimi, Oleg would go make sure Dale was good and dead. He'd send a picture of the body to Zoloto. She'd probably like to see that.

Zana saw the man running toward him with a rifle in his hand, a kaffiyeh fluttering at his neck. He hadn't seen Reza in many years, so he wasn't sure what exactly to expect. The man sprinting his way certainly had the look of an operative. Who else could it be?

Even though he believed he was finally looking at Reza, he also thought he wasn't yet out of the woods. Reza had just shot Zoran, thinking him a threat. What if Reza also thought Zana was some kind of enemy? What if the CIA man didn't recognize Zana after all these years? With Zoran's shattered head fresh in his memory, Zana walked forward with his hands raised high.

The man he thought was Reza saw him and waved without breaking stride. He kept running forward, straight at Zana. Though sorry about Zoran, Zana felt a wave of relief. It was the signal he'd been looking for. It would all be over now. Finally.

But then his heart sank. He heard the faint growl of a heavy vehicle. Glancing to his right over the otherwise black desert scrub, he saw the distant bounce of headlights heaving wildly as a vehicle rushed forward. With at least another hill to cover, it would still take some time to get to them. But the way the engine howled, the way the headlights bounced indicated to Zana that the vehicle was trouble. It wasn't even trying to hide itself.

Only the Army would do that, Zana thought. *The IRGC.*

He ran forward, anxious to tell Reza what was happening.

CHAPTER 46

KASEM AND THE IRGC SERGEANT HAD DRIVEN A FEW HOURS DOWN TO this little point of land that jutted into Iraq. They were in a three-axle flatbed truck with a mounted fifty-cal. Until now they'd been waiting over on the border road, prepared to make a run for Dale at the first sign of trouble. For a while they'd just waited and listened to the radio calls. It'd seemed like a bust.

Far from it.

The captain back at the school had been an enormous help. He'd stayed there, monitoring the net, keeping the line of communication open with the Quds lieutenant colonel. The IRGC captain had a good relationship with the NAJA force that had been conducting the search of the roads. The captain had relayed the news of one dead Iranian youth south of Saqqez. Another kid was in critical condition, saved by a hastily tied tourniquet over the bullet hole in his leg. The tire marks showed that the perpetrator had headed south.

That was when Kasem knew he was right. If nothing else, the dressing to the kid's wound was a dead giveaway. Kasem was living proof of that. The CIA man who'd saved Kasem's own life in Iraq was now on his way. If Kasem could arrest him and Rahimi together, the CIA man would redeem the Quds officer's life all over again.

But it was still a porous border. Kasem couldn't know exactly where he and the sergeant should position themselves. They'd set up on a high bluff, using their night-vision goggles, looking and listening, waiting.

Then the captain had called on the HF radio net. A villager had phoned the police with reports of gunfire, not four kilometers from where Kasem was parked. Kasem had ordered the sergeant to get moving. They'd get more details on the way.

The villager had said it sounded like it was up at the last farm against the hill. That made sense to Kasem from a tactical point of view.

There were no obvious roads connecting to the farm from this side. They left the border road and began overlanding it in a rush, picking their way through the wadis, smashing through low vegetation like a charging bear. It was a rough, wild ride, but Kasem kept urging the sergeant on. Only the seat belts kept them from flying out as the big truck lunged forward. It had been a lucky odyssey to get this far. Kasem wasn't about to blow it now.

Oleg grabbed Rahimi by the arm and dragged him to the ground. He too noticed the distant truck trundling up the hill, headlights bouncing. He told the Iranian to get his head down. They couldn't be seen.

Oleg had spoken in English. Rahimi had called him Reza, thanking him, saying some other things that didn't make a lot of sense to Oleg.

The Russian would sort it later. It didn't matter. What mattered right now was getting out of the open, getting to cover.

He pulled and prodded Rahimi to race across the corral, to get to the other side and dive down an embankment. It was a longer run in the open, but it went away from the truck coming up the hill. Once he got some concealment, he'd deal with the vehicle.

The pilots had piped communications with the ops center directly through to Meredith's headset in the helo, which was speeding low and fast over the desert toward the Iranian border. They were taking orders from her now. The blond guy from the Agency who had been in charge had basically delegated everything to her, they'd said.

Meredith and the DEVGRU SEAL team were supposed to see drone video that bounced off satellite relays to the ruggedized tablet strapped to a bundle of equipment in the center of the helo. But frustratingly, all Meredith saw were blinking vertical lines as the Air Force worked out the kinks. She asked the ops center for a sitrep (situation report).

They said over the sat radio that the man identified as their officer was up again, moving forward. He had the IR reflector, so they had a confirmed PID on him now.

The IR reflector was especially important, some colonel added, because as the helicopter arrived on-site with its nose-mounted forward-looking infrared (FLIR), the gunners would be able to tell who was who.

Meredith nodded at that, looking at the SEALs bunched around her, who were also listening in. She prodded the arm of the ranking senior chief riding across from her to make sure he really understood. The last thing she wanted was friendly fire, a blue-on-blue engagement, a shot at John by mistake.

In the flickering dark of the cabin, his face greased with black paint under his helmet, the team leader made an acknowledging motion with his head.

That wasn't anywhere near good enough for Meredith.

"Hey!" she shouted into her boom mic, grabbing him by the front of his combat vest just above the hand grenades.

The startled frogman reacted with an uncertain jerk, steadying himself against a nylon strap.

"I need to hear you've got good copy on that, Senior Chief," she said over the intercom. "Our man is up and moving. When the helo's FLIR lights him up, he's the good guy. *You fucking read me?*" She kept holding on to him.

His eyes widened. "Yeah. Check. Copy all," the team leader said, recovering, pushing her arm off his chest.

Chuckling, one of the other SEALs said over the intercom, "Hey, Senior, you *sure* you got all that?"

More chuckles.

"All right, all right," the senior chief replied, waving the other men off with a gloved hand as the helo banked.

The tablet screen came to life with drone video. Finally. They all leaned over it. Meredith saw the white dot of the IR reflector: John. She pointed it out to the others.

The team leader asked the flight crew for an ETA. In five mikes they'd have a FLIR scan of the target area from the helo's onboard ball turret mounted up on the nose. Landing two mikes after that.

The team leader studied the screen's drone video and relayed instructions about what they'd do on touchdown, pointing out terrain features. He reiterated where Meredith was supposed to go, that she was supposed to stay close to Tex at all times. That was nonnegotiable.

Tex, Meredith's seatmate, grinned as he listened, white teeth on black face paint. Meredith couldn't understand the grin, didn't like it one bit. She looked at the SEAL, tugged on the M-4 barrel resting on his knees to get his attention. Once she had it, she pointed at the tablet, at the small white dot that was the IR reflector, their man, John.

"We're getting *that guy*," she said to Tex, tapping the screen, the white dot. "You copy?"

Tex nodded, still smiling. Meredith was about to yank his combat vest too, get his head in the game, wipe that stupid smirk off his face.

But before she could, Tex did something unexpected. He gave Meredith's forearm a little squeeze. He said, "Glad to hear he's okay, ma'am. Don't worry. We'll get him."

Dale heard the low grinding vibration of a vehicle struggling across the landscape. It was still some distance out, but it sounded heavy. Heavy meant military, troops. Not good.

He'd regained the function of his legs now, but his ribs still hurt like hell. Every breath felt like a naked crawl across barbed wire. But with that truck growling away, he couldn't afford to pay attention to the pain.

He'd made it back to the edge of the corral, approaching it as low as he could. Though his wound hurt, the last thing he was going to do was present himself as a target again.

He skulked forward with the Glock in his right hand. He wasn't sure what the hell he was going to find up there, let alone what was happening with that truck. But he got to a position that worked. He dug in at the end of the field, waiting, watching.

Then, looking up, he saw something amazing. The man he'd previously identified as Rahimi was running right toward him. He was held by the arm by another guy, who had an AK-12 in his hand.

Who the hell is that?

Didn't matter.

Lying prone, Dale took aim at the guy with the AK. But it was a distant shot and they were running. Worse, the stab of pain in Dale's rib as he extended his arm for the shot made him unsteady. He fired a three-round burst.

All missed.

The guy with the AK dove into a copse of weeds, dragging Rahimi down, both of them disappearing in the brush. The sound of Dale's gunshots echoed helplessly against the hills. After they'd faded, Dale heard the truck again.

He swore under his breath. He'd lost the initiative. Trapped between the truck behind him and the assaulter in the field across from him, he was now a sitting duck. The only thing he had going for him was the darkness, but under the half-moon, even that was thin.

Fuck! he thought impotently, hearing the crackle of distant branches as the truck rambled on. After all he'd been through, the IRGC had still managed to set a trap for him.

Pangs of fear welled up from their demonic depths. Evin Prison, torture, death. He fought each one of them off, concentrated on an inventory of the tactical assets he had at his disposal. Six rounds left in the mag, another in his pocket.

Compartmentalization of thought was everything now. He traded the half-empty mag for the full one, slamming it in place with the heel of his hand. Even that move hurt his ribs, but he was learning to ignore that.

He rolled twice to the side, each revolution inflicting a searing jolt. He stopped at the bottom of a low, stumpy tree, nowhere near wide enough for cover, but maybe offering a shred of concealment. It would have to do. He swept for a target. Nothing. His ribs throbbed.

Fuck!

He touched the IR reflector on his shoulder, ensuring it was still there, wondering who, if anyone, was up there watching him.

CHAPTER 47

OLEG LAY ON TOP OF RAHIMI, SMOTHERING HIM. HE'D WANTED TO LEAP up instantly to aim at Dale, but in the tangled fall with the scientist, he'd lost a few seconds. Now, rolling off the Iranian, Oleg found a gap in the bushes and raised his AK. He scanned through the dark across the corral, looking for movement on the other side. No sign of Dale.

Grovno, Oleg cursed, annoyed with himself for not finishing the kill when he'd had the chance. With that truck getting closer, the delay in hunting Dale would be costly. He didn't need this wrinkle.

Then again, it should be quick. Oleg had seen Dale go down with the earlier rifle shot. He must be injured—and outgunned. Dale's weak attempt at an assault told Oleg that the CIA man was lightly armed and alone.

Rahimi said something to him in Farsi. Uncomprehending, Oleg looked down at him and considered zip-tying the scientist's wrists and ankles, treating him like a hostage. Oleg didn't need the extra hassle of Rahimi running off. Especially with Dale still out there.

The scientist switched to English. "Reza, you hear the truck, yes? Is that how we're getting out?"

Hearing the name Reza reminded Oleg that Rahimi thought he was in the company of John Dale himself. No need for the zip ties, then. They'd serve only to spook the scientist.

"No," Oleg replied carefully. His English had a slight Russian accent that he'd never quite gotten rid of. He hoped Rahimi wouldn't notice.

"The truck is probably IRGC. I have a car down there. But first I have to neutralize that shooter. Then we run for it."

"Yes. Who is he, the shooter?"

"Someone who wants to kill us both," Oleg said.

The Russian rolled onto his back. He retrieved his NVGs from a cargo pocket and flipped them over his eyes. He lay still, allowing them to warm up, staring up at the starry sky. When the image turned green, he rolled back to his stomach, raised himself on an elbow, and scanned the bilious terrain.

With the spindly black tubes over his eyes, leaning on his elbows, the man next to Zana looked like an insect, a praying mantis.

The insect turned to Zana. He grasped the Iranian's shoulder tightly.

"You stay right here," the goggled man said. "Do *not* move. Understand me?"

Zana nodded. The man he thought was Reza rose to a crouch and crept forward, a rifle cradled across his forearms.

Kasem asked the sergeant to stop the truck. They were on a low rise, a reasonable vantage point. A short valley stood before them, a few hundred yards across, veiny shadows at the bottom that indicated dry creek beds. Once they entered that valley for the final push to the farm, Kasem would lose his high ground.

He climbed onto the flatbed. Leaning against the fifty-cal, he scanned the farm with his IR scope.

Jackpot. He saw a man creeping forward in a tactical crouch at the edge of the field, toward the valley in front of him, an assault rifle at the ready. Kasem swept the scope farther right, anticipating the man's path, wondering who he was and what he was hunting.

There. Another white blob, a man lying prone at the field's edge, a pistol in his hand.

Was that everyone? Everything?

Kasem swept the rest of the landscape. Sheep pen. Small house. Farther afield he saw a vehicle, a small car, still warm from its travels.

Farther still there was another one, barely visible because its engine was nearly cold.

Kasem sensed opportunity. Whatever egress the CIA man had plotted for his spy was now fouled. There was a gunfight playing out here, now, right in front of him. He, Kasem, stood between them and the Iraqi border. They had no chance. He smiled behind the scope.

"Radio the garrison at Saqqez," he said to the sergeant over the rattle of the idling diesel engine.

Once the captain was on the line, Kasem ordered a surge of all air and ground assets to Alut. He gave the precise grid coordinates, referencing the truck's GPS. He ordered the advanced guard to come by the fastest air possible toward the border. He told them he'd meet them there to set up a perimeter.

He emphasized the urgency, used all his juice as a Quds man, Soleimani's former adjutant. It worked. They were on their way.

Riding the truck back toward the border road now, Kasem allowed himself to relax in the bucking cab. He'd found the spies. The jig was up. Whatever was playing out over there in that field didn't much matter anymore. Dr. Rahimi would be held to account. Kasem would be a hero. Kasra could come home.

"We've got FLIR!" one of the SEALs said over the helo's intercom.

They all looked forward over the tablet in the center of the cargo bay. The nose-mounted FLIR turret was painting a flickering picture that looked like a blurry photo negative.

"Whoa!" Tex shouted.

They were watching a man with an AK in front of him edge along the side of a field. A dozen yards to his rear was another man, lying flat in a thicket. The FLIR video shifted right, indicating a brilliant white flash.

"IR reflector," said the senior chief, asking the copilot to adjust the gain so they could get a more detailed view. The focus improved.

When a clearer picture emerged, they saw the man with the IR reflector lying prone. He seemed to be aiming a pistol in the general direction of the man with the AK.

"That's our guy!" Meredith shouted, smacking them all on the shoulders. She put her finger on the tablet screen. "That guy there, he's our officer. This guy in the middle with the rifle needs to die. *Quick!*"

The SEAL team leader asked for an ETA. Two mikes out, answered the pilot.

Meredith shook her head, cursing.

"We got this," Tex said.

All the SEALs started tightening straps, snapping gear in place.

"We've got a problem," said the Air Force colonel over the radio from back at the ops center, Hammer.

What fucking now? Meredith thought. She asked the colonel to spit it out, quick.

"Bandits speeding toward your pos," he said. "Flight of two MiG-29s just took off, climbing on burner, turning your way. We've also got two MI-8 helos heading toward you from the north."

Fucking hell. "How much time have we got?" Meredith asked the colonel.

"Wait one."

Intent on the tablet screen, she watched John holding his pistol, vulnerable, his hands before him, elbows bent, as if in prayer.

We could use a divine intervention, she thought.

"One minute!" shouted the senior chief.

He'd flicked clear goggles down over his eyes. Tex indicated to Meredith to do the same. Over their helmets they had their NVGs tilted up, at the ready.

The helicopter slowed, barely. It banked left, hard, throwing Meredith against the bulkhead.

The colonel came back on the line. "We assess about fifteen minutes on the fast movers, maybe a few minutes more for the helos to your pos. Lot of air defense radars lighting up your area too. This may be a hot LZ."

Meredith acknowledged the colonel's call.

Tex was fiddling with more straps on her vest, asking her for a thumbs-up.

She ignored him. "What's our antiair?" she asked the helo's copilot.

"Not much against MiGs, ma'am. Flares if they launch heat seekers. Nap of the earth flying if they hit us with radar-guided stuff. The good news is that there are no SAMs in the area. We'll only have to worry about those fighters."

That's the good news? Meredith thought. *What a clusterfuck.*

The senior chief yanked the fabric of Meredith's shirt up near her shoulder, repaying the treatment she'd given him earlier. "The guy with the AK just hopped into a ditch or something." He pointed at the tablet screen. John hadn't moved, but AK man had somehow disappeared from view. With that threat now unaccounted for, the SEAL leader directed a landing at a different spot, orienting the helo so the door gunner could cover their egress, guarding against the threat.

"Thirty seconds!" the SEAL team's number two shouted.

Tex pushed Meredith forward, steadying a hand on her back, ready to shove her out.

"Ma'am? You ready?"

"As I'll ever be," she said.

Coming from higher ground, Oleg had seen that this dry creek bed wound a broad semicircle toward the spot where Dale had to be hiding. If he guessed right, it would end in a flanking position to the CIA man's left. If he guessed wrong, he'd be surrendering his higher ground, losing a tactical advantage.

But Oleg didn't have time to wait Dale out. He had to flush him out of his hide. That truck was still out there somewhere. He thought he also detected the faint, distant sound of a helicopter. If he was to kill Dale and nab Rahimi, he had to act quickly before the IRGC moved in. The flanking maneuver was worth the risk.

The floor of the creek bed was soft, sandy, quiet. There were few obstructions, so Oleg was able to cover the distance quickly. As he approached, he paused frequently, looking for movement.

He saw something. A blocky shift against a low tree just ahead. He raised the AK, put the stunted tree in his sights, straining to discern the shape of a man through the leaves. He thought he recognized the shape of a head in NVGs, a dark circle, potentially a nose. It moved slightly.

Yes.

Oleg was certain now. He exhaled slowly, stilling himself, preparing to fire.

CHAPTER 48

DALE HAD TO ASSUME THAT THE MAN WITH THE AK WOULD BE COMING for him. AK man had had the high ground up at the corral and a better weapon. Dale had no hope of mounting an assault of his own. His only option would be to ambush his pursuer, acting like armed bait.

Easier said than done.

A successful ambush required spotting the target, which required Dale to move around. But to move was to give away his position.

He tried to balance both objectives, listening, straining, sweeping left and right with small movements, long pauses between them, the IR scope perched to his eye.

But he heard nothing, save for the far-off whine of that truck. And the faint approach of a helicopter.

He'd been hearing the rumble of distant helicopters all night as the IRGC conducted its search of the roads a dozen miles north. But the airborne rumble he heard now had a different pitch, different rotor cadence—a familiar one. He realized now it had to be a 60, a Black-hawk, probably the Special Forces variant. He knew the sound well. It was getting louder.

Thank fucking God.

The MH-60 Pave Hawk dove over the final hill and flared. The nose tilted up. Men leapt from the open door, five feet from the ground.

Choking on dust, Meredith felt rough hands thrusting her forward into the night, spilling out at the edge of the corral.

Weighed down by gear, she stumbled in the loose dirt. Tex wrenched her up by an arm, then nearly tackled her as they sought concealment in the brush at the field's edge. Two other SEALs were on either side of them, setting up a security perimeter. The rest were still in the helo, which had already flown off in a hurricane of whirling dust. They were to set up a secondary security position to guard against any approaching IRGC forces along the border road.

"You see anything?" she asked Tex once they'd settled and things had become quiet again.

"No," he said. Then he angled an ear, raising his helmet slightly.

She heard gunfire. Tex raised a fist, telling her to be still, quiet. The shots were somewhere down the hill, a hundred yards off.

"That sure as shit sounds like an AK," Tex said, rolling away from her for a different view across the field. He said into the radio, "Charlie One, I've got enemy contact at my two o'clock, hundred fifty yards. No visual. Estimate single shooter."

Meredith heard two more three-round bursts in the field across from her. AK man had made his presence known. By order of the senior chief, still aloft in the helo, the two SEALs to either side of Meredith sprang up and ran forward, across the corral, toward the sound of the gun.

Behind Meredith, another man stood, walking forward, arms raised, surprising them all.

Tex swung his rifle at the man.

"That's our asset!" Meredith shouted, diving at Tex, knocking his rifle off its aim. She sprang to her feet, waved her arms crazily.

"Dr. Rahimi!" she shouted, running to him.

Oleg blamed the arrival of the helo for the miss. Just as it had popped over the hill, Dale had rolled away, making the shot go wide. Now Oleg couldn't find the CIA man anywhere.

The Spetz operator guessed that the helo was American. It didn't sound like the MI-8, the recent Russian upgrade for the IRGC, a machine with which Oleg was intimately familiar. It meant the team that was coming for Dale's extract had finally made it. Everything had suddenly changed.

Out of frustration, the Spetz Alpha operator had shot up the brush behind Dale's position and run forward to see if it had achieved anything. But on inspection of the area, he saw no movement whatsoever. It seemed that Dale had somehow managed to make it to a different spot, probably preparing to race toward his rescuers.

But there was still a chance. Even if he'd missed Dale again, Oleg was reasonably sure that the CIA man was injured from the original sniper shot. He could still chase Dale down, shoot him before he could rendezvous with the now-orbiting helo, catch him in the brush. Even if he never got back to Rahimi, he'd still get Dale.

To Oleg, that was the meat of the mission.

The Russian crept forward to the area he'd just shot up, climbing in and out of the dry creek bed as necessary to cover ground efficiently while still maintaining concealment. He arrived at the shredded leaves and snapped branches where his previous AK burst had done its damage. He poked around with the barrel, looking for blood. He saw nothing.

The wadi he'd been using zigzagged to his right, headed away from the hill. Oleg wondered if Dale had followed it. It would have taken the CIA man away from the helo's likely landing area, but it would have been easy to traverse if Dale had had to make a run for it.

Oleg climbed into the wadi. He turned, avoiding a boulder, a few other scattered rocks, dark forms in his NVGs.

One of them moved.

Dale had heard the Russian coming. He'd been lying still among the rocks, listening to the fading clatter of the 60 as it receded behind a hill. He wasn't sure what maneuver his egress team was executing up there, but with the IR reflector on his shoulder and an AK-armed assaulter hunting him down here, he figured it was safer to get cover than to present himself as a target. So he just lay there, listening, watching.

This kind of hide was second nature to him, drilled into his head over his years as a sniper, a hunter. He'd covered himself with branches, taken still, shallow breaths, even made himself *think* like a rock.

Finally, when the echo of rotors had faded, there was another sound. First one, then two rustles in the bush back where Dale had just come from.

He guessed that AK man was poking around at Dale's former hide, up there among the stunted trees above the creek bed. Dale thought about breaking cover, going for the shot, surprising the man. But he knew he was a little off with his rib injury. And he had only six rounds left in the mag. Going for an assault on a better-armed operator could be a fatal error. He waited. The rustle of brush got louder.

The hunter was coming to him.

Dale saw movement through a crack in the branches over his eyes. The man swept the AK back and forth, walked slowly, carefully, just as any trained operator would. NVGs were flipped down over his eyes. He wore a kaffiyeh over his head. The exposed skin of his face was marked up with camo paint. Dale could see a triangle of exposed flesh at the collar. Likely no body armor, then. He sure as hell hoped that was the case. A head shot would be too risky.

Now.

Ignoring the flash of pain that ran down his ribs, Dale rose to a sitting position, lifting his Glock.

The man turned and shot, but didn't know exactly where to aim.

Dale put six pistol rounds into his target's chest. The man fell back, dropping his AK, dead.

Kasem had stopped the truck about two hundred yards from the corral when he first heard the helo. They'd been racing toward the border road, preparing to meet the incoming IRGC forces, when they heard the aircraft sweep into its landing.

At first Kasem assumed it would be the arrival of the advanced guard of the IRGC. But then the Iranian's heart sank. He recognized the helo's shape as an American Blackhawk. It touched down briefly, deposited a team, and took off again, speeding away. It seemed to be darting in and out of the hills now, its rotor echoes occasionally bouncing off them.

Kasem killed the truck's lights. He ordered the sergeant up to the fifty-cal, telling him to try to hit the helo if it came within sight. He told the sergeant to train the guns toward the sound of the echoes. He was sure the helo would be circling around again.

As the sergeant searched for the helo, Kasem walked a dozen yards away and found a good vantage point. He raised his IR scope and surveyed the corral. He saw soldiers there moving across the field, gathering at its far side. Occasionally he swept the hills around him, looking for the approach of an IRGC vehicle. But none came.

He swung the scope to his right. The American helo's turbine engines whined, sounding like they were girding for a landing somewhere not too far from them. The sergeant rotated the fifty-cal toward the noise, pulling a lever.

"Over there!" the sergeant yelled, before letting loose a handful of pink tracer rounds from his fifty-cal that skittered off the dirt, deflecting away into the night sky. He fired again, higher, anticipating that the helicopter would emerge from behind the hill.

But the sergeant was swept from the truck then, spilling backward over the side of the flatbed, silencing the big gun, which swung back and forth from the momentum of its own recoil.

A sniper's bullet had pierced the sergeant's neck.

Standing there in the dark a dozen yards from the truck, unarmed, Kasem assumed the next sniper bullet would be for him. He dropped to his stomach and crawled into a ditch.

Meredith had been hastily debriefing Rahimi. In halting English interrupted by his rapid breathing, Zana told Meredith of Zoran, the PDKI fighter who had brought him there. He also spoke of Reza, who was wearing a kaffiyeh. Zana explained that Reza had scooped him up and tackled him in the weeds, told him to wait there while he chased down some other assassin.

No, she'd countered. The situation was reversed. The man with the kaffiyeh was bad. Her husband was still out there, looking to come in. Rahimi had been tricked. The scientist blinked at that, confused.

Tex and another SEAL were huddled near them in the weeds at the edge of the corral.

"Weapons down! Weapons down!" Tex shouted, relaying the order that had come across his headset. "Friendly coming in!"

He turned to Meredith and Rahimi. "Sounds like we got your man," he said, grinning, his teeth brilliant against his painted face. He pointed.

Meredith followed Tex's finger. There, on the far side of the field, she recognized John. He was limping, hunched, hanging on a SEAL's shoulder as they made their way forward. She ran to meet him.

Dale looked up at her, filthy, his hair hanging from his neck like a dirty rag. "What the fuck?" he said, breaking away from the SEAL who'd been holding him up.

She wanted to hug him, but with all the gear and the nearby commandos, there was simply no time for it. Instead, she waved away the SEAL who'd been helping John and crept under his arm, supporting him, taking the SEAL's place.

"Told you I'd get him," John said to Meredith as they limped together back toward the edge of the field.

She could feel his warm breath against her ear. "Yeah," she said, "you did. You fucking did."

When they arrived at the spot next to Tex, Zana Rahimi turned his gray beard toward both of them.

"Dr. Rahimi, I presume?" John said, hoarsely.

The older man nodded. They hastily shook hands, said a few words of greeting in Farsi.

One of the SEALs then laid Dale flat, opened his shirt, and inspected the deep bruise from the sniper round he'd endured below the body armor. Meredith was right there next to the SEAL, fussing over his every move.

Tex watched her, smiling. "Yeah," he said, raising his voice to be heard over the sound of the incoming helo, the 60 coming back to the LZ to get them all. "Is it true you guys are married? That's the rumor going around the CP."

"Sort of," Dale said in a half groan, looking up at Tex with a lopsided grin. The smile turned to a wince as the other SEAL prodded his chest, dabbing the wound with some kind of solvent.

"Well," Tex said, "if 'sort of' actually means no, then please step aside, sir. 'Cause I'd like to propose to this here woman myself."

CHAPTER 49

"WHO THE HELL IS THIS?" MEREDITH ASKED WHEN THEY'D ALL strapped into the helo, John right beside her. She was looking at an IRGC officer, his arms zip-tied behind him, a lieutenant colonel if she remembered how their insignia badges worked.

The helo was twisting among the hills, low and fast. The MiGs were almost within range.

The senior chief said, "We took out a technical with a mounted fifty-cal that tried a few potshots at us. This guy came out of the bushes with his hands up. Speaks English, says he could help us, that he's an officer. Thought he might be good intel, so we bagged him. If you'd rather we just shoot and dump him before we leave Iran, we can. Your call, ma'am."

Jesus, Meredith thought, *I have to decide this?*

Whatever her decision, it had to be done quick. They were only a minute away from the safety of Iraqi airspace, racing against the MiGs. Meredith put a hand on John's knee, asked him what he thought they should do with the IRGC man.

Dale didn't immediately respond. He'd gone pale, staring open-mouthed at the Iranian officer who sat bound across from him.

The Iranian officer asked for a set of headphones to speak on the IC. Meredith said it would be okay.

"You remember me, don't you?" said the IRGC man once the mic was over his lips. He spoke with a cultured English accent.

Dale kept staring.

The Iranian officer then asked if one of the soldiers might unbutton the top two buttons of his shirt and hold it open for a moment so that the man could show them something. The SEALs thought this odd, but everyone agreed that it would be okay. He'd already been frisked.

"Put a light at the base of my neck," the Iranian said. "Please."

The light shone on a raised scar that went near the base of his ear, all the way to his sternum.

"Yeah," Dale said over the IC then, "I thought that was you."

"I'd shake your hand again," the IRGC man said in his polite way, "but I seem to be otherwise engaged."

"To put it mildly," said Dale, slowly smiling. "But I don't get it. What are you doing here?"

"My job was to catch you. And him." He nodded toward Rahimi.

"Well, ma'am," asked the senior chief, "what do you want us to do with him?"

She looked at Dale. "John—what's going on? Who the fuck is this?"

Dale nodded toward the Iranian. "He's the guy I waved to on the drone tape five years ago near Mosul. The one that made me a so-called security risk." He looked up at the Iranian. "That caused me a shitstorm of trouble, by the way."

"Sir, whatever your name is, you have no idea the trouble you've caused me," Kasem answered.

Meredith borrowed the flashlight from Tex. She shone it into the Iranian's face. "Who?"

"That man saved my life once upon a time," the Iranian said, clarifying, squinting against the light. He looked at Dale. "I don't suppose you'd care to do it again?"

"Who *are* you?" Meredith asked the Iranian, shocked.

"Lieutenant Colonel Kasem Kahlidi, at your service. I'm the former adjutant to the late General Soleimani of the Quds Force. I presume you're more familiar with him."

"Huh," said Dale. "I always wondered what happened to you."

The Iranian said, "The question still stands. Care to save my life again?"

"Why would we do that?" asked Meredith. "We killed Soleimani with good reason. We should probably kill his adjutant too."

"Because," he said with a nod toward Rahimi, who sat crumpled with exhaustion against his seat, "much like your man here, I'm willing to start working for you."

Meredith looked between the faces of John and this strangely polite Iranian officer.

The senior chief looked at Meredith again. He shifted a boot to lightly kick her in the foot. "Ma'am, seriously. Need you to make a call. The border's right up here. Is he a keeper?"

Meredith thought about it for a few seconds, looking between John and the Iranian. "Yeah," she finally said. "One way or the other, they're both keepers."

GLOSSARY

Active Archer—Code name for the CIA's program to disrupt Iranian enrichment operations.

Alut, Iran—Small Kurdish village near the border with Iraq.

AOR—Area of Responsibility, designated geography for a military operation.

Arak, Iran—A city in central Iran. Location of a secret Iranian heavy-water reactor that can be used for enriching uranium to weapons grade.

Baradar—Farsi for "brother," a term of comradery.

Baramar—The Dubai-based export-import company that provides centrifuge equipment to the Iranians.

CP—Command Post, term used by the US Army and Air Force to designate a deployed headquarters.

CPT—CIA Counterproliferation Division, charged with stopping the spread of nuclear weapons.

DEVGRU—Naval Special Warfare Development Group, shorthand for the tier one commandos of SEAL Team Six.

DGSE—French General Directorate for External Security, subordinate to the Ministry of the Defense. Responsible for military, strategic, and signals intelligence. Also responsible for counterespionage outside of national borders.

Echelon—NSA-administered voice-intelligence intercepts of foreign telecom companies.

Elahieh, Iran—Upscale neighborhood in Tehran's District One on the northern edge of the city. The Elahieh neighborhood houses many foreign embassies, including Russia's.

Erzurum, Turkey—City in southeastern Turkey, high in the mountains of Anatolia. Easternmost airport for access to Iran.

FOB—Forward Operating Base, a remote US military outpost.

FSB—Russian Ministry of State Security, heir to the KGB, based in Lubyanka Square, Moscow.

HQS—Agency shorthand for CIA headquarters in Langley, Virginia.

IAEA—International Atomic Energy Association. A UN-chartered organization that monitors the development of nuclear materials and compliance to the NPT.

IFF—Identification Friend or Foe, an automated radio interrogation system used to identify an aircraft in flight.

IG—CIA Inspector General, charged with ensuring the lawfulness of Agency operations.

Interpol—International crime-fighting organization with more than a hundred member countries and a recognized UN charter. Headquartered in Lyon, France, Interpol maintains database submissions from member countries for tracking across borders. These submissions include fingerprints, DNA samples, travel documents, and face photos. Interpol maintains an encrypted network called I-24/7 that provides access to databases. Many member countries can access the I-24/7 system at airports and border-access points. Interpol can issue a Red Notice, which is equivalent to an international arrest warrant with the expectation of extradition.

IR—Infrared.

IRGC—Islamic Revolutionary Guard Corps. IRGC was formed by the Ayatollah Khomeini as a parallel military force, since the shah's military could not be trusted. IRGC has since evolved into all service branches—Air Defense, Navy, Air Force, Army. The IRGC has been officially designated as a terrorist organization since October 2018 by Bahrain and Saudi Arabia and since April 15, 2019, by the United States.

ISIL—Islamic State of Iraq and the Levant, also known as ISIS. Sunni Muslim revolutionary army operating in northern Iraq and Syria.

ISR—Intelligence, Surveillance, Reconnaissance.

Jon—A Farsi term of endearment appended to a given name, equivalent to "dear" in English.

Karzkak—Turkish oil company.

M-4—Standard assault rifle for the US military, 7.62mm.

Mahdi—The messiah; some devout Shias believe the Mahdi is the Twelfth Imam hiding in the Occultation since the year 872. At the end of days, the Mahdi will reappear and institute a new world, per Allah's will.

MOIS—Ministry of Information and Security, the Iranian intelligence service.

MRAP—Large armored multipurpose Army combat vehicle. MRAP stands for Mine Ready, Ambush Protected. The MRAP was designed and built partially in response to the vulnerabilities of Humvees to IEDs in Iraq.

Natanz, Iran—A city in northern Iran. Location of a deep underground Iranian enrichment facility exposed by the CIA in the early 2000s.

NCA—National Command Authority, composed of the most senior US officials who decide national security policy.

NPT—Nuclear Non-Proliferation Treaty, administered by the UN.

OPSEC—Operational Security, procedures used by US national security organizations to keep general operating details confidential.

Pasdar—Farsi for a revolutionary of the Islamic Republic, guardian of the revolution, used as a term of respect.

Pasdaran—Farsi for Islamic Republic revolutionaries.

PDB—Presidential Daily Brief, the CIA's rundown of intelligence delivered every morning to the president by a CIA briefer.

Quds Force—The elite arm of the IRGC charged with foreign intervention through paramilitary forces. Quds (or Qods) Force (meaning "Jerusalem Force," after the Israeli holy city that they someday hope to conquer) is tasked with intelligence activities, unconventional warfare, and foreign operations.

Razi—Border town in western Iran, just east of Turkey.

ROE—Rules of Engagement, guidelines presented to combatants to establish offensive or defensive weapons use.

S-400—Advanced capable SAM exported by Russia to Iran. Considered a significant air defense threat by NATO forces.

SAC—Special Activities Center, the CIA paramilitary arm.

SAD—Special Activities Division, the name for the CIA's paramilitary arm before it was renamed to SAC in 2018.

Salam—Arabic greeting, short form of *Salam Aleikum*, "Peace and God be with you."

SAM—Surface-to-Air Missile.

Saqqez, Iran—City in central-western Iran, Kurdistan Province.

SCADA—Supervisory Control and Data Acquisition, a computer system for gathering and analyzing real-time data. SCADA systems are used to monitor and control a plant or equipment in industries such as telecommunications, water and waste control, energy, oil and gas refining, and transportation.

SES—Senior Executive Services, the level of US civil service employees equivalent to military general or flag rank.

SIGINT—Signals Intelligence.

SOAR—Special Operations Aviation Regiment. US Army unit that operates with special operations teams. Their primary aircraft is the MH-60 Blackhawk helicopter, equipped for special operations missions.

Spetsnaz—Storied Russian special forces unit. Spetsnaz operatives can be assigned either to complement conventional military forces or to assist the SVR in covert activities.

Spetsnaz Alpha—Specially trained Spetsnaz special forces soldiers assigned to work undercover for the SVR. Plainclothes Spetsnaz Alpha soldiers were visibly active in the Russian invasion/annexation of the Crimea in 2014.

Mk 12 SPR—Lightweight enhanced 5.56mm sniper rifle in use by US Special Forces in Iraq and Afghanistan.

SSE—Sensitive Site Exploitation, a procedure to search for opportunistic intelligence in a physical location.

SVR—Russian foreign intelligence service, equivalent to the CIA, headquartered in Moscow's Yasenevo District. S Directorate SVR officers operate in secret under nonofficial cover. PR Directorate SVR operatives operate in embassies under diplomatic cover.

Tabriz, Iran—City in northwestern Iran, home to Tabriz University. Site of the underground Tabriz enrichment facility.

Tor missile—NATO designated SA-14 SAM, used by Iran to shoot down the Ukrainian airliner in Tehran in January 2020.

Twelvers—Those who believe staunchly in the Mahdi, the Twelfth Imam in hiding.

Van—City in eastern Turkey near the Iranian border.

Y-12—An all-purpose twin-engine cargo aircraft manufactured by the Chinese company Harbin. It is used by the IRGC for various utility missions.

Yasenevo—Russian suburb of Moscow. Colloquial reference to SVR S Directorate.

Zaqqum—The tree that grows in the depths of hell, as noted in the Quran, fruited with the heads of demons. Used as the code name for the Iranian program to obtain sustainable nuclear-weapons capability.